The Orthogonal Galaxy

Galaxy Series
— Book 1 —

Michael L. Lewis

First Printing, 2014

ISBN: 1501099078
ISBN-13: 978-1501099076

michaellewisbooks.blogspot.com

DEDICATION

To my supportive and loving wife, Suzanne, whose encouragement
turned this work of fiction into reality.

Chapter

1

In a quiet alcove of the federal courthouse in Atlanta, Georgia, a middle-aged man stared out of a rain-splattered window. His dark hair was betrayed by streaks of gray on either side of his head. Although a model of physical fitness, he leaned against the wall for support while watching the heavy rain that splashed down on the sidewalk five stories below. He watched as cars drove by purposefully and pedestrians with umbrellas dashed along trying to avoid the streams of water that rushed off into the street. Occasionally, his focus was directed to the window as beads of water raced erratically down the glass pane.

While he stood in this motionless position, he envied every car, bus, taxi, pedestrian, and—yes, even the lone bicyclist—in their ability to travel to their intended destinations. How he would have traded positions with any one of them. Even the bicycle was a symbol of freedom that he currently was not able to enjoy. How much longer that privilege would escape him was up to a jury of seven men and six women who had just settled into the courtroom not far away.

"Paol?" a soft voice from behind him blended smoothly with the subtle sound of rain splashing against the window. It was so soft that the distracted man completely missed it.

The sound of heels clicking on the polished tile floor grew louder as they approached the man, but even this noise did nothing to arouse him from his thoughts. Only when a gentle hand was placed on his shoulder did he turn with a start.

"It's time, Sweetheart." The gentle words were warm and encouraging in spite of the façade. Paol knew that his wife was agonizing ever so much as he was, and while he was grateful for her strength, he ached to know that she had to carry this burden so gracefully.

As his bloodshot eyes gazed into her smiling face, a corner of his mouth turned up sadly. With a deep breath, he held out his arm. She received it happily and turned towards a man that had been waiting at the back of the room.

"We'll beat this, Paol! I'm confident that if there are any on the jury who are yet unconvinced, they will be on our side before the end of the day."

Wearing a dark pin-striped suit, well-pressed white shirt, and cobalt blue tie, the lawyer was dressed as confidently as he sounded. Spinning around, he walked with deliberate poise down the hall. Following his lead, the couple pursued the man and disappeared into courtroom number 523.

As he crossed the threshold, he contracted some of the encouragement of his defender. After all, Paol Joonter knew that he was innocent of the charges filed against him. Surely, the best judicial system in the world could not make the wrong decision.

Chapter

2

In a different location of the galaxy, Joram Anders studied his new surroundings that appeared perfectly earthlike. The sky was blue, the grass green, the collection of oak, maple, and willow trees rustled in the gentle breeze just as they did on Earth, and the strong golden Sun beamed its warmth in approval of the setting. Yet, for Joram, it felt as though he were on another planet. Motionless, he looked slowly to his left and then to his right. He saw a vast number of human-like figures traveling on brick-lined pathways in all different directions, each arrayed in a varying degree of fashion and quality of grooming. The sound of cars on nearby streets and an occasional bird singing high in the treetops confirmed that, indeed, Joram had not been mysteriously transported to another planet.

Yet it all seemed so dreamlike, so surreal. And perhaps it should! As far back as Joram could remember, he had dreamed of the day he would stand in front of the building he had seen in hypergraphic photos from the moment it was dedicated. That was eight years ago—just two weeks after his thirteenth birthday. For several minutes, Joram kept reading the words "Carlton H. Zimmer Planetarium" and each time he felt his heart race with excitement, anticipation, and anxiety. For a while now, he had stood in a statuesque manner, moving just enough to occasionally twist his arm for a glance at his watch. In just a few minutes now, the farm boy from Wichita, Kansas would begin his astronomy studies as a graduate student at the California Institute of Technology.

Naturally, he was intimidated to enter the planetarium for his first class of the term, where his boyhood idol and legendary astrophysicist, Carlton

Zimmer, would instruct Astrophysics 21: Galaxies & Cosmology. Joram took a deep breath and approached the building slowly while other students passed by, paying no attention to this nervous newcomer. With one last glance of his watch, he grabbed the door handle. While he was seven minutes early to enter the building, this was by design. He wanted to take in the whole setting by stationing himself in the middle of the arena, partly so he could be lost in the crowd, but mostly, because he wanted the perspective of being at the nucleus of this great building.

With the door closing behind him, he paused to allow his eyes to adjust to the darkness. The room was dimly lit from recessed lighting that circled the room shining directly up onto the ceiling, which was as black as any midnight Joram had experienced back on the farm in Kansas. The front of the room was brightly arrayed from a string of track lighting lining the wall behind the lectern. Lights along the floor helped Joram find his way down the red carpeted stairs towards the center of the room. Making his way into an aisle marked with the letter "I", Joram slid down to the middle seat. Surprisingly comfortable, he brushed his hand against the velvet upholstery, and reclined almost all the way to the floor. For the first time all day, his anxiety gave way to a deep soothing sigh.

Instantly, he was transported back to the family farm where he would spend hours at night every summer evening, laying on a blanket near the darkest side of the house. In the stillness of his Kansas farm and with a pair of well-worn Star Goggles, he could see the faintest of stars viewable under the thick atmosphere of the Earth.

"Joram," his mother would call out from a window, "it's nearly midnight, Son. Come on in outta this night air and get you some rest. You know that your Pa needs your help with the chores in the morning."

"Just a few more minutes, Mom. Barnard's Star is about to set."

"Barnyard Farm! What are you talking about, anyway?"

"Not Barnyard Farm, Mom," Joram said with an exasperated tone. "It's Barnard's St—oh, never mind. Just five more minutes, Mom. I Promise." Joram allowed his mind to depart Earth one last time to wander among the stars and particularly to Barnard's Star. While Proxima Centauri is the closest star to our solar system, it is never visible from Kansas. He would love to see Proxima Centauri some day, although he knew that the difference between

4

4.2 light years and 6.0 light years didn't really mean much. Both are invisible to the naked eye from Earth, so both would require the assistance of the Star Goggles. Yet Proxima Centauri was his star—the one he dreamt about, the one he longed to see with his own eyes.

His fascination with Proxima Centauri centered on his dream to visit the stars. While he eagerly attended to all of the news regarding the scientists who were racing to develop the first interstellar shuttle, nobody had produced anything that would approach the velocity required to travel to other star systems. Should interstellar travel ever be feasible, he would have to think that the Proxima Centauri star system would be among the first targets for exploration.

Hearing the window fly open again, Joram absently shouted out, "Just two more minutes, Mom."

An audible huff and the shutting of the window left him to his perfect silence one last time, as he continued to gaze at Barnard's Star, trying to imagine in his finite mind how far 6.0 light years really is.

. . .

A sudden burst of light brought Joram back to reality. Restoring his chair to its upright position, he looked behind him as students began to enter the planetarium. Embarrassed to be seen reclining in his first grad school classroom, he scrambled to raise the seat back up. Fumbling for the wooden desktop in the right armrest of his seat he began to empty the contents of his backpack, comprising just two small electronic items. The first was his brand new Digital Note Tablet, currently empty of any entries, but would soon be put through the paces of digital note-taking. The second item was his iText Reader. This device had already been slightly worn, evidence of his early perusal of the texts which his professors had assigned to him for his coursework this term. Most professors transmit books during class, since each classroom is equipped with its own private Wireless Services Access Point, so there was no need for Joram to have downloaded them over the Internet first. But, his love of science—and particularly astronomy— drove him to download all of his textbooks from the university intranet the moment they were announced to the students.

Joram, however, knew that it was more survival than ambition that generated this behavior. To come all the way from a dairy farm on the plains of the Midwest through Wichita State University to this prestigious institution in Southern California would require all of his abilities. He was now placed in an atmosphere where intellect and knowledge were practically innate. He had come from an insufficiently educated farm family, so he was not oblivious to the challenge that would face him in this highly competitive setting.

"I hear these seats are really comfortable," interrupted a young lady as she took a seat next to Joram.

"Yeah, they are," Joram blushed slightly as he looked up at his classmate. The blush wasn't so much intended for the attractive brunette with emerald green eyes who had engaged him in conversation as it was for his state of relaxation that some must have noticed as they entered the room earlier. Joram had hoped that the lighting would have still been too dim to notice, and that the newcomers' eyes would have not had enough time to adjust to the darkness yet.

"Have you taken a class in the planetarium before?" the brunette asked.

"No," admitted Joram. "Seeing how I arrived a couple of minutes early, I thought I'd give it a try. Let's just say that it's more comfortable than anything in my apartment."

"Tell me about it. What isn't lumpy at my place is either broken down or completely missing its upholstery. I'm Kather Mirabelle, but my friends call me Kath." Kath extended her hand, which Joram accepted graciously.

"I'm Joram. Joram Anders." Joram was grateful for the hospitality and acquaintance. Since arriving at CalTech a few days earlier, Joram had had little opportunity to meet any of his new Southern California neighbors.

"Nice to meet you, Joram," Kath said cheerfully. "What year are you?"

"First year grad student," replied Joram. It still seemed amazing to hear himself say it. The first college graduate of his family, many back home found Joram's penchant for education, and particularly science difficult to grasp.

"Really! So am I!" said Kath. "Are you in the astronomy department, then?"

"Yes," answered Joram. "And you?"

"Naturally. My undergraduate degree was in meteorology," Kath responded, "but I've always thought astronomy to be fascinating."

"Have you heard anything about Professor Zimmer", Joram inquired of his companion.

Kather cocked her head in surprise, and replied, "Well, yes. He's the most famous astrophysicist in the world."

"Well, yeah," Anders smiled slightly at his poorly phrased question, "but what I meant was, do you know anything about him as a profess—".

Joram's words were cut short as he noticed an immediate quieting of the chatter throughout the room. A door had opened in the front of the room, which Joram had not previously noticed. Through the opening, a tall man in his sixties with graying hair strode through confidently and quickly. He was attired conservatively with dark gray slacks, white shirt, navy blue striped tie, and black leather shoes. Shutting the door behind him, he lunged for the rostrum in the center of the stage and tapped on the microphone a couple of times. Responding readily to the test, the man cleared his throat and introduced himself.

"Good afternoon. My name is Carlton Zimmer and it is my good fortune to have an opportunity to instruct you in this astronomy class this term." His voice was raspy, yet confident. He articulated smoothly delivering his words with a pleasant tone that matched a warm smile. With a full head of hair, more white than gray, Zimmer showed signs of his age. Joram sensed that the dark rings around his eyes indicated both a lack of sleep and an abundance of stress. Joram wasn't surprised to make this observation, as he had already presupposed that the successes of a world-renowned scientist would not come without significant workloads.

Joram's heart started racing again. Standing just thirty feet before him was a man he instantly recognized. How many times had he seen his picture next to an article in the astronomy journals he kept up with on the Internet? How many times had he seen him interviewed on the Science Channel or other television programs honoring him for his prolific career? While he did appear taller in person, and his voice certainly deeper than it did on TV, he nevertheless recognized him almost as well as he would recognize his own father.

"Many of you have varying degrees of interest in this subject," Zimmer continued as he pierced the room with an intense glare, as if he were determining a priori those who would succeed—or fail—in his class. "Some of you are undergraduates with a minor interest in astronomy. Others are first year grad students trying to make a life out of this. Others simply needed the elective, and the time slot just happened to fit your schedule. But whatever your motives are for being here, my job is to make sure that it is worth your time and effort.

"While these great facilities make it possible to obtain a varied degree of instruction," the Professor gestured to the vast dome overhead with his right hand, "I hope that your expectations are such that you are not just here to enjoy a good light show. While we will certainly have opportunity to fire up the sky overhead, I find that the seats are too comfortable to allow for much real learning to occur when they are reclined."

Professor Zimmer then proceeded to announce some important policies which each student must respect. He made clear that the doors would be locked by five minutes after the beginning of class each day, in order to avoid any "disturbances in the force" of the educational process. The attempt at humor was not a success, simply because he often forgot that his students, so far removed from his generation, usually didn't recognize obscure references to the rather ancient pop culture with which he was at least familiar through his studies of all things science fact and fiction. He reiterated, just as the signs did outside each entrance that while the room may have the appearance of a movie theater, food and beverage were strictly prohibited. He allowed the students to then synchronize their Readers with the selected readings of the class. Everybody except Joram rifled through their backpacks and extracted their iText Readers.

As Kath began her download, she raised her brow slightly and whispered in Joram's direction, "Aren't you going to download the texts?"

Smiling, Joram responded, "I downloaded it—" Refusing to appear too zealous, Joram paused in order to replace the phrase 'three months ago' with "—before the semester started."

Turning his head back towards the front of the room, he thought he noticed the professor staring at him with a slight frown on his face. Joram's stomach sank. What a lousy first impression to make on the man he most admired. While the noise of backpack zippers would've certainly drowned out the exchange between the two new friends, he was sure that Zimmer had noticed the verbal exchange between the two classmates. While he had hoped that sitting in the center of the room would make him less noticeable, the opposite had actually occurred, because he was now sitting right in front of the professor at his eye level.

Once the room had been restored to its previous state of attentiveness, Professor Zimmer continued.

"By way of introduction to our study this semester, who can tell me why the study of astronomy is important in our society today?" This was a loaded and sensitive question to ask, for in this society, there was a decreasing public opinion of the field. Professor Zimmer knew as well as anybody that many murmurings were taking place in Washington D.C. regarding federal funding of astronomy programs. "We should keep our feet on the ground and worry about the problems that are right next door, instead of those that are thousands of light years away," was a common call among some aspiring politicians.

As Zimmer had expected, there was no response from anybody in the class. "Now surely some of you are here, because you believe there is merit to the field of astronomy. Why should we study astronomy?"

Joram saw a rather tentative hand slowly rise down in the front, right side of the room. Professor Zimmer, clipping a lapel microphone to his tie, ventured towards the student.

"What is your name, young man?" asked Professor Zimmer.

"Farrem Tanner," answered the young man.

"Well, Mr. Tanner," continued the professor, with a smile, "I'm glad to see there is somebody in my class who is here for a good reason, someone who believes there is some value to this field of study. Tell me. Why should we study astronomy?"

"Well, sir," Farrem began, "It gives us a better understanding of ourselves and our position in the universe when we study astronomy."

"Well said, Mr. Tanner." Zimmer nodded his approval and warmly congratulated his student for his answer and his courage to be the first to speak up on a controversial subject. "We can't gain a comprehensive understanding of the physics which rules our world, if we limit our field of vision to the Earth. A study of geology can teach us much about the world we live in, but a study of astronomy can teach us much more about the universe we live in, can't it?"

9

Zimmer returned to the center of the room, and leaned against the lectern in an attempt to provide a more casual feel and thereby encourage more participation. "Anybody else care to continue on this course of discussion?"

Another answer came from somebody sitting a couple of rows behind Joram. "Professor, there are tangible benefits as well. By understanding the forces in the universe, we are able to place satellites into orbit, which improve our quality of life."

"Do you mean," prodded Professor Zimmer, "that you are able to get thousands of TV stations from around the world in your dormitory lounge?"

A few laughs indicated that the class was relaxing.

"No, sir," corrected the student. "I'm thinking about the safety of airlines that use the advanced Precision Global Positioning System and weather warning satellites to avoid collisions and hazards."

"Very well," nodded the professor. "Please accept my apologies for a premature judgment of your thoughts, Mr..."

"Johnson. Marrett Johnson."

"Thank you, Mr. Johnson for your response."

With yet another hand, Professor Zimmer acknowledged that he could see deep into the back of the arena, in spite of the track lighting which shined brightly onto the professor.

"Yes, the young lady in the back," professor Zimmer craned and gestured to the back row.

"Professor, my name is Cintera Fernandez, and I have a relative who enjoys the benefit of occasional zero-gravity therapy sessions as a relief from severe rheumatoid arthritis."

"That's marvelous, isn't it, Miss Fernandez?" began the professor. "I was thrilled to see the cost of low-orbit travel become reasonable enough in the last couple of decades to allow the passenger airline industry to venture above the atmosphere so readily. With the low-cost of extra-atmospheric travel, doctors are able to prescribe these therapy sessions that you mention. Thank you, Miss Fernandez."

Zimmer was growing bored with all of the trite answers and decided to shift direction a little "But, class, I fail to see why any of these excuses gives us any reason to consider galaxies which reside many, many light years away

10

from us. And yet, we're going to be doing just that in this classroom this year. What benefits will you as a student receive by such a study?"

For the first time, Zimmer saw his students reaching deep into their intellect, straining for the answer. He was pleased with the effective result of a few moments of silence.

"Let me ask what I hope to be an easier question." Zimmer spoke more quietly now. He had the attention of his students, but he wanted it to be more focused. "When you look at the night sky with the naked eye, you can see a few thousand stars." He paused. "That is... when you are *not* standing in Pasadena, California," Zimmer paused for the laughter to subside, "but rather on Palomar Mountain, where our university's observatory is located just a few hours away from here, you can *indeed* see a few thousand stars with the naked eye. Which of these stars is closest to our own Sun?"

Joram's heart gave a leap. Carlton Zimmer was now asking a question about his star! Joram looked around, but no hands went up to indicate knowledge of that. Come on! This was a bright group of people, and not one of them could answer that question? Maybe they were all still being too timid on the first day of class. Joram tried to keep his hand from shaking nervously as he projected it slowly into the air.

"Yes, sir," acknowledged the professor without any apparent recollection of his earlier disapproval of the interlude between Joram and Kath. "Please tell us, if you will, the star which is closest in proximity to our own Sun."

"That would be Proxima Centauri, Sir." answered Joram confidently.

"That would be correct," approved the professor. "What is your name, young man?"

"Joram Anders, sir."

At this, the professor appeared to hesitate for just a moment, as if straining to remember why that name should sound so familiar to him. It came to him.

"Ah, yes," interjected Professor Zimmer, "Joram Anders... from Kansas, is it?"

Joram gave a start. How on earth did one of the world's most renowned astrophysicists know this obscure farm boy from Wichita? As if reading his mind, the professor proceeded. "Sorry, Mr. Anders, if I have concerned you by knowing more about you than you would have expected. I do assure you that I am just an astronomer, and not also a mind-reading astrologer." Roars of laughter ensued.

"After returning from a summer in South America, I had been reviewing all of the first-year graduate applications just last week, and I happened to remember your name, because I don't believe I've had the honor of instructing anyone from Kansas before, especially one with such amazing credentials with which you come to this institution."

It was always the way Professor Zimmer treated others. He was naturally complimentary, and in spite of being one of the world's greatest intellects was never condescending. Few ever doubted his intentions, for in the well-established career and character which he had developed, there was never any reason why he should ever have to ingratiate himself to anyone. And certainly not to a first-year graduate student from Kansas.

Before Joram had an opportunity to fumble for a response to this somewhat embarrassing recognition, the professor continued, "Mr. Anders, I suppose that you will be able to tell me the distance from our own Sun to Proxima Centauri."

"4.2 light years, Sir."

Zimmer whistled lowly through his lips. "So that means that if I could travel at the speed of light from Earth, I would arrive at the nearest of these thousands of stars in just 4.2 years?"

"Naturally," responded Joram somewhat conversationally now.

The professor thought for a moment. "Are there any rest stops along the way?" More laughter.

"Mr. Anders," implored the professor. "Why should I care about Proxima Centauri, if I could never practically travel there to see it?"

"Sir, there is much we can and have learned from the stars without having to travel to them," responded Joram. "Besides, I thought the race was on to discover the means of interstellar travel."

"Are you referring to all of the warp drive nonsense that the media is so colorfully pitching these days?" Professor Zimmer stared inquisitively at Joram.

Slowly responding to the professor's question, Joram refused to commit an opinion on the matter, although he was certainly very opinionated and excited at the hopes for interstellar travel. "I'm not sure about the details or

12

the validity of all of these projects, Professor. But it does seem like every scientist in the country is in hot pursuit of interstellar travel these days. Somebody must be thinking that it's possible." Joram paused to weigh his next words, but emboldened by the excitement of the discussion, he breached his better judgment anyway. "What do you think of interstellar travel, Professor?"

Before Zimmer could begin to formulate a response to that question, the door in the back of the room opened up, allowing a flood of sunlight to penetrate the room. Every student looked back to see a man enter the room. Joram squinted at the silhouette but didn't recognize the man. He did suspect that he was another professor, judging by the whiteness of his hair—at least that little bit which remained on the sides of his rather bald pate—not to mention the fact that the conservative style of his attire was similar to that of Professor Zimmer. The man and Professor Zimmer exchanged nods and smiles knowingly while the man allowed the door to shut. He remained standing along the back wall, while the students returned to their previous postures.

"Let me answer that question in the following way, Mr. Anders," began the professor. "During your course of investigation into the astronomy program here, you may have become aware of a little research project of mine involving the possibility of parallel star systems. Do you suspect that I am engaged in this activity, because of an overwhelming stack of evidence suggesting that parallel universes do indeed exist?"

The professor shook his head, and then appearing to address the man in the back of the room, he continued in a more animated manner of hand gestures and body language. "Contrary to popular opinion, living a life of science isn't always about facts and evidence. Many very important discoveries have been made more from the hunch and imagination of the scientist than the data with which he is presented."

His attention returned to Joram as he took two steps towards him. "Mr. Anders. Let me answer your question with a question. Do you think I would be engaged in such a research project, if I believed that interstellar travel would prove to be impossible? Do you think I would want to make a discovery of a so-called parallel solar system, and then not be able to travel there to study that star and its orbiting bodies?"

Joram's question was answered.

At this, the professor paused for a few seconds, and the campus chime was heard ringing from some distant point. Joram looked at his watch. What? Could the entire 50-minute lecture be over already? Why, certainly no more than five or ten minutes had elapsed.

But he was wrong, and he knew it. Along with the rustle of items being haphazardly returned to backpacks and the hands of his analog wrist watch, Joram knew that his first lecture from Professor Carlton H. Zimmer had officially adjourned.

. . .

Professor Zimmer waited in the front of the room while all of his astronomy students left the planetarium. After the last one exited the room, he made his way up the stairs of the theater while the man in the back of the room met him half way down.

The man greeted Professor Zimmer warmly with a firm handshake. "Carlton, nice to see you. How was the trip?"

"Oh, it was fine, Ballard," answered the professor. "But, it's good to be back home."

"I'll be eager to see your official report, Carlton, but how about a preview. Any news from Chile?"

"Well, it was a busy summer down there for us, but we continued to narrow down our list of target stars in the South. We had about 800,000 stars when we started this summer, and have narrowed that list down to just under a half million. But that's still too many to start targeting any data collection efforts using the Kepler3 telescope. I do believe, however that we have a darned good team assembled down there to continue their work and should whittle that list down by 50% before I return next summer."

At this, Zimmer thought he'd detected a slight frown from his longtime friend and Dean of Astronomy at the University. "Ballard, you know that this is the proverbial needle in the haystack. These things don't conclude overnight."

"If there is a needle, Carlton," countered Ballard with an apparent allusion to his disbelief in Zimmer's research project.

Changing the subject, Professor Zimmer offered, "Hey, how is your son doing on the Star Transport team at the Jet Propulsion Lab?"

14

"I just had dinner with him over the weekend. He's pretty stressed right now." Ballard gladly accepted the change of direction. "He mentioned a pretty big design review coming up, and he believes that his team will get highly scrutinized this time. Although, I must say, if your research is the needle in the haystack, then I think this interstellar transportation stuff is the Holy Grail. Yes, I know… the theories abundantly support the concept of travel at the speed of light, and yet, I have a hard time swallowing the practicality of such a maneuver."

"I believe you may have heard a similar doubt from one of the grad students just a few moments ago," smiled Zimmer.

"Yes," chuckled Ballard with a playful wink. "It seems you are having a harder time winning converts to your cause these days, Carlton. These kids these days come in here with their heads the size of Betelgeuse. In the old days, they used to come in respecting their professors. Now, they enter thinking they know more. But, just as will be the case of Betelgeuse, their education will explode like a supernova if they are not careful."

"Do you know who that student was?" asked Zimmer impatiently.

Ballard looked back at the door, as if he might still be able to catch a glimpse of the student walking away from the room. "No, I only saw him from the back. Should I know him?"

"That was Anders." Carlton lowered his voice as if worried that somebody, perhaps Joram himself, would overhear the conversation.

Ballard's look turned serious. "You mean, Joram Anders?"

Carlton nodded.

"The kid from Kansas?"

More nodding.

"The same kid who had the highest astronomy entrance exam of any entering grad student in the last decade?"

A final nod convinced Ballard that Joram Anders was indeed a real person, and not just a figment of his imagination. He'd always had a very hard time believing the results on Joram's exam.

"Well then, I'll be very interested in getting to know this young man better."

"Me too!" exclaimed Professor Zimmer.

Looking at his watch, Ballard noted, "Gotta run. I have an appointment with the NASA folks in a little bit. Hey, I have a free hour this afternoon at four o'clock. Can you meet me at my office? There is a lot to catch up on, and I want to hear about the new telescope down at Cerro Tololo."

Carlton looked at his watch. "Sure, I'll stop by at four."

...

Kath and Joram emerged from the planetarium squinting from the bright Sun that was just starting to lower in the sky. He shielded his eyes with his hands, while she fumbled around her backpack searching for her sunglasses.

"Well," Kath said casually as she put on the dark sunglasses. "It looks like my study partner selection instincts have served me well yet once again."

"What do you mean?" Joram asked while twisting his head to see her face. It was as much an attempt to look away from the blinding Sun as it was to interpret the expression on her face.

"Let's see," Kath said playfully, and then lowered her voice. "Such amazing credentials you have, Mr. Joram Anders, from Kansas." Returning to her normal voice, she explained, "I seem to recall Zimmer saying something of that nature, didn't he?"

Joram blushed. "I would hardly consider myself the teacher's pet just yet. And just look at my note tablet. It's still perfectly blank!" Joram was appalled and disappointed in his lack of note-taking on the first day of class. "By the way, did you see any look on his face while we were talking at the beginning of class?"

"No," she said honestly. She was among the rest of the students focused on synchronizing the course textbooks to their Readers at the time that Joram had spotted Zimmer looking their way.

"So, you're from Kansas," Kath changed the subject conversationally. "I've never been there."

"Not surprising," Joram admitted. "There's not a whole lot there, you know. Just miles and miles of farmland."

"Did you grow up on a farm?" asked Kath.

"Yeah. My father is a dairy farmer."

"He must be so proud of you, coming here to CalTech," Kath boasted.

16

"Yes, but I'm not sure that I convinced him that CalTech is any better than Wichita State," Joram smiled upon recollecting his conversations with his father about why Joram had to go so far away.

"He kept asking me, 'Are there any more stars over Southern California than there are here over the farm?'"

Joram enjoyed sharing the laugh with Kath as they strolled along the winding paths and well-manicured landscape of the university. Conversation came naturally to the new friends, and Joram found out much about the Southern California native, who seemed to have many interests as well as the energy to keep up with them all. She was a regular at the gym early in the mornings, unless the conditions were just right to go surfing. As an avid tennis buff, she placed fifth in a state-wide tournament in high school. Her father was a chemical engineer who spent most of his career working on alternative energy sources. She was not ashamed to admit that she was proud of his accomplishments and was quick to mention how he had helped transition the world away from its addiction to non-renewable sources of energy.

In turn, Kath was amazed to discovery that Joram had a deep love for astronomy and had amassed quite a wealth of knowledge in the field. She began to understand that it was more than just the Kansas connection that compelled Professor Zimmer to quickly recall the name of Joram Anders. She was enamored at his description of life on the farm. It was so different from her own upbringing, and she could tell that some of Joram's physical features stemmed from his time on the farm. His golden, almost leathered complexion spoke on the amount of time he spent in the blazing sun. His broad shoulders and barrel chest were certainly the result of real work, and not that of so many other weight-lifting, muscle-pumping goons she'd met time and again at the gym. If only she'd had a dollar for each nauseating pick-up line from some arrogant muscle-flexer who assumed that every woman owed them for their existence. Of course, even she wasn't oblivious to how much she enjoyed being attended to at the gym, and it was a fun hobby of hers to record and review her little book of pick-up lines. Even so, it still irritated her to think that these guys really believed that they could "charm" a girl through such triviality. It was just so offensive to her intelligence.

At the end of their conversation, Joram was simply amazed that he had spent an hour and a half with her on the patio of the Red Door Café, where Joram nursed his lemonade and Kath finished off two iced coffees. Where had the day gone? His first astronomy lecture had flown by, and now his acquaintance with Kath had seemed but a flash.

"Wow, how the day has flown!" Joram commented as he looked at his watch. "I have to be going now, Kath, but I'll see you in class on Wednesday."

"Sounds great," Kath acknowledged.

With that, the new acquaintances bid each other farewell, until Wednesday, when they would meet again in Professor Zimmer's class.

...

Zimmer took a long stride as he walked into Dean Scoville's office. As he sat down in the chair opposite of the dean's desk, he wasted no time in getting to the point. "How was the meeting with NASA, Ballard?"

Scoville's face turned austere. Just as Zimmer was settling into his seat, the dean stood up to look out of his window overlooking the campus.

"Things did use to be more simple around here, Carl," Ballard admitted. Then turning back to look at Zimmer while gazing on the well-manicured grounds visible from his fourth floor office, he continued. "I didn't know exactly how the meeting with NASA would turn out, but I was worried when they called yesterday to schedule an urgent discussion for this afternoon. NASA almost never works on a schedule like that, unless it's pretty serious."

Zimmer listened attentively, fearing the worst. Actually, he had already been fearing the worst for the last three years, precisely when he began the extended summer research at Cerro Tololo. He was starting to feel the pressure on his research budget, and knew that he had to step up his efforts. He needed to throw a bone to NASA to ensure that his funding would persist.

"The research funding committee flew out from Washington to visit us on our research programs. Darn it, Carl, you know how everything has to be so political these days. Politicians are riding the public appeal of interstellar travel, because their constituents want to travel all over the universe. But they don't seem to care as much about the real science of astronomy."

"But Ballard, they've promised us—in writing—at least two more years of funding," Carlton announced.

"Yes, they mentioned that as a tactic to apply pressure. They're threatening to pull the plug at the end of this year if they don't start seeing results from your current research. It seems like every senator who's aspiring for the Oval Office is flapping their jaws about limiting unessential research. Some are even so bold as to threaten NASA with extinction!"

Zimmer hung his head. "Ballard, they promised two more years."

"Funny money, Carl. A bill that is signed into law today will have a counter-measure erasing its efficacy next year. You can't trust anything that these guys put down on paper, because they can simply legislate it all away."

"What are their demands?" Professor Zimmer immediately put himself into problem solving mode.

"They want evidence, Carlton. Hard, rock solid evidence that this parallel solar system concept is valid."

"Ballard, I've provided them with the statistics. The universe is—well, it's universal. With the vast number of class G2 stars out their, the mathematical models provide compelling evidence a copy of earth is out there."

Dean Scoville sat back down in his black leather chair, leaned over his dark walnut desk, and looked Professor Zimmer straight into the eye. "Carl, when are you going to find that needle?"

Zimmer hung his head again. He had no answer, and was starting to see his lifelong dream slipping away from his reach.

Hanging and shaking his head slowly, Carlton responded. "I don't know Ballard... I just don't know."

Chapter

3

As Paol Joonter took his seat at the defense table, he poured himself a cup of water from the pitcher in front of him. He looked down at a legal pad and scribbled a few notes. The notes were intended as a distraction to keep him from looking up at the jury or the district attorney, actions which his lawyer suggested could cause him to appear desperate, and that could sway the jury against him.

"Warron?" Paol whispered leaning somewhat to the left to get closer to his lawyer. With his chin resting in the palm of his hand, the lawyer bent his ear towards Joonter's head, after which he spoke a brief statement that only the lawyer was able to hear.

Scribbling quickly on a corner of his legal pad, Warron ripped off the note and turned back to hand the scrap to a paralegal, who nodded and quickly departed the courtroom.

As the door to the back of the courtroom opened, the court bailiff announced, "All rise. The honorable judge Walldar J. Etherton presiding."

All stood in unison as directed and watched as the judge entered and assumed his seat at the front of the room. Looking down at a flurry of papers in front of him, he put on a pair of wire-rimmed spectacles, assessed that all was in order and looked up at the courtroom. He counted the jury and studied the counsel tables to make sure all were accounted for. Looking at the audience, he saw many of the same individuals who had been present for the duration of the case.

He observed the concern on the face of Joyera Joonter, who sat as normal directly behind her husband within arm's reach. He saw a few additional individuals seated on the opposite side of the courtroom, and understood that more of the victims' family members were showing up now that the case was nearing its conclusion. To say that it was a somber setting would be an understatement. Faces devoid of color hinted at anxiety. Dark shadows expressed a lack of sleep. Bloodshot eyes betrayed the tears that flowed freely previously.

"Please be seated," he instructed. Looking at the district attorney, he continued, "Is the prosecution prepared for closing remarks?"

"Yes, your Honor," stated the lawyer with his hands folded over his legal pad.

"Please proceed, then."

Chapter

4

For Garrison O'Ryan, it was the experience of a lifetime. As the most common route taken on nearly all manned space missions these days, astronauts call it "the interstate" of space travel. As a 26-year old astronaut, Garrison was making his first journey along this well-beaten path. NASA engineers are quick to point that this interstate is actually safer than the one frequented during the morning commute. There had never been any incident along this well-traveled corridor, and Garrison was confident that he wouldn't be the first, even though he was a bit nervous about having to fly solo.

As it turns out, there are actually two legs to "the interstate." The first leg is a relatively short 250,000-mile two-day trip from Kennedy Space Center on the Florida coastline to the "rest stop" at Camp Moon. Garrison will stop here and take a day to get several hours of rest. From there, he will leave his rocket-intensive Moon Shuttle behind for the more cramped but speedy design of the Mars Shuttle, on which he will travel the second leg of "the interstate" all the way to Mars. Due to its weaker gravitational field, the Moon makes a more desirable location for launching a vehicle towards Mars. Once in flight, the shuttle will transport Garrison to Mars in just over a month of travel. While NASA always plans this second leg to be as short as possible—that is, when the Earth and Mars are relatively close to each other—this part of the trip will still take Garrison an additional 60 million miles away from his home. Astronauts claim that you feel every one of those miles too, because while the Mars Shuttle was designed for speed, comfort ranked pretty low on the list of design constraints.

On the first leg, Garrison was overwhelmed at how massive the Earth appears when viewed from several thousand miles above sea level. The vastness of his home and the space surrounding him diminished his own sense of worth in the universe in which he lived. As he orbited the moon to prepare for landing, he was amazed to see the incredible detail of the deep, shadow-laden craters. He was astounded at how much effort it took to walk on the Moon, especially considering that he only weighed thirty-three pounds there. He also noted how Camp Moon felt like a well-preserved ghost town, particularly because he was the only person present on the ten-acre site of buildings and hangars. He was not, however, surprised at how little he was able to sleep. With the anxiety of the long trip ahead of him, he only nodded off for a couple of hours, and found himself in a confused state when he awoke, wondering if all of this was nothing more than a dream.

Walking from his dorm to the hangar where the Mars Shuttle waited for him, he observed a crescent Earth that hung precariously over the horizon. He ate his breakfast consisting of a protein bar and pomegranate energy drink, both scientifically calculated to minimize the amount of waste he'd incur on his flight to Mars. Then he suited up, left his pressurized room, and made his way out to the runway, where his Mars Shuttle waited.

The Mars Shuttle was designed for horizontal takeoff and landing, both easier propositions for a solo pilot. It sat at the beginning of a relatively short runway indicating its readiness for service and its ability to accelerate into space very quickly.

Garrison knew how small the space craft was, for he had already become familiar with the cockpit in several prototypes. What amazed Garrison, however, was the comparatively massive solid rocket boosters bolted underneath each wing. The boosters were so large that the bottom of the vehicle was twenty feet off the ground, meaning that the boosters had to have landing gear of their own in order to propel the shuttle down the runway. Garrison knew that the boosters were necessary. In order to obtain high velocity, the shuttle requires a massive volume of rocket fuel to obtain the required speed, even in this low-gravity environment. Once jettisoned, the boosters would be able to return to Camp Moon via automated computer navigation. The same landing gear would be used to touch down on the satellite and then taxi off of the runway for future use.

Looking up at his tiny home for the next month, Garrison paused momentarily, wondering whether he really wanted to be confined to this miniscule capsule for a month. But, he knew that he had not spent years preparing himself for this moment, only to turn around and abort the mission now. Climbing the ladder structure to the top of the rocket booster and then walking the length of the booster to his cockpit, O'Ryan paused just a moment to admire the Earth and wondered if his wife was looking up at him at the same moment.

Throwing his body down into the cockpit, he sealed the hatch above him, and listened as a rush of air pressurized his environment, allowing him to stow his helmet in a compartment under his seat. Running through a checklist, he inspected gauges and monitor readouts to ensure that all systems were prepared for launch.

"Mission Control, this is Captain O'Ryan, prepared for takeoff in the Mars Shuttle Iowa" Garrison announced formally to NASA engineers at the Johnson Space Center in Houston, Texas.

"Iowa," responded a mission control specialist, "this is Mission Control. We're going over the last set of data from the vehicle to make sure we are a go for launch in T minus 32 minutes. We'll confirm system check in twenty minutes, Captain."

"All systems checked from visual inspection of the vehicle, Mission Control", Garrison confirmed confidently.

"How ya' feeling, Garrison?" asked another specialist more casually.

"Certainly not as comfortable as you, Halton." Garrison recognized the voice of his astronaut mentor, Halton Cooke. Cooke had recently retired from the astronaut program, but still served as a mission advisor to NASA on retainer.

"D'ya sleep well?" Halton knew that the chit chat would help keep Garrison's mind occupied during the pre-launch routine.

"What do you think?" Garrison answered the question with one of his own.

"Yeah, I copy you on that, O'Ryan." Halton couldn't help but smile as he leaned back with his hands behind his head, making sure not to pull off his headset. "After your third or fourth trip, you'll be sleeping like a baby in that bed on the moon."

"Sleeping like a baby?" quipped Garrison. "You don't know the O'Ryan baby apparently. That little tike didn't sleep until he was two years old it seemed."

"Then, you'll get to know how he felt," volleyed Halton quickly. "By the time you get to Mars, you're going to feel like you've gone two years without any sleep."

"And that's supposed to make me feel better?" asked Garrison.

"No," admitted Halton. "It's supposed to make you feel prepared. This is going to be a long trip, Garrison. I hope you're ready for it."

"Of course, I'm ready," lied Garrison. "I wouldn't miss it for the world."

"My prediction is that you will certainly miss the world before you come home a couple of years from now." The brutal honesty of Halton did not escape his friend. He was used to it, and it was that ability to say things exactly as he saw them for which O'Ryan had always admired his mentor. However, while Garrison had known that he'd be gone for nearly two years, the realization of this was just starting to settle in. He thought even more profoundly than previously how Timmer would be six years old by then. He wondered if he would even be able to remember his father after that much time.

All astronauts served a twenty-two month rotation on Camp Mars. A pair of astronauts was stationed there at all times. Garrison was hitting the early part of the window where Earth and Mars are sufficiently close to make the trip. He would relieve an astronaut, who would return in the Mars Shuttle back to Camp Moon shortly after he landed. Then in a month, another exchange would occur, relieving Garrison's companion of his duties in a similar manner. After that, the Earth and Moon would continue to diverge, as Earth raced around its orbit at twice the rate of Mars. After one year, the Earth would be back in the same position it was today, but Mars would've only traveled one half of its orbit, placing it on the other side of the Sun from Earth. Both planets would need to travel another nine months around their orbit in order for their positions to be close enough for Garrison to be relieved of his duties on the red planet.

"Iowa," interrupted the mission control specialist from Garrison's nostalgia. "All systems check. You're good for launch in T minus six minutes."

25

Halton announced to Garrison that it was time to resume business as the last several steps of launch preparation would need to be completed. Upon hearing the commotion from mission specialists on Earth, images and thoughts rushed through his head like they did back in Florida just a couple of days ago. And then in a flash, it happened.

"10... 9... Iowa, you have horizontal acceleration. Rockets are engaged at 100%... 4... 3... 2... 1... Mars Shuttle Iowa has lifted off from the runway. Second leg mission clock has commenced at four hours, twelve minutes, and seven seconds GMT."

...

Even though Garrison had already seen Earth and the Moon from the sweeping view of space, Garrison was even more stunned as he stared out of his shuttle down onto the surface of Mars. While orbiting the red planet, he was able to identify some of the most prevalent features that he'd become so familiar with.

He easily noticed the massive scar-like canyon, Valles Marineris. The deepest, widest, and longest canyon in the solar system, even from several hundred miles above, Garrison was stunned at its massive structure. On Earth, Marineris would stretch from Los Angeles to New York City, with depths up to 25000 feet, and would span a distance of 125 miles wide. By comparison, the Grand Canyon would look like a small ditch. He observed massively fractured canyons jutting off of both sides of the main canyon walls, until Marineris narrowed tightly into a maze of slot canyons, called Noctis Labyrinthus.

The Labyrinth of the Night was Garrison's favorite feature of Mars. He was thrilled to discover that part of his mission on Mars would entail a visit to this feature, along with a significant investigation of the geological—or, because it was Mars, and not the Earth, areological—forces of this region. With his mouth open in surprise, he attempted to gain a perspective a the massive sand dunes he saw swirling up onto the canyon walls. He imagined that these structures might rival anything found in the Sahara Desert, since the canyon walls were as tall as 10,000 feet.

The shuttle whisked him away from the Labyrinth quicker than he would hope, and in craning his neck to see the last of it, he hadn't realized that he was directly over the Tharsis Region mountain peaks: Arsia Mons, Pavonis

Mons, and Ascraeus Mons. Ranging from fifty to sixty thousand feet in elevation, these three mountains arranged in a straight line were easily identifiable.

The jaw dropping experience of the Tharsis Mountains had dazed the young astronaut, but he quickly recovered to remember exactly where to locate another impressive feature. The aptly named Olympus Mons—Mount Olympus—sat on the western edge of the Tharsis region. While no longer active, the solar system's largest volcano grew to its stature over a period of about 100 million years. Every astronaut will attest that nothing can prepare you for awesome sight of Olympus Mons from the ground. Towering at nearly 90000 feet or 17 miles above the mean level surface of Mars, you would have to stack three Mount Everests on top of each other to understand the degree of reverence this behemoth commands. As he passed just to the south of the mountain, Garrison stared down into the 60-mile wide caldera. Seeing the six impact craters at the top, Garrison could understand just how difficult it would be for a meteor to actually miss the top of this mountain. It just looked like a magnet the way it leapt off of the plains surrounding it.

On a second orbit of the planet, Iowa entered Mars' thin atmosphere with hardly any indication. The shuttle began a sharp decent and leveled off directly over a feature that Garrison had missed earlier. The Hellas Impact Basin impressed Garrison greatly as he was only about thirty miles above Mar's largest impact crater. He shuttered to think about the violence required for an impact to leave a hole 1500 miles wide and over five miles deep. In fact, seeing the landscape peppered with hundreds of thousands of craters-within-a-crater caused Garrison to shudder with concern for his own safety at Camp Mars. However, he had to remind himself that this landscape did not occur overnight, and that his odds of being hit by a meteor on Mars was only a little better than being hit by lightning on Earth.

As he left the Hellas basin, Iowa started issuing a series of lights and buzzers that reminded Garrison it was time to get down to the business of touching down on the runway of Camp Mars, just moments away.

Compared to all of the massive features that he'd been experiencing, it was a good thing that the computer navigational system knew where to pinpoint the relatively tiny three-mile wide crater that was home to Camp Mars. The landscape was littered with craters. As he strained to find his crater, he couldn't help wondering whether he would be able to spot such an inauspicious feature. Fortunately for Garrison, the crater glowed with artificial lighting. The greens and oranges of the lighting towers focused his sight to the camp, and eventually to the red ground lights lining the two-mile long runway. His approach and landing was incredibly smooth, a point which he would first mention proudly to the pair of astronauts eager to make introductions with their replacement.

"Did you see that landing?" Garrison asked as he made his decent from the shuttle onto Martian soil. "I should've become a commercial airline pilot."

"Well, Stud," interrupted one of the astronaut companions. "Before you pat yourself too hard on the back, just remember that you're in a much thinner atmosphere here… there's not as much turbulence and wind, at least not here near the equator."

"Oh, yeah. Good point" Garrison's bubble had burst. "Gentlemen, I'm Garrison O'Ryan reporting for duty. It's a pleasure to make your acquaintance."

"No," answered the other astronaut with a Russian accent. "The pleasure is ours. We are glad to see the first replacement. It has been much privilege come to Mars, but I am eager to see family again. Come, we show you the barrack now. You must be exhausted."

"Am I ever!" Garrison yawned and stretched, and as he took his first step, he faltered. While the cockpit of every Mars Shuttle was equipped with exercise mechanisms needed to keep limbs from freezing up. It had been over a month since he had actually used his limbs in any meaningful fashion.

"Oh," said one of the Martian veterans. "I'm so sorry. I forgot that it's nearly impossible to walk upon touchdown here. Let us help you."

With that, each astronaut flanked O'Ryan and assisted him into the barracks, where he was able to strip out of his spacesuit and collapse in a heap on a bed wearing only his long underwear.

…

After a few hours of rest—it seemed more like a couple of minutes to him—Garrison's two colleagues woke him up from a deep slumber.

"Rise and shine, Sleepy Head," called out one astronaut.

With an achy head and blurry eyes, Garrison responded, "What time is it?"

Looking at his watch, the other astronaut offered, "Well, it's 2:30 PM, Tharsis Standard Time."

"Ok," nodded Garrison. "Thanks, but why did I even ask that question? Let me try again. How long have I been sleeping?"

"Well, you arrived this morning at precisely 9:17 AM, so it's been a little over five hours."

"Really?" Garrison sat up in his bed and looked around now that his eyes were beginning to focus.

"How are you feeling, Garrison?" The first astronaut held out a hand for Garrison.

"Ayman!" Grasping his hand firmly and joyously, Garrison recognized his astronaut fellow from some training sessions they had performed together a few years ago at Kennedy. "I'm fine… a little tired, but that's nothing that a few days of sleep won't solve."

"Well, I'd love to grant it to you, but I need to depart for Camp Moon before the sun sets. We have just a couple of hours to give you the grand tour here before I head back home." Then, turning to the third astronaut, he said, "Garrison O'Ryan, I'd like you to meet a great friend of mine who has served marvelously at my side these last couple of years. This is Dmitri Boronov. He will be your companion here for the next couple of months until his replacement arrives."

"Ah, yes," Garrison warmly bowed and grasped the hand of his new companion, "We met earlier, but I was a bit out of it. By the way, I didn't get a chance to thank you for helping me walk into the barracks earlier."

"You should be slow to stand now," counseled Dmitri. "It will take few minutes to use legs."

Heeding his advice, Garrison stood slowly from his bed and while steadying himself on the wall next to it, took just a few experimental steps. "I must agree with you, Comrade."

"We will give you a few minutes to adjust and dress, Garrison," said Ayman. "To encourage you, there will be a hot bowl of soup, fresh-baked bread and juice waiting for you in the dining room."

29

Garrison didn't realize how hungry he was until he heard this discussion of food. "That sounds great!" admitted Garrison. "I'll be there as quick as I can... um, where is the dining room, anyway?"

"As you leave the room, turn left and proceed to the end of the hallway. The door is right at the end. See you there soon."

Garrison thanked the pair as they left his room, where he stretched his limbs and began learning how to walk all over again. He found a sweat suit in his closet, exactly like those being worn by Ayman and Dmitri, with the name "O'Ryan" embroidered on the left chest pocket. The door to a private bathroom was open, so he stepped in. After splashing water on his face and hair, he washed his hands and felt much better. He would've liked to take a shower, but his appetite and time constraints gave way to the temptation. Toweling himself off with a large white towel, which also had the name "O'Ryan" embroidered on it, he ventured back into the bedroom to dress.

As if his legs might still give out under him, he walked slowly and cautiously out of the bedroom and into the hallway. He peered down both ends. So far, the barracks had a more homey impression than he might otherwise have expected. The cream-colored plush carpet led down towards the dining room at one end and the foyer at the other end. Framed pictures and artwork, depicting some of the impressive features of Mars lined both walls. Towards the foyer, he could see all of the typical NASA-produced hypergraphs of each Martian-based astronaut lining either side of the hallway.

The door to the dining room was open, and he could hear the soft din of a casual discussion taking place between Ayman and Dmitri as he approached. He could only make out the occasional word or phrase: "Home", "your family", "what an adventure."

Ayman and Dmitri quickly stood up as Garrison appeared, as if needing to help him to a seat.

"I'm fine," He waved them off. "I'm actually adjusting rather quickly. I suspect that it's because of the lighter gravity that my legs are feeling back to normal so quickly."

"True," admitted Ayman. "Keep in mind, however that the adjustment will not be so sudden when you return to Earth. Part of our daily regimen is an exercised routine prescribed by NASA trainers to ensure that we do not lose muscle tone in our arms, back and legs. This is because the gravity here

30

is so much less than it is on Earth that muscle atrophy would cause a serious impediment to an adjustment to Earth life."

At this, Ayman noticed that Garrison was bracing himself on a chair, and realized that he was still laboring a little bit to get his full strength back.

"I'm sorry, Garrison... please, have a seat." Ayman gestured to the chair. He sat down to a place setting as Dmitri walked over to a counter. From under a heat lamp, he grabbed a steaming bowl and a plate with all of the contents as promised. Garrison noticed that the remains of the other astronauts' lunches remained on the table.

"Cheese steak sandwiches and potato salad?" asked Garrison curiously. He was famished and thought that he should be able to partake in the more wholesome fare of his colleagues.

"Sorry, Garrison." Ayman hung his head in apology. "For the first few days, NASA has ordered a strict diet of soft foods for you. You've been so unaccustomed to eating 'real' food that it will take some time for your digestive system to adjust."

"No worries, Ayman." Garrison understood his predicament. "After a month of those cardboard bars and watered-down powder, this chicken soup and bread look more like a steak and lobster meal to me."

With that, Garrison commenced to devour his supper while Ayman briefed him on the duties of the afternoon.

"As soon as you're done there, Garrison, we'll need to show you around. We'll start with the central facilities, including the barracks here, and the workshop and bunker just outside. Then, we'll drive the Mars Terrain Vehicle to the outer portions of the crater to show you all of the support structures which make life and work possible for us here at Camp Mars.

"Dmitri and I have already taxied the Iowa into the hanger and have fueled up and positioned the Nevada for my trip back to the Moon, so we'll finish the tour at the runway, so I can take off while there's still some sunlight. NASA always prefers us to have the best visual conditions as possible when landing or launching from the crater."

Dmitri interjected an important item which Ayman had omitted from the agenda. "We must remember to get new headset at SAR pad. It should be there now."

"Thank you, Dmitri," said Ayman. "I almost forgot that my communication headset has been flaky the last couple of days. I certainly want to make sure that I depart with a set that I know will work on the trip back to Mars. It would be awful to lose communication from Mission Control."

After he had finished his meal, Garrison felt adequately refreshed and strengthened for the tour. They began, logically enough, with the barracks. Comprising four bedrooms, each with a private bath, the barracks were sufficiently appointed for comfort and peace. Each bedroom had a full-sized bed with unaesthetic, yet comfortable, bedding. Each bed had a wall-mounted light bright enough for reading. Next to the bed was a nightstand with a lamp. The lamp was designed to provide soft lighting, and certainly wasn't sufficient to read by. It was, however, adequate to extract any personal items off from the drawer of the nightstand or make a trip to the bathroom. There was also a large wardrobe, consisting of underwear, sweat suits, and spacesuits for outside activities.

The dining room and kitchenette were cozy, yet adequate. A round kitchen table was could seat four astronauts, since there were rarely anymore than this on Camp Mars at any given time. In the kitchen area, there was a sink, microwave oven, and a small refrigerator. Garrison opened the fridge to reveal that it was only stocked with beverages and condiments. Cupboards revealed dishes, glasses, mugs, utensils, and spices for meals as each astronaut may desire. There was also a stock of snacks—pretzels, popcorn, chips, and candy bars—available to the astronauts as desired.

In the middle of the hallway was an exercise room

A trip down to the other end of the hall revealed a small foyer with some plush seating and tables with magazines and newspapers. Two rooms extended off of each side of the foyer. The first revealed a study with plenty of books for reading—fiction and non-fiction were equally represented, and there was a sufficient amount of light reading and some that looked calculated to help an astronaut endure an evening of insomnia. There were two reading stations, which consisted of an overstuffed recliner, a throw blanket, pillow, and an audio station with wireless headphones. A side table was within reach of each chair, allowing the astronaut to store his current book of interest and any beverage or snack that he might be enjoying at the time.

The second room on the opposite side of the foyer was a room that Garrison was frankly surprised to see. He had not been told about the entertainment room, and this proved to be a significant perk. By far the largest room in the barracks, this room consisted of two plush theater-style rocker-recliner chairs that sat in front of a coffee table directed towards a bare eight foot wall. On the ceiling behind the chairs was a high-definition digital projector, whose image covered the top half of the wall, for a full eight-foot wide image. A media center between the chairs came equipped with a high-quality Holographic Video Disk player and sizable library of HVDs. The latest audio technology was included in the form of a 540-degree surround sound system. Developers used the term "540-degree", because it provides a more immersive audio experience than the 360-degree system. At 360 degrees, there is a full wall-length speaker on each of the walls in the room, so that sound can come from all angles. The 540-degree effect comes in from the set of four speakers mounted on the ceiling as well, to give a more dome-like effect to the audio. A video game console was also connected into the projector, and a few titles were available, but this was not as popular a piece of equipment for many of the astronauts. Either way, Garrison thought he was sure to give it a try, since he would have plenty of time ahead of him for the next couple of years. Behind the chairs was a fully equipped mahogany pool table with a billiard lamp and two bar stools.

"This is amazing!" Garrison admitted. "Why hadn't I heard about this."

"It's actually a well-guarded secret," smiled Ayman. "After enduring the long journey, all Mars astronauts have agreed that this little fringe benefit really makes their day."

"Or in our case," Boronov interjected, "it makes our two years. It is, as the American say, icing on cake, I think?"

"Icing on the cake?" Garrison reacted. "This is the whole darn bakery, Dmitri."

"Come," Ayman put his hand on Garrison's shoulder. "You'll have plenty of time to enjoy this room. First, we need to show you the rest of the compound."

They exited the foyer and wandered back down the hallway. They opened a door, previously unexplored by Garrison, and turned on a light inside. This was not a room but instead a staircase which led down to a

33

tunnel under the ground. The tunnel was lit by fluorescent lights mounted to the concrete ceiling. The walls and floor were also concrete and were sealed to maintain the pressure and oxygen needed by the astronauts. After walking for about thirty feet, a staircase took them back up to another closed door, which Ayman, leading the way, opened up for the three astronauts.

As Garrison emerged from the door, he found that he was in a very large open room, clearly a workshop. There were tools and electronic devices of all different types. Workbenches complete with electrostatic discharge mats allowed the astronauts the ability to work on all types of electronics. A twenty-foot tall roll-up door was visible at the end of the building. Just inside the door was a vehicle which looked like a jeep but had four axles underneath the chassis. Each axle had two wheels on a side for a total of sixteen wheels. This was the Mars Terrain Vehicle or MTV. He recognized it instantly, as he had practiced driving prototypes through obstacle courses at the China Lake Naval Weapon Center just outside of Death Valley, California. He knew how this little vehicle could climb over boulders, and almost vertically up the sides of canyon walls, a useful ability, considering the vast number of cratered walls that would have to be encountered and handled on Mars.

After a brief introduction to some of the equipment and safety procedures of the workshop, Ayman confessed that there would be much about this building that Garrison would have to become familiar with due time. Dmitri would provide him with full training on all of the facilities within the next month. During the three or so months of transition, there would be no scientific missions or planetary explorations in order to allow the new astronauts a full briefing of the camp.

The group returned back down the stairway and then proceeded into a different corridor that Garrison did not notice during his first trip down the tunnel. It led to a bunker 150 feet below ground. The bunker was a huge cavern about 300 yards wide by 500 yards long. Despite its size, it was well-lit with a regular array of fluorescent lighting along the ceiling and walls. There were racks full of emergency supplies. Should anything go wrong on Camp Mars, the astronauts would be able to survive in the bunker for three months—long enough for a rescue mission to arrive and return the astronauts safely back to Earth.

The most likely and devastating scenario for such an emergency was a meteor impact. Mars was situated very close to the asteroid belt, which made it particularly vulnerable to meteor impacts. Fortunately, the thin atmosphere was still sufficient to mitigate the threat of constant meteoric bombardment, so the odds of a meteor landing in the vicinity of Camp Mars were very remote. While the possibility of this event was certainly weighed by NASA early on in the planning of the Camp Mars project, there was still good reason to justify the 120 billion dollars that the mission has cost NASA since its beginning a couple of decades earlier.

Ayman was proving to be an excellent tour guide, effectively showing Garrison the most important aspects of Martian living and working. They now returned to the workshop and suited up to go outside. Garrison was surprised at how quickly his fellow astronauts were able to fully suit up, and while he was finishing this laborious activity, the others had already rolled up the large garage door, fired up the MTV and drove it into the decompression garage.

After Garrison joined them in this new room, Dmitri pressed a button on a control panel to close the garage door behind them. Then, pressing another button, a loud hissing sound indicated that the room was losing most of its precious oxygen. Once the valves and gauges of the pressurization system had detected nearly equivalent pressures inside and outside of the garage, a second roll-up door slowly elevated.

A dull brown sunlight began to splash into the garage, and it was the first time that Garrison realized that he had not seen sunlight since he arrived on Mars. He'd forgotten that due to pressurization differences between the inside and outside of the buildings, windows were features that could not be added. Instead, solid concrete and rock walls, five feet thick were needed to ensure a safe, pressurized environment in which the astronauts could live.

Ayman climbed into the driver's seat of the MTV, and Dmitri gestured for Garrison to take the passenger's seat. The MTV was really built just for two passengers, since that was the typical operating procedure. However, a flat and uncomfortable platform in the back of the vehicle served as seating for additional passengers.

"No," said Garrison to his senior companion. "You should sit up front, Dmitri."

"It is not so," Dmitri responded quietly. "Ayman will show you much about the compound. It will be better learning for you in front seat."

Garrison yielded reluctantly to this logic, and with all three astronauts configured in the vehicle, Ayman nudged the accelerator, and the MTV lunged for the paved driveway outside of the garage. Garrison lowered his sunshield over his helmet. While the Sun is not quite as bright on Mars, it was still brighter than inside. Further, there was a dusty glare through the atmosphere that made it even more difficult to see.

With jaw dropped, he surveyed the landscape for the first time. Upon his arrival, he had been too exhausted to notice anything. He looked down at the rust-colored dirt off to the side of the black asphalt. He could see lava rocks protruding from the layer of fine-grained Martian sand. He looked up to the rim of the crater. With a quick 360-degree examination, he could see that he was in the center of the crater with steeply-sloped walls that rose hundreds of feet above the ground. With only one exception, the camp was completely surrounded by cliffs. After vast deliberation and somewhat heated arguments at NASA headquarters, it was the exception which Garrison was now observing that compelled NASA to select this crater as the site of the camp.

Camp Mars was located in a crater that was very similar to most of the impact craters originally. However, a lava flow from Arsia Mons surrounded this particular crater and eventually broke through one of its walls, flooding it with lava. As a result, this crater was an extremely desirable location. At three-miles wide, it was just the right size. It had walls to protect the camp from high winds and dust storms. It had a natural opening that gave easy access into and out of the crater. And unlike most craters which are significantly deep because of the impact, this crater had been filled in, such that it was at the same exact elevation on the inside of the crater as it was on the outside of it.

High up on one cliff, he saw large American and Russian flags perched next to each other, but noticed the discoloration caused by the Martian atmosphere. The American flag appeared to have brown and yellow stripes and yellow stars set on a background of purple waved in a gentle breeze while a smaller-than-expected sun shown in the tawny sky above. Garrison and Dmitri remained quiet as they allowed the surrealistic nature of O'Ryan's new home to settle in.

Due to the electric engine and smooth suspension of the MTV, Garrison didn't realize that they had just made their first stop. He was still enraptured with his new surroundings.

"Garrison," Ayman stated in grandiose fashion. "This is the SAR pad."

Garrison snapped out of his amazement and returned to the task at hand. He saw a huge building about a half-mile long and five stories tall. It was by far the largest and most dominating of any building in the crater. However, its design was similar to the other buildings around camp, so there was nothing particularly aesthetic about it. Four concrete walls and a flat steel-reinforced concrete ceiling did not give Garrison anything to write home about. However, this building, he knew to be one of the most significant and well-used facilities on the premises. Indeed, the SAR pad was absolutely essential to life on Mars.

...

Sub-atomic replication was an earth-shattering invention that occurred just before Garrison was born. A team of physicists under contract with the U.S. government worked on a project so secretive that it rivaled the efforts of the Manhattan Project which brought the world into the nuclear age way back in the twentieth century. Their efforts landed themselves a Nobel Prize in physics for their invention.

The concept of sub-atomic replication is simple enough. Everything that has mass is made up of atoms. These atoms have sub-atomic building blocks—neutrons, protons, and electrons. The theory for years had been that if you could take an atom and reconfigure the number and relationship of these sub-atomic particles then you could literally turn any atom into a completely different atom. For this reason, the project was dubbed the Midas Project, with the thought in mind that if the project succeeded, then it would literally be possible that anything could be turned to gold.

Once the physicists were able to demonstrate the successful reconfiguration of an atom, they could then turn their alchemistic efforts to the molecular level. The problem which hampered the scientists for so long was how they could reconfigure an object of significant complexity. The usefulness of the solution was very limiting, because they were only able to demonstrate sub-atomic replication to the most basic of materials. Such would be of little use to the government.

A significant breakthrough occurred when a particular electrochemical reaction was discovered that facilitated the stripping away of layers of complex objects, but there were still two problems that remained. First, the massive amount of computation and data storage that was required to understand the object's exact sub-atomic ingredients and relationships were daunting. Second, because layers were literally stripped away one at a time, only solid materials could effectively be replicated. Liquids and gasses would escape their container as they were stripped away sub-atomically. For example, if the SAR machine were to strip away the layers of glass, there would be no glass to hold the water. Thus, before the layers representing the water could be reached, the contents of the glass became a mere puddle on the floor, making it impossible to reconstruct its original state inside the glass.

To solve the first problem, the team worked long and hard on an algorithm using photonic computing. Photonic computers utilize a different approach to calculation than do classic computers. While the latter relies on bits which can take on one of two binary states—0 or 1—the former relies on colored photons of light that race around nano-optic cables. Each photon conveys 32 bits of data that represents a unique signature of the color and its brightness. The fact that they travel at the speed of light makes it even faster to move data around. In order to solve the second problem, the team used magnetic refrigerators in order to produce temperatures near absolute zero. At sufficiently cold temperatures, all matter freezes. Once frozen, it is then possible to strip away the layers to compose a full chemical map of the object. It turned out that magnetic refrigeration made the entire process more robust. Because of the lack of heat, the state of the sub-atomic particles showed very little variance during the process of decomposition, and as a result, the map was less likely to be in error when the object was replicated. This, then, was the silver lining that paid out gold for the Midas Project.

The project proved to be a tremendous success, and talk of "teleportation" became a household standard. Yet, because of the manner in which the problem was solved, sub-atomic replication only applied to non-living material. Scientists would have to go back to the drawing board if they ever wanted to teleport people seamlessly from point A to point B. Once the myth was dispelled that NASA had no astronauts that could bark the command, "Beam me up, Scotty," interest among the lay person diminished.

But as time went by that interest was rekindled in the business sector. Entrepreneurs began to realize the potential of sub-atomic replication. Imagine the money that could be saved in the transportation industry if long-haul truck drivers could be replaced with regional SAR pads. Manufacturers salivated at the thought of producing a map of one superior product which could be cloned by throwing a bunch of sand into a machine. At one point, Coca-Cola was known to request licensing the technology for a one-time fee of $600 billion, because they recognized how quickly they could recover the price when they would only need to come up with massive quantities of very low-price raw materials—dirt, rocks, garbage—that they could be fed into a SAR generator and thereby crank out bottle after bottle of refreshing carbonated beverages. When the U.S. government promptly shut down discussions, Coca-Cola renegotiated based on a potentially more lucrative royalty-based proposal. It would offer the U.S. an opportunity to reap the profits directly from the manufacturer instead of through the tax structure. While such a proposal had many on Capitol Hill scouring calculations about what such a proposal might do to release the U.S. of an ever-blossoming budget deficit, many experts were quick to point out the socio-economic devastation that might result.

Fears were justified just months after the second Coca-Cola proposal was nixed. A ring of NASA scientists were scandalized for unauthorized usage of the SAR pad. They had crafted a way to bypass certain security mechanisms such that there was no record of their entry. However, federal agents investigating a counterfeit money scheme eventually discovered the operation. After convictions and sentences were issued to the participants, NASA tightened security at each earth-based SAR pad to prevent further corruption. In the meantime, progress on Camp Mars was hampered such that the project completed two years behind schedule and caused great public outcry for its budget overruns.

Now recognizing the potential problems that such a technology would cast onto a fragile international economy, the U.S. government thought it wise to treat sub-atomic replication as secret as nuclear technology. Further, the number of sub-atomic facilities had been limited to just five. These were located at Edwards Air Force Base in California, Kennedy Space Center in Florida, Johnson Space Center in Texas, Camp Moon, and Camp Mars. Each was equipped to decompose or replicate any object from encrypted data which was transmitted to its receiver from any other site via satellite.

It is impossible to argue against the fact that SAR technology was absolutely required for sustained life on Mars. Through the technology, astronauts obtain everything from chisels to cheese-steak sandwiches to the very chemicals and supplies needed to run the SAR pad. From a constant supply of mass acquired through waste materials, astronauts are able to restock everything they need to sustain life.

The only additional requirement to make life on Camp Mars possible is the constant demand on energy to make all of the chemical transitions. Fortunately, the sun is a constant source of energy on Mars, for which the astronauts can tap into without any atmospheric obstructions making solar energy a very reliable source of power.

. . .

As the crew staggered towards the massive building in the awkward gravity of Mars, Dmitri was the first to reach the steel door. He released the latch mechanism and slowly swung the door open with some effort. Garrison peered into utter darkness while Ayman crossed the threshold and flipped a large circuit breaker. The room flooded with a bright light that caused Garrison to squint at first. He walked inside to see a cavernous concrete box. Very little adorned this wide-open building, but upon close scrutiny, Garrison did notice that the back wall was lined with tall chemical canisters and pipes running out of them in a chaotic looking manner. They ran this way and that up the wall and into the ceiling. There were tiny darkened windows about twelve inches square all the way around the interior about half way up each wall. There was a room in one corner of the building that had a large window about 15 feet off of the floor. Through the window, Garrison could see a series of control panels with yellow and green lights sparsely spread across each panel. Garrison's attention was then drawn to the center of the room. He peered intensely and noticed that there was a tiny object adorning the floor of the room a couple of hundred yards away.

"What's that?" Garrison asked, gesturing to the object?

"Ah," exclaimed Ayman. "That would be my new headset. I'll just go pick it up and meet you two in the control room."

Ayman then hopped onto an electric scooter and proceeded to drive to the headset a couple of hundred yards away. Dmitri led Garrison to the control room, first entering the decompression chamber. With the door to the SAR pad sealed, Garrison heard the now familiar sound of air filling the chamber. The two proceeded through another door and proceeded up a stairwell into the control room. After removing their helmets, Garrison looked out of the window to see Ayman driving the scooter back in the direction of the control room. Within a minute he had joined them.

"NASA has asked us to send them the faulty headset so that they can assess the problem," Ayman informed Garrison as he swapped the faulty set out of his helmet for the good one.

Ayman returned to the center of the room on the scooter and set the faulty set down. After returning, he handed Garrison a pair of dark goggles. Noticing that Dmitri had already put a pair of goggles on himself, he followed the lead of his colleagues.

"I show you the SAR controls," Dmitri gestured at the main control panel. "First, we decompose the headset. Because it is such small object, this will only take few seconds."

The first button that Dmitri pushed extinguished the lights from the main room. Then, he dimmed the white lights from the control room, leaving a faint glow of red lighting that shined directly onto the control panel.

"Now, we replenish environment with correct chemical vapor level," Dmitri depressed another button, which initiated a whistling sound that persisted for a couple of minutes.

"Environment sensors in room inform computer how to correct vapor levels. Once correct levels are reached, this light here will turn on."

When the team of astronauts saw the square green light with the words "Environment Stable" on it, decomposition could begin. Dmitri slowly turning a knob clockwise, and while doing so, Garrison could see a green glow develop in the main room. He could see a slight haze from the chemicals which had recently been injected as well. In a flash, he saw a steady stream of lasers scanning the room from the windows along the walls. Green, red, and white lasers splashed throughout the room for about six seconds, and then a sudden darkness and quiet enveloped the whole of the SAR pad.

Pushing one last button, the lights were turned on in full and the three astronauts removed their goggles. Garrison looked out into the room and noticed that the headset which sat on the floor was now gone. Decomposed into a fine dust which he could not see due to the distance, the headset became nothing more than a stream of 0s and 1s rushing up to one of the four satellites orbiting Mars. Within fifteen minutes, the data would arrive on Earth, allowing technicians there to replicate and study the headset to determine the source of failure and improve the design in the future.

"And that's all there is to it, Garrison." Ayman said grabbing O'Ryan on the shoulder. "One of the most technologically complicated inventions of the millennium boiled down to the push of a few buttons.

While Ayman and Dmitri were the first to place their helmets on their heads, Garrison's head continued to shake his head in awe of the scene he had just witnessed.

...

The team of astronauts left the SAR pad and continued on their tour, first stopping at the well house on the Southern end of the crater. Before studying the underground world of Mars, NASA knew that the SAR pad could be used for delivering water to the astronauts. A 55-gallon barrel of ice could easily be decomposed and sent once to the camp. That formula could then be saved into the computer, allowing the astronauts to create as many barrels as were needed. However, after sufficient investigation, areologists were quick to conclude that there likely were large reservoirs of water underneath the surface. After drilling in several locations on the crater, a reservoir had indeed been found several thousand feet below the crater floor. While there was no cycle of precipitation to replenish the reservoir, experts had calculated that the reservoir that had been tapped into should last for a few decades of use in the camp.

The road from the well passed along a couple of smaller craters, evidence of impact since the main crater had been established. O'Ryan was tempted to ask whether his colleagues worried about meteor impacts. An impact was the one thing that Garrison feared the most during his time on Mars. Remembering the lesson that his trainers had engrained in him memory, he shook his head and said to himself, "Stop it, O'Ryan! You're much more likely to be killed by lightning on earth, than to be killed by a meteor impact on Mars."

On the west side of the crater, Ayman pointed out the communication towers to Garrison as the team stopped briefly in front of an array of ten large satellite receivers and various radio transmitters all pointed in different directions. After Ayman enumerated the uses and functions of each tower, the team drove on, passing by two large fuel tanks used to store the propellant needed by departing shuttles. Here, the road parallels the two-mile long airstrip. Garrison could see a Mars Shuttle down the runway just outside of the hangar. He knew that this was Ayman's aircraft, and that soon, the crew on Mars would consist of just himself and the Russian.

Now at the north end of the crater, Ayman parked the vehicle at an electric sub-station on the other side of the crater. The station tied into a vast field of solar panels that filled in the entire crater north of the airstrip. Because of the distance from the sun, solar electricity was less efficient than it was on Earth, and that meant that the power needs of the camp would require a two square mile area of solar panels collecting as much sunlight as possible. Ayman led Garrison on a tour of the sub-station and the solar field. As they returned back towards the vehicle, the sun was getting lower on the horizon.

"Well, gentlemen," announced Ayman. "I will be leaving you here. I need to get that thing off the ground before the Sun sets."

"Thanks for the tour, Ayman." Garrison was appreciative of the hospitality but also felt tentative of his departure. While Dmitri was certainly a capable host, talk had been intermittent, since he deferred much of the orientation to his American companion.

"You're welcome, O'Ryan. And good luck with your mission here." Ayman saluted Garrison, since handshakes were not feasible in the spacesuits. He turned and saluted Dmitri as well. "Mr. Boronov, it has been a pleasure serving here with you for the last two years. I'll look forward to seeing you at our joint press conference and debriefing in a couple of months."

Dmitri bowed and saluted. "It has been much pleasure of mine to work with you here on Mars."

With the farewell complete, Ayman turned on his heels and walked towards the shuttle. Garrison and Dmitri watched as their fellow astronaut climbed the ladder into the cockpit and heard over the common channel that Mission Control had cleared him for takeoff as soon as he was ready.

Garrison could see the burn of the engine just before the sound reached his ear. And then, in a flash, the shuttle was down the runway, in the air, and soon out of sight.

...

"Looks like he's gone," Garrison turned to his companion. "What do we do now?"

"Well, friend," Dmitri began. "We have instructions to repair valve gauge on fuel tank number one. When we fueled the Nevada shuttle, we noticed a malfunction on gauge. NASA gave instruction for fixing it."

"Ok, then," accepted Garrison. "Let's go do it."

"Boronov to Mission Control. The Nevada has successfully taken off and we are heading to fuel tank number one for pressure gauge malfunction assessment and repair."

After this brief announcement, the pair walked back to the MTV where Dmitri took over the controls. As he began to back away from the solar field, he stopped abruptly. "Oh. I forget to grab toolbox. We will need to go back to bunker for tools."

Arriving back at the workshop garage, the two astronauts exited the MTV and stopped abruptly on either side. Turning quickly to his colleague, Garrison exclaimed, "What was that?! I just felt something odd."

Dmitri turned slowly to face his partner. "I do not know. Did it feel like... like..." Dmitri grasped for words in English to describe the sensation.

"Almost like a breeze passing through my spacesuit from behind." Garrison turned around, almost expecting to find the source of the mysterious sensation, but all he saw was the massive SAR building on the east end of the crater. No wind. Nothing out of place.

"Yes," panted Dmitri. "I feel same thing too, but it went as quick as it came."

Garrison had a bad feeling about what had just happened. He couldn't explain why, but the concern gave him the sensation of goose bumps on his arms, and a tingling of hair on his neck. He knew that it wasn't just his imagination, since Boronov also felt it. Worse still for O'Ryan was the fact that his companion didn't seem to recollect ever observing the sensation before. Silence fell over the pair, as they grasped to make sense of the matter. A breeze? Inside their space suits? Impossible!

Chapter

5

Walking confidently toward the jury, the District Attorney began wrapping up the case from his perspective. "Ladies and gentlemen, first let me thank you for the full attention that you've given this case over the last couple of weeks. I know that each of you have very busy lives, and I appreciate the devotion and service you have given to see that justice is served.

"What we have before us is a classic case of a crime of passion... a very serious, violent crime of passion. It is a case where the defendant seated over there"—the attorney whirled around and pointed a long index finger at the suspect, who did not flinch at the attention, but who inwardly did despise the man standing before him, trying his best to wrongly ruin his life—"lost better judgment to greed. It is a case where money, in all of its ugliness, cost the lives of two hard-working individuals, murdered in cold blood. Oh, how vain and senseless is the almighty dollar at ruining the lives of people who should know better.

"This man, Paol Joonter, a high-flying executive, flew from his home in Seattle, Washington to Atlanta, Georgia, in order to prevent further risk to a failed business deal. He arrived on March 27th of this year, in order to mitigate the loss of vast corporate wealth, which he, in part is responsible for losing. When he could not succeed in his task, we have shown the unfortunate sequence of events which ensued.

"We have shown through documents and eyewitness that Mr. Joonter purchased a .38 caliber pistol at a local gun dealer on March 28th. We have shown surveillance video of his late-night entry into the office of Mr. Rawson

Becker on the evening of the 28th. We have provided a chilling recorded audio of the exchange of words—and bullets—which experts have matched to the mouth and gun of the defendant. We have given forensic evidence of fingerprints matching those of Mr. Joonter so clearly that Detective Johnson of the FBI was quoted in the courtroom as saying, 'Those prints leapt right off the gun.' There is motive, there is clear, irrefutable evidence, and there is a man who must be punished for his crimes. Paol Joonter is clearly responsible for the cold-blooded murder of Mr. Becker and his assistant, Ms. Shannyl Cox. I'm confident that you will see justice done in this case. Thank you for your time."

As confidently as he approached the jury, he returned to his table convinced of victory in this case. His opponent exchanged some hushed words with his client before proceeding with his closing remarks. While he was one of the most renowned defense attorneys of his day, he couldn't help feeling that the odds were stacked against him. What made him such an excellent lawyer was his ability to remain composed, and to observe and utilize any holes in prosecution's defense. As a result, he did not give the impression that he was on the losing side of the case.

Chapter

6

On his second day of Zimmer's class, Joram was working his Digital Note Tablet much harder than he did on the first day. He was soaking up every word, every thought, which the professor had for the class. Sitting at his left once again, Kath also found herself scribbling frantically, and enjoying the concepts placed before them.

"Over the next several weeks," started the professor, "we'll be studying various examples of the different types of galaxies. We'll discuss how and why they form their characteristic shapes, and compare and contrast these in vast details.

"You should know," attested Zimmer as he paced in front of the class with his wireless lapel microphone broadcasting his lesson clearly to the entire class, "that there are three major classifications of galaxies. These are spiral, elliptical, and irregular.

"Spiral galaxies are perhaps the best known of these, and this is certainly because our own galaxy, the Milky Way, is indeed a spiral galaxy. However, the photos that you may have seen of spiral galaxies come from those which may be indicative to the Milky Way, but certainly do not mirror our own galaxy. For obvious reasons, it is rather difficult to acquire a detailed image of our own galaxy, since there are no spacecraft far enough away which might give us a portrait of our own system. Nevertheless, there are several superb computer renderings that depict our galaxy as shown on this slide."

The professor then gestured behind him, where a computer-generated image of the Milky Way was depicted for the class.

"As you can notice from this image, there is a bar of stars which emanate from either side of the extremely bright galactic center of our galaxy. These bars eventually give way to several spiral arms. This type of galaxy is called, appropriately enough, a barred-spiral galaxy. There are others, as the one in this next image, which do not demonstrate this type of barring effect. In the Hubble Classification, we designate spiral galaxies with the letter 'S', and barred-spiral galaxies with the letters 'SB.'"

At this point, the professor advanced through a series of slides demonstrating other types of galaxies. The class took fastidious notes as Professor Zimmer rattled off a quick and elementary overview of galaxies. This was a graduate class, so he would have to quickly launch into great details about the makeup and classification of galaxies, so he was brief in his introduction.

"Now that I have described to you the various classifications of galaxies in the known universe," Professor Zimmer gestured to a screen where a slide was being projected, "it is prudent for us to begin our study of each type. We will begin, appropriately enough, with our own galaxy, the Milky Way."

The professor was interrupted here by the opening of door to the back of the planetarium. He looked up to see Dean Scoville enter and assume a standing position in the same exact place as last time.

Joram whispered to Kath, "That guy is making a habit out of disrupting the professor right at the end of class."

"That guy," breathed Kath lowly, covering her mouth to be less conspicuous, "is Dean Scoville."

Joram's head whipped back again to see a rather urgent look on Scoville's face. "He looks—" Trailing off, he recalled the awkward episode that occurred on Monday, and snapped a worried glance up to Zimmer. Fortunately, the professor did not notice the two friends' discussion, but instead looked intently at the dean. The two seemed to exchange knowing glances for a moment before the professor turned back to his class.

"But that discussion," began the professor, "will begin on Friday. Also, please take a look at the course website for the first set of selected readings. We will begin discussion on those readings next week. Class dismissed."

Rather than wait at the back of the class this time, Dean Scoville swept down the stairs and onto the stage to meet up quickly with Zimmer. Joram watched the pair intently, while the rest of the class turned off their note tablets, and fumbled for their backpacks. There was no exchange of words as the two met up. Instead, Scoville gave a slight nod and gestured towards the door in the back of the room where the two swiftly disappeared from sight.

"What do you think that was all about?" Joram asked Kath.

"Huh?" Kath asked looking up at Joram as she zipped her pack. "Oh, you mean Scoville and Zimmer? Don't know... it looked pretty important though." Then, shrugging off the incident, she continued, "Hey, I'm thirsty. Let's go get something to drink."

As they left the planetarium, Joram looked back towards the closed door as if expecting to see it reopen or otherwise gain some knowledge as to the urgent departure of the two professors. Realizing that he would gain no further insight, he shrugged his shoulders and bounded up the stairs to rejoin Kath.

...

At Johnson Space Center, two engineers sat quietly in a control room where panels of computer screens monitored activity on Camp Mars. The main screen contained an image of the camp as captured from a digital camera mounted on a satellite orbiting the planet. Other screens contained various waveforms and pulses which monitored environmental and meteorological activity. Side-by-side screens titled Boronov and O'Ryan contained the vital signs of the two astronauts. Another charted the progress of the Shuttle Nevada recently departed from the crater and heading on a direct bearing for the Moon.

Staneck Rodgers and Physon Edwards had worked this station together for years. They were intimately familiar with the operations and mission of the astronauts on Camp Mars.

"Hey, now that Ayman's up in space, it looks like everything is stable here," announced Rodgers. "I'm going to go use the rest room. Be back in a few minutes."

"Sure, no problem," Edwards agreed. "I'll stand watch. It should be pretty boring for a couple of days, while Boronov shows O'Ryan the ropes."

As the door shut behind Staneck, Physon received a communication from Mars: "Boronov to Mission Control. The Nevada has successfully taken off and we are heading to fuel tank number one for pressure gauge malfunction assessment and repair."

Physon leaned back in his chair and cradled his hands behind his head. "Yep... it's gonna get boring around here until mission operations resume next week."

After a few minutes of idle daydreaming and casual monitoring of the data, Physon's life got less boring very quickly, as he heard a pulsing beep coincide with an alarm light on control panel in front of him. He leaned forward to examine the alarm.

"Odd," he said to himself. "I've never seen that alarm malfunction before."

The alarm read "Satellite Two Communication Failure."

Within moments, another pulsating sound: "Satellite Three Communication Failure." With this alarm the main screen showing the video image of the Camp Mars crater went blank.

With the blackness of the screen ahead of him, Fossaman leaned forward in his seat, his mind reeling at this puzzling chain of events. He considered the events. "That's not good... what could cause two satellite link failures within moments..."

Physon was trained to not panic in these situations. False alarms were part of the business of inter-galactic communications. Solar events, asteroid eclipses, even the Earth's own magnetic field would occasionally interrupt the otherwise weak signals emanating from the Mars satellites.

Quickly, however, Physon was required to enter a state of panic, because a litany of alarms went off simultaneously, and all of the monitors on the wall went dark. "Satellite One Communication Failure," "Astronaut One Vitals," "Astronaut Two Vitals," "Satellite Array Failure," "Audio Comm Failure," "Shuttle Comm Failure."

The room was awash with flashing lights and beeps and buzzes of various volumes. Physon quickly muted all of the alarm sounds and reached for his two-way radio.

"Stan, do you copy?" Physon voiced eagerly into the radio.

"Yeah, Physon. What's up?"

"Where are you at? I need you to come quickly."

"I'm on my way back right now. I just stopped at the break room for a cup of coffee. What's wrong, buddy?"

"We have a massive communication failure with Camp Mars right now. I've never seen a comm interruption of this caliber."

"Be right there." Physon's voice and sprinting footsteps echoed with anticipation, as he returned his radio to his holster and raced back to the control room. Within moments, he threw open the door and found Staneck quickly pacing the length of the control panel to assess the situation.

"What have we got, Stan?" Physon asked eagerly for a briefing of the situation.

"Three satellite failure alarms, and a complete link loss to the surface array."

"So, we are still receiving signals from one of the satellites?" queried Physon as he rubbed his forehead with his hand.

"Yeah. Sat Four is still online, but we're only receiving heartbeats, since it's not in range of the camp."

"What's its orbital ETA to line of sight?"

Physon raced to the other end of the panel, assessed the current orbit of Satellite Four, looked at his watch for the current time, punched a few numbers into the computer, and returned the results. "Sixteen hours, thirty-three minutes." Physon looked up at his colleague with concern.

Stan sighed deeply and shook his head yet maintained a calm voice. "You mean the only satellite we got yapping right now is on the opposite side of the planet?"

"Pretty much," confessed Physon bleakly.

Stan ran to the control panel, quickly scanned the situation and immediately picked up a phone and dialed a four-digit extension.

"Vurim, Edwards here. We have a serious communication failure. You better get in here ASAP."

Staneck hung up the phone and looked up at Physon, who appeared sullen. With eyes wide open and perspiration forming around his temples, he raised his eyebrows at his colleague questioningly.

"I know, buddy," Physon's voice trailed off with a hint of concern. "You know, these things rarely implicate something catastrophic, but darn it all, if it doesn't get your heart racing, and turn your hair gray..."

Physon was distracted as his eyes scanned the control room panels. "Stan, come take a look at this."

Stan started when he turned his head and saw Physon grow pale, a horror-stricken stare flaring from his wide-open eyes. Stan was at Physon's side in just a couple of steps and looked at the panel that Physon had motioned towards—the panel labeled O'Ryan.

"Had you noticed O'Ryan's vitals just before the comm failure?" Physon asked his partner.

"No, I... I hadn't," he confessed. "It shows that his heart and breathing rates increased rather abruptly about... oh... 30 seconds before the comm failure. But there's nothing unusual about Boronov's vitals."

"Look closely," Physon rebutted, pointing to the ECG waveforms. "Right here, it looks like Boronov skipped a beat. No racing like O'Ryan, but it looks like there is a synchronized event... perhaps something that startled the pair."

"What do you make of it?" asked the junior engineer.

Physon could do little more than shake his head slowly and shrug his shoulders in dismay.

After a brief pause, Stan asked his more experienced partner, "Weren't you in the control room when mission 79 had to be aborted?"

"Yeah," said Physon breaking into a forced smile. "That was a grueling three-day event that taught me to keep a level head and a stock of Tums on hand."

"But those guys were only a hundred thousand miles from Earth?" pointed out Stan. Our boys are millions of miles away right now, cut off from all communication, perhaps for quite a few hours."

"Indeed." Physon pointed out and reached inside a drawer. Then with a slight smile, he gave one last word to his younger partner. "Tums?" he reached his hand out to his companion with a tube of the antacid in a subdued, yet calming voice, hoping to alleviate some of the tension. He didn't like the symptoms he was seeing at all, but he also knew that it was premature to jump to any conclusions, and also that there was nothing he could do about it at present.

...

With lengthened stride, Scoville rushed down the corridor leading away from the planetarium and back to his office.

"What is it, Ballard?" asked Zimmer who was lagging the dean by a couple of steps.

"I've got NASA on hold."

At this, Professor Zimmer stopped dead in his tracks. Noticing that the sound of the extra pair of footsteps had ceased, Scoville turned back and looked at Zimmer.

"Are they cutting off the funding, Ballard?"

Ballard lowered his head and took a couple of steps back towards Zimmer. "No, no... it's... it's something... worse." With the last word, his voice trailed off. He turned again, and restored to his former swift gait. "You'll be briefed presently."

They rushed into Scoville's office and quickly took seats opposite of each other at a round conference table. A telephone with a blinking red light informed Zimmer of the urgent party waiting on the other end.

Taking the phone off of mute, Scoville announced their return. "Vurim, I'm back. I have Professor Zimmer with me. I believe that you two have met."

"Yes, we have met," answered Vurim affirmatively. "Dr. Zimmer, this is Vurim Gilroy. I'm the director of the Mars Mission here at Johnson Space Center."

"Ah, yes. Dr. Gilroy. We met a few years ago at the International Conference on Modern Astrophysics, didn't we? As I recall, you presented some results and conclusions from your first subterranean drilling explorations of Mars, right?"

"That is correct."

"What can I do for you? I understand you have a matter of some urgency you wish to discuss with me?"

"Unfortunately, yes we do." His voice was hushed, and an audibly deep breath ensued before he began his briefing.

"We are currently studying a set of data regarding a series of disturbing events which happened a few hours ago regarding our Mars mission. We hope you may be of assistance in brainstorming possible astronomical phenomena which might account for the singularities we have witnessed."

"Ok," said Zimmer attentively. "I'll do what I can to help." Zimmer's gaze was fixed on Scoville, as if searching his expressing for clues. Scoville's shrugged his shoulders and shook his head to convey that he knew next to nothing yet himself.

"First of all," stated Gilroy hesitantly, "we'd like to request your presence here at Johnson where we are convening a team of experts to examine the data first-hand."

Scoville looked up at Zimmer, twisted his head, threw up his hands, and nodded slowly. "Well, I just began a new term of courses and research here at the university. Any leave would have to be approved of by Dean Scoville."

"He has assured us full cooperation in this matter," announced Gilroy in a business-like manner.

Zimmer looked at Scoville in a puzzled manner and tapped the mute button. "Ballard?"

"Carlton, we're treading lightly on the funding for your research. We need to bend over backwards for these guys. I'll be sure to cover for your class and research teams. It'll only be for a few days."

After taking the phone off of mute, Zimmer continued. "Ok. When do you need me to leave?"

"I have a chartered plane that will be landing in Burbank at 1:20 PM Pacific Time."

Zimmer looked at his watch, which read 12:17 PM. "Why, that's just an hour away. I'll need some time to pack and…"

"No packing!" Gilroy interrupted shortly. "We'll get everything you need here. You can communicate those needs from the airplane once you're in the air."

"Ok," agreed Zimmer in an overwhelmed manner. "Can I ask what the urgency is all about?"

"I'm afraid that's not possible. We are conversing over an unsecured communication channel, and this is a matter that is currently classified as secret… You do still have a security clearance, Professor?"

"Yes, yes. I'll depart for the airport immediately."

"Thank you for your understanding and support. We'll talk in a few hours."

The phone went dead.

"Ballard, what is going on?"

"I don't know anymore than you, Carlton. But, my hunch tells me that something has gone wrong on Mars. NASA doesn't operate like this unless there is genuine concern for the well-being of their astronauts."

"But, why me? I'm an astrophysicist, not an aerospace engineer. If there's a problem millions of miles away, what possible help will I be?"

"I don't have answers for you, Carlton. But, once you find out what is going on, I'd appreciate hearing from you. I'll need to know what arrangements need to be made here in the department during your absence."

"Will do, Ballard." Zimmer stood up and bid farewell to the dean. He disappeared through the office door and rushed down the corridor for his rendezvous with the jet that had been arranged to pick him up a couple of hours before he himself knew of it. Like Scoville, Zimmer was beginning to fear the worst. NASA was too eager, too quick, too quiet to not cause these two CalTech astronomers significant concern.

...

Professor Zimmer landed in Houston at 6:15 PM. Dr. Gilroy had a car waiting for him to quickly usher him to Johnson Space Center. Gilroy was waiting on the curb for the astronomer when he arrived. He opened the door for Zimmer and shook his hand warmly and gratefully.

Zimmer noticed that he showed signs of fatigue and stress. His complexion was pale, and his eyes deeply red. As they shook hands, the professor could note that Gilroy's hand was tremulous and sweaty.

With a subdued voice, he said, "Thank you for coming, professor. I will escort you through security and into a conference room, where we have compiled a set of data that we hope you can decipher for us."

"I certainly hope that I may be of assistance to you, Doctor," started Zimmer.

The conference room was ample and bright. Entering through a glass door, the professor noted an open feel to the room, because of the windows which wrapped around three sides of the conference room. Along the far wall, which contained no windows, a long counter contained coffee pots, cups, napkins, and a water dispenser. In the center of the room, a long, elliptical table had seating for 12 people, and every seat except for two was occupied. Gilroy offered the professor a seat at the end of the table, and took the seat immediately to his right.

"Professor Zimmer," announced Gilroy, "I'd like to introduce you to a few members of our team. "Starting to your left, we have Staneck Rodgers, Physon Edwards, Kinnet Brothers, and Christian Popolous. These men are mission control specialists for the Mars Mission. Following is our team of engineers. Lawton Jacobsen is our lead telecommunications hardware engineer. Then we have two of our top aerospace engineers, Sharli Cartwright and Cordic Huford, both from Kennedy. Our materials scientist, Lane Wells, is from Ames. And I believe you may know our Martian experts, Draven Sillieu, and Marselline Jones."

"Stan, would you please explain to the team the reason why we have convened this meeting?"

"Certainly," stated Stan with a deep sigh. He slowly lifted himself out of his seat and progressed towards the end of the room opposite of where he unrolled a large map depicting Earth and Mars. Several post-it notes of different color were placed around the map, but Zimmer could not read the writing on any of them.

"At 07:22 this morning local time, an alarm went off indicating that one of the four Martian communication satellite links demonstrated a failure here." Rodgers gestured with a laser pointer to one of the post-it notes on the map. "In three seconds, we lost comm with another satellite here, and this one stopped communicating about two seconds later. For some reason, satellite number four, which was right here at the time of the failures, has continued to transmit, and is currently located here. At first, we assumed that there was an electromagnetic incident which took the satellites offline, but typically, interference lasts a few minutes." Stan paused to look around the room to see how this information was being received.

"Have you calculated a correlation with the timing of the loss of failure?" asked Zimmer.

"Yes," answered Rodgers. "And what we found was that all three satellites failed at exactly the same moment in time. The fact that we observed the alarms at different times is due to the differences in the distance of each satellite from the Earth as well as the latency of the various signals traveling over those distances. Satellite Two was closest to the earth, while

Satellite One was the farthest. As a result, we received these just moments apart due to the extra distance required to reach the Earth."

"I trust they all operate off of the same software code base?" Zimmer quizzed suggestively.

"Yes that is true," Stan's gaze met the floor while his voice tapered off.

Physon stood quickly to relieve his partner. "Professor, we have eliminated the possibility of a software bug causing the failure at the same exact clock cycle."

Zimmer's forehead wrinkled as he gestured for the mission specialist to continue with the details.

"You see, less than thirty minutes before the incident, there was a shift change. An astronaut departed Camp Mars in a shuttle, and we also lost communication with him as well."

Zimmer leaned forward in his seat as if to better comprehend this last statement.

"Communication loss with the shuttle is also calculated to be synchronized to the same exact moment in time." Physon paused to compose his words precisely. "The clock in the shuttle is not synchronized precisely to the satellite array... and the shuttle software team was completely isolated from the satellite software team. In other words, the software code is entirely different for the shuttle. The probability of a synchronized bug between two entirely different pieces of complicated software code... well, it's just not practical to suggest such a correlation."

Zimmer stood on his feet and turned away from the table. Stroking his forehead and cheek, it was clear that his mind was working feverishly. He wheeled around quickly. "A visual... we must get a visual. Surely we can see the satellites and shuttle from a terrestrial-based observatory. It's not all that far to Mars."

Vurim chimed in from his seat. "Madrid has been working on that for the last several hours, but they have not been able to identify a visual on any satellite or on the shuttle."

"Well, their results are bogus! You have told me that there is still one satellite which is communicating. They simply must get a visual on that one."

"At present, it is too close to the horizon of Mars to pick up a visual on it," clarified Vurim. "But we should be able to do so in about two hours." He looked at his watch. "Maybe a bit less than that."

"Madrid should send us their data… we need an extra pair of eyes on it," suggested Zimmer.

"We've got a team of astronomers assembled upstairs… they're looking at the data right now," claimed Vurim.

Zimmer took a new line of suggestive data collection. "Any clues from the data of the remaining satellite? I trust that it is able to communicate with the camp? Can it give us a visual of Mars?" Zimmer brainstormed.

"We've been looking at images of the planet, but nothing looks out of the ordinary… Well, there is a slight dust storm that we're noticing, but that is not unusual. What we're waiting for right now is for Number Four to get into range of Camp Mars. Presently, the Camp is on the opposite side of Mars. Earthrise on Camp Mars won't be for another seven hours, but Satellite Four will have a visual lock in about five hours… we should have at least visual data of the Camp around midnight in order to check on the status of the astronauts there."

"You've been thorough in your analysis, Doctor Vurim," Zimmer admitted. "I'm not sure how I can be of help."

Vurim pleaded with Zimmer, "We need theories, Professor… astronomical, physical theories on what could have caused an event like this to occur. We're at an absolute loss to explain this anomaly."

"I think we're going to need more data," announced Zimmer. "I'd like to take a look at the Madrid data, while we are waiting for Sat Four to get in range. Then, I will want to do some study myself this evening at Palomar. But first, I have a few phone calls to make."

…

Joram Anders rushed up the steps of the apartment complex, bypassing every other step with great strides. At the third floor, he rapped on the door intently. Kath opened the door slowly and playfully.

"Who is it?" she said with a cheerful voice.

Joram gasped for breath. "Ah, Kath… it's me, Joram."

"Joram? I'm sorry, Joram who?" She tried to be coy, but gave herself away with a snicker as she completed the inquiry.

"Ok, Kath," Joram shook his head. "You win... I owe you an apology." Then with a deep breath, he let out, "I'm sorry."

The door opened wide revealing a very light apartment. Joram's shaded his eyes for a moment in part to get used to the light, but mainly to get a less blinding visual on his new friend, who he admitted to himself appeared more and more attractive each time he saw her. This time was no different. Kath looked as beautiful as ever, and he wondered if his tardiness didn't allow her more time to prepare herself for perfection.

Shyly, he looked down at the floor. "I'm really sorry, Kath." Then looking up to meet her eyes, he admitted, "I got so caught up in reviewing my notes from the day that I completely lost track of time."

"Why didn't you answer your cell phone?" she asked.

"I had my Ear Cups on," he explained.

"Oooh," Kath took a step back. "You have a pair of Ear Cups? I'm starting to see more and more of those, but I'm not sure if I like them."

"Why not?" asked Joram.

"They're so... so...," Kath strained for the right word, "unfashionable."

Joram laughed. "They're not supposed to be *fashionable*... they're supposed to be *functional*. My parents got me a pair for my graduation this year. I was so surprised, because they are really not very technical people... I didn't even know they knew about them, since they're so new! They're much more comfortable that head phones or ear buds because they just cup right over your ear, and the slight suction effect keeps them on snug. The sound quality is amazing, and I'm surprised at how well they cancel the surrounding noise... which is the reason why my parents got them for me. They were all, 'You know it's gonna be noisy around that college. You should have something to help you study without all of the distractions.'"

"Well, I'll just have to try them for myself sometime," Kath conceded. "But you still won't catch me with them at the gym."

"No," Joram chuckled. "I guess I wouldn't."

"Well, let me just grab my purse and we'll be on our way then."

Joram waited outside the open door, but he studied the apartment, looking for clues about Kath's interests and tastes. It was sparsely decorated, a common practice among all college students, but it looked comfortable nevertheless.

"So, I hear Louie's makes the best pizza," Joram offered as they strode together down the stairs.

"It's really, really good," Kath admitted. "I'm sure I must be in there once a week. Goodness, I'm starving just thinking about it."

"Well, you wouldn't be if your dinner partner would've been on time."

Kath touched him lightly on the forearm. "It's ok, Joram, really. I understand."

At Louie's, Joram was in heaven. The pizza was indeed delicious and Kath's company was simply delightful. He couldn't help feel a little jealous for all of the guys at the place that seemed to know her. He had thought about how his life had changed so quickly. Why, just a week ago, he was still on his rural farm outside of Wichita, Kansas helping himself to a hearty plate of meatloaf and mashed potatoes before heading out to admire the stars in the night sky. Now here he was in bustling Pasadena, California, enjoying the company of a lovely young lady in a very active and trendy restaurant. He snapped himself out of the daydream.

"So there I was," Kath continued in the middle of an animated story. "drenching wet, and the police officer asks me, 'is that what you normally go swimming in?'"

Joram forced a laugh, wishing he had actually paid more attention to what must have been a fascinating tale. Just as Kath's raucous laughter began to subside, Joram's cell phone rang. He pulled it out of his pants pocket and looked at the caller ID.

"Oh sure," Kath tilted her head slyly and allowed a wisp of hair to cover her winking eye. "In your quiet apartment you can't hear my phone call, and now in one of the most noisy restaurants in Pasadena, you can hear it just fine."

Joram smiled with feigned irritation. "I don't know who it is… it's a local call. I wonder who it could be."

"Well, the best way to find out is to answer it," Kath allowed the distraction.

"Hello," Joram answered jovially. The smile eroded from his face, and he sat upright in his chair.

"Um, yes, professor, right... um... hello... how are you on this fine evening?" He winced in embarrassment while hearing how lamely he had greeted the caller.

His grew quiet and pale.

"I'm sorry... it's a little noisy here." He covered one ear as if to hear better. "Did you say tonight?"

He looked at his watch and appeared ready to rebut, but thought better of it. "Where? But, I don't understand... Well, okay, I'll see you then. Good Bye."

After a moment of tense silence, Kath attempted to ease any discomfort that Joram may have been feeling. "You know if you're going to hold your mouth open like that, you might as well start on another piece of pizza."

He decided to use his mouth in a different way—by explaining to Kath the mysterious nature of the phone call.

"That was Professor Zimmer!" He said in confused excitement. "He said that I need to..."

His explanation was cut short. Now it was Kath who had a call on her phone. "Hold that thought... I'll just be a moment."

"Hello," she answered.

Her mouth dropped as she cupped her hand over the microphone. "It's Professor Zimmer," she whispered in amazement to Joram, who threw up his hands in amazement and leaned in over the table as if proximity to Kath would help him solve the mystery. He listened intently as the conversation continued.

"Tonight?"

"Wha...? Where?"

"What's this all about, Professor?"

She stared at Joram intently, searching for him to give her clues about the situation. He could only stare blankly into her eyes while shaking his head.

"Okay... uh... bye then."

She slowly placed her phone back in her purse.

"Tonight?" Joram inquired on the edge of his seat.

"Uh-huh," She mouthed back.

"At the Burbank Airport?"

"Uh-huh."

"The private terminal."

"Uh-huh."

"Rendezvous with a helicopter?"

"Uh-huh."

"Heading to Paris, France?"

"Uh-huh... No, wait." Kath collected herself. A smile slowly appeared on her face as she admired Joram's trick to pull her back to reality.

"No, Mount Palomar, silly... the same thing he told you, right?"

"Uh-huh," Joram playfully mocked Kath with a falsetto voice intended to mimic her responses to him.

"Very funny, Joram Anders." She looked at her watch. "We have to get going... we don't have much time to pack before Zimmer meets us at the airport... What do you think this is all about, Joram?"

"I don't know, but what the heck... a helicopter ride to a mountain observatory for some star-gazing... sounds wonderful to me. Let's go!"

"Yeah, it sounds rather..." Kath caught herself and blushed slightly as she pulled the word "romantic" off of her lips and responded, "Rather wonderful."

...

Kath and Joram paused as they entered the helicopter terminal together. Kath pulled a roller bag behind her, while Joram had a duffel bag on his shoulder. They both looked around for Professor Zimmer who was to meet them here.

"I'll just check at the counter," Joram said.

With sleepy eyes, Kath watched Joram approach the counter and engage a young man on the other side. The young man motioned to his right and exchanged some words and a smile with Joram, who nodded and turned back towards Kath.

"We need to wait in room 109 right over there," Joram offered as the two continued towards the meeting room.

As they entered the small, well-lit room, they saw another individual slumped in a seat. As he heard them enter, he stood up and peered at them, straining to identify them as someone he knew. Joram was the first to recognize the individual as the person who entered the planetarium on the first day of class when he was relaxing in his fully-reclined seat.

"You're in Professor Zimmer's A21 class, aren't you?" Joram offered his right hand.

"Yes," said the young man accepting Joram's firm handshake. "As I recall, you were the first person in the room on Monday weren't you?"

Joram blushed, realizing that he had been caught off guard that first day of class as he had expected.

"Yes," he chuckled. "I suspect you caught me in a rather vulnerable position there didn't you."

Kath cocked her head slightly and gave Joram an inquisitive glance.

"I arrived early to class that first day, so that I could acquaint myself with the planetarium. I was experimenting with the controls of the seat, and got a little comfortable when I reclined it all the way."

At first, Kath snickered, but she quickly regained her control... for just a moment before she had a chance to visualize Joram being caught in that position. The thought, coupled with her fatigue, made her burst into such a fit of laughter that her new companion joined in heartily as well.

Joram rolled his eyes and nodded, blushing even more.

"I'm sorry, Joram," Kath said. "I know it's not funny, I just..."

"It's ok, Kath," accepted Joram. "Actually, it is pretty funny, so I don't fault you."

Kath now turned to her classmate, "I'm Kath Mirabelle."

"Oh, I'm Reyd Eastman," their fellow student introduced himself throwing his right hand out in front of him quickly. "It's nice to meet both of you."

"Reyd," Joram grabbed his colleague's hand and bypassed the chit chat, "do you know why we're all here?"

"No, I have no idea, Professor Zimmer just said..." Reyd was cut off abruptly.

"I can tell you why we're here," announced Professor Zimmer, looking rather haggard from his second flight of the day. "But please follow me to the helicopter first."

The trio of graduate students retrieved their luggage and obeyed the professor quickly and quietly as they proceeded out of the room and down the hall of the terminal.

63

For an aging professor, the trio of students was surprised at the quickness of his gait. After briskly catching up to him, Joram's curiosity won out over discretion. He turned his face towards Zimmer and asked, "Professor, what is this about?"

"I'm not at liberty to say here in the terminal, Joram," the professor looked straight ahead and continued his rapid pace. "While the situation was declassified just moments before my plane landed, NASA is scheduling a press conference later this evening, and I am not at liberty to speak of the matter here. I'll tell you everything once we're aboard the helicopter."

Joram tried to piece the clues together. Situation? NASA? Press conf… Joram looked at his watch… a press conference later this evening? It was already 11:45 PM. Why would NASA schedule a press conference this late in the evening? Something was obviously very urgent. And then, didn't the professor say something about a plane landing? But he was just in class with him about 12 hours ago. Where could he have gone—and returned—so suddenly?

The professor continued his pace with the students following along with him silently all the way to the tarmac where a helicopter's blades were already whirring overhead. A pair of airport personnel rushed out to meet the party and assist the group and their luggage into the helicopter. A pilot assisted Kath into the cockpit first and then helped Joram, Reyd, and lastly the professor. Each seat had a headset on it, and each member placed it on their heads. After the pilot gave some brief instructions, all of the passengers were harnessed into their seat and clearance was granted from air traffic controllers for departure.

The helicopter lifted slowly off the ground, and the three students gazed out of their windows to see the lights of Southern California stretch to the horizon in nearly all directions. A smattering of lights could also be seen in the mountains to the north of the city. They watched until the ground disappeared under a dense marine layer and soon all that could be seen was the flashing lights of the helicopter itself and the moonless sky filled with a vast array of stars of various brightness and color. Joram admired the scene overhead. He had only been in Southern California for a week, and he was already missing the expansive, star-filled sky over his home in Kansas.

Joram looked back over at the professor who was studying the contents of a manila folder intently. After a moment he looked up at the pilot, who was engaged with final departure communication from the airport. The pilot looked back at Zimmer and nodded.

Reaching for a button on his headset, he engaged his microphone. Looking at his perplexed trio, he spoke, "Can you all hear me okay?" They each nodded and leaned towards the professor with intent curiosity, as if by proximity they would be able to hear him through the noise of the helicopter better.

"You'll recall that Dean Scoville came into my classroom today as lecture was finishing up. He led me to his office, where I was given a very urgent assignment from NASA. I have been to Johnson Space Center, where they have briefed me on a situation of utmost concern." He paused, not sure how to continue. "It is our lot to solve a rather perplexing astronomical puzzle as quickly as possible, which is why I have summoned the three of you to travel with me to Palomar tonight."

He caught himself with that statement, "By the way, I have failed to thank you for your willingness to do this without sufficient preparation or explanation. My apologies for not being clearer... I had to be brief on the phone because this situation was classified when I spoke to you."

Another longer pause ensued, as he was not sure he wanted to precede his briefing with the following introduction. "There are at least three astronauts whose lives could be in jeopardy at this very moment."

At that, Kath gave a start, and covered her gasping mouth with her hands. Joram leaned back in his seat, horrified at the implication. Reyd dropped his head in realization of the seriousness of the situation.

Zimmer gave his students the details as they had been conveyed to him by Gilroy's task force.

"Now, we had hoped to have a visual on the camp by now, seeing how the lone communicating satellite is directly overhead. However, a severe dust storm has completely obscured visibility of 60% of the surface of the planet. Even so, the satellite should be able to communicate with equipment at the camp, but..." with this Zimmer lowered his head, "... but, I'm afraid that there is no signal. Now, the timing is not as desirable as we'd like," Zimmer began to wrap up his briefing. "At this late hour, we will only have a few good hours to collect data."

With an introduction to the situation out of the way, Professor Zimmer instructed his graduate students in the plans which he had devised on the plane trip back from Houston. "Joram, you will accompany Reyd, who has familiarity with the setup at Palomar. Reyd received his bachelor's degree last Spring in Computer Science with a minor in Astronomy. He will be able to work the system to process the data in any manner we need. Kath, as the only meteorologist currently in the program, I have called on you to study the dynamics of the dust storm. This is not a storm of any typical nature that has ever been observed occurring on our neighbor. I, in the meantime, will control the telescope to collect what I believe will be the most useful set of data for us to process. For the time being, I advise you to get what little rest you can before we land at Palomar. If you have any questions, just press the red button on your headset right here."

Kath was the first to deploy her microphone. "Professor, you are correct that I have studied meteorology, but only as it pertains to Earth. I have no notion of the atmospheric dynamics on Mars to be able to adequately perform this study."

"I suspect that you will learn quickly, Miss Mirabelle," began Zimmer, "As soon as we touch down, you will have complete access to a team of Martian meteorologists in Israel. They are prepared to teleconference with you and have been given express instructions to give you full access to their knowledge. Ask them any question that you need. Call upon them for any report of data that may help. Your job is to communicate to the team assembled at Palomar any and all details as they unravel from the team in Israel."

Kath nodded her head. She did not feel adequate to the task, but also did not want to let the professor down, and she certainly did not want to let down the three astronauts whose lives could depend on the teamwork of everybody involved on their behalf.

"Any more questions?" probed the professor.

Joram had many, but he knew that he could defer many of them to Reyd once they were on the ground, so as to not distract the professor from any data processing or theorizing on the matter for the remainder of the flight.

After a moment of silence, the professor returned to his seat, reclined the seat back slightly, and rested his head, heaving a burdened sigh as he closed his eyes.

Kath, who sat next to Joram took off her headset and spoke above the noisy helicopter into Joram's ear. "How exactly are we supposed to rest with this racket?"

Joram reached under his seat and pulled out a pair of objects from his duffel bag. "You said that you were wanting to try these, and well... I thought they might come in handy for you on the flight."

Kath smiled in amazement. In the little time that Joram had to pack for the trip, he was thoughtful enough to remember his Ear Cups... for her!

She placed them over her ears, and was quite shocked to discover that they worked amazingly well. She could hear almost nothing. In his ear, she said, "You're wonderful, Joram Anders," and proceeded to kiss him on the cheek.

The two exchanged a warm smile with each other before Kath got comfortable, resting her head on Joram's broad shoulder. In an instant, she was asleep as if resting in her own bed, and not on a noisy helicopter bound for a mountain observatory 100 miles away.

Chapter

7

With a commanding presence, Warron slid his seat back deliberately, causing a slight squeak as it rubbed on the tile floor. He stood erect and turned to face the jury. Beginning at the lower left of the jury box, Warron ensured that he had the attention of each juror. Scanning the last juror seated in the upper right corner, a young male college student, he felt confident on whom he should focus to provide the desired results.

Obviously, he needed all twelve to be able to acquit his client, and that was the ultimate goal. However, success could also be measured with a single "not guilty" verdict, since a hung jury would reset the entire legal cycle, which favored his client in two ways. First, it gave Warron even more time to build a better case through the learning he had acquired during the first trial. Second, lengthy legal proceedings would stretch the resources of the district attorney's office, causing the state-appointed counsel to weary of the case.

While he was one of the most renowned defense attorneys of his day, he couldn't help feeling that the odds were stacked against him. What made him such an excellent lawyer was his ability to remain composed, and to observe and utilize any holes in prosecution's defense. As a result, he did not give the impression that he was on the losing side of the case.

"Ladies and gentlemen of the jury," he began. "You will recall that when you were selected a little over two weeks ago, Judge Etherton shared with you some instructions that you must apply during your tenure as a juror in this court. First, he mentioned that the defendent must be presumed innocent until proven guilty. As you look over at Mr. Joonter, I trust that none of you have looked at him as a guilty man during the course of this trial. When you walk into your room to deliberate, you must then decide whether there is ample evidence to convict this man of the serious crimes with which he is charged. Because my client is innocent of any wrong-doing, you hold the fate of his future in your hand.

"Second," the lawyer started pacing slowly along the jury in order to make direct eye contact with each of its fourteen members, "the judge instructed that you do not need to determine his guilt beyond a shadow of a doubt, but instead, you must determine whether there is 'reasonable doubt' in the evidence presented to you by the prosecution. With that said, it is my duty to convince you that there is most certainly reasonable doubt in this case. In talking with my client, in reviewing the details of this case, in hearing the arguments put forward by the district attorney, I can certainly assure you of that fact.

"Take a look at the character of Mr. Joonter. He was born into the most unfortunate of circumstances. His parents, murdered by a carjacker, left him orphaned at the age of two. A kind couple adopted him and gave him a chance to succeed in life. As an adolescent, he admits that he was grateful to his adoptive family, and yet always felt that he didn't quite fit in, being the only athlete in a family of cultured artists and intellects. We have learned how devastated he was when his athletic ambitions ended prematurely from an unfortunate injury that he incurred while playing freshman football. And even in that time of tremendous depression and soul searching, he was reached out to and befriended by his football coach, who saw great potential in him. Stunned that his coach would take such a personal interest in the life of a youngster who could no longer play for him, Paol grew curious about the life of this good man. Finding out that he was a devout Christian, he sought religion in his life, and has become an admired member in his congregation today.

"I have brought before you many of the acquaintances of this fine man: neighbors, fellow parishioners, co-workers. All have vouched for his character. All have confirmed that the crimes committed are not only inconsistent with his character, they are simply inconceivable. Consider that while this business deal turned out very unprofitable for his high-tech company, we have shown convincingly that there have been other deals which he has championed that have even gone worse. Yet, nobody

69

associated with that deal mentioned that it angered or embittered him to any degree. He simply learned from his experience, and capitalized on his mistakes to improve the quality of business.

"Now let's review some of the details of the case. The district attorney has reminded us that fingerprints leapt off of the gun, yet surveillance video shows that he wore latex gloves during the incident. Why would my client buy a gun, smear his fingerprints all over it, and then wear gloves during the shooting?

"And what of the discovery of the murder weapon? It was found in a dumpster of the Atlanta Airport, where four different eye-witnesses claimed they saw Mr. Joonter in the airport terminal in the late night hours of the 28th of March. Yet, his itinerary showed that his flight was not until the 30th, because he had yet another day of meetings on the 29th. Why, then, would he go through the trouble of driving to the airport just so he could discard the weapon there, and then show his face in such a crowded public location, only to drive back to his hotel and surrender to local authorities in his hotel room?

"But then we must ask ourselves, what of the audio and video? As for video, we know that it is too easy these days to create very realistic masks of anybody. Halloween shops are able to receive portrait and profile photos of an individual and create a very personalized mask that will fit a specific person used to masquerade as somebody else. Several suspects have been acquitted in other cases where this technology was utilized in order to frame the suspect of a crime he or she did not commit.

"As for the audio, experts have said that—and I quote—'the quality of the speech waveforms implicated Mr. Joonter, although they did not match his voice perfectly.' Under oath, they pointed out that the voice was slightly deeper than that of my client, even though the shape of the waveforms were sufficient to give 'a high degree of confidence' that the voice recorded at the scene of the crime was that of Mr. Joonter.

"I now ask you jury members, how confident are you? Experts did not say that they knew 'beyond reasonable doubt'. They said, 'with a high degree of confidence.' There are many questions that remain unanswered in this case. Does that not give you 'reasonable doubt'?

"Finally, let me remind you that one of your peers has already been removed from their service by the court for suspicious interactions, leaving

70

two alternates left here today. We do not know exactly what these interactions entail, but we believe that they were approached by an unscrupulous individual seeking a verdict against Mr. Joonter. It was a very odd development in the case which only left this courtroom filled with more questions, and fewer jurors."

Warron paused to take a deep breath and looked earnestly over at his client. "This man, Paol Joonter, is a good, hard-working businessman, whose award-winning accomplishments as CTO of LifeTech, Incorporated are widely-known in his industry, and are widely-appreciated in our homes and lives. I implore you to know what I know—that this man is innocent of the crimes for which he is being charged, and to return a verdict of not guilty. Thank you."

With his case closed, he nodded to the judge as he took his seat. Without fanfare, the judge gave final instructions to the jury, and adjourned them for deliberations. Paol Joonter watched as the jury was led out of the courtroom by the court clerk. As the door closed, he knew that the fate of his future— and that of his family—was left in the hands of this group of people who certainly did not know who the real murderer was any better than he did. He was completely powerless in the matter now. The jury now contained full discretion over his future.

Chapter

8

Joram Anders looked at his watch as the helicopter touched down on Palomar Mountain. 12:50 AM. He did not feel the exhaustion of his studies of the day, his meal with Kath that evening, the surprise summon to meet Professor Zimmer at the Burbank Airport, or the relaxing helicopter ride, where Kath rested on his shoulder during the entire flight. Instead, adrenaline was flowing from the excitement and fortune of being at an astronomical observatory at the invite of his boyhood idol. Attempting to orient himself to his surroundings, his eyes searched the darkness without success. The CalTech observatory was strategically located as far away from light pollution as Southern California would allow. As he stepped onto the helipad, all he could see were the flashing lights of the helicopter, a rim of lights circling the pad, the canopy of stars overhead, and a dimly lighted path.

"Please follow me," the professor instructed as he set out for the path. His trio of blurry-eyed graduate students followed with a quickened pace, as if Zimmer had not the least been fatigued by his day of instruction in the planetarium, the flight to and from Johnson Space Center, the intense focus and study on the troublesome data from Mars, and now, the helicopter ride to Palomar.

During the hike from the helipad, the darkness was met with silence. The stunned students did not know what to say, or if anything should be said at all. At last, they arrived at a white dome-topped cylindrical structure. Joram suspected that this wasn't the structure which housed the 200-inch Hale telescope, famed as the largest telescope in the world for several decades of the twentieth century.

"Students," Zimmer announced, "this is our very modern and accurate 26-inch telescope. It is one of our very best for studying near-earth objects, such as our very own solar system. With this, I believe we will obtain the best possible quality images to help us with our study surrounding the events which have transpired on Mars. Please follow me to the control room, where you will be performing all of your data collection and studies this evening."

As they entered the control room, aptly stacked with computers, monitors and control equipment, Zimmer oriented them as quickly as possible to their workstations. He began with instructions to Kath.

"Kath, you will work here." He gestured to a workstation. "Your first task will be to get on the phone for a conference call to Israel to discuss Martian atmospheric and meteorological conditions with experts there. According to our observatory administrator, there should be a sheet instructing you on the headset and the contact information of the individual who has been studying the situation.

"Joram, Reyd will acquaint you with the equipment over here." Zimmer pointed out a large panel of instruments and controls, equipped with several large flat-screen monitors, already containing a set of initial data on Mars.

"I will be up on that platform over there, fine-tuning the controls of the telescope as needed in an effort to obtain the necessary images. Camp Mars is currently in view from Earth, and will be so for the next 4 hours. My first effort will be an attempt to get as many visual clues as to conditions in the vicinity of the camp. Once Earthset has occurred—that is, when Earth will not be visible to the astronauts—I will then search for clues surrounding the missing satellites and shuttle, as well as to lock a visual on the lone signaling satellite, which we know to still be functional. I would like to give you a much better briefing and overview of the equipment and task on hand, but time is critical. Are there any questions?"

Reyd was familiar with Professor Zimmer's terse manner of instructing research students in their duty, and shook his head knowingly. Joram and Kath, on the other hand, returned glassy-eyed stares to the professor, still in shock over this sudden change of activity in their lives. Zimmer drew closer to them in a gesture of understanding.

"Joram, Kath," his voice softened. "Any questions?"

"Well, not yet," Kath was the first to answer. "I'll just head over there, peruse my instructions, and get on the phone with the team in Israel."

Zimmer smiled and nodded. "Thank you."

"Joram?" Zimmer prompted, staring at the individual whose potential the professor was eager to explore and develop.

Joram did have a question, but he was hesitant to ask why on earth the professor had chosen him for this trip. Reyd, of course, had the expertise on the equipment. Kath had credentials from her studies of meteorology. He was just a star-gazer from Kansas. Prudence took control of his curiosity, and he realized that the professor could not be bothered with a question of such a trivial nature, when the lives of astronauts were at stake. "No, sir. I'm sure Reyd will bring me up-to-speed quickly."

"Great!" Zimmer clapped his hands together, wheeled himself around, and was the first to reach his station. Kath filed off next in the opposite direction, while Reyd took his seat at the console. Joram remained rooted for just a moment as he watched the professor begin his work. Then excitement and adrenaline took over. With an excited spring in his step, he caught up to Reyd and took a seat next to him, ready, willing, and eager to learn the controls of the observatory, with which he hoped to become intimately familiar.

...

"Ok... yes, I do see that now... Aha... Yep," Kath's tired yet pleasant voice spoke into the headset. "Yes, I'm starting to figure the system out, Ravid. I'm sorry about this... you don't really have the time to be helping me ramp up on this computer, while there is important research to be done on the weather.... Well, thanks for your encouragement. I hope I can be of some help as well."

The sound of Kath's voice filled the room, but was occasionally interrupted by an exchange between Reyd and Zimmer. "Is that any clearer, Reyd."

"I still can't make anything out, Professor. The features just aren't coming through that clearly. Even the common areas of varying light intensity aren't coming through as expected."

"Ok, it looks like the dust storm is still pretty intense down there then. I'm going to try to zero in on Olympus Mons. We should be able to at least

74

calibrate our image quality there... the peak has got to be above the dust storm."

Joram focused on the images of Mars, and while he knew enough about the planet to find his way around the geographical features, he admitted that he was lost with this view. Finally, however, as the telescope zoomed and focused in on the massive dormant volcano, he gasped at the sight of it. He was surprised to see the mountain come into view.

"Something wrong?" Reyd turned to Joram with concern in his voice.

"It's delightful!" Joram exulted boyishly. "I've just never seem Mars so clearly depicted."

Indeed, the reddish-brown caldera and impact craters deep on the top of the volcano were in exquisite view. Anders easily discerned which impacts were older based on the portion of the crater which was obscured by more recent impacts.

"That looks good, Professor," I'm seeing the top of the mountain in clear view. Looks like we could use a little sharpening... That's better... better... perfect!"

"How much of the mountain is in clear view, Reyd? How far down are we obscured by the dust storm."

"I'm not really sure. I'm not very familiar with the features of the mountain. I'll have to digitize the image and compare it to the database. It should just be a couple of minutes."

Lowering his voice, Reyd continued to speak to his fellow student. "So, to get to the image database, Joram, simply gesture with your finger like this to pull down the database menu, select Solar System, and then Mars. You can see a list of objects here. We'll select mountains and just scroll down the list here... Nereidum Montes, Oceanidum Mons, Octantis Mons... Ah, there we are, Olympic Mons.

"Now the default view, as you can see is straight above the top of the mountain, but we'll want to rotate the 3D image to coincide with the angle of the satellite. Hover over the mountain with your finger and drag like this... Ok, it looks like we have an approximate angle, judging by our picture on the right. Now, we just need to spin the mountain around to the correct side. To do that, we move our finger in a little bit closer and swipe with a curving motion like this to spin the digital image around, and there. Now, we'll pull down the tools menu, and select the measure tool. We'll pull it to about here. Well that looks like a pretty close match."

Reyd pointed to a feature on the side of the mountain in both the left and right frames of his monitor where the digitized image and the live image of Olympus were depicted respectively.

"Ok, so that gives us the distance along the slope, but we need to know the elevation difference between these two points, so we gesture with a spiral—like drawing a lower case 'E' in the air—to give us the elevation."

Another voice interjected from the back. "Thirty-two thousand feet!"

While Joram focused on the controls of the system, he didn't notice that Professor Zimmer had now appeared behind the two students observing the data.

"Wow!" Joram exclaimed. "That's some elevation... several thousand feet taller than Mount Everest altogether! But then again, Olympus does stand eighty thousand feet above the surface of Mars! Does that means we're seeing a dust storm that is nearly fifty thousand feet deep?!"

Zimmer frowned as he turned to look at Kath, hoping that her time spent on the phone may provide some additional clues.

"Yes, I do see the wind patterns and speeds now on my computer, Ravid." Kath was quickly ramping up on the weather simulations that the team in Israel had been putting together for the last twelve hours.

"So, if I understand correctly, we have a ton of dust in the air, but not much wind. It looks like average global wind speeds are about fifteen kilometers per hour, and that the maximum is about fifty, right?"

"Yes that is correct," said Ravid. "It is actually a calm day on Mars. This dust just makes no sense."

"This thing seems to cover the entire planet, right now. How large can dust storms get to, Ravid?"

"Well, storms can cover the entire planet, and when they do, they can last for a month."

Kath let this last comment settle. "Ravid... are you telling me it could be a month before we get a visual on the astronauts up there?"

"I don't think so in this case, Kath. The typical scenario for a global dust storm is that wind speeds reach one hundred kilometers per hour. This kicks up dust, which absorbs sunlight and heats the atmosphere. This heating then creates convection that only increases the wind even more. By the time these atmospheric conditions subside, we're talking easily a month of global dust cover. However, the winds are too light in this case."

"But you just told me that dust in the air will heat the atmosphere…"

Ravid completed her sentence, "… and increase the winds. Yes, this is what has us very concerned, also. If that proves to occur, then it may be weeks before we are able to assess the status of the astronauts. At this point, we don't believe that will happen and must hope for the best. We need to break through visually as soon as possible to understand how the astronauts are coping with this atmospheric anomaly."

Kath's eyes raced across the screen. She rotated the planet to the east, west, east, and west again in order to get a better picture of the wind patterns across the globe. She tilted it north and south in order to assess the differences between the polar and equatorial patterns.

"Ravid," she spoke into the phone after a long silence. "So we've assessed that this is not a typical wind-induced solar storm. I don't want to ask stupid questions, but could this be caused by an impact?"

"No, it is not a stupid question. We keep coming back to that question ourselves. However, we have seen impacts, and it doesn't have the characteristic signature of an impact. For example, impacts are always more localized. This layer of dust covers 75% of the surface of the planet."

"How about a really big impact, then?" Kath offered.

"An impact that you are suggesting would have to come from a known object. Radio astronomers would have certainly detected an object this large as a shadow in the magnetic signature of the solar system. Besides, an impact of an object that kicks up this much dust would have to be large enough to alter the orbit or rotation of the planet. We have no indication that this has happened."

"Lots of little objects, then?"

"Again too much dust. Small objects could kick up some dust, but not likely this much."

"Can we tell how high the dust has been? Perhaps the objects kicked up the dust, and then the wind continued to agitate it, by kicking it up higher and higher into the atmosphere. No that sounds ridiculous, again, because the winds aren't strong enough."

Kath received a tap on her shoulder. She gave a start and turned around quickly to see who had been watching her.

"Kath, can you put Mr. Avram on the speakerphone for me," Professor Zimmer asked.

"Ravid, I'm going to put you on the speaker. Professor Zimmer would like to talk to you."

With that, Kath looked around to find Joram. He was still engaged with Reyd. Their voices were low, but she could tell by their gestures that Joram was engaging Reyd in a question and answer session on the control panel they were working together. Reyd pointed to a series of buttons on the control panel, and Joram responded with a nod. Another gesture, another nod.

"Ravid, this is Carlton Zimmer."

"Good evening, Professor. How are you?"

"Tired, naturally, and perplexed. Hey, I couldn't help overhearing that you two were wondering about the depth of the dust cloud?"

"Yes, we think it would help us to understand how much volume we are talking about. We suspect that it is thousands of feet deep, based on the obscurity of features that we have observed. However, we cannot tell for sure with the images we are working from."

"We just got a visual lock and measure on Olympus Mons which indicates the depth of the cloud to be nearly 50 thousand feet at this region."

There was silence on the other end.

"Ravid, are you still there, can you hear me ok?"

"Yes, professor, but… that just can't be! How can it be that deep? Typical dust storms kick up no more than ten kilometers into the atmosphere. Here we are talking fifteen kilometers… and there is no wind to do this. Are you sure of your calculation?"

"It looks accurate to me. Unless—it could also be that the dust has whipped up on the slope of the mountain as well, giving us the impression that the cloud is really that deep."

"Professor, the atmosphere is so thin at those elevations that the dust should settle quickly above even thirty thousand feet, let alone fifty thousand. It's a fascinating data point, but it only creates more questions and fewer answers. I will have to share this with my team and see if we can make sense of it."

78

"Well, I will let you get back to Ms. Mirabelle. She's probably got more questions for you as well. In the meantime, I'll go take a look at the Tharsis region. If the cloud is truly at fifty thousand feet, then we will be able to assess this from the elevation of the cloud on these mountains. If the cloud is simply whipping up on the slopes of these mountains, then we may see a different elevation profile on these mountains than we do on Olympus."

"That will be a very helpful piece of data. Thank you, Professor. Keep us informed if there are any further developments."

"We'll do just that, Ravid. And good luck on your end as well."

Kath placed the headset back on her head again as Zimmer walked back to the telescope. From the sound of the conversation, she quickly returned to her brainstorming session with the Israeli areologist. He approached Reyd and Joram to inform them of their next data collection effort.

"Gentlemen," Zimmer stated as he sat down in a vacant chair next to Reyd. The two students leaned away from the console which had engaged their attention for nearly an hour. "We are going to the Tharsis Region. Dr. Avram, an atmospheric specialist with whom Kath is speaking, is baffled by the dust patterns on Mars. We believe that we have found a fifty thousand foot cloud of dust covering much of the surface of Mars. However, we're not sure if the cloud really isn't lower, and that we're seeing dust coming off of the surface of Olympus Mons itself.

"In other words, we need to figure out if the dust has only kicked up a few hundred feet from ground level all the way up the slopes of the mountains. If we look at a smaller mountain peak, where the atmosphere is more dense than it is on the upper reaches of Olympus Mons, we might get a clearer idea of how much dust we really have swirling around up there."

Wheeling back to the telescope platform, Zimmer announced, "Give me a few minutes to dial in the coordinates and calibrate the surface angle for best imagery. You guys might want to warm up the image database for the Tharsis Mountains. We'll be performing similar elevation calculations there as well."

The professor returned to the telescope and began calculating coordinates for Ascraeus Mons, the tallest mountain in the Tharsis Region, and the second highest peak on Mars.

Reyd whispered to Joram, "My money is on the professor's theory, and the dust proves to be a thin layer that's just being stirred up to low levels all over the planet."

"But all of the circumstances have just been bizarre enough so far that I wouldn't be surprised if we really have a fifty thousand foot tall dust cloud," Joram rebutted. "Remember that this dust is really just a barrier to the real task at hand here. We need to find out how a group of satellites and a shuttle just disappear into thin air, or thin space. I'm guessing there is a link to the disappearance and the dust... hopefully, if we solve one mystery, we get all of our questions answered."

"That's a good point. Either way, let's start taking a look at the Tharsis Mountains, shall we?"

Reyd started negotiating the database menu again, when he stopped suddenly.

"What's wrong?" asked Joram looking at his companion.

"Well, I'm trying to recollect the names of the mountains that the professor needs us to look at... but I'll just go to the 'regions' portion of the database to find the names of the Tharsis mountains. I know I've heard them, but I forget now."

"Ascraeus, Arsia, and Pavonis," Joram said.

"What?" Reyd didn't grasp that his peer had just named all three Tharsis mountains in two seconds.

"Oh, I'm sorry... I gave them to you in order of elevation. Did you want them in terms of their geographic alignment. Ascraeus is the northernmost, Arsia is on the south end, and Pavonis sits right between them."

Reyd's jaw dropped as he stared at Joram. "Where did that come from?"

Joram blushed a bit. He did not intend to condescend, but being caught up in the moment of research, he couldn't help blurting out a little too much knowledge perhaps. "I'm sorry... I read a book on Martian geography a couple of years ago. The chapter of Martian mountains really left an impression on me, I guess."

"Apparently so." Reyd flushed slightly as he shook his head in amazement and turned back to the console. He got ready to dial into the Ascraeus database in an attempt to beat Zimmer to the punch, while the telescope was quickly zooming towards its new subject. "Ascraeus Mons... there it is."

Zimmer called out, "How does she look, Reyd."

"It looks great, professor. However, we don't have quite the same angle on the slope of the mountain, as we did for Olympus. It might be tricky to pick a spot that we'll want to measure from the digital image."

"The lava flows might help us find our spot," Joram pointed out on the database image. "They extend all the way around the mountain."

Joram pointed to the northeast and south sides of the mountain where dark slits cut all the way around the mountain. Larger gashes where those of dried up lava flows at the surface of the mountain.

"Those are really amazing geologic structures there," admitted Reyd. "At this zoom level, those flows make the mountain look more like a scratching post than a volcano. It makes for a very distinguishable feature. However, they may be too low in elevation for them to be any use to us. Wow... look at the scar over on the west side of the mountain where it looks like a landslide has left a huge gash in the mountain. Again, that's way too low to be of use to us, but what about this?"

Reyd pointed to the east side of the mountain. "These pits here may be caves or perhaps the end of lava tubes opening up on the surface of the mountain. Some of these might be high enough. Otherwise, there isn't a whole lot of distinguishing features around the mountain to tell where a cloud may end."

"Take a look at the live image right there." A long finger belonging to Professor Zimmer had reached between the pair of students and pointed to the live image on the monitor. Just above the cloud was a distinguishing feature, either a cave, or perhaps a large boulder, but it was easily spotted by the shadows being cast by the afternoon Sun.

"Let's see." Reyd worked quickly to spin and focus on the object. "That's just north of west on the mountain. Interesting, I didn't remember noticing many features on that part of the mountain. Could that be a new exposure or perhaps a crater?"

Silence ensued for a few minutes as the two teams examined both the left and right frames, as if watching a rapid volley at a Wimbledon tennis match.

"Right here," Joram pointed on the left side of the screen. "Look at the database image. The lighting isn't as favorable, but I think there is a slight difference in coloration which may match to the shadow in the live image."

Zimmer suggested, "Hey, Reyd… can we scan the remaining images in the database? It would be nice to find an image with similar afternoon lighting in order to pinpoint that structure."

"Yes, sir." Reyd negotiated through the menus quickly to bring up the full catalog of images available. He set the default 3D model to provide a west-side angle.

The team scanned through image after image for a couple of seconds each. After flipping through more than a dozen pictures, Zimmer shouted, "There!" He pointed at a pinpoint of a black spot, not as large as that of the live image, but certainly in the same location. "It's a shadow," Zimmer stated confidently. "It's not being cast as long in this image, certainly because it was taken earlier in the day, but make no mistake, that's our spot."

With accepting nods from his students, Reyd went quietly to work, clicking and measuring. He leaned back in his chair and clasped his hands behind his head, as the trio of astronomers clearly understood the data they were looking at.

Professor Zimmer nodded approvingly. "Kath!"

Kath gave a start and spun around quickly.

"Kath, do you still have Dr. Avram on the phone?"

"No, Professor, but I can call him back. What did you find out over there?"

"Thirty thousand feet, Kath. The cloud is at thirty thousand feet on Ascraeus Mons. On Olympus Mons, it was fifty thousand feet above mean surface level, so it would appear as if the height of the dust cloud is relative to the surface features."

"That means there isn't as much total volume of dust in the atmosphere, right, Professor?" asked Joram buoyantly.

"Yes that is correct, which means…"

Kath, the meteorologist, finished his sentence. "…it won't absorb as much heat, won't generate as much wind, and will settle out quicker. Maybe we'll be able to see our astronauts soon!"

Professor Zimmer looked at his watch. 3:30 AM. He dashed back to the telescope controls. "Reyd, small mountains… give me coordinates to one of the smallest mountains on the planet."

Reyd's eyes opened wide as he grasped Zimmer's plan.

"If we find the dust low on a small mountain, then we will know for sure that the dust is not thick. I'll dial up the list right away."

Reyd spun back to the control panel quickly, and worked the menus again. Within moments, a spreadsheet emerged on the screen with a long list that Reyd sorted by ascending elevation.

"Professor," Reyd announced abruptly. "Some of these features are below the zero elevation. What elevation should we start our search at?"

"Reyd," Joram pointed to the screen. "Can we eliminate all of the patera from the list? These are usually low-lying craters that won't benefit us. We need just the mons features that actually project upward from the surrounding surface."

"Yes," Reyd nodded. "Good point. Let me filter farther."

While Reyd worked, Joram jumped to his feet, startling his partner at the control panel. He raced towards Zimmer. "Professor! What about Valles Marineris? Rather than iterating on various mountain elevations, we should look at Marineris! The canyon is of varied elevation throughout, and if the cloud is relatively low to the nape of the planet, then we'll be able to see the canyon walls, and we'll be able to tell exactly how deep the cloud is inside of the canyon. Besides, Marineris is to the east of Tharsis, where the sun will be setting soon. We'll have good afternoon shadows to give us perspective of the canyon walls."

Zimmer smiled at Joram and hopped down from the telescope. "Ok, then… give me coordinates to Marineris and an image of the canyon system. That is one long trench, and we'll need to figure out where to start looking."

Within moments, an elevation-shaded relief map of the deepest canyon in the solar system was portrayed on the full widescreen monitor, replacing both the live and historic images of Ascraeus Mons.

"Well, let's start right here in the middle," the Professor stated.

"The Candor region," interjected Joram. "Excellent choice, Professor. We could start here in the Candor Chaos and work our way to its chasm, where the elevation differences are varied, and the walls are more step-like than the main branch of the canyon. We can tell based on which steps are exposed, the elevation of the dust cloud, I believe."

Joram didn't notice that both Reyd and Zimmer were staring intently at him as he focused on the screen.

Reyd was slowly shaking his head. "How... how do you know all of this?"

Zimmer's eyebrows were raised. He wasn't certain whether to be irritated or impressed with this upstart college kid. "Candor, it is! Coordinates, please!"

Zimmer bounded back to the telescope and arrived in time for the coordinates from Reyd. He worked rapidly at the controls. "What do you see gentlemen?"

"A lot of dust," answered Reyd sharply.

"Can we side-by-side the current coordinates, Reyd?" asked Joram. "We need a clear reference to see where we're at here."

Once again, the screen was split with the live image on the right and the best database image on the right. Both images were bounded by the same exact coordinates, guaranteeing that the mouse cursor hovered over exactly the same location on both images.

"Wow!" Joram exclaimed. "Look at that, Reyd."

"Professor, can you zoom in on grid cell D6? Joram's found something interesting here."

Both students leaned forward in their chairs.

"Professor?" called Reyd. "You should come see this."

Zimmer scaled down the telescope platform again and met up with his students. He turned to Kath. "Kath, can you come take a look at this?"

"Absolutely, Professor." She looked over Reyd's left shoulder intently. "What exactly am I looking at?"

The professor briefed her on the discovery. "This, Kath, is Valles Marineris, the longest canyon in the solar system, and if some sources are to be believed..." He cut a glance over at Joram "...we are looking around the Candor region."

Joram blushed while shrugging his shoulders almost imperceptibly.

The Professor continued: "Anyway, look at this billowing cloud of dust. This is down inside the canyon. And right here, you can see the border of the canyon wall. Any ideas what might cause a dust cloud like that to occur?"

"I'm having a hard time with perspective here. How wide and deep is the canyon here?" asked Kath.

"About one hundred miles wide and three miles deep," answered Reyd.

"Three miles deep? That thing is three miles deep? And I thought the Grand Canyon was impressive… My goodness."

Professor Zimmer brought Kath back to the task at hand. "Any ideas about this cloud, Kath?"

"Well, it looks like it's bubbling up from the middle. I'd say that there must be wind rushing down both sides and creating a violent turbulence right in the middle."

"What could cause that?"

"A sudden drop in barometric pressure inside the canyon perhaps? That could cause a vacuum-like effect and suck the wind from the plateaus above… or a sudden change in temperature inside the canyon to cause convection… or…"

"Or…" Joram interrupted while he pushed the mouse cursor along the canyon wall in the database image. "Or… the canyon wall is crumbling."

Zimmer couldn't help chuckle at this suggestion, mainly because of the matter-of-fact nature of Joram's idea. "What do you mean by that, Joram?"

"Well, Professor, at first, I thought the images weren't lined up very well, because look at the cursor here on the south side of the canyon. It is set some distance inside of the live image. But then, if you point the cursor to the north canyon wall, it also looks offset from the canyon wall, but in the opposite direction. Simply put, the width of the canyon is narrower in this satellite photo than it is over here in the live image."

Zimmer offered an explanation. "Perhaps the zoom factor is different? Reyd, can you calibrate the two images?"

"I don't think so, Professor," countered Joram. "Look up here in the Candor Chasm. There is a ridge right here. It is inside the rim of the canyon, and yet it overlays perfectly on both images."

"Joram… this is ludicrous. Mars is not a geologically-active planet. There is no rain to erode the surface features, and there isn't enough wind to cause landslides like this! For centuries, we have relied on pretty much the same exact look at Mars. Today, you're telling me that Marineris is growing wider?"

"Professor, it fits with the billowing cloud. If the walls of the canyon were crumbling, tons of rocks and sand would rush down the slopes, creating a downdraft that would meet in the middle and balloon up from the canyon."

The professor buried his head in his hands and rubbed his eyes deeply. He turned away from the students. "How does this happen?" Sarcastically, he offered, "Has somebody just nuked the surface of Mars? That might explain all of the dust, and crumbling canyon walls."

"Professor," Kath interjected. "I would propose in this case that the wind patterns for a nuclear reaction would be too violent for this. We aren't seeing the kind of wind needed."

"Agreed, Kath. It was a ludicrous theory to being with, but it's just that this is growing more and more frustrating," he whispered as much to himself as to his students. Turning back, he completed his thought. "Team, what we really need are *more* answers and *fewer* questions. It seems that with every turn, this whole mystery grows more and more complicated."

Reyd was the first to try to console the professor. "There does appear to be one answer, Professor."

Zimmer looked up and gave a half-smile to his student.

"We now know that the cloud is not deep enough to obscure the entire canyon. We can see some of the walls. The cloud may be a couple of thousand feet thick, but certainly is not fifty thousand feet thick."

"We might be able to get a better estimate," began Joram. "If we scan the telescope along the canyon to the west, it will bring us to the Labyrinth, where we will be able to see various depths of the canyon and whether the cloud fully covers these more shallow regions or not."

Without saying a word, the professor scaled the telescope platform again. Slowly guiding the telescope towards the west, they continued to see the occasionally billowing cloud of dust, indicating that the dynamics of the event causing this phenomenon were not local to the Candor region. Where clouds were not billowing, they saw a flat layer of dust hanging off of the valley floor. As they approached the western edge of the canyon, a massively wide expanse ended abruptly into a series of canyon narrows which intertwined in a chaotic, mazelike structure known as the Noctis Labyrinthus.

Joram broke the silence. "The Labyrinth of the Night. Professor, this is wonderful! We are nearing the end of the labyrinth where the canyons get narrower and shallower and yet we are still able to make them out."

"What is the depth of the canyon here?" asked the professor turning away from the telescope controls and looking at his trio of helpers intently.

Reyd clicked the mouse a couple of times and noted the elevation on the plateau above and the floor below. "Twelve hundred feet, Professor!"

"Twelve hundred feet," the professor nodded approval. "That sounds much better than fifty thousand feet! Kath, please call Dr. Avram again and let him know of our results. See if you can get him to assess a time frame for when this type of dust will settle out and give us a visual on the camp."

"Yes, sir." Kath raced back to her station and quickly placed the headset on her head.

"Gentlemen," proceeded Zimmer. "It is time for us to turn our attention to the satellites. I'd like to get a visual lock on Satellite Four. Could you please calculate its current position and provide me with coordinates? If we can find this satellite, then we'll be able to tune our telescope accordingly, and spot the remaining satellites in their current locations. Then, we'll turn our attention to the shuttle, although it might be tougher to calculate its precise location and distance. Looking at my watch, I can see that we only have about an hour of nighttime left, so we'll still have much to do tomorrow night as well."

While Reyd pounded at the keyboard in front of them in an effort to make some very hurried calculations, and while Kath reintroduced herself to Ravid Avram to notify him of their discovery, Joram was beginning to feel a bit more helpful. His knowledge of the Martian terrain and suggestions for where to turn to for answers was proving to be a valuable asset to the team after all. Turning in his chair, he saw Professor Zimmer reclining in a chair with his hands behind his head and his eyes closed.

"Mr. Anders," the professor spoke without opening eyes or appearing to be awake at all for that matter.

"Yes, Professor."

"Thank you for your suggestion on using Marineris to assess the dust cloud. A very astute suggestion that has provided us with a significant answer to an important question."

Joram's head lowered in humility for this recognition from a giant of an astrophysicist. "Thank you, Professor. I really just want to be as helpful as possible."

The professor maintained his position and did not respond, but nodded his head slowly and took a deep breath.

"Professor," interrupted Reyd. "I believe I have the coordinates for you, but I'm afraid that Satellite Four is behind Mars presently. It won't emerge for another 6 hours."

"Ok, if it wants to play hide-and-seek, then so be it. In the meantime, I think I'll simply zoom away from the planet and put ourselves into needle-in-a-haystack mode of operation. In the meantime, can you calculate the remaining satellite coordinates?"

"Yes, sir."

As Reyd typed again, Joram sat back and watched the show. The telescope slowly zoomed away from the labyrinth revealing Marineris on the left and Tharsis on the right. Olympus shortly came into view and a host of other unidentifiable features, but for the most part, the entire planet seemed to be covered in a cloud of dust. Joram was stunned that a dust storm could occur on such a global scale.

Presently, the entire globe was within the view of the telescope, and continued to diminish just a little more before the professor locked its position. Joram continued to wonder at the view and dream about what it would be like to be on Mars. How he envied those astronauts who had been able to step on its surface and study its features up close. And then… he saw… well… he saw something, but did not quite know what to make of it? He leaned forward, tilting his head and wrinkling his brow.

"Reyd, what the heck is this?"

Reyd looked up to where Joram was pointing at a dim undulating yellow stripe in the upper right hand corner of the screen. He shrugged his shoulders and stated indifferently. "Imaging anomaly, I guess. We see some strange things from time to time depending on the lighting situation and the optics."

Reyd went back to typing on the keyboard, but Zimmer overheard the conversation and wandered over to take a look at what Joram had noticed.

"Can you try to clean that up, Reyd? It's a curious piece of imagery."

"Do you think that is necessary, Professor? It's surely just some image problem," Reyd rebutted.

"It may not be necessary," responded Zimmer honestly. "However, I always lose faith in my data when optical abnormalities need to be filtered."

"Understood, Professor."

For a few minutes, Reyd and Zimmer worked on their stations respectively, talking back and forth about their efforts to remove this figment. While the stripe was in the image, Zimmer worried about their ability to pinpoint the satellites. He figured that image problems would only turn their task of looking for a needle in a haystack into something much worse.

After persistent attempts to clean up the image, Reyd and Zimmer grew increasingly frustrated. This was not the time to be having technical difficulties. In just minutes now, the earliest light of dawn would begin.

"Professor, may I make a suggestion?" Joram spoke out.

"Absolutely."

"Would it be prudent to zoom out a little bit more and see if the optics will clean up the stripe?"

"Couldn't hurt."

Zimmer slowly retracted the telescope and the red globe began retreating slowly from the screen again. The yellow streak persisted.

"Maybe we should try to pan as well," suggestion Zimmer. "In case there is some pre-dawn light that might shift out of view with a different horizontal angle."

This, however, drew more perplexing concern from the team, since the relative position of the stripe remained fixed, and as the red planet dipped out of the bottom of the image, the yellow stripe continued to pulse its dim straight beam of light just as a flashlight might do inside of a dark, dusty cave.

"Well, it just can't be a real object," stated Zimmer. "There must be some technical reason for this stripe to persist in our system. I'll have our maintenance team look at it today..." He paused... "and yet, the stripe remains straight as an arrow. I would expect an imaging problem to demonstrate more curvature, because of the curved nature of our lenses."

"Could it be a tail of a meteor or some other object, Sir?" suggested Joram.

Zimmer shook his head readily. "No, this... thing appears to be emanating light. Look at the undulating pattern. If this were a tail of some object, we might see some reflectivity of sunlight coming off of the dust and ice, but this pulsating... waving... geez... it almost looks like an Aurora in a straight, thin yellow line of light. Very strange."

"I agree, Professor," joined Reyd. "It may not be an imaging problem, but it may be some rendering problem with the image digitization software."

"We definitely need maintenance to look at this."

A few moments of thoughtful pondering and wonder was broken by the ring of a cell phone.

Zimmer tapped his ear implant and answered, "Hello, Carlton Zimmer here."

"Hello, Professor, this is Vurim Gilroy at Johnson. Have you been able to assess anything this evening?"

"Yes, Dr. Gilroy. We've noticed that the dust cloud is much thinner than originally anticipated. We are talking with Ravid Avram now to assess a time frame for visual assessment."

"Anything else odd, Professor?"

"No, nothing else at the moment, we will certainly continue our study tomorrow evening. Hopefully, Madrid can make some good progress tonight as well."

"Professor, there is a report..." Vurim paused.

"A report, Doctor?"

"Yes... it appears that an amateur astronomer from the Mojave Desert called in a report at 4:15 AM pacific time. NASA has been notified that he discovered a faint yellow streak across the south-eastern sky stretching to both horizons."

Zimmer stopped dead in his tracks, grew pale, and fixed a gaze at the telescope monitor, walking towards it slowly.

"Professor?"

"Vurim! We are seeing it as well, but we assumed an imaging problem. This thing has no visual signature that I can ever recognize seeing."

"There's one other thing you should know, Professor."

90

"Go ahead," Zimmer said while remaining fixed on the yellow stripe.

"There are reports of a spike of electromagnetic activity on portions of Earth."

After a brief pause, Zimmer asked quietly, "What kind of radiation are we talking about, Vurim?"

"Well, we're not sure yet, but it is some form of high-energy ionizing particle radiation that is detectable, but not identifiable. It was a very quick, sudden, and low-volume burst... we don't believe there is any harm to communications at this point, but there is something very odd about it, Professor."

"Go on."

"The time of impact coincides with the Martian anomalies, and only the portions of the Earth which were facing Mars at the time of the incident report any such detection."

"So, you calculate the impact to be about the same time as the satellite disappearance."

"Not 'about', Professor. Exactly the same time."

"Sounds like a significant piece of the puzzle, Vurim. Martian satellites disappear due to a radiation event, and the event is detected after the radiation hits sensors on Earth."

"Professor, there is no after. Let me clarify. The radiation is detected synchronously at several stations on at least three continents. Then, three minutes and forty-seven seconds later, an alarm event in our control room indicated that we'd lost communication with the satellite up there. Considering that we are about forty-two million miles from Mars, three forty-seven is precisely the time it takes for signals to travel from Mars to Earth. That means, the exact point in time when the satellite stopped transmitting was the same point in time when the radiation hit the Earth. They are perfectly simultaneous events."

Zimmer weighed this new information for a moment, stood up and clapped his hands.

"Vurim! This is great news."

"What do you mean, Professor?"

"Well, what has stumped us the most is the exact timing of the loss of signals between objects at different distances! Now, we can relate this to a radiation event which probably knocked out all of your sensors at the same point in time… on Earth, not up on Mars."

"Yes, it would seem so, but we've been studying the sensors, and they seem undamaged. They are able to receive signals from test sources in the labs here at the space center… And there's one other thing."

"Yes?"

"A solar observatory in South Africa noticed a flash of intensity from the Sun—"

Zimmer paused, not wanting to admit he knew the point Gilroy was about to make.

"—at the exact same time!" Gilroy concluded. "Well, the clock at the African facility wasn't accurate enough to show exactness in simultaneity, but they can confirm that the event occurred approximately at the same time, plus or minus three seconds."

"I'm guessing the radiation couldn't have screwed with those solar readings?"

"South Africa was not in the radiation path, Professor. They were on the opposite side of the planet when the rays hit."

Zimmer shook his head vigorously. "I'm sorry, Vurim, but I'm not convinced. There simply must be a correlation. Sensor failure is the only rational explanation. The solar event could be a coincidence." Then he glanced back at the yellow stripe. A sickening feeling hit his stomach. His voice grew quiet, as he spoke more to himself than to the NASA administrator. "But then again… there hasn't been anything very rational about this whole mystery, has there? Dr. Gilroy, thank you for the call. We will continue to investigate."

As he tapped his ear to terminate the communication with Gilroy, he stared at the streak in the image. Briefing his researchers on the situation, he explained, "So, we have a yellow streak in the sky, the likes of which have never been seen. Further, we have a communication failure from Mars, a radiation event on Earth, and a solar flare on the Sun that all happened within three seconds of each other."

"But, Professor," Reyd protested. "Light takes twelve minutes to travel from the Sun to Mars. No single event would be synchronized between these three heavenly bodies within a matter of seconds, unless the source of the event was equidistant to all three orbs."

"Or, perhaps three different synchronous sources which were all equidistant to their respective locations," suggested Kath.

"You realize," Joram chimed in, "that either of those answers would suggest something orchestrated."

"But, but whom? And why?!" Zimmer spoke more to himself than to the students as he fixed his gaze on the yellow undulating beam in the large video monitor overhead. "And what does that yellow beam have to do with it?"

As the world's foremost expert on all things astronomical, he tried to formulate a theory, but failed to think of anything reasonable. The entire room was embraced in silence. Zimmer, flanked by three confused graduate students, looked back up and continued to watch the yellow streak until the light of dawn persisted in obscuring it completely from view.

Chapter

9

Summer thunderstorms blackened the sky outside of the Atlanta courthouse. The thunder and driving rain were a stark contrast to the quiet hall in which Paol Joonter was found pacing back and forth. The defendant, his wife, and attorney were all speechless as they waited for the second day of deliberations to finish. He looked at his watch. It now said 4:38 PM, just four minutes past the last time he glanced. He turned on his heels and began pacing the opposite direction. As his anxiety level was increasing, his lawyer looked more and more comfortable.

"I'm telling you, Paol," the lawyer broke the tense silence with a cool voice, "the longer this jury hashes it over, the more likely they are to acquit."

"Or hang," sighed Paol as he stopped to face the man who had given it his all to help his cause. "And then, we'd just have to start all over again. Warron, I don't think I can go through this again."

"Even if they hang, Paol, it gives us great confidence. Then we know that we can inject doubt into jury members. If we can do it once, we can do it better the next time around, because it buys us more time to create an even better case."

"Warron," Paol broke a faint smile onto his pale face. "I'm sure glad you're here. Thanks for believing in me. It's just that this is torture, waiting around to hear the verdict."

They heard footsteps rapidly approaching down the hall. As a lady in a gray skirt and white blouse turned the corner hurriedly, she looked at the lawyer and panted.

"Warron," she gulped for more air. "They're ready."

"Thanks, Monay," responded the lawyer. "Please inform the clerk that we'll be present in two minutes."

She vanished down the hall as quickly as she arrived, echoes of footsteps trailing off quickly.

"If the worst happens, Paol… we'll appeal, you know." Warron assured confidently.

Paol did not return an answer. Instead, he faced his wife, grabbed her hand, and began the walk towards his fate.

The courtroom was empty, except for the district attorney, who was pacing in front of his table with his hands clasped behind his back, and the court clerk, looking through a stack of papers on her desk just beside the judge's bench.

They took their seats and other court participants and spectators began to file in. Paol watched the jury enter intent on picking up body language that might indicate the decision which was reached. Warron was less interested in this technique, because he'd been wrong on these clues too many times—usually in his favor. In the end, Paol wasn't sure what to make of any facial expressions or other body movements as each of the twelve jurors took their seat. He suspected that most were eager to finish up this ordeal and get back to their normal lives. He only hoped that they were going to afford him the same privilege.

"All rise. The honorable judge Walldar J. Etherton presiding."

"You may be seated," Etherton offered just before taking his seat. At Warron's request, Paol always remained standing until the judge was comfortably seated in his own chair—a sign of respect for the authority who presided over Paol's future. Warron noted that defendants typically received lighter sentences than might otherwise be the case, when his clients followed all of his courtroom instructions perfectly.

The judge looked over to the jury stand. "Ms. Foreperson, has the jury reached a verdict?"

A middle-aged woman dressed in a tan business suit stood and faced the judge. "We have, your Honor."

"Will you please read your verdict to this court?" asked the judge.

"We will, your Honor," she paused as she unfolded the verdict form she had filled out just moments before. "On count number one, we find the defendant, Paol R. Joonter… guilty of first degree murder against Rawson Becker. On count number two, we find the defendant, Paol R. Joonter… guilty of first degree murder against Shannyl Cox."

Joonter bowed his head and stared at the table. While he managed to maintain his composure emotionally in spite of the quiet sobbing of his wife that word guilty echoed violently through his head. It was the last word he would hear before he was nudged by Warron.

"Mr. Joonter," the judge addressed him. "Do you understand the verdict which have been given by this jury of your peers?"

Paol stood and faced the judge. He could not blame this man whose life service was in the performance of justice. In fact, he did not know who to blame for the failure in justice being delivered to him. "Yes, your Honor."

"Ladies and gentlemen of the court, I thank you for your patience and service here in this courtroom. Jury members, I thank you and release you from the service of this court. My clerk will provide you with instructions upon your return to the jury office downstairs. This court is adjourned until a date for sentencing can be arranged."

With that, the gavel came crashing down onto the judge's desk, and the sharp noise made Paol flinch. With wide eyes, Paol watched the jury file out of the courtroom, but nobody returned his gaze. As the door closed behind the last juror, he knew that this day would be a tremendous turning point in his life and in the life of his family. However, even he could not begin to comprehend how tremendous that change would be.

Chapter

10

"Ah, here is box of tools we will need." Dmitri Boronov had rifled through the contents of one workbench after another in the under-ground bunker. He looked up at his new colleague. "I must apologize. I am not usually so careless with equipment. I am some little off routine with your arrival."

"No problem, Dmitri," accepted Garrison O'Ryan. "I knew we would find the toolbox. Even Martian gravity is sufficient to keep things from floating off into—"

The junior astronaut was cut short by thick darkness, so complete that in looking all around him, he could make out nothing—not a scrap of light to be found anywhere.

"Dmitri, what happened?" called O'Ryan loudly, as if the sudden darkness had greatly increased the distance between the two astronauts. After a series of load clicks were heard, a faint blue-green light filled the room. Thankfully, O'Ryan's companion, toolbox in hand, was still right by the workbench just a few feet away from him.

"We lose power," Dmitri answered. "Emergency battery system has engaged, which is why the light is so dull now."

"Dmitri," Garrison's voice cracked with concern. "How often does this happen?"

"Must be less than once every two years. I have not seen this happen since I come."

"What could cause a power outage?"

"My guess is malfunction in power delivery grid." He set the toolbox down. "This will likely put our gauge repair work on back burner." He said this lightly and with a smile, hoping to ease the concern of his new comrade.

He placed the headset from his space helmet over his head and turned in on. "Mission Control, this is Boronov. We notice power failure in bunker at local time…" He looked down at his digital watch, which kept track of two different time zones. "…Local time: 17 hours, 21 minutes; central time 07 hours, 22 minutes. Please advise of repair work or maintenance procedure required."

Boronov looked up at his companion. "We should hear from mission control in 10 minutes. Meantime, we go look at power array control panel."

"Yeah, maybe it's something simple that we'll spot quickly, like a plug that fell out of an outlet?" He smiled in order to prompt Boronov on his joke. The Russian returned the smile and began walking back to the bunker entrance. As O'Ryan placed a firm grasp on the lever of the steel door connecting to the underground tunnel, Dmitri noticed a sensor panel next to the handle.

"Het!!!" shouted the Russian slipping into his native tongue, but the warning was too late.

With a click of the latch, the door flew outward and O'Ryan fell face first onto the concrete floor. Blood stained the spot where he landed, lacerating his forehead upon impact. He clawed at the ground, but found himself being dragged slowly on the surface by a gale force wind, as if a vacuum was sucking all of the oxygen out of the bunker. Boronov embraced a support beam on a workbench near to the door and gasped for oxygen as the rushing wind of the bunker replenished the depressurized tunnel. He shielded his face and head as best as he could, while small objects flew by. An assortment of hardware glanced off of the Russian's body as they sped through the recent breach in the environment. Worried about his partner, he peeked under his arm to see the body pulled by the unseen force, a small trail of blood marking the straight trajectory of the body as it slid down the poorly lit tunnel.

As Garrison gasped for oxygen, he felt his lungs filling with more dust than air. Realizing how helpless he was during this violent turn of events, he attempted unsuccessfully to scream for Dmitri's help just as everything stopped as abruptly as it began. He lay on the ground, drained of energy and choking in a mix of dust and blood that was trickling into his mouth. He looked up to see a pair of astronaut boots arrive.

"Garrison, you alright?" asked a voice in a thick Russian accent.

Coughing more than answering, O'Ryan rolled to his back, lifted his head and nodded. "I—think—so."

Boronov collapsed to the ground and rested his back against the wall. Breathing heavily, the two astronauts took some time to recover in the dusty, dark tunnel. At last Boronov raised himself and ran down the tunnel towards the greenish hue where Garrison was standing at ease just a couple of minutes before. The sound of footsteps dimmed, faded away, and then quickly resounded their echo into the tunnel. Dmitri kneeled at the head of his colleague. Lifting his head with one hand, he slowly poured water into Garrison's dry mouth with the other. As the liquid trickled down his throat, it had the effect of a life-giving elixir.

Raising up on his elbows, Garrison's senses were returning. "Dmitri, what happened? What is going on here?"

Boronov took a deep breath. "When you went to open door, I remember environment sensor. Green light means environment on other side of door is safe. Red light is not safe."

"So, the light on the sensor was red?"

"No, the light on the sensor was out. It had no power. On Mars, one must never assume environment is good."

Garrison hung his head. "Dmitri, I'm so, so sorry. I—I—"

"Friend," whispered Boronov. "It was easy mistake, with big lesson. At least we are both ok."

As O'Ryan's faculties slowly returned, he looked around him. The tunnel was too dark to see anything. He could only see the entrance with its green glow about 15 feet away along with a dark black streak marking the trace of blood left by his head as it was dragged down the tunnel. "Dmitri... if the atmosphere was depleted, then why didn't all of the oxygen escape..." He lowered his voice, "...and continue to drag me unprotected to who knows where?"

Boronov answered by flashing a torch towards the dark end of the tunnel away from the bunker. Garrison looked around to see a steel door sealing off the tunnel about three feet from where he lay.

"I still don't get it," said O'Ryan shaking his head slowly. "What caused the breach in the environment if that door is closed?"

"There is mechanical pressure release on every door leading away from bunker. With sudden drop in bunker pressure, a latch releases the doors from ceiling, and closes off the breach."

Garrison was trying to piece the puzzle together. "Ok, so when I opened the door, this tunnel was vacant of oxygen, the sudden change of pressure created a wind that felled me like a tree to the ground and dragged me here. Then, this huge door drops out of the sky and seals off the bunker and tunnel."

"Yes."

"Do you realize that if the mechanism had released any later than it did…" Garrison gulped for more air. "…I'd either have been crushed by that door, or I'd be outside flopping around for air like a fish out of water?"

Dmitri did not need to answer that question.

"Come," said Dmitri. "I help you up off floor. There is cot in bunker where you can rest."

Dmitri helped his companion off the ground. O'Ryan's head throbbed violently. Holding his forehead with one hand, he braced the other on Boronov's shoulder as the two walked back into the bunker. The slow walk to the cot proved painfully long for O'Ryan, as his head continued to pound with each step. At last, he swooned onto a cot which, by comparison, felt more comfortable than any bed he had ever slept in. His eyes fell closed, blocking the blue-green light from view until Boronov returned with a first aid kit and dressed the wound. Garrison winced as Dmitri dabbed antiseptic all around his forehead. With the bandage in place, O'Ryan fell into a state of restful unconsciousness.

…

A voice echoed in the distance. "Boronov to Mission Control. I still have not received response. Please copy."

Garrison O'Ryan opened the eye which was least swollen and at first saw nothing but a green hazy glow about him. Opening the other eye as far as he could, he focused and looked around to see racks of boxes. The perspective was not helpful, so he sat up to get a better look around. His rebellious head did not approve of the maneuver as a pain shot from his forehead to the back

100

of his neck. Looking around again, he saw another cot across the way, identically to the one on that he was on. He saw a small stand next to his own bed with a tumbler of water and a dish with large round cracker-like bread. He suspected that Dmitri had set this down for him in order to nourish himself after his accident. Since his mouth was dry and throat parched, he first drained a few ounces of water from the glass and took a bite of bread. "Ah, yes." He thought to himself. "A meal fit for an astronaut. How does NASA come up with this awfully engineered stuff? It's like I'm back on the Mars shuttle again."

Regardless of his disliking for the nutritive, he knew that his body needed the sustenance, so he methodically consumed the plate of bread, chewing only as fast as his head would allow without convulsing in pain.

Dmitri returned to check on his colleague and sat down on the edge of the cot opposite of Garrison's, looking dejected, concerned.

"Dmitri," called Garrison quietly as he looked up with his head askew and with eyes half open. "How long have I been sleeping?"

"About three hours."

"Dmitri, about the door… I'm very sorry."

"No need to worry. All is fine," reassured the senior astronaut.

"What have you heard from Mission Control on this whole affair, Dmitri?"

"Nothing."

O'Ryan paused to grasp the meaning of this short answer. "You mean they don't know what has caused the power failure?"

"No, I mean I have not heard anything. It appears that along with power failure, there is comm failure too."

"I would've hoped that communications were on battery backup."

"They are supposed to be. The failure must be worse than we fear, since we have lost power and comm," Boronov pointed out.

Garrison tried to stand up in anxiety for their welfare, but his head began to throb intensely as he did, so he laid back down on the bed with his hands clasping his temples.

"Dmitri."

"Yes, Comrade?"

101

"If we can't communicate with Mission Control, then we must assess the situation and figure out what to do."

"I agree," said Boronov flatly. "As you have slept, I have been thinking of this too. The main thing we must do is assess why power failure has occurred. We must restore the power if we are to evacuate."

"Evacuate?" inquired O'Ryan, sitting up to the edge of the bed again. "Well, you don't think it is that dire, do you, Dmitiri?" I'm sure we can make repairs for anything that might have problems."

"But, we will not be able to speak with Mission Control on repairs needed. We have some maintenance manuals here in bunker, but any difficult repair instructions need to come from experts on Earth."

"Okay, but you just said that we'll need to repair power to evacuate. Why do we need power, and more importantly, what if we are not able to repair the power or comm problems ourselves?"

Boronov weighed these questions, drew a deep breath and began to explain. "To answer first question, we need power to operate SAR pad. It requires much power, and cannot operate on battery backup. The SAR pad is necessary, because without it, we have just one parachute."

Garrison strained to understand, but didn't understand why a parachute was needed. He raised his eyebrows, and threw up his hands in the air.

"Garrison," said the Russian leaning forward on his cot. "Iowa is only Mars Shuttle on site. You flew it here from Moon. It only carries one person. Without SAR pad, we cannot replicate other shuttle to carry both of us back to Earth."

"Dmitri, I think we're crossing bridges before we come to them. Let's first go see if we can assess the problem with the power, and then we'll start planning any contingencies that might be needed to solve our problem."

"It is nighttime now," pointed out Boronov. "I believe we must wait for daylight to venture above ground."

"But what will we do if we can't restore power?"

"Ah, yes. If that is case, you will become very familiar with this room, as we will remain here until rescue."

"Wait, here? Until rescue? How long will that take?" Concern rang through O'Ryan's voice.

"Do you not recall emergency procedure? In worst-case scenario, we must wait in here, as it will provide up to three months of nourishment, water, and oxygen."

"Let me guess," Garrison said rolling his open eye. "The CO_2 scrubber doesn't work on battery backup either, huh?"

"Yes, it does, but battery will not last forever, neither will food or water. Three months. We must hope rapid preparations are made on Earth if rescue should be required."

"Is three months long enough to be rescued?"

"One piece of good fortune, my comrade, is that you just arrived. We both know that this means the distance from Earth to Mars is nearly at its closest proximity. Support vehicle carrying rescue crew travels slowly compared to Mars Shuttle, but three months will be enough time for them to arrive."

After a few moments of reflection on the part of both astronauts, Garrison broke the silence with another question. "Dmitri, didn't you say that the depressurization sealed us off with those steel doors?"

"We will not be able to exit through tunnel. We must take trap door, instead."

"Trap door?"

"In back of bunker is emergency exit, complete with pressurization chamber. We can safely enter the chamber without risk of much loss of oxygen since chamber is very small. This chamber opens into tunnel which goes up to manhole cover, which we called 'trap door' if I recall correct from training."

"Oh, yeah… I remember too now that you mention it. I'm a little slow right now with this head injury." Dmitri looked up as if to see the wound on his forehead, and felt it with an index finger. It was well-dressed, but moistened with blood and needed to be changed. Knowingly, Dmitri picked up a first aid kit from the floor and placed it on O'Ryan's side table.

"Thank you, Dmitri. I should redress this."

"Yes, and then we must both try to rest until daylight there isn't much else we can do for now, except…"

Dmitri stood and faced away from his companion, as if trying to hide something. He turned on his headset and spoke, "Boronov to Mission Control, do you receive communication? Please copy."

He returned and sat back down, watching Garrison change the bandage on his forehead slowly, but thoroughly. As he did so, he counted the seven stitches that his companion must have given him while he was unconscious. Garrison looked up at the green cast lights, looked back down at his companion and began to chuckle lightly.

"What is funny?" Boronov asked with as much curiosity as irritation.

"In this room with its light, I can't help thinking about how we must look like little green Martians in here."

Boronov's lips slowly curled upward as he snickered at the thought. "Yes, we must be an odd set of life forms in this universe... Anyway, we must lie down and rest now. Tomorrow we will need energy and good thinking to figure out what we need to do."

As Dmitri lay on his cot and cover himself with a light weight blanket, O'Ryan sat for a while longer on the edge of his bed, but without conversation, found that he was feeling effects of extreme exhaustion, so he lay down and both astronauts fell into a restless sleep.

. . .

Garrison woke up feeling groggy and looked over to find his companion's cot empty. He sat up and called out for Dmitri. At once, he heard the steps of boots on the concrete floor approaching.

"Garrison, how are you feeling?" Dmitri asked with concern in his voice.

"Better. Say, what time is it, Dmitri?"

"09 hours, 13 minutes," answered Boronov, consulting his watch.

"We must go look at the power array."

"Yes, yes, but you must eat first." Boronov gave Garrison an energy bar and drink for breakfast. "I have already breakfasted this morning."

Garrison smiled and shook his head knowingly at the nourishment. "Ah, yes. An astronaut's manna, this. Still no cheese steak sandwich for me, eh, Dmitri?"

"I fear there will be no more for either of us, until we get this camp back in order."

104

"Well, I guess if it worked for me on the ride in the shuttle for a couple of weeks, I can gag down a few more of these bars. I wonder how they compress the sawdust into such perfectly shaped rectangles." He shrugged and accepted the nourishment. Standing slowly, he found that he was actually better on his feet than he expected. Suiting up took about ten minutes, while Boronov disappeared to do senior astronaut work, apparently. Placing his helmet under his arm, he ventured off, not knowing exactly where he was in this cavernous bunker in relation to the entrance the pair of astronauts had come through the night before. Wandering amidst stacks and stacks of well-supplied shelves, he studied his surroundings. At last, he heard a rustle somewhere to his left. He ventured down an aisle to follow the noise, and discovered Boronov working at a workbench.

"Right. You are ready, then?" asked Dmitri when he spotted his partner approaching.

"Yes," said Garrison. "Let's solve this problem and get back to the mission at hand."

"I'm just packing some tools and manuals that we will want in our investigation of the system." He patted the top of a large spiral bound manual.

Garrison looked at the cover. *'Camp Mars: Power Subsystem.'*

Dmitri closed the box and started away with determination. Garrison followed shortly behind as they ventured deep into the recesses of the bunker, until they came to a door, similar to the fateful door which O'Ryan will never forget opening in error.

"There's no light on the panel, Dmitri."

Nodding, he replied, "I expect that to be. We will chance this door, for two reasons. One, it is a small pressurization chamber. Very little oxygen will be lost. Two, we must trust that the containment door dropped on this passageway as well. It is a chance we must take."

The pair placed and sealed their helmets, and Garrison deferred the job of opening the door to Dmitri this time, fearing that he should make another critical mistake. As the door opened, there was no rush of air. The environment on the other side was identical. O'Ryan peeked in to see another door just a couple of feet away. Boronov stepped inside and motioned for O'Ryan to do the same. Upon closing the door, Dmitri reached

105

for a lever which opened a vent. The sound of rushing air reminded Garrison of the tour that he made with Ayman and Dmitri just the day before, when the garage of the workshop was depressurized in preparation for departure in the Mars Terrain Vehicle.

Dmitri grabbed the handle on the outer door of the pressurization room. "Nobody has stepped into this next tunnel," stated Dmitri with an air of concern and suspense as he looked at his companion.

"But we must go on," reassured Garrison. "What could you do so wrong, Dmitri, after seeing what I did to us last night?"

Encouraged, Dmitri pulled the lever release and opened the door without incident. Both astronauts leaned forward, gazing into the darkness. Dmitri lit his torch first and shined it into the tunnel. The beam of light shown through a haze of red dust particles. Garrison flicked on the beam of light from his torch and followed Dmitri into the narrow tunnel, barely tall enough to fit their statures comfortably. They walked for 50 yards until arriving at a stair well.

"Going up?" asked Dmitri playfully in an effort to release the tension.

"After you," teased Garrison.

They climbed into a stairwell which seemed to go on for many stories of back-and-forth climbing. Neither astronaut counted the number of steps, but both were glad that they were doing this climb in the gravity of Mars and not Earth. At last, they arrived on a low landing where the concrete stairs ended abruptly. There was about four feet of distance from the floor to the ceiling, so both astronauts were kneeling here. Shining their torches upward revealed a yellow painted square which marked the boundary of the trap door. Reaching up, Dmitri felt for a release mechanism and found a handle with a trigger. With a click and a grunt which was audible through their helmet comm system, he tried to force the door open.

"Won't budge?" asked Garrison.

"No," grunted the Russian as he pushed upward with his arms and back, attempting to gain leverage on the door.

Garrison came to Dmitri's side and assumed a similar position. As the two pushed together, they could feel the door give about an inch or two, and after several moments gave up the effort.

"It feels like there's something blocking it," pointed out Garrison.

"I can't imagine that would be true. We do not have junk just lying around the crater."

"Either way," shrugged Garrison. "What are we going to do now, Dmitri. This door, as you have said, is our only hope to assessing the power failure at the array. But why can't we go back through the main entrance. With the pressure door deployed, we can use it as a pressurization chamber."

"We lose too much oxygen in main tunnel. We would risk not surviving a rescue effort, if this situation gets that far."

"Well, we've got to get through there, Dmitri, somehow."

"Do you have a crowbar in that tool box? Perhaps we could pry the hatch open?" Garrison brainstormed out loud.

"I didn't bring crowbar. It didn't make much sense for a power repair. But, it is good idea. I should return to get one. You wait here." Dmitri began his descent into the bunker.

"Dmitri, wait."

Dmitri turned, flashed his torch upward to look at Garrison.

"Is it a good idea for us to separate?"

"Perhaps not," admitted Boronov. "But you are not at 100 percent health. I prefer you not to have to climb stairs again so soon. Our headsets will remain in range should we need to communicate."

Garrison deferred his judgment to that of the senior astronaut and sat down on the landing with his back against the slab of concrete forming the wall of the tunnel. He turned off his torch to save battery, and watched as the dim light of Dmitri's light descended deeper and deeper into the ground until it had disappeared completely from view.

Garrison was not sure how long Dmitri had been gone, as he nodded off in the quiet darkness of the tunnel, until his partner had arrived with the crowbar. The two worked with the crowbar for some minutes before having to admit defeat again.

"It's budging farther with the crowbar," admitted Garrison, "but we still can't get it to open enough to exit. I don't get it, Dmitri."

"The hinges must be frozen from inactivity."

"We really need to get out there and assess the situation." Garrison lowered and shook his head, frustrated at the chain of events that was starting his mission so ominously.

107

"I have two ideas. First, we try light explosive."

"Explosive?" asked O'Ryan.

"We have small charge which can blast the hinge without damaging tunnel."

"I don't know, Dmitri. If the explosive causes a cave in, then we cut ourselves off from our only exit. Let me hear your second idea."

"Cutting torch. We cut through steel, but the torch will be difficult to bring way up here. It is big and heavy."

"Then, we'll take turns carrying it up," offered Garrison. "The idea of an explosive… it sounds too risky."

"You are not at full health," pointed out Dmitri. "It would not be advised for you to carry the torch."

"Dmitri, I'm well enough. We simply must get through that door. Besides, you have been exhausted walking up the stairs twice. You'll need to do yet a third trip. That's nearly 500 feet of stair climbing in one day."

"Yes, but at a third of gravity, it's more like 150 feet, or 15 flights of stairs. It is no problem, really."

"But you pointed out that this next trip will be a bigger deal, dragging up a heavy cutting torch up—Dmitri, let's not argue. I will come down and help you bring the torch up."

The senior astronaut yielded to the persistence of his younger companion, and the two shared the job of hauling the torch up 500 feet of stairs, a task which proved less tiring since they were able to have periods of rest while the other grunted up the stairs.

Boronov did the cutting, which proved tedious because of the thickness of the door, and the fact that the work was entirely overhead. Since there was little room to work on the top landing of the stairwell, O'Ryan remained on the landing below to watch his companion work. Boronov began cutting by making four perforated straight cuts along each side, just next to the yellow lines marking the edge of the square door. Then he connected one perforated edge to another to form corners of cuts. He worked on connecting the corners closest to him, so that when the door finally gave on any remaining connected steel, it would drop down from the ceiling in such a manner as to swing away from him.

"Just two more cuts to go," Dmitri called to his companion.

A hazy brown light from outside began to filter through the cracks where the cuts had been made. He set the torch to work on the second to last cut, and jumped back when he noticed a sudden increase in light indicating that the door was finally collapsing into the stairwell. The door swung away from Boronov as anticipated, but what he wasn't expecting was the vast quantity of debris which came flowing into the tunnel as well. Broken chunks of concrete and asphalt mingled with Martian dirt rushed into the tunnel, forcefully knocking Dmitri to the concrete ground.

"Dmitri!" screamed Garrison shielding himself from a shower of rocks which were now bouncing down the stairs. He jumped away from the falling debris until the commotion ceased. Working past rubble on the landing and stairs, he was finally able to make his way to the upper landing. Obscured by dust, Garrison at first was having difficulty assessing the situation. "Dmitri! Are you okay? Can you hear me?"

There was no immediate response from Boronov, and O'Ryan feared that he might have been knocked unconscious from the blow. As the dust settled, he saw nothing but a pile of rubbish filling much of the upper landing. Boronov had been completely buried. Garrison furiously pulled chunks of concrete and asphalt off of the landing using nothing but his hands for tools. With each effort, the sound of rock and concrete bouncing down the stairs kept rhythm with O'Ryan's effort to extricate his companion. After fifteen minutes of work, he felt a soft lump, which he quickly recognized as the spacesuit of Dmitri. Working harder, he continued to sweep the debris away, until he had removed his companion, who was able to sit up against the wall of the stairwell, still shaken from the incident. He looked up to see streams of light through the pile of debris.

"Dmitri! Can you hear me? Are you in pain?"

"What—happened?" Dmitri asked in a daze.

"When the trap door opened, a flood of debris came down on top of you. Are you in pain?"

"A little, but I do not think injuries are too bad," Boronov stated. "I simply do not understand. There should be nothing blocking this emergency hatch. Camp is kept free of stuff like this, and yet it is clearly garbage from camp. Blocks of concrete, road asphalt? There is a landfill, but it is on east side of crater near SAR pad, where junk is recycled as material for SAR operation. This hatch should not lead us there."

"Well, we will know where this came from once we can get above ground and see what it is and where we are at," pointed out Garrison looking at the streams of ruddy light. "But that will have to wait. We must see to your injuries first. Do you think you can stand?"

Boronov nodded, and slowly, Garrison helped him to his feet with a few grunts and Russian words which O'Ryan assumed to be cursing.

"This is very frustrating, Garrison. All day long we have been just feet away from ground level and we just cannot seem to get there." Dmitri looked at his watch. "17 hours 13 minutes. Even if we can clear this pile today, it will be dark again, and we will not be able to work on power array."

"We must not work on it today," insisted Garrison. "Your injuries must be tended to, and then we must rest and hopefully return to complete this stubborn job tomorrow."

Defeated, the pair of damaged astronauts walked slowly and quietly back down the stairs, Garrison sulking in the misfortunes of the last 24 hours, and Dmitri hobbling on a swollen foot.

...

Through the slits in his eyes, Garrison saw the same green glow that had greeted him the morning before. He sat up, yawned, and saw his companion tightly wrapping his right ankle with a bandage.

"How is it, Dmitri?" asked Garrison. "The foot?"

"It is some swollen, but not so much as I feared. I can walk, and this bandage will help us with our day of work."

"Well, let's get packed." Garrison stood on his feet and clapped his hands together. He felt optimistic about the day ahead of them. Besides, it couldn't get any worse than the last couple of days, could it?

"I have packed some hand tools to help with debris," Dmitri mentioned. "Hand shovel and small pick axe should get us through tunnel and onto Martian soil. But, do eat some breakfast first."

Garrison was beginning to wonder if Dmitri ever slept. By the time he awoke in the mornings, his partner had already finished breakfast and began preparations for the day. He completed his meal while Dmitri was gone. By the time he was finished suiting up, Dmitri had returned and the two proceeded into the depressurization chamber and ensuing tunnel again. They climbed the stairs slowly, feeling the muscle fatigue of yesterday's climbs as well as the pain from their respective injuries.

When they reached the top landing, they discovered that there was not enough room on the stairs for both to safely work, so Boronov began by removing debris from under the trap door and O'Ryan cleared a path off of the stairs, while trying to dodge rocks and dirt flying from his companion's shovel. Every now and then, the pair would trade roles in order to catch a breather from the digging and shoveling, but later in the morning, they were able to extricate enough of the material to give an opening large enough for an astronaut to fit through.

"I think we might be able to make it now." It was Garrison's turn on the pile when he announced the opening to his partner.

Dmitri was a couple of flights down, spreading the debris evenly down the stair well in order to not create a barrier in their return to the bunker. "I will be there in one moment."

As Dmitri made it to the pile, he saw a dust-filled chamber filtering an orange glow from the hole above, now adequately sized to allow the pair to climb out of the tunnel. Garrison was already scaling the remaining rocks and disappeared slowly through the hole.

"What do you see?" asked Dmitri. "Where are we, and why is this pile of junk here in first place?"

"I really can't tell," responded Garrison. "The visibility is simply awful. This must be one of those dust storms that they taught me in Martian Weather 101."

"I come up and see too," Dmitri replied with both curiosity and concern.

The curiosity and concern only deepened when he reached the surface, and saw a lot of dust in the air, and a lot of uneven debris on the ground.

"Well, it is dust storm, but it is not right." Dmitri said sullenly.

"Why?"

"Little wind," pointed out Dmitri matter-of-factly. "Dust storm of this nature requires much wind. Where is wind?"

"So, you haven't seen this kind of activity before?"

"It is most unusual weather."

"Let's take a look around and see if we can find our way out of the landfill," said Garrison.

"Garrison, this is not landfill."

"But what about this pile of junk underneath us?"

"I don't know, but I know what landfill looks like. There is too much concrete and rocks and... broken asphalt?" Dmitri wandered slowly through the uneven terrain and came to a section that consisted of more significant amounts of asphalt, which was only used on the road surfaces of Camp Mars. No road work had been redone during Dmitri's mission, and there was none that he could recall at the landfill either.

"Dmitri, does it make sense to go to the power grid with all of this dust? Will we be able to see anything to make a diagnosis?"

"No, it does not make sense. Nothing makes sense right now."

"Should we head over to the barracks, at least? We can wait out this dust storm there to make a better assessment."

Dmitri was leaning down onto the pile of debris picking at the pile with the axe.

"Dmitri?" Garrison carefully stepped over rocks and jagged concrete to meet up with his companion. "Dmitri?"

"This is road, here." Dmitri indicated with the end of his axe.

"What?"

"The road goes here, under these rocks. The asphalt is largely broken up and tossed about, but here, I see asphalt, but over there it is just dirt."

"I don't understand."

"This concrete," Dmitri said as he sat on a rock and hefted a concrete chunk. "It is rounded. Based on the arc, I believe this is part of very large cylinder."

He paused to see if Garrison understood.

"It is fuel tank, Garrison."

"The fuel tank blew up, then, and left this pile of rubble here? But how does that relate to the pow—". O'Ryan stopped in mid sentence as he was able to piece together a theory. "Shrapnel! Dmitri, shrapnel from the tank must have flown over the runway and landed on the solar array as well, or worse, all the way to the other side of the crater to the distribution subsystem.

Oh, no... the communication array. Dmitri, this is a huge blow to our camp."

Dmitri shook his head. "We must not draw hasty conclusion. "The atmosphere is not sufficient for that kind of explosion of fuel."

"An earthquake, then?" suggested Garrison eager for answers.

"We would feel a marsquake in bunker. Besides, you know that Mars is not geologically active."

"We must explore the camp and assess the extent of damage, Dmitri."

"No," said Dmitri quickly as he stood up. "We must not risk becoming lost in this dust storm. Remember... since Mars is one of few planets with no magnetic field, we only rely on visual landmarks, sky navigation, or vehicle navigation system."

"Okay, so we can't see landmarks, but we can see a faint bright circle through the dust that indicates the position of the Sun. We can use the Sun to help us reach the MTV and then drive around the camp to assess the extent of damage."

"Too risky. We must first wait out dust storm."

"Dmitri, why can't we wait in the barracks instead of the bunker?"

Boronov's voice raised slightly. "What if we find barracks damaged also, and then we grow disoriented and can't find hole in the ground with this sea of debris around it? Too risky, Garrison."

Garrison nodded, and turned around, straining to survey anything through the haze of dust. At last, he asked, "How long will the dust last, Dmitri? When will we be able to venture about and restore some sanity to this camp?"

"Winds are not strong. I am hopeful that tomorrow, we will have clear day to assess damage and make repairs."

A frustrated sigh was audible to Dmitri.

"I'm sorry, comrade. We must return to bunker and wait."

Dmitri lead the way back to the trap door. Pausing, he kneeled down and picked up an object that Garrison did not recognize.

"What is it, Dmitri?"

Boronov showed Garrison the contents of his hand. "It is fuel gauge that needed repair."

Garrison hung his head and sighed. "Looks like it's going to need more than repair now, my friend."

...

Joram Anders sat upright in bed, his heart started by the sound of a telephone ringing next on a table next to his bed. He answered the phone.

"Hello."

"Joram, this is Professor Zimmer. Can you meet me in the common room?"

Joram looked at his clock. 11:25 AM. He just went to bed a couple of hours earlier after a third straight night of investigating the Martian dilemma. Rest had not come easily, either, as his body was struggling to cope with his sudden change of schedule. In fact, this was the first morning where he was able to quickly go to sleep, and even if it was Carlton Zimmer on the phone, he couldn't help feeling agitated at being awoken from such a sound sleep.

"Um... Yes, professor... I'll be there in just a minute."

Joram's room on Palomar observatory was smaller than a motel room. It held a twin size bed, night stand, and a small closet for a few changes of clothes and personal affects. He went into a tiny bathroom, washed his face in cold water, dabbed with a towel, and proceeded to put on a pair of clothes he had tossed in a corner.

When Joram entered the common room, which really was a library stocked with astronomy and science texts, he noticed that Zimmer was already conversing with Kath and Reyd. Spinning around towards the door, Zimmer clapped his hands. "Ah, right. Let's head to the video conference room at the observatory, then."

"What's going on, Professor?" Joram prompted Zimmer for a briefing of their morning activity.

"Ravid called Dr. Gilroy a couple of hours ago. He is confident that we will get a visual of the camp during this Earthrise. We will be getting a live video feed from an observatory in Istanbul which is already focused on the eastern Martian horizon, waiting to get the first visual into our hands."

As Zimmer led his trio out of the dorm facility, Joram buttoned up the wind breaker that he put on, due to a morning autumn wind which had deposited a light frost on the ground the night before. Reyd, likewise zipped up his jacket, and Kath embraced herself sporting a jacket and scarf, which

114

was flowing freely in the wind. Zimmer, who was familiar with the weather on the mountain, wore a long sleeve dress shirt and tie.

As they entered the dimly lit room, the party of four took seats along a conference table closest to the large projected display which was already showing clear images of the Martian horizon. Long shadows filled the breach between night and day, cast by mountains and craters and were replaced by even longer shadows as the frigid surface rotated, groping for sunlight.

Zimmer dialed on the speaker phone in the center of the room.

"Dr. Gilroy, this is Professor Zimmer. I have my students with me here at Palomar Mountain."

"Thanks for calling in, Professor! We know that your team has been working through some exhausting evenings, and we apologize to bring you back this morning. I have Ravid Avram on the phone in Israel, as well as Camp Mars specialists here at Johnson and Kennedy. The team at the Istanbul University Observatory is also online. We really hope that we can get a visual on the astronauts during this Earthrise and begin to establish a plan for their safety."

After a brief pause, a different voice came over the phone. "Dr. Gilroy, do you plan to make an announcement about Ayman Hardy today?"

"We are not inclined to give up our efforts yet," Gilroy replied.

"He has been non-communicant for more than 60 hours now, Doctor."

"Yes, but as far as we know, his shuttle is carrying him as safely as ever back to the Moon, even without communication. The shuttle can sustain life for four weeks."

"But you have also failed to make visual contact with the shuttle through either visual light or infrared which should detect the heat trail of the shuttle."

"Understood," Gilroy sounded annoyed. "We are guarded in our comments to the press, but we are also conveying realistic scenarios as well. We simply will not give up until the full two weeks have elapsed. If he does not arrive on the Moon in that time frame, then we will announce our fear of the worst."

Joram looked across the table at Kath, who was staring down at the floor motionlessly. He returned his gaze to the projected image.

"Two minutes to visual, Dr. Gilroy," announced a scientist who was calculating the estimated time of Earthrise on Camp Mars.

"Doctor, the edge of the crater is in view now," said another voice that appeared to be in the same room as Gilroy.

"Thank you, Stan," replied Gilroy, and then speaking into the phone gave instructions to all who were dialed in. "If you will all fix yourselves on the upper left corner of the horizon, you will see the edge of the crater, distinguished by its opening to the plains surrounding it. We should be able to start to see camp facilities in less than a minute now."

Joram leaned forward in his chair. Kath looked up at the crater rim while manicuring the nail of an index finger with her teeth. Reyd straightened his eyeglasses to improve his vision. Professor Zimmer stood, muted the speakerphone, and paced towards the back of the room with hands folded behind his back.

"What do you expect to see, students?" asked Zimmer with his back to the projection.

All three turned in their chairs to look at Zimmer, but none gave a response.

"See for yourselves." He wheeled around and gestured with his right hand. "This is what we've been anxious to see for three days now."

The three turned back to the view. The phone was silent of any significant conversation, but indistinguishable mumbling could be heard from a couple of sources.

"Professor," Kath was the first to speak. "I—I really don't recognize anything. Are we too zoomed out to make out any structures?"

Zimmer shook his head and spoke softly. "There are no structures, Kath."

Her eyes grew wide in recognition.

"Oh no," gasped Joram as he stood and drew closer to the projected image. "It's—It's…"

"…a pile of rubble!" exclaimed Reyd. Leaping to his feet in horror, Reyd turned to the professor. "Professor Zimmer, what happened? How? How can this happen?"

Zimmer shook his head slowly. "I do not know, Mr. Eastman. It is an unspeakable tragedy. We have lost three astronauts."

"Three, professor?" asked Kath in surprise. "Are you sure that the shuttle was destroyed also?"

"Ms. Mirabelle," answered the professor carefully. "Whatever leveled Camp Mars also took out three of the four satellites. It also sent a flurry of unidentifiable radiation to our very own planet and caused a sudden flare of brightness on the Sun. Whatever force we are dealing with here, it is very powerful. That shuttle didn't stand a chance."

"But one satellite survived, Professor. Couldn't the shuttle be safe as well?"

"That satellite survived, Kath, because it was sheltered from the destructive path that has left an indelible mark on our inner Solar System. However, the trajectory of the shuttle was not in the shadow."

Kath did not understand. "In what shadow, Professor?"

"In the shadow of the yellow beam, Ms. Mirabelle. Mars protected that remaining satellite, as it sat in the shadow during that one fateful, destructive moment."

The three students gasped.

"Professor?" Joram asked quietly. Deliberately, he phrased his questions. "Are you suggesting that the yellow beam is the source of the radiation?"

"Yes, Mr. Anders, I believe that is exactly the case."

"Then, you know what this yellow beam is, then, right?"

Zimmer sighed heavily. "I have no clue, Mr. Anders. But you three are going to help me find out. Consider yourselves assigned to your graduate research here at CalTech."

117

Chapter

11

Paol Joonter broke an awkward silence in an attempt to calm his nerves. "It seems just like yesterday," he said as much to himself as to those around him. He was staring out of a window in a very familiar hallway of the courthouse. The last time he was here, he was awaiting a verdict in his murder trial. Now, he waited to hear his sentencing.

"What seems like yesterday, Paol?" His lawyer accepted the prompt, knowing that it would help pass the time, if not the stress.

The client turned to his council as he answered the question. "It's just that I remember sitting in that bench over there for two days—or was it eternity—waiting to hear the verdict. Now, here I am again waiting to hear another jury decide my fate."

"How do you feel this time, Paol?" continued Warron.

"Frankly, I'm still disturbed, but I'm not as nervous. I think I'm beyond that now. I'm hardened, calloused inside. Maybe it's numbness and the whole thing hasn't really settled in yet." Turning back to the window, he paused for a moment. "At least this time, it's a beautiful day out there. The sun is shining, not a cloud in the sky. Maybe that's a good omen. But how good can it possibly be?"

"Paol, remember what I've told you. We will appeal, and we will win. You will not have to spend any time in jail. Since this is a first-time offense, I should have no problem getting bail during the appellate process, especially because it's a first offense, and nobody is considering you to be dangerous."

"Yes," countered the frustrated businessman, whose optimism had given way to cynicism in recent weeks. "You also pointed out how lawmakers on

Capitol Hill were encouraging federal courts to wield harsher sentences on white-collar criminals these days."

"True," admitted Warron. "I did warn you that things could be different, but typically, those new laws are because white-collar crime continues to grow at alarming rates. Tax evasion, fraud, money laundering, and embezzling were wreaking havoc on the national economy. The intent of Congress was to increase penalties on these monetary types of crimes that have been impacting our economy for years." While Warron believed that this was the case, he was also concerned about how these laws might be interpreted by federal judges and juries, particularly in the case of his client.

Paol Joonter retreated from the window and returned to the bench to sit beside Warron. Staring at the tile floor, he refused to continue to distract himself with the beautiful autumn day that was occurring outside. It was too painful for him to think that he may never be able to see a beautiful sunny day in a downtown park setting ever again.

"The way I see it, Warron, it's either life in prison with parole in no fewer than 20 years or the death penalty. Right?"

"Wrong!" Warron refused to look at the glass half empty. "It's neither of those scenarios... it's appeal, Paol. Appeal and acquit."

Paol smiled weakly. "Thanks, Warron. With your confidence, I am hopeful that you will find a way to restore justice to the system."

Warron stood erect with the sound of echoing footsteps. "That would be Monay."

Paol heaved a sigh of concern. "Here we go again."

Chapter

12

"Hello, Reyd," said Kath cheerfully as she leaped through the door of the common room.

Reyd Eastman gave a start. "Kath. Joram. Glad you could finally make it." He frowned while looking at his watch. "Zimmer's been asking for you guys for a while now."

Joram's eyes widened in concern. "What did he say, Reyd?"

"Something about finding some more *reliable* grad students to make history by studying one of the most bizarre astronomical phenomena to occur in the last century." Reyd's smirk gave away his practical joke.

Kath, who by now had approached to within arms distance, slugged Reyd in the shoulder. "You need to practice your poker face! By the way, why didn't you ride down with us?"

"Oh, I have an aunt who lives in Lake Elsinore, so I stayed at her place last night. It breaks up the drive nicely."

The trio turned towards the door as they heard it fly open. Professor Zimmer marched briskly into the room. "Ah, Joram. Kath... Glad you could finally make it. I was beginning to wonder if I was going to have to find some more *reliable* graduate students to make history by studying one of the most bizarre astronomical phenomena to occur in the last century."

With jaws dropped, Kath and Joram turned quickly to Reyd, who could only shrug his shoulders with as much surprise as they. Did Zimmer overhear their conversation?

"Just kidding, you two," smiled the professor.

"Professor, you seem rather chipper this evening," Kath observed.

"Ah, that's because I have just heard some great news, Kath!"

"What's that?"

"I received a call from Dr. Gilroy at Johnson. An observatory has yielded an encouraging piece of evidence. It appears that our Martian astronauts are…" Zimmer paused for effect and then lowered his voice to a whisper, which was betrayed by the twinkle in his eye, "…alive!"

Kath let out a screech, Reyd sighed with much relief, and Joram applauded.

"How did they discover that, Professor?" asked Joram eagerly.

"Turns out that they left a message with some of the rubbish: S.O.S, it spells. They were able to trace two sets of footprints leading to the opening where they were able to lay out the letters with a series of beams to make the three block letters needed."

"Professor, I saw the destruction," pointed out Reyd. "There was nothing left standing. How could they survive that?"

"Apparently, the last communication that we had with the astronauts occurred while they were in the bunker—deep under ground. They were supposed to be on their way to a maintenance task, but they had forgotten a set of tools in the bunker."

Kath breathed deeply. "What a stroke of luck… what a miracle!"

Changing conversation abruptly, Zimmer announced, "Now, I must inform you that I will not be able to assist your efforts in the observatory tonight. I must attend a meeting of some urgency. You three will have to proceed on your own. You have the information from our meeting on campus earlier this week, correct?"

The three nodded their heads as Zimmer eyed his three students for their affirmative response. "Good!" he said clapping his hands. "You may proceed to the observatory to begin your preparations for the evening."

Zimmer left the room, closing the door behind him with a pace that was quicker than his entrance.

"I wonder what that was all about," Kath mused with her hands on her hips.

"Dunno. But let's go make history!" Joram directed with excitement. This was the team's first trip back to Palomar, and he had been eager to continue exploring ever since they returned back to the university.

...

The trio of graduate students huddled around the main control panel of the observatory. For the first couple of hours, the team organized themselves as best as they could without their mentor. They poured over the data that had been collected from the resident astronomers, as well as that of other observatories around the globe.

First looking at optical data collected from their very own 26" telescope, they were able to conclude that the brightness of the yellow beam was growing steadily in intensity. In the past week, the apparent magnitude of the beam had gone from a barely visible 6.3 when it was first detected to its present 1.3, making it as bright as some of the brightest stars in the sky. They had been able to calculate that the beam was about 120 miles wide and passed by Mars at a minimum distance of 12,500 miles—a near miss in astronomical terms—and that the line was perfectly parallel to the plane of the Milky Way. This was a significant contribution, and allayed much of the tension and concern surrounding the beam.

There were still many lay people who were swayed by the media to conclude that it had to be an alien spaceship, but the scientific community had concluded convincingly that this was very likely a galactic phenomenon, because of its orientation to the plane. Nevertheless, in the back of everyone's mind was the fact that some radiation event began exactly in the direction of the beam, and that it was detectable from Earth, from the Sun, and on Mars around the same point in time—evidence, say the visionaries that it must have been a space craft emitting the radiation as it passed by at very high speeds—perhaps even nearing the speed of light—and that the trail left behind was simply the exhaust of the passing UFO.

Reyd was the first to broach the subject. "You know what the media is saying don't you?"

Kath shivered at the allusion. "It's easy for them to spew off irrelevant theories. It's harder for me to scientifically study this phenomenon with the thought that just maybe I don't want to discover what the source of it is."

"Oh, Kath," rebutted Reyd. "It would be a marvelous discovery to learn of extra-terrestrial intelligence. You know Zimmer has been eager in this subject for some time."

"What, the parallel earth?"

"Sure, I mean, what comes with a parallel earth?" Reyd paused too short for either of his peers to craft an answer. "Parallel beings! That's what comes from a parallel earth!"

"But if that was a spaceship, then we have no parallel. And if the conspiracy theorists are right, our solar system just got buzzed by some alien ship scouting out our neighborhood. And look at the damage which that one ship caused on Camp Mars. Now that the scout has buzzed us, the rest of the troops will move in and take over. It could be the end of us, Reyd. I don't want to discover our Armageddon."

"Kath, you worry too much." Changing subjects Reyd asked her, "So what is your theory, then? What is that thing?" Reyd pointed to the screen where some of the latest images of the beam twinkled mysteriously.

"I... I don't know."

"Jor. What do you think?" Reyd turned to his other colleague.

"Wha? Huh?" Joram had completely missed the conversation as he scoured the data.

"Could this be a UFO, Joram?"

"UFO? C'mon, Reyd," Joram snorted. "You need to pay more attention to the data, and less attention to the media."

Quickly changing the subject back to their research, Joram announced, "There is no telling how long this thing is. I mean, it could be several light-years long."

"What?" Reyd and Kath synchronized their stunned response.

"Why is that so surprising?" Joram turned away from the monitor to look at his colleagues. "Just because we've only seen measurable effects from our inner Solar System... don't think that the thing is local to us. Where does the beam begin? And where does it end?"

After a pause, Reyd said, "Why don't you tell us, Joram? You seem to be the authority on the subject."

"No," Joram tried to avoid a confrontation. "I'm just like you two... trying to learn what the heck this is."

"Sorry, Joram," Reyd reined in his aggressiveness. "So tell us. Why do you think it is so sizable?"

"Visual clues indicate that for at least 7000 Astronomical Units in both directions, the beam has at least the same absolute magnitude. Thus, I wonder how much farther the beam extends in both directions before it fades? But more importantly, what the heck is causing such a phenomenon? It is so strange."

"It must be some jet of radiation, and if we can figure out which way it is coming from, we can go back and find the star that is giving it off," suggested Reyd.

"Which way do we go? We don't really know which way it originated? Nor do we really know its heading. We only know how far it is from Mars," Joram responded.

"Well, we can figure out its heading if we get one or two more location points. Can we measure it against any other planets?" Kath asked. "If we can get some triangulated data, we should be able to calculate its distance to other planets via parallax."

Parallax is exactly what astronomers used to calculate its distance from Mars. By collecting visual data from two different observatories, at extreme latitudes, they could see the relative difference in the two images. In an image shot from a North American observatory, the beam would appear to be just South of the Martian equator. The opposite would be the case for a South American observatory. Since Mars is relatively close enough to Earth to perform just such a calculation, scientists were able to observe that the beam passed by Mars at a distance of just 12,500 miles. This allowed astronomers to calculate that its distance from Earth was over 100 times as much at about 1.4 million miles.

Earth-based parallax—using points on opposite sides of the Earth—worked very well for finding distances when the measurement was in the inner Solar System. But such calculations would be more difficult when trying to measure the distance of the beam from, say, Neptune, or Jupiter. Instead, the team would need to use a point farther away from Earth.

As the team had mentioned this point, Reyd suggested, "The Kepler3 telescope! A moon-orbiting telescope should enhance our parallax, don't you think?"

"Um… we don't exactly have access to Kepler3," pointed out Kath.

"Actually, we sort of do!" said Reyd. This piqued Kath and Joram's curiosity as they shot a quick glance at each other. "Zimmer has access to the Kepler3 through his Parallel Earth team. I actually know a couple of the team members. If I explain our situation, I think we can get some help from the team."

"Well, giddyup!" Kath said as she slapped Reyd on the back.

With that, Reyd dialed his cell phone and engaged in a conversation with a fellow graduate student. Kath and Joram strained to follow at least half of the conversation. Within a couple of phone calls, and a few minutes of precious observatory time, Reyd hung up his phone and gave a thumbs up.

"Keelor Jefferies is gonna call me back in about 10 minutes. He's briefing the current Kepler3 astronomers. What we need to find are planets in the vicinity of the beam."

Reyd sat down at the main control terminal and dialed up the database on the Solar System. Within one minute he had a space map depicting the current locations of all of the planets.

"Boy, not too many are in good position. They're either on the other side of the Sun, or they're simply not close enough to the trajectory."

"Yeah, we're looking for a line like this," Joram indicated as he drew an invisible line on the monitor with a pencil he found on the console.

"Could Uranus work?" Kath said. "A bit far, but maybe we can get an image with the beam and Uranus together. I'm thinking that Saturn is a better choice, but it would be nice to have a third point along the line, so we can convince ourselves that we have the line correctly calculated."

"What about some dwarf planets, Reyd?" asked Joram.

"Good question. Let me dial those into this map."

As a handful of the larger dwarf planets appeared on the map, Joram pointed to a promising candidate. "Eris! Right there!"

"Good call, Jor!" Reyd congratulated. "I like the fact that we can find a point farther out in the solar system, too, as that will give us two pretty distant points to more accurately project the line. Hey, wasn't Eris discovered here as well?"

"Yeah, I think you're right," said Kath. "That's kind of cool... using Eris to help us with another important discovery right here at Palomar."

"Let's get this thing pointed at Eris," Reyd said as he stood and proceeded towards the telescope platform. Joram and Kath followed, as both were eager to see and learn the controls of the telescope. Reyd was the only member of the team to have previously been trained by Zimmer on the telescope controls.

Within a few minutes, Reyd had the coordinates dialed into the telescope, and it whizzed to its new location.

"Joram, do you remember enough of the console to be able to feed back the quality of the image to me?"

"I think so."

Joram descended from the telescope platform, and Kath followed behind as Reyd's cell phone rang.

"Keelor! Thanks for calling back… yeah… point that thing at Eris, would you… be sure to grab the exact coordinates from Palomar-26. They're currently dialed in exactly where we want, so you should be able to get them from the intranet… We'll also need an image on Saturn… Just give us something with the beam, we can adjust the zoom of the image to overlay with ours later… Yeah, I'll bring up Kepler live on the monitor in just a moment… Hey, thanks man… this is really going to help us move this effort forward… sure… I'll give you a call tomorrow and let you know… Yeah, you too."

When Reyd hung up, Joram announced, "Looks good, Reyd, but we can zoom in a little to get a better calculation from the image."

"Sure thing… how's that?" Reyd asked.

"Great. Come take a look." Joram responded. "We got really lucky with Eris, because it has such an eccentric orbit."

"How so?" asked Kath.

"It's way out of the plane of the solar system, but it's close to intercepting the plane right now, and the positioning couldn't be better to measure a second point along the line."

Reyd rolled up his sleeve, and looked at his watch. 10:49 PM. There was still plenty of time in the evening for making some observations and calculations. For a couple of hours the students pointed the telescope at Eris and Saturn respectively, collecting images, comparing them to Kepler3, situated nearly a quarter million miles from Earth. With scientific calculators, computers, and plain old pencil and paper, the students worked out the various calculations based on parallax between Palomar-26 and Kepler3.

"Ok, there's our line!" said Reyd after looking at his watch. "2:12 AM! Where does the time go?"

He stood up and walked away from the console with both hands behind his neck, working out some tightness in his neck and shoulders. He looked back to see Joram huddled over the console, while Kath watched intently. She knew Joram Anders well enough to know that he was concerned with something.

"I think we need to rework these numbers," he announced.

"What do you mean?" asked Reyd. "We got three points, and they come darn near to as straight of a line as can be expected."

"But it's not perfectly straight," Joram answered.

"Well, of course not... there will be some error in measurement, and perhaps some round-off error in our calculations." Reyd returned to the console, agitated at his colleague's perfectionism.

A look of deep intent and concern clouded Joram's expression. He drew his lips into a tight line before blurting out, "Look, guys. Our so-called line bends in towards Saturn. Either we've calculated the distance to Saturn too close, or the distance to Eris too far."

"Or," Reyd suggested, "we don't have a valid measurement for the distance to Mars."

"I think Mars is our reference point." Joram shook his head. "It should be the one we can get closest too. Besides, several different teams of professional astronomers all agree on the number. We're just a trio of grad students. I'm guessing we're more likely to be wrong. Let's just rework the numbers."

"Joram, that'll take another hour!"

"It'll be an hour well spent."

Reyd disagreed, especially when he looked at his watch at 3:04 AM when a fresh stab at the calculations provided effectively the same exact results.

"We need to go back to the drawing board and grab fresh images. Perhaps we botched the time or coordinates of one of our shots." Noticing that Reyd was displeased with this suggestion, he continued. "I'm sorry, Reyd. I just think that if we can't nail this line exactly down, then when we trace it back to find its source, the margin of error is going to cause us to miss the source of the beam altogether."

"Ok, we still have tomorrow night to start our trace," Reyd agreed.

Kath jumped in. "I agree with Joram. Besides, this is our research project, gentlemen. We're not just in this for the weekend, but for the long haul. Let's not forget that it could take an appreciable amount of our graduate education to solve this puzzle. We just need to be patient and careful with our work."

With a fresh set of images, and a clean slate for calculations, the team ended up with yet the same results.

"I can't believe this," said Reyd. "It's 5:15, and we're no farther than we were hours ago. Well, now we're running out of nighttime to do anymore data collection for today."

Joram didn't hear Reyd's tirade, but instead continued to focus on the data. Just as Reyd was about to storm out of the observatory, Joram called. "Reyd! Kath! I think I know what's happening!"

"Whatcha got, Joram?" Kath was the first by his side.

"It looks very close to a line, because it is very close to a line, but it's really an arc—an orbital arc."

"An orbit!" exclaimed Reyd in disbelief. With a deprecating smile on his face, he asked skeptically. "What exactly would it be orbiting, Joram?"

Joram looked up at his colleagues. "It's orbiting the Milky Way—in other words, it is orbiting our very own galactic core. It's an orbital object, you guys!"

"Explain," replied Reyd skeptically.

Joram retraced his calculations with his partners. "Our solar system is 26000 light years away from the galactic core, right? That's a circumference greater than 10^{10} Astronomical Units. The distance from Mars to Eris is about 100 AUs, so we're talking a ratio of 1 to 10^8. Now, on my calculator, if I divide 360 by 10^8, and then multiply by 60 arc minutes and follow that with 60 arc seconds and then by 1000 for milliarcseconds. We're looking at a mere milliarcsecond. That small of an arc is always going to look like a line, but the deviation that I had pointed out matches perfectly with the arc that I just described."

"So you think this thing is orbiting the galaxy?" Reyd wrinkled his brow as he let the concept settle.

"Yes." Joram affirmed. "Definitely!"

Both heard a suppressed sob from behind them and turned to see a horrified Kath staggering backwards and growing very pale. Joram jumped out of his seat and raced to her and braced her by wrapping his arm around her waist.

"Kath, you're not feeling well. What's wrong?" Joram asked as Reyd arrived with a chair.

"Sit down, Kath," instructed Reyd.

Her gaze was fixed towards the console, but the blankness of her expression was clear that she was focusing on some point much farther away... perhaps on the yellow beam itself.

Shaking her head vigorously, she came back to her senses. "Guys, listen... this thing is growing brighter, isn't it?"

"Well... yes... we do know that," Reyd answered.

"Don't you see? Maybe it's not actually orbiting the galaxy. Maybe it's emanating away from the galactic core. It's... it's like a ripple. Throw a pebble in a pond, and the ripple continues outward, right?"

"Great point, Kath!" Joram said. "All this time, we were assuming that it was a trail of some sort, but maybe it is some light coming from the center of the galaxy."

"Not just light, Joram! It's carrying some sort of annihilating radiation with it. Something powerful enough to obliterate Camp Mars."

"Not so, Kath." Joram argued. "The beam is on the inside of Mars with respect to the galactic core."

"Joram... that's just the visible ripple. There must be another invisible ripple ahead of it which is carrying the destructive force." She looked up at the two men, each more concerned about her well-being than a beam of emanating radiation. She propelled herself out of the chair and raced to the monitors where a smattering of the evening's images were still available, each showing the glow of a yellow streak.

"Guys, listen to me! You don't get it, do you? That thing is heading... towards... Earth!"

Now it was the men's turn to grow pale.

"Kath, are you suggesting what I think you're suggesting?" The dawn of realization was setting in for Joram Anders.

"The thing is going to destroy half of the Earth, leveling every building it hits, and crushing every living thing. They'll be the lucky ones, because they'll not even know what hit them. The inhabitants on the other side, however, will not be so lucky. On land, we'll see a dust storm just like we saw on Mars. It will block out the Sun's rays for weeks, plummeting temperatures to inhospitable levels and freezing crops worldwide. On sea, it will wretch sea water miles into the air. Gravity will force trillions of tons of moisture back into the oceans, creating global tsunamis that will wash every coastal area on the planet into the depths of the oceans."

Kath's voice trailed off into sobs. Joram and Reyd stood rooted to the spot in horror of Kath's scenario.

"The astronauts," Joram pointed out. "They lived by going underground."

"Sure, you can come back out of your hole in a few weeks, but what are you going to eat. How will you keep from freezing in the severely global winter. There will be no survival." Kath was devastated.

"Scientists for a long time have known there are cycles of mass extinction." Reyd pointed out. "Could this be some cyclic radiation event coming from the black hole that forms the center of our galaxy? Perhaps so much energy gets sucked into it that the black hole must eventually belch out a burst of violent energy… kind of like a geyser bursts out water to relieve it of the pressure build-up of super-heated water and gasses."

Trembling violently, Kath pulled a cell phone out of her purse and began to dial.

"Who you calling?" Reyd asked as color continued to flush from his face.
"Zimmer."

"You have Zimmer's cell phone number?" Reyd was impressed.

"It's on caller ID from when he called us that first evening, remember?"

"But didn't he say he had something more urgent to attend to."

Kath's jaw dropped as she threw up her hands in despair and shot an irritating and disgusting glare at her peer. "Urgent?! More urgent?! You id—

"Professor Zimmer. This is Kath Mirabelle."

…

Carlton Zimmer was escorted into a conference room by Dr. Vurim Gilroy at the Johnson Space Center in Houston. Gilroy had convened an investigative task force for the emergency mission that would be required to rescue the astronauts whose life support system was being quickly depleted.

"Carlton, thanks so much for coming back so quickly."

"Well, I'm glad to assist in any way I can, Vurim."

Dispensing with pleasantries, the NASA program manager got right to business. "Since we've already lost one astronaut this week due to the bizarre phenomenon, we'd highly value your input as to what we're up against. I know that you've told us that you really haven't yet figured out what we're dealing with, but you are still the most knowledgeable, and your opinions will be highly respected among the entire team I'm sure.

"Carlton, we don't want to lose Boronov and O'Ryan, but we'll be in even hotter water if we lose the rescue crew. They'll be completely vulnerable up there in the unprotected expanses of space."

Zimmer paused for a moment. "Vurim, you're not suggesting that we might leave those astronauts up there are you?"

"No—at least not at the moment—but we need to consider all of the risks."

"If you go to the American public and tell them that you do not intend to at least attempt to save the astronauts, there will be outrage."

"The rest of the team will be here in 15 minutes Carlton. Let's lay everything on the table then. You'll recognize most of the members of the team from our last meeting. However, the director of NASA will also be in attendance. This thing is out of my hands, Carlton. The ultimate decision will come from Washington.

"Can I get you anything to drink?"

"A bottle of water will be fine, thank you."

Gilroy left Zimmer in the quiet conference room to gather his thoughts while he went to collect a bottle of water for his guest, but within a couple of minutes, others began to convene in the conference room. Zimmer remembered everyone from the last time he was at Johnson, although he did not recall most of their names. The atmosphere was slightly more relaxed this time, considering that the team at least knew that two of the astronauts were still alive.

As Gilroy returned to the room, he not only had a bottle of water with him but also a man Zimmer immediately recognized as the director of NASA.

He was attired in a dark suit, blue tie, and black wingtip shoes. He was the very appearance of diplomacy and policy making, and Zimmer was sure to not appreciate his presence at the meeting, simply because these were the types of people so far removed from scientific discovery and understanding, yet they were also very crucial in its funding.

"Ladies and Gentlemen, I'd like to introduce all of you to Dr. Marrak Henley, the director of NASA." He then went around the table introducing each team member to the director.

The meeting began at 1:35 AM. There was a general briefing on the situation, and all known data points were provided. After a 40-minute overview, Gilroy led the team in a frank discussion about a rescue mission. Launch windows were mentioned and astronaut availability determined. It was generally agreed by all that rescuing the astronauts was extremely feasible, and that well-studied emergency plans were already in place for just such a rescue. Through the ninety minutes, Zimmer had been quiet, yet attentive to the discussion that he thought may be wrapping up, when Henley turned towards the astrophysicist.

"Dr. Zimmer, we've been hearing much from the media, from the scientific community about this yellow beam. We've heard enough to believe that it is directly linked to the Camp Mars disaster as well as to the loss of Ayman Hardy. When our rescuers get up into the completely unsheltered expanse of space between Earth and Mars, how can we be certain that another event does not cause the loss of more astronauts and resources?"

"Well that is the question of the day, right?" Zimmer stood from his seat to create a position of strength. He began walking slowly along the length of the table. "I mean, if we can answer that question, it will help us determine conclusively whether the benefit of the mission is worth the potential risks. We do not know what the yellow beam is, and we have not proved that it is related to the destruction of Camp Mars. However, it is highly reasonable to assume that it is. I can't give you my word that this thing will not again attack our inner Solar System, but here are my thoughts about making the decision to save the astronauts. First, America will expect—perhaps demand—an effort. If it fails, will they blame you? Certainly. If you don't make the effort, will they blame you? Definitely. There are always risks involved in manned space exploration, but you have devoted astronauts who are determined in this effort in spite of those risks.

"My guess is that you already have enough astronauts willing to make the effort that you could fill three or four teams of rescuers. They will gladly risk their lives to make the attempt. If you don't give them the chance, they will always live with the decision to allow Camp Mars to become Graveyard Mars. They won't be able to sleep at night, and I'm hoping that you wouldn't be able to sleep either if you make the decision to not go."

"Fair enough," said Henley without emotion. "I appreciate your candor and your opinion, Professor. I was already mostly off the fence in favor of the mission. Your insight helps convince me that we will go. Dr. Gilroy, I will expect daily reports between now and launch next Thursday as to the status of the preparation of the vehicle and its crew."

"Absolutely. I will have those daily reports to you by 5:00 PM central time."

"Well, gentlemen. If that's all…"

Zimmer was surprised at how easily Henley was convinced to run the mission. Emboldened, he added, "Vurim, if I may add just one more thing before we conclude, I know that our highest priority is the rescue of the astronauts, but I think you do yourself and NASA a disservice without looking ahead."

"Looking ahead, Professor?" Gilroy's eyes narrowed in curiosity.

"If we cannot determine what this beam consists of, we may never know what exactly it did to destroy the camp. The future of manned space exploration may be in jeopardy if we cannot comfortably comprehend the forces that can alter our exploratory efforts."

"What do you propose, professor?"

"Since we are sending a crew millions of miles away to rescue the astronauts, why not spend an extra day or two on a side trip to study this phenomenon."

"I do not feel comfortable with that idea, Professor," announced Henley, as the team members once again took their seats in realization of a drawn-out discussion. "You're asking us to fly one of our ships into the beam that could bear highly destructive forces. This needs to remain focused as a mission of rescue, not discovery."

133

"I understand that Dr. Henley. I'm not suggesting that we fly into it, but I believe we have some ruggedized probes that could be easily deployed from a distance in order to study the beam close up. Of course, the craft would keep a safe distance, and I realize that it would come after the rescue. And... if either Boronov or O'Ryan are in physical or medical peril, we would scrap the experiments, and rush them back home."

"Define safe distance, Professor." Henley continued to press. "Who would be able to determine with any confidence how close we can get?"

"The ship would have to come no closer than it already is approaching. We'll already be within 10000 miles of the beam according to our calculations. This is already a distance which is certainly closer than desired, but the probes can be launched from the ship and traverse the remainder of the distance themselves."

"Really, Professor," dismissed the NASA director. "We simply cannot worry about experiments when the lives of astronauts are at stake."

"I understand your position, Dr. Henley, but I think it would be prudent to consider the future. If we can't identify the beam—if we can't understand the physical phenomenon that leveled Camp Mars, then we can no longer feel comfortable with space exploration in general. We'll always be too frightened of the unknown. For the future of NASA and scientific space exploration in general, we simply must figure out what this thing is, and to do that, we're going to have to visit it. It can't hurt to add the probes to the payload and spend an extra day in the orbit of Mars to get them dispensed."

Dr. Henley weighed Zimmer's arguments. If Zimmer was right, then public opinion could sour on the mission of NASA, and that would put his own job in jeopardy.

Henley turned towards Gilroy. "Vurim, we have less than a week to organize the rescue effort. Would we have time to consider these experiments as well?"

"I would need more people, Joe. My team will be tasked 24/7 with the task of getting the rescue effort put together before then. But, if there was another team available who could also work full throttle on the experimental payload, we might be able to pull it off. Of course, we'd need your help, Carlton."

"You would have my full attention over the next week on any issues that come up. I need to return to my research team in California to collect the data and observations that they have made over the weekend, and with that data, we will comprise a set of experiments which should help us figure out what we're dealing with here."

After a brief pause, Gilroy dismissed the meeting, and on the way out of the room, Zimmer felt a vibration in his coat pocket. He pulled out his cell phone, looked at the number, but did not instantly recognize it. "It's 5:30 AM in California... who would be calling me at this hour."

"Hello, this is Carlton Zimmer."

Zimmer answered to hear a quavering, distraught voice on the other end. "Professor Zimmer. This is Kath Mirabelle."

Chapter

13

"All rise…"

Paul rose in unison with the rest of the room, but he didn't hear anything else from the court clerk until he took his seat a second after everyone else had.

"You may be seated," the judge announced as he took his seat. "It looks like the jury is accounted for. Have you reached a decision, Mr. Foreman?"

"We have your Honor."

This time, it was Warron who was more intent on the outcome of the jury, mainly because of those white-collar laws. He was curious to know if the courts would implement them to their fullest in this case. As for Joonter, he figured life in prison was another form of death penalty. At his age, could he possibly live 20 or 30 years in prison and live to see parole?

The foreman stood and read the statement prepared by the jury. "In the case of Paol Joonter, your Honor, we recommend a penalty of life in prison for the murder of Rawson Becker with parole review in 20 years. Further, we recommend the death penalty for the murder of Shannyl Cox, as we consider her to have been an innocent bystander at the murder scene who was completely absolved from any responsibility in the business proceedings of Mr. Joonter and Mr. Becker."

"I understand," reiterated Etherton, "that you are recommending one life in prison sentence and one death penalty sentence. Is that correct?"

"Yes, your Honor."

"Will council please approach the bench?"

Paol was now very intent as sweat began to bead up on his face. His wife, just behind him, was sobbing, but rubbed his back in an attempt to show her continued support of her husband.

"Your Honor," Warron was quick to launch the first words in his sidebar with the judge. "This is simply unprecedented. Two different sentences for effectively the same crime?"

"You heard the jury's argument. They could perhaps understand a crime of passion, since you've shown the unscrupulous manner in which Becker handled some of his business affairs. However, Ms. Cox was not involved in any decision that should've turned your client's weapon against her. It was a cold-blooded deed your client dealt her."

"My client will appeal, I assure you... he is innocent. However, this is his first offense. His record of ethical business dealings speaks for itself. He has contributed greatly to our society. And he could possibly do no harm when he is released from prison on parole. In other words, even if he had committed the crime, I believe that all recognize that he is not a violent criminal. Why will we throw the book at him?"

"Your Honor," The district attorney stepped in. "This jury, which was selected by yourself, and both counsels, has seen all of the evidence, they have spent ample time deliberating. I believe they have made a conclusion consistent with the Congressional White-Collar Act of..."

"Henry," interrupted Warron. "You know as well as I do that the White-Collar Act was intended against crimes of economic import. This case has nothing to do with that act, and yet, I'm afraid that the jury has been distracted by this law and has been confused on its interpretation."

To this argument, the judge responded, "The act says nothing about the type of crime involved."

"An oversight by Congress that simply needs to be resolved sooner than later as this case apparently dictates. Gentlemen, we all know why Congress was motivated to pass that law. We must be sensitive to their intent."

"I interpret the law as I read it. The intent will have to be determined by a higher court of law than this one. In the meantime, I have to agree with the jury, and with the prosecutor. The request of the jury will stand. In the meantime, I suggest you begin the paperwork on the appeals of the United States v. Paol Joonter *and* on the Congressional White Collar Act."

"May I ask, your Honor, what you will consider a reasonable bail for the appeal? The paperwork has already been submitted, and the appellate court has accepted it."

"Bail?" asked the judge in surprise. "The Congressional White-Collar act states that any sentence handed down to an executive officer of a for-profit incorporated firm must stand as declared by the judge without possibility of bail. Part of the reason for the act is that constituents affected adversely economically by the actions of corporate officers are simply tired of seeing these men convicted and let free while the vast numbers of white-collar appeals sit on the benches of judges for years. Where is the justice of a wealthy criminal who is convicted of effectively robbing from his employees and investors and then is allowed to enjoy his wealth in the comforts of his own home for the rest of his life while appeal after appeal is filed on his behalf?"

"Your Honor, I must protest," began Warron. "Murdering these two people did not make Mr. Joonter any richer. He will not be enjoying much of anything while an incorrect judgment has been passed on him."

"As for the judgment, my court has done everything in its power to render a correct verdict. I trust that my juries have done everything in their power to make these decisions as just as possible. I would appreciate that you not suggest ineptness on the part of my court."

"Your Honor, I mean no disrespect, but we all know that one juror had been corrupted."

"And I handled that as judiciously as possible," answered the judge, growing more irritated with the defense attorney with each attempt to persuade the court to change its mind. "Even you agreed to the handling of that juror yourself, did you not?"

"I did, your Honor."

"Then, if you have no further arguments, may I proceed with this session?"

Enraged at this failure of the judicial system, Warron conceded defeat, "You may, your Honor."

"Mr. Prosecutor, do you have anything further in this case?"

"No, your Honor."

138

"Then, I believe we are done here." The judge dismissed the attorneys with a severe look.

After the lawyers returned to their seats, Etherton addressed the suspect directly. "Mr. Joonter, after discussion with the defense and prosecution in this case, I have decided to accept the jury's recommended sentences. You are to serve one life sentence which is superseded by the death penalty sentence. As I have explained to your council, I am disallowed, by law, to grant you the possibility of parole during appeal, but I will grant you one week before you are to report to the federal penitentiary to begin your sentence in order to allow you to put any remaining personal affairs in order. You will be under house arrest during that period of time, and will be accompanied by a federal agent at all hours of the day. Because your appeal has already been accepted, I would expect that the appellate court will initiate your case within three to six months. At that time, the appellate judge will determine whether there is ample evidence to grant you bail at that time, or whether you will continue to serve your sentence until the jury determines a new verdict and sentence. Do you understand these directions?"

Vacantly, Paol gazed into the eyes of the judge and affirmed. "Yes, your Honor."

Chapter

14

Conversation was light in the Palomar dining room on Saturday evening. The stresses of the evening before coupled with the grind of nighttime work in the astronomy induced significant fatigue on the part of Professor Zimmer's graduate students. Each would eventually shake off the slumber of the day through their microwave dinners and choice of caffeinated beverages. Joram had already consumed half of his bottle of Coca-Cola, Reyd was sipping at his hot coffee, and Kath was savoring her peach-flavored iced tea. Engulfed in silence, the trio looked up from their meals as they heard the door to the room open.

"Professor Zimmer!" Kath exclaimed, relieved to see her mentor appear.

With bags under his eyes, it was clear that the toil of the last couple of weeks was even taking its toll on this seasoned astronomer, all too acquainted with nocturnal living.

"Hello!" Zimmer nodded and smiled. "I'm glad I'll be able to assist you with your efforts this evening. I'm very sorry I left the three of you alone in your duties last night, especially considering the scare that you gave yourselves. However, I'm impressed with the accomplishments that you were able to make last night."

"Accomplishments?" sneered Reyd, cutting a glance at Joram. "We spent the whole evening regenerating the same set of numbers from the same set of calculations."

"Ah, but in the end, you made a discovery that has become a great piece of the puzzle," Zimmer stated in a congratulatory manner.

After a brief pause, Kath broke the silence in an imploring tone, "Professor?"

"Yes, Kath."

"I'm sorry that I jumped to such ridiculous conclusions last night."

"Nonsense, Miss Mirabelle. They were not ridiculous at all. I was singularly impressed with your theory. It fit Mr. Anders' calculations. It fit the manner of the brightening of the beam. It was a really clever piece of deduction."

"Clever, indeed. It only took you five seconds to disprove it. I... I didn't think it through enough."

"Only because of experience, Kath. I've been around the block enough with scientific discovery that I'm constantly trying to analyze all of the data in an effort to disprove any theory which I might concoct, as it is always easier to prove a theory wrong than to prove one right. For example, take Einstein's theory of relativity. It has dominated the thought process and laws of physics for centuries now, yet it cannot be proven. Just because we've observed that it holds true in a million and one experiments which have been conducted over many years doesn't mean that experiment number one million and two will not provide evidence to disprove it—or at least provide a singularity to the theory. It would take infinite observational prowess to prove a theory, but it takes just one contrary piece of data to disprove it.

"That said, as you set forth your theory to me last night, my first objective was to disprove it. And so, I realized that the calculation of the distance from the beam to Mars was calculated by several teams over several days. All of these teams came up with the same number. 12,500 miles. This indicates that there was no motion of the beam towards the planet Mars, thus it could not be emanating away from the center of the Milky Way as you had proposed.

"Further, any such radiation would propagate through the empty expanses of the galaxy nearly at the speed of light. Had the beam been approaching from the center of the galaxy, we would have been hit with the radiation only minutes after it had rained its destructive powers down on Camp Mars.

"Further, we know that the radiation had *already* hit Earth, just not with the same punch that it had on Mars—which is most fortunate. We know that there was an unidentifiable impact of radiation on the side of the Earth which is facing in the direction of where the beam rests now. The Sun also received a radiation event at the same time as well."

At this, Joram interrupted Zimmer. "That's what's got me confused, Professor. How can the event be synchronized between Earth, Mars and the Sun? How could it be omni-present at the same exact moment in time?"

"That, Mr. Anders... has cost me many a night of sleep in the last couple of weeks. It is a serious piece of the puzzle that must be understood, and as you know... in order to do that, we would be better served spending time over at 26, instead of here in the dining room."

All three students got the hint, and each returned to their dinner and drink. Zimmer pulled an apple out of an oversized pocket on his windbreaker and instructed the team to meet him at the observatory as soon as they were finished with their dinner. The distinctive crunch of the juicy apple was clearly heard as the door shut behind him.

"I think your theory was brilliant, Kath," Joram complemented. "You had Reyd and me convinced, you know."

"It's not so much the theory that's bothering me." Kath shared. "I really am starting to wonder if I really want to do this type of research. I'm afraid of what we might find."

Reyd attempted to console her. "You know, Kath, even if we discover it without you, you'll eventually know what the yellow beam is. As soon as the phenomenon of what happened here is understood, it will be broadcast to the world. You should be thrilled—honored—to be a part of it."

"I know, but what if we actually come in contact with extra-terrestrial life, Reyd?"

"Well, they're just as likely to be friendly as they are to be ornery, aren't they? Besides in thousands of years of human history that we can piece together, what do we have to show for it in terms of any alien interaction?"

Joram, attempting to lighten the situation, fired off a fast answer to the question. "Well, we do have all of those accounts of alien abductions and UFO sightings."

Kath pursed her lips and playfully slugged Joram in the shoulder. "Oh, stop it, Joram Anders."

142

Joram simply shrugged his shoulders, covering up his smile by stuffing the last piece of lasagna in his mouth.

"Well, anyway, what do I really have to contribute to the team, anyway? I'm just a meteorologist, remember? I'm not an expert astronomer, or a computer whiz."

Joram got serious. "Kath, you are a first-year astronomy graduate student, just like Reyd and me. We have an education in front of us. What better way to obtain it than to be on a research team, obtaining our knowledge of the universe from one of the world's foremost astrophysicists. I have a feeling that we're going to learn a lot as we continue to work with Zimmer. This project he's assigned us to—it's large, very large! When there are questions that Zimmer cannot answer..." He trailed off. Realizing that he had made his point, he opted to use his mouth to consume the remainder of his garlic bread and soft drink.

Being the first to stand up, Reyd and Kath took their lead from Joram and followed him to another evening of research.

. . .

On that evening, the four astronomers organized a plan to continue their study of the beam. They used computer models to calculate the trajectory of the circle around the Milky Way. After dispelling Kath's emanation theory, the team returned to an orbital theory. That is, their major assumption at this point was that the beam was the trail of an object orbiting the center of the Milky Way, since the arc calculated by the team just the evening before perfectly represented an orbiting body.

For a couple of hours they tried to zoom in on the beam and study its undulating pattern. They had hoped to orient the direction of its travel, but they could not make out from the near-randomness of the oscillations which direction any of the radiation was traveling.

After a midnight break, the group returned to their stations to resume their work. The beam was undulating on all of the monitors, precisely where they left the telescope focused on it.

Shortly after sitting down, Reyd turned in his chair. "Hey, Kath. What's the forecast for tonight anyway?"

"Clear skies. Why do you ask? Are you hoping to call it an early night, partner?" Kath winked playfully at him.

"No, but I do believe my eyes are clouding over, because it looks like the beam is more dim. I thought that maybe there was a light haze or perhaps marine layer developing."

Professor Zimmer squinted at the screen from behind Reyd's chair. "Are you sure it looks more dim, Reyd?"

"Well, it looks like it to me, but maybe my eyes are just fogging over during these late night studies."

"Joram, Kath, what do you guys think? Does it look like it's dimming?"

Joram shook his head, and Kath shrugged her shoulders.

Zimmer slapped his forehead. "Drats!" he exclaimed while stepping away from Reyd's station. He quickly pulled out his cell phone and paced anxiously around the observatory.

"Hi, Stan. Carlton Zimmer here... Listen, I completely forgot that we should start a bolometer on the beam... I'd like to use the AstroLab for greater precision, and round-the-clock capability... Yeah, that's all. No, wait... First, let's go get the tangential points along the horizon of the curve. That should be about 7000 AU away... Thanks, Stan. I'll be in touch on the analysis."

After hanging up the cell phone, he could tell by the gaze of his students that an explanation was needed.

"That was Stan Rodgers, a mission specialist at Johnson. In fact, Stan was one of the specialists on duty the morning of the disaster on . Dr. Gilroy has given me 24-hour access to his team, and this happens to be Stan's shift.

"Anyway, I can't believe that I didn't start bolometric analysis on this thing the moment it appeared in the sky. We should be measuring its luminosity constantly to see if we can determine what is emitting the light, how much energy it is giving off, and how quickly the energy is dissipating."

Turning his focus back to the yellow beam, he continued, "I just hope that the adage 'better late than never applies now' because that is a huge oversight."

"Professor." Joram asked. "Did I understand that you were going to get measurements at either end of the beam?"

"Precisely," Zimmer smiled at the observation. "As you no doubt had calculated, the orbit is 1.4 million miles away from here. At that, we can see about 7K AU away before we get to the visible horizon of its orbit. By taking a quick luminosity measurement at either end, we should be able to assess the direction of travel, since one end will be brighter than the other. The bright end is the one where the origin of the trail was more recently attended. That will help us determine the direction that this thing went as it flew by."

Kath wanted to ask Zimmer a question, but she was afraid that this might not be the time, as he returned to the computer monitor where he stared intently at the live images of the beam on the monitors. Focused on the image, Kath whispered to Joram, "What the heck is a bolometer?"

"It measures electromagnetic radiation intensity. If the radiation is in the visible light spectrum, it is used to calculate the luminosity. No doubt Professor Zimmer would like to have the data on this beam as it has come into existence. If it is the tail of some orbiting object, then we can be certain that it will disappear. The rate of dissipation could help us determine what..."

Joram stopped dead in his tracks as the professor spun around with wide eyes. His first thought went back to that first day in class when he was sure that Zimmer noticed him whispering to Kath. He now thought to himself that Zimmer must have a very keen sense of hearing. Joram began to offer a lame apology for distracting the professor's attention on his work.

"No, No, it's not that," Zimmer replied. "There's something I just noticed about the beam that is very perplexing."

The three students stood at attention waiting for this latest nugget of information from their mentor.

"Come look," he pointed to the screen. "You see the thickness of the beam here. Since it is dimming, it appears as if the light is not solid, and yet, I can see no light coming from behind it. And now look at the edges of the beam here. It appears that there is a dark band both above and below the beam. Even where this beam is not giving off light, it appears to be obscuring the light behind it. Reyd, can you bring up the star atlas on the other monitor. I'd like to see what we're missing in the sky if this beam is truly obscuring its background."

Within a minute, the left monitor had an image very close to the one on the right, except that there was no yellow beam. This image was a digitally-rendered simulation of the same section of the night sky for their present location, date, and time. "Ok, so what I'd like to do, Reyd, is to follow the beam to the star Deneb," Zimmer said.

"Alpha Cygni!" exclaimed Joram Anders. "Great choice, Professor. It should be right in the galactic plane such that it would be obscured by the beam."

Zimmer turned in his seat and peered intently at his first-year graduate student. "Actually, Mr. Anders, if my calculations are correct, Deneb will still be perfectly visible in our sky. It will clear the beam to the north of the galactic plane. However, Deneb—or as you point out, Alpha Cygni—is the brightest star in the constellation Cygnus, as well as one of the brightest stars in our sky, with an apparent magnitude of 1.25. While it is about 3500 light years away, its radius is more than 200 times that of our own Sun, making it about a quarter of a million times brighter."

Kath pursed her lips together and let out a soft whistle. "200 times the size of our own Sun?"

"Yes, Kath," confirmed Professor Zimmer. "As you may be aware from your primary school science instruction, there is an elementary analogy that demonstrates the difference between the size of the Earth and the size of the Sun."

"Oh, yes," Kath recalled excitedly. "If the Earth were the size of a garden pea, then the Sun would be the size of a basketball."

"Great memory, Miss Mirabelle. Now, if our Sun were the pea, then you would have to be a giant to play the basketball of Deneb, because it would be over five feet in diameter."

Kath reeled at this imagery. It was hard enough to imagine the size of the Earth, let alone the Sun. Now to find out how massive Alpha Cygni is in relation to our own Sun was simply hard to fathom.

"So, if I understand correctly, Professor," said Joram closing in on Kath. "If the Sun is the size of a pea—" he said bending over slightly and holding his finger and thumb about a pea's diameter apart in front of Kath's abdomen. "—Then Deneb would be a five-foot tall basketball," he said placing his other hand on top of Kath's head.

Reyd attempted to suppress his laughter, but instead let out a bursting snort that was clearly heard by all.

Kath turned the corners of her mouth down and narrowed her eyes in feigned irritation. "Very funny, Mr. Anders."

146

"Indeed," said Zimmer dryly in mock agreement with the prank. "Anyway, Deneb will be very easy to find, and it gets me in the ballpark of the object I really want to look for—NGC 7000."

"The North America Nebula?" asked Joram with some confidence in his question.

"That is correct, Mr. Anders."

"Why that feature, Professor?" asked Kath with curiosity.

"NGC 7000, Miss Mirabelle, is about the size of the Moon in our night sky. And it will be very easy to see with our 26 here. While looking for stars only gives us certain points in the vicinity of the beam, the nebula will give us a cloud of ionized gas that we can use to find the border of obscurity and perhaps measure the width of the beam. Turning to Reyd, Zimmer restated his direction. "To Deneb, Mr. Eastman."

"Yes, sir," nodded Reyd and gave a glance towards Joram just before returning to the console.

Zimmer returned to the telescope platform to dial in the adjusted coordinates of Deneb as Reyd reeled them off. Joram and Kath watched as Reyd and Zimmer worked towards the bright star.

"How does that look, Mr. Eastman?" Zimmer asked.

After a pause, Reyd turned towards Zimmer. "Professor… I don't see Deneb in this image."

"Perhaps I misheard your coordinates, Mr. Eastman. Can you please repeat them?"

"Right ascension: 20 hours, 41 minutes, 25.9 seconds."

"Got it."

"Declination: Plus 45 degrees, 16 minutes, and 49 seconds."

"Yeah that looks right," Zimmer said shaking his head in dismay.

After several attempts, the team had to admit defeat. Deneb was nowhere to be found in the sky above the beam. Reyd pulled up both the live image on the left monitor and the digitized image on the right.

"I don't understand," Zimmer said quietly. "You can see that the beam's obscurity borders are just below the indicated position for Deneb, and yet while other stars are visible, Deneb just isn't there."

"Deneb is a white supergiant, Professor." Anders suggested. "As such, it is in its last phases of life. You don't suppose…"

"Supernova, Mr. Anders?" Zimmer asked in amazement. "We would not have missed that event. And what are the odds of Deneb dying precisely with the beam?"

As silence ensued for a few moments, the team pondered this new mystery. Kath was the first to be heard. "Well, this may be a crazy idea…" Her voice trailed off, as the entire team wheeled around to see what Kath was thinking about.

"Go ahead, Miss Mirabelle."

"Well, what if the yellow beam *is* the death of Deneb."

"Not a bad piece of thinking," Zimmer admired while rubbing his chin. "However, such an idea would only hold under your previous emanation theory. That is, the light would be emanating at the speed of light right past us if Deneb had already exploded some 3500 years ago—the time it would've taken for the light to reach us—and as we know, this beam is just not radiating in that manner. But, do remember, Team that we must not dismiss any crazy notion. Please speak every thought that comes to your mind."

For some time, the team continued to stare at the two images. The next to break the silence was Joram. "Reyd, is there a way to overlay these two images?"

"Yes, I can make a transparent overlay of the digital image on top of the live image. However, you won't really see anything new, because all of the stars in the digital image will simply sit on top of stars in the live image."

"I'm not so sure that they will, Reyd."

"What are you suggesting, Mr. Anders?" asked the professor as he leaned farther over in his chair.

"I'm not sure, Professor, but it looks like light may be bending towards the beam. As such, the light from Deneb would be pulled southward enough to be in the region of obscurity."

"Well, ok… However, keep in mind that what you're suggesting is that the beam is carrying a vast amount of mass to produce the gravity necessary to bend light, right, Mr. Anders?"

"I know, Professor. It's a crazy idea."

"But… as I said, no crazy notion dismissed." Professor Zimmer conceded. "Go on, Mr. Eastman. Let us overlay the images. Heaven knows I have nothing better to suggest at this bizarre turn of events."

148

Eastman worked the keyboard quickly, dialing in the correct menu settings to overlay the two images. The resulting image was a noisy chart of pinpoint lights of varying brightness and size all over the monitor.

The entire team leaned forward staring at the image with captive attention. At length, Zimmer's eyes grew wide in recognition. "Reyd," he said softly and calmly, as if in shock. "Falsify the color, please."

"Professor?"

"The digitized image. Can you falsify the color of the stars? Perhaps turn them all fluorescent green."

"Oh, yeah, coming right up."

With a couple of mouse clicks, the live stars maintained their yellowish-white glow while other green dots appeared across the screen.

The rest of the team quickly understood what they were seeing. Far away from the beam, the green dots overlayed perfectly with the stars, but going closer into the center of the image, where the yellow beam sat, pulsating its mesmerizing light, the green dots remained farther and farther away from the beam, while the live starlight grew closer and closer. And at least one green dot, the digital location of the star Deneb, was alone in the night sky, with its live counterpart completely missing. The light was indeed bending towards the beam, and those stars which were closest to the beam found that their starlight was completely consumed behind the obscure background of the beam itself. Another momentous discovery had been made, but as have been the case with all discoveries thus far, more questions were created than there were answers afforded.

While Reyd and Kath congratulated Joram on this huge find, Zimmer remained at the monitor studying the image. He began pacing and mumbling incoherently. The noise level of the trio of graduate students diminished as they understood that Zimmer was still consumed in thought and concern. The tension of silence resumed and was broken by a tension even greater in the form of a phone call.

"Dr. Gilroy," breathed the crackling voice of Zimmer into his cell phone. "We have a huge problem... about the rescue mission... I'll need to come to Johnson immediately."

...

A voice droned and echoed throughout the domed room. "Apparent magnitude can be calculated as follows. The variable M-sub-x denotes apparent magnitude, where x denotes the specific band of electromagnetic radiation for which apparent magnitude we are measuring. Thus, M-sub-x equals negative two point five times log base ten of F-sub-x plus C. F-sub-x is the flux in the band x, and C is a constant calculated for the band of interest. As you already know from Maxwell's equations, the flux can be derived by calculating the surface integral of an electromagnetic vector field..."

Kath could barely keep her eyes open. As her head began to nod, she forced herself to attention once more.

"... equation by John Henry Poynting, where S, representing the energy flux in watts per square meter, equals one divided by mu-sub-zero times E cross B, where mu-sub-zero is the magenetic constant, defined as four times pi times ten to the minus seven power..."

It was no good—Kath could not stay focused. She looked to her left and noticed that she was not alone in her inability to follow the monotone nature of Dean Scoville, filling in for the absent Zimmer. She looked to her right and saw more of the same. Heads propped up by hands on desks, gravity-afflicted bodies slinking out of seats towards the ground, and—you gotta be kidding? One student taking fastidious notes, consumed with rapt attention. A smile formed on Kath's face. She couldn't resist the moment.

"P-S-S-S-S-T." The letters formed quickly on Joram Anders's Digital Note Tablet inline with the notes he was rapidly copying from the whiteboard which Scoville had filled for the third time during the lecture. "One divided by the quantity two times mu-sub-zero times P times S times S times S times S times T all multiplied by E-sub-zero squared."

Irritated, he looked up and glared at his fellow student. As Kath shrugged her soft shoulders in a most flirtatious manner, Joram felt a tingle in his stomach and knew that he couldn't be the least upset with his delightful research partner.

He shook his head, fixed the equation, and returned his attention to Scoville—sort of. He could still feel Kath staring at him, and glanced over as she gave him a wink. He gave a sigh, looked over and mouthed the words

"Stop it", concerned about how easily she was able to steal his attention away from weightier matters.

After class, Joram had to scold her. "Note passing, Kath? Isn't that a bit juvenile?"

"How could you focus on that lecture, Joram?" Kath attempted to change the subject.

"Kath, it's not the speaker that I care about—it's the subject."

"I know, I know," Kath surrendered. "I'm sorry, Joram. It's just that I've been having a hard time sleeping. These weekends at Palomar are really throwing my body into sleepless disarray. I'm not sure if I'm cut out for astronomy, Joram."

"Don't say that, Kath." Joram loathed the idea of losing Kath from the program. "Give it some time, you'll adjust. It's just been two weekends so far."

"And then, with Scoville... I swear if Zimmer doesn't get back soon, I'll become infamously known throughout the department as Kath Van Winkle."

"Speaking of Zimmer," Joram took advantage of the segue, "What do you think he's doing?"

"I suspect he's still at Johnson."

"Really? But he left on Sunday. Three full days?"

"Yeah, I suspect the longer he's gone, the worse news it is on the rescue mission, not being able to figure out how to counteract the effects of gravity on the beam so close to the spaceship." Kath's voice trailed off.

"What's wrong, Kath?"

"I just can't help wondering about the astronauts. How awful it will be if we have to leave them up there. I understand they can survive for several months. What a miserable demise it will be to be left waiting that long. Talk about a slow death." Kath stopped on the sidewalk and turned to Joram. "It could've been worse, you know."

Joram returned a curious stare. "What do you mean?"

"If you hadn't discovered the gravitational effects of the beam, we might have sent up a team of rescuers to an most unexpected and unfortunate doom. You have probably saved a handful of lives, Joram."

"Well, before you award me with that medal of honor, the act wasn't anything close to heroic, Kath. I just stumbled across something, that's all...

any of us could've done that. Besides, it was Zimmer's decision to go find Deneb. Any other star, and we probably would've just looked over the detail."

"Do you think a rescue mission is still possible?" Kath asked the question that had weighed on her mind all week long.

"I'm confident that Zimmer will come up with a way to save them—and study that beam too."

"But how, Joram? What would you do to save those astronauts in light of the gravitational risks of the beam?"

"I really don't know, Kath. I suspect that we might need to take advantage of the beam's gravity. Use it as a slingshot to hurl us away from Mars and then bring us back in a sort of orbit around the beam perhaps. It might take a lot longer to get there, depending on how strong the gravity of the beam is, but what's a few more weeks, or even a couple of months if need be to bring those astronauts back. Any politician who loves his career is going to do all that he can to bring those men back alive."

"I sure do hope you're right, Joram."

The pair resumed their course through campus at a leisurely rate, when Kath's cell phone rang in her backpack. Opening the phone up, she looked at the caller's phone number and gasped. "It's Zimmer!" she said quietly to Joram, as if the professor might overhear her.

Without saying a word, Joram gestured anxiously for her to answer.

"Hello, Professor... Really? Oh, that's great news... launch on Friday... oh, I'm so relieved. But what about the gravity? I'm sorry, say that again... But... I don't understand... Houston, you say? Weekend after next... Wow... yeah that will be great! Joram? Oh, he's probably too busy reviewing Dean Scoville's notes after the last lecture to turn his cell phone on..."

Joram's jaw dropped as he threw open his backpack and rummaged through its contents looking for his phone.

"Yeah... he says he's really enjoying the dean's lectures... he's absolutely smitten with the man's intelligence..."

Joram looked horrified. This little prank was just going too far, and he made gestures to get her to stop—frantically waving hands, jumping up and down, making slicing motions across his neck, reaching out as if to strangle her for this level of imprudence.

152

"Just kidding, Professor... he's right here with me. We just got out of 21, you know... yeah, I'll let him know... See you on Friday."

Kath roared with laughter. "You should've seen your face, Joram Anders."

Joram stood there motionless, not wanting to give away any emotion, but as he watched her jubilantly engaged, with her soft brunette hair bouncing around her face he felt his irritation, once again, melt into attraction.

Taking a deep breath, she composed herself once again. "Let's go to the Red Door Café, and I'll tell you all about the call."

Joram jumped at the offer, all too eager to hear progress of Zimmer's activities. Joram prodded her for information all the way, but Kath refused to divulge any details until she had a peach-flavored iced tea to drink.

"Well?" Joram asked as he and his raspberry lemonade took a seat next to Kath.

Kath held up a finger to hold off Joram just a moment longer. She took a swig of her tea along with a long drawn out breath.

"Are you quite sufficient to talk now, my lady," Joram said bowing to his regal companion.

In a burst, Kath let out all of the details of the conversation in the longest run-on sentence that Joram was ever aware of hearing. "Zimmer said there's no worry about gravity; after studying the gravitational effects of the beam on Mars, they realized that the light was not bending because of gravity, but for some other phenomenon, because the beam had not shown any effect whatsoever on Mars; of course, we're going to have to figure that one out now too, you know, but Zimmer said he'll brief us on that the next time we're at Palomar, which won't be for a week and a half, but let me get back to that little detail later; anyway, the mission will resume with just one day of delay, so the launch will be on Friday afternoon instead of Thursday morning; the professor needed extra time to add a few items for studying the light-bending phenomenon up close; the mission is going to launch the experimentation equipment prior to landing on Mars in 18 days, which means that the experiments will begin on our next research weekend, not this weekend but the next one, but of course, you already know that; what you don't know, however, is that we'll not be going to Palomar that weekend, we'll be going to Houston instead, in order to be in the rescue mission control room while the experiments are under way; Zimmer thought it would be best for us to be there collecting data in real time; by the way, Zimmer was steamed that you didn't answer your cell phone when he tried to call you first..."

"What?" Joram's jaw dropped. "But... but... but c'mon we just got out of class. I didn't have a chance to turn it..." Joram cut himself short recognizing the look in Kath's eyes. "Oh, I am so gullible. Would you just stop doing that to me? How many times will I fall for it?"

Kath chuckled. "Hook, line and sinker."

"Yeah, but just you wait, Kather Mirabelle. I'll start recognizing your bait before long, and then you'll have to pick up and move to a different pond, because this fish ain't gonna bite anymore."

Kath feigned an expression of seriousness. "Oh that will be a sad day, Joram Anders... a sad, sad day." Looking at her watch, she finished her tea hurriedly. "Would you look at the time? We should get going. I'm meeting a friend at the tennis club for a game this afternoon, and you need to start reviewing those notes from Scoville."

With a quick peck on the cheek, Kath immersed herself in the crowded walkways of the CalTech campus. Joram watched and admired her gait for as long as he could see her. After she disappeared, he allowed the moment with Kath and the news from Zimmer to settle in while enjoying the rest of his lemonade.

Chapter

15

After doing his best to encourage Paol as they left the courthouse, Warron and Monay walked quickly together towards the parking garage, each holding a black umbrella to protect them from the rain. The storm was starting to clear, but a dampening drizzle encouraged them to seek shelter as they walked.

The silence began to disturb Monay. She was not one for awkward fits of silence, even if it was her boss. "Warron," she engaged the sullen attorney, "do you still really believe that Paol is innocent?"

"Absolutely," he affirmed. "I can feel it. I have no doubt that he is innocent. We just need to find better answers to the questions of the case. I really wished the jury had been more convinced that these questions were pertinent and serious. If I can find an answer or two, I'll convince them in the appeal."

"The case seemed so open and shut to me," she confided. "If I was on that jury, I would've voted him guilty also."

"I know, I know, I would have too. That's why this is so difficult for me to swallow. I have a client who is a good, honest, and *innocent* man. I have failed to represent him adequately, and now he's been sentenced to serve a prison term he does not deserve." He stopped in his tracks and gazed intently at his paralegal. "But I will not fail him in the end, Monay. Mark my words. Paol Joonter will be acquitted."

She turned one corner of her mouth up in a half smile. "I'm sure you will find a way... that's why I work for you, you know."

Distracted, she turned back towards the window front of an electronics store that the pair had stopped in front of. Televisions of all sizes, synchronized to the same channel were just starting to broadcast the evening news. A pair of speakers above the window allowed passersby the opportunity to watch and hear the broadcast.

A male news anchor dressed in a dark suit coat, white shirt and red paisley tie announced, "Our top story of the night comes from Houston, Texas, where our reporters are picking up the latest details from the incident on Camp Mars. Rilynn Stewbridge comes to us live from the press room at the Johnson Space Center. Rilynn, can you fill us in on what we know so far."

The television screen split to show both the anchor and field correspondent side-by-side. A caption at the bottom announced, "Tragedy on Mars."

"Well, Milas," began the correspondent, strategically placed with an empty press podium and NASA logo in the background. "Dr. Vurim Gilroy just gave an announcement that NASA will attempt a mission to rescue the astronauts on Camp Mars. Communication has still not been made between Mars and Earth, and there is no word on the status of astronauts Garrison O'Ryan and Dmitri Boronov.

"He stated that a team of NASA specialists have been assembled, as well as renowned astrophysicist and CalTech professor, Carlton Zimmer, to assess the cause of the incident. We talked with Dr. Zimmer earlier today about the incident."

"A newsreel then showed the interview with Zimmer. Warron lowered his umbrella, since the rain had completely ceased now, and took a couple of steps closer to the largest TV.

Wow!" he exclaimed. "Would you look at that?"

Monay playfully hit her boss over the head with her umbrella. "What is it with you men that make you drool every time you see a large-screen TV?"

He turned abruptly. "No!" he said. "I'm not talking about the TV... I'm talking about how haggard Carl looks."

"Carl?" Monay asked as she turned back to the television. "Just because you're one of the top lawyers in the country doesn't give you a right to be on a first-syllable basis with every important scientist, you know."

He turned away from the store window and began walking away from Monay. "Not unless that important scientist just happens to be your brother."

Monay's jaw dropped. "Carlton Zimmer is your brother! I... I... I had no idea!"

She bounded several steps quickly in order to catch up to Warron Zimmer, the younger, and certainly less popular sibling of the Zimmer family.

"I mean, sure you have the same last name and all, and maybe Zimmer isn't all that popular, but I never would have made the connection."

"Well, we certainly took a different course in life," Warron said. "I was still in diapers when Carlton was already intently studying every move of NASA. Every young boy his age was captivated by the announced development on Mars. Carl just took it more to heart, I guess. He knew the first astronauts' names. He monitored construction of the camp intently. He became quite the areologist."

"Airy what?" asked Monay.

"Areology," began Warron, "refers to the study of Mars. Carl made sure I knew the correct word, when I kept referring to him as a Martian-ologist. The poor chap looked exhausted in that newsreel, I'll tell you that much. I don't think he should continue to work at the pace that he does... he's just starting to get too old for that to be any good on his health."

"Well," retorted the paralegal. "I'm not so sure he looked a whole lot different than you during your pre-trial efforts."

"That's different," the lawyer countered. "I'm younger than he is... by eight years." He cut a glance out of the corner of his eyes, spying on a reaction from his assistant. He was disappointed when all she did was roll her eyes.

"Anyway," Monay switched the conversation back to the current event. "I saw a headline this morning in the newspaper regarding the Mars incident."

"What did the paper have to say about it?" Warron asked.

"Nobody seemed to know what was going on, but it sounded like a couple of astronauts may were in serious danger."

"And that's how my brother comes in. NASA called on him to help them find a solution to saving the astronauts. Well, if anybody can do it, he's their man. The best problem solver I know. He'd have made a better lawyer than me."

"Well, he certainly makes a better Martian-ologist, or whatever you call it," Monay asserted. "Your brother is Carlton Zimmer, and I know more about what's going on at Mars than you do?"

"It's not like Carl works on the Mars thing anymore. He's chasing bigger challenges at this stage of his career."

"Oh, that's right. Didn't he attempt to study black holes?" asked Monay.

"That was his main project a couple of years back, and I don't think it ended on a positive note. It was a beginning of a rough relationship with NASA funding of his programs. It turns out that it's really hard to understand something you can't observe, and since black holes are known to be gravity sources so large that nothing—not even light—can escape, well, it's not like you're landing an astronaut on one of these things to take soil samples, are you? He mentioned that it was one of his toughest and most frustrating pieces of research. I know that he wasn't happy with the results. Either way, he's really been interested in just one objective practically since he was in grade school."

"What's that?"

"He's trying to find a parallel earth out there. You know, I really respect his dream, but it seems so unreasonable. I hope he's not chasing some dead end path. But... he is the expert, and I know he has his theories for good reason. I just don't understand it all when he explains it to me."

"Well, I wish him the best. He's made some fascinating discoveries along the way. It sounds like a parallel earth would be a crowning achievement for him"

"It really would be. I sure hope he can find it."

Chapter

16

Carlton Zimmers' research team stepped out of a white shuttle van in a large parking lot. Zimmer looked more tired than ever, while the students looked like energetic, bright-eyed children on a field trip. Nonchalantly, Zimmer thanked the driver of the van and walked towards the adjacent building—an inauspicious off-white structure of four stories in height with no windows and only the identifying number 30 placed high on its wall.

"Not much to look at, huh?" Reyd said, breaking the silence.

"No, you're not!" Kath shot back at her fellow student as she turned and slugged him on the shoulder for his irreverence at this space exploration monument.

"It doesn't have to be much to look at," Joram rebutted. "Just think of the history, Reyd,"

Zimmer settled the squabble once and for all. "Would you all prefer to stand out here and debate the architectural merits of Mission Control, or would you like to go inside and get a closer look at our beam."

Without a word, the three followed the professor inside the foyer of the building, where a tall middle-aged man was waiting with an outstretched hand.

"Dr. Zimmer."

"Stan... so kind of you to meet us here."

"It's no problem, Professor.

"Students, this is Staneck Rodgers—mission specialist for the Mars mission." Zimmer introduced each of his students to the NASA engineer.

"I'm glad you all could come see the mission. I, for one, have lost plenty of sleep—mostly over the astronauts, you'll understand—but also out of curiosity over this mysterious object. I really hope this mission will shed some light on its origin and makeup."

Walking towards a security desk at the foyer, Stan proceeded with business. "I'll need each of you to sign your name and provide our security guard, with a set of fingerprints."

Reyd went first, and Kath remained close by to follow after him. Joram lingered a little behind in order to bend his ear towards the conversation ensuing between Rodgers and Zimmer.

"No, professor," Joram overheard Staneck as he shook his head. "There have been no anomalies with the mission. Everything is going smoothly. We had a clean separation of the USL from the shuttle at 0913 hours this morning. In approximately 45 minutes, we should have paddle separation. Data collection should begin within a few minutes of trajectory correction for each of the twelve paddles." Stan looked at his watch. "Things should start getting busy, and hopefully interesting, in about an hour or so."

"And the astronauts, Stan?" inquired Zimmer with a concerned tone in his voice.

"No fresh evidence, Professor—" Stan answered as Zimmer lowered and shook his head. "—but remember, they are simply following strict protocol to preserve the environment in the bunker. Once they are awaiting rescue, they must remain locked inside, otherwise they compromise too much oxygen."

"Come on, Stan," Zimmer protested. "Protocol or not, what would you do? Tell me that you wouldn't come out during Earth-sight with a field scope and look for a high-luminosity morse signal. You would have to have nerves of steel to wait inside your Martian gravesite, not knowing if or when you were going to be rescued."

"Astronauts are trained to follow every instruction, Professor."

"Then why are we sending the signal, Stan? We have stations on three separate oceanic islands, constantly transmitting a night-time light source in morse code, so that the astronauts know about the mission and its timeframe. If we thought they wouldn't emerge, we wouldn't send the signal."

"The astronauts are never notified of the emergency communication signal. They have no idea that such a procedure exists, simply because we don't want to tempt them to surface too often and squander their environment. The signal is only intended for them to see under dire circumstances."

Zimmer laughed in ridicule. "So we tell our men to wait it out, but we send a signal that they're never supposed to see anyway. I just don't understand these emergency procedures very well."

"I'm sorry, Professor. Even I didn't know about the emergency light signals. Until this had occurred, they were highly classified. Remote islands with no human contact were selected in the South Pacific, North Atlantic, and Indian Oceans. High-intensity solar-powered light sources with remote satellite communication capabilities were set up and known only by a few top NASA personnel until they were turned on. Even though these islands are ridiculously remote in most cases, any airplane within a few thousand miles could see the light shining way up into the atmosphere at nighttime. NASA had to declassify them with a formal press release the moment they turned them on."

"Did Gilroy know?"

"Yes, Professor."

Zimmer shook his head in disgust.

"Well I am glad that they declassified it, so that every future astronaut in the inner solar system will know that he can still receive communications from Earth. I just think it is atrocious to make those two men suffer the constant emotional stress of imagining death by slow suffocation in a lonely Martian chamber. To build into emergency procedures the knowledge that Martian astronauts in distress are to be left in the dark—perhaps both figuratively and literally—I don't think the public is going to be too happy with NASA once they realize—"

"All done, Professor," Zimmer was too busy opining on the state of the astronauts that he entirely missed Kather's appearance, nor did Kath realize until it was too late that she had interrupted a conversation in a rather tense moment.

"I'm sorry—we'll just—just wait over here." Kath stammered.

"No, no, Miss Mirabelle. Your timing is appropriate. Mr. Rodgers and I were just finishing our conversation, and I know he has some pressing matters to look after."

"My apologies, Professor. There really is nothing more we can do except get that shuttle down to Camp Mars as quickly as possible and return those astronauts to Earth. This is our top priority, I assure you."

"I am glad to hear it." Then changing the subject, Zimmer proceeded, "Why don't you show us to the control room, and we'll let you get back to getting those astronauts back!" He smiled and gestured that there were no ill-feelings. Deep down, he did know that NASA was doing everything they could to return the astronauts to safety.

Stan gestured to the group to follow him down a long sterile hall awash with bright LED lighting from two contiguous rows of lights along the ceiling and another along each of the walls. At the end of the hall, he turned to his right, and all followed him except for Joram Anders.

"Excuse me," he called out.

The entire party halted and turned to Joram.

"Shouldn't we be going that way?" indicating the opposite direction in which Rodgers was leading them.

Kath looked intently down Joram's hall way, and then back to Stan's chosen hall. "Joram Anders, why on Earth would you suggest that? These halls look identical."

"It's just that the Mars mission control room is down that way," Joram stated matter-of-factly.

"What?" Reyd said rolling his eyes. In exasperation, he probed, "How would you possibly know that?"

"I've been on the observation deck of the control room for the Mars mission." Noticing that all were still perplexed, he sighed and continued. "In high school, my family came to Houston to visit relatives. They indulged me in a trip to the space center here, where a tour took us onto the observation deck of the Mars mission control. Perhaps the control room has moved since then?"

"No, Joram," said Stan with a smile. "The control room is still down there. By the way, I'm impressed that you remembered that little detail all of these years. There are no windows in here to retain any sense of direction."

162

"Yeah… it's odd that I remember. I guess I was just so enthralled by the visit that I still remember it like yesterday."

"Wow," Stan exclaimed with genuine amazement. "Anyway that control room is devoted to the current activities of the rescue mission. You will not be going down there right now. Instead, I'll be taking you to a different control room, which is monitoring the remote controlling and data collection of the unmanned mission to examine the beam."

"Once the Unmanned Space Lab—or USL—left the rescue vehicle, a set of engineers has been assigned to handling the activities of that mission down here. Follow me, I won't lead you astray."

With a smile, Stan turned and did not lead them astray, as promised. He opened a door to a control room, somewhat smaller than the Mars control room that Joram had visited during his adolescence. There were just two small rows of consoles on the main floor, and a smaller arena encased with glass for civilian observation of the control operations.

Joram was surprised to notice that the room was fairly full of individuals with visitor's badges and laptop computers. As if noticing the question on Joram's face, Stan spoke up.

"As you can see there are already a fair number of individuals representing the press here," Stan pointed out. "We do have four reserved front row seats for your party, Dr. Zimmer."

"Thank you so much for your generous hospitality, Stan."

"Press?" asked Kath. "I'm actually surprised they are all here instead of monitoring the rescue mission down Joram's preferred hall." She cut Joram a playful glance, who returned with a feigned smile.

"Actually, the press will be thronging the control room down there tomorrow when the rescue shuttle makes its descent and landing outside of the Camp Mars crater."

"Outside the crater?" asked Joram. "Why not land in the crater."

"Well, the runway is useless, as it is littered with shards of solar panel debris. The shuttle will have to make a somewhat risky vertical landing outside the entrance to the crater and then make their way to the bunker in the middle of the crater. With the landing in the morning, they should be able to recover the astronauts sometime by tomorrow afternoon, assuming they can find a relatively unimpeded entrance to the bunker."

"That should be easy, shouldn't it?" asked Kath. "We know that the astronauts had already surfaced after the disaster."

"You are right, Kath," answered Zimmer quickly, "but you'll also recall that we didn't get to see the state of the camp for a couple of weeks. It could be that the devastation was not a single event, and that obstructions have since blockaded all entrances. For example, we have not seen the astronauts wander out since the dust has settled. As you know, there has been about as much tabloid-generating drama by the media on both the astronauts and on the beam. These individuals want to be the first to write up the scoop on the beam. I hope they don't engender a sense of panic in their reporting of our experiments. We certainly don't need or want mass-scale fear or panic. Riots, looting, chaos."

"Do you think it can get that bad, Professor?" Kath asked quietly.

"Not if I have anything to say about it. I have been trying to allay much of the public concern, and will continue to do so. Let us not worry about that now, and take our seats. The show is about to begin, Team."

With that ending, Stan excused himself in order to continue with flight operations for the rescue mission. Zimmer and students entered into the observation room and took their seats with great anticipation for what would soon unfold.

...

Conversation was light among the trio of research students. The anxiety was apparent. Kath twirled her hair with her left hand. Reyd nibbled on his fingernails and cuticles. Joram, already at the edge of his seat, gazed at the various monitor displays. A main central display showed a live image of the beam, representing the closest imagery ever obtained. On the right, there were six smaller displays that were presently black except for a caption at the bottom of each. "Paddle one." "Paddle Two." And so forth. On the left, a sea of data indicated the status of the mission. Finally, just below the central monitor, a thinner display contained a digital map indicating the locality of the USL with respect to the beam. The USL was represented as a needle-like projection with twelve red dots on top of it.

Joram noted that the map indicated that the USL was beginning to decelerate as it neared the beam, with reverse thrusters fully engaged. Soon, the USL would stop and launch its twelve research stations, called paddles, towards the beam.

"This is the Public Affairs Officer of Mission Flashlight," the students heard a voice from speakers overhead.

Joram scanned the various stations of mission control to find the source of the voice. Silver placards were placed along a counter-top that ran the length of both rows. In all capital letters, the placards spelled words and acronyms such as CONTROL, NETWORK, FIDO, GUIDO. Ah, there it was… PAO. In the middle of the second row of stations, Joram saw the bald spot on the back of the head of a silver-haired engineer who sat at the public affairs station. This is the man who would exclusively communicate all mission activities to the press booth and anyone listening to the appropriate communication channel around the country. He was currently engaged in conversation with a middle-aged woman with short blonde hair sitting in the front row, at a station labeled FLIGHT. She nodded her head to the PAO, and then spoke into a headset as she returned her gaze forward, looking at the data scrolling by.

"The FLIGHT officer has noted an ETA of just under 4 minutes, 30 seconds. PAYLOAD is powering up and confirming the status of each paddle. Power-on-self-test should complete in approximately 6 minutes. So far, all systems are a 'go' on payload delivery."

"Well, team," Zimmer whispered as he glanced over at his wide-eyed astronomy students. "This is where I get off."

Eyes growing wider, the Professor explained. "I'll be spending the rest of the mission down there." Zimmer indicated an empty chair at the FLIGHT station, next to the blonde, who was now standing and relaying instructions to somebody seated at the NETWORK station at the other end of her row. "NASA has asked me to provide real-time decisions in light of data received from the paddles." He paused briefly and took a deep breath in realization. "The next time I see you, we'll have lots to talk about. Take good notes on every idea that comes to you, and enjoy the show."

At that, all three students watched the professor open the door and leave them for the more spacious and hectic atmosphere of mission control. Seating himself quietly, he greeted the engineers around him, promptly put on a headset, and sat back in his chair, while others around him maintained their efforts.

The PAO announced the next milestone in the mission. "FLIGHT informs me that the lab has obtained resting velocity and has turned over main mission operation to PAYLOAD. Payload chamber doors are sequencing. NETWORK is providing real-time imagery of the hatch for mechanical observation."

The main monitor no longer showed the growing brightness of the yellow beam, but instead changed its view to a camera looking straight down on top of the USL. A long rectangular chamber was coming to view as curved doors slid underneath the cylindrical body of the vehicle. Within moments, the doors were fully open, and the inside of the chamber depicted its payload of a dozen three-foot round iridescent objects each sitting at a 45-degree angle with the doors of the chamber.

These paddles were loaded with observational and telecommunication equipment. Cameras, sensors, and on-board laboratory equipment would be able to instantly detect, measure and determine the impact of material and radiation. Tens of thousands of sensors made up the array of each paddle, which would be able to communicate the pattern of any material being emitted by the beam.

"Launching paddle number one."

The forward-most paddle began to lift seamlessly from the chamber. Once the round disk had emerged, a long shaft used for steering and guiding the paddle indicated exactly why the term 'paddle' had been used for the objects. It resembled a holographic video disk on a silver Popsicle stick. The paddle cleared the payload bay, rotated, and straightened, yielding a burst of color reflected from the Sun.

"Paddle one is heading for rendezvous on the far side of the beam as paddle two begins launch."

One at a time, the first six paddles were each successively launched in this manner, and the trajectories, marked by six red dots on the map display, began their journey towards the beam. Monitors for paddles one through six also began to convey statistics and images from each of the paddles. They approached the beam in a precalculated manner, such that all six pointed directly towards the beam in sixty degree intervals, thus allowing a full study of the beam on all of its sides.

Complete silence from inside the observation deck as well as from the PAO indicated growing tension and curiosity. Activity from the control floor bustled as a flurry of directions were passed back and forth from CONTROL, NETWORK, and PAYLOAD. Zimmer—still reclined in his seat—appeared to be the only relaxed individual in the front row, but Joram could see enough of his face to note that he was devotedly attentive to the data as it came across the various monitors and displays.

The paddles all appeared to be in position, and after a nearly unbearable silence, the team began to wonder why the mission seemed to be on pause. The PAO appeased their doubts, "Paddles are now in position for deployment into the beam, but FLIGHT has recommended a delay for delivery of sensory data. Deployment into beam is estimated at fourteen minutes."

While the students felt that they couldn't bare another moment of anticipation, the more-experienced Zimmer knew that patience and data collection was needed at the moment. It would be inexcusable to compromise the mission after millions of dollars had been spent on it should a hasty judgment jeopardize the entire effort. Further, Zimmer knew that the world had already waited for weeks to obtain answers. Another fourteen minutes would not break the bank.

In silence, the students waited anxiously. Kath had to place a steadying hand on Joram's knee to remind him to relax once and then twice. On the third attempt, Joram turned and whispered, "Sorry, Kath, but the suspense is killing me. What are they waiting for?"

Kath only shrugged, but Reyd, seated on the other side of her leaned across her and breathed an explanation. "Zimmer is a very deliberate person. He never makes hasty decisions, but weighs all of the data first. You won't have to work with him too long to realize this."

"The NETWORK officer advises the team that the paddles are all in good health, and that no extraordinary sensory information has been obtained by any of them. FLIGHT advises that the mission proceed ahead. The mission has calculated that the paddles are presently located 25 kilometers or 15 miles away from visible extent of the beam, and that the minimum diameter of the beam is calculated at about 12000 kilometers or a little less than 7,500 miles. CONTROL is advised to begin coordinated acceleration of the paddles up to 1 kilometer per minute, which is a little over 35 miles per hour."

The map began to indicate the movement of the six paddles towards each other as they closed in on the beam. Joram fixed his focus on the six displays of the paddle's cameras, which were pointed directly toward the beam. Each image simply contained a bright yellow light with very little form or shape to it. There was a flickering of intensity and it appeared that the light leapt all around, as though a million fireflies were densely packed together in a glass jar placed in the blackness of outer space.

Superimposed on the bottom right of each image were two vertical bars with gradient shading from blue at the top to red at the bottom. One labeled 'light intensity' had about a third of the meter filled with red. The other bar was labeled 'particle density'. It had just a hint of red for each of the paddles. On the bottom left, he saw a pair of numbers indicate the speed of the paddle and its distance to the center of the beam. He watched as the paddles accelerated from 20 to 30 to 40 and eventually to 58 km/h. He also saw the distance decrease from 12,050 km... 12,010 km... 11,080 km.

As the distance decreased, he noticed that the light intensity was increasing uniformly for each paddle. He leaned forward and furiously scribbled notes on his Digital Note Tablet, stopping mid-sentence as a cold shiver passed through his spine. His head whipped up to look at Zimmer, only to find an empty chair. Furiously, his eyes raced through the control room to find his mentor, and spotted him standing on the right hand side of the front row, scanning the paddle imagery and data. His head slowly turned back to the observation room, where he could just make out the wide-eyed stare of Joram Anders. Zimmer gave a single and nearly imperceptible nod of recognition. Teacher and pupil were in sync with the same discovery.

Kath noticed the exchange. "What's wrong?" she implored.

Joram looked behind him to notice the throng of media and realized the need for discretion. He raised a finger to indicate that he needed a moment and returned to his tablet in order to finish his observation and conclusion. With an exclamation mark, he handed his notes over for Kath and Reyd to read.

"1912 hours. Paddles reach visible extent of beam at a distance of 12000 km from center of beam. Light intensity is uniform at all six positions around the beam, and yet paddle 2 is on the sunny side of beam, while paddle 5 is on opposite side of beam from sun. Conclusion: beam does not reflect sunlight… it generates light from within!"

After reading Joram's notes and understanding the magnitude of this discovery, Kath and Reyd looked back up to the displays and noticed that indeed, all of the live camera images from each of the six paddles had the same intensity of yellow flickering light. The predominant theory was that the beam was just the tail of a comet reflecting a large density of ice or rock chunks, but discovering the brightness of the beam on its side opposite of the Sun proved that this clearly could not be the case.

The thoughts of the students were broken by an announcement from the public affairs officer. "Paddles are communicating a slight radiation increase as they begin to enter the visible extent of the beam. Some sensors are detecting impacts of small quantities of highly-quantized positively-charged particles. Mission specialists indicate that extremely small masses indicate a very fine dust of atomic-sized materials."

Joram watched the paddles and noticed that the 'particle density' bars were showing more red now, and that the red was slowly beginning to fill the bars of each paddle, at which he noticed the image of one of the paddles—paddle three, to be precise—went black.

"NETWORK indicates a sudden communication failure with paddle three. They are seeking to reengage the paddle via commands to the Unmanned Space Lab."

After a lengthy pause, the commentary continued, "NETWORK is currently studying whether a radiation spike inside of the beam may have caused the failure, but… we have… yes… NETWORK confirms outage in paddles one and four. A significant and unanticipated communication breach has occurred now with three… four paddles, as paddle two has also lost comm with the USL. Paddles five and six are now spiking heavily with impact sensory data, as they receive as much as 12000 fine-particle impacts per second. CONTROL is beginning to rotate direction of paddles five and six to reduce the amount of direct impact density in case significant and irreparable damage has been incurred…"

The voice trailed off shortly after the remaining two images went black. Joram noticed that all six red dots that had submerged into the beam had disappeared completely from the map. By all indicators, the beam had simply eaten up all six paddles.

Reyd placed his head in his hands, while Kath's trembling right hand was covering her mouth firmly. Joram looked to the control room floor, where Zimmer was observed relaying orders into his headset while fixing his stare on the monitor at his station. He stood up, dropped his headset down onto the station, and paced to the back of the control room, where he attempted to gain a better big picture of what little data remained on the wall in front of him.

"Mission control confirms the loss of communication with all six paddles. NETWORK is attempting to reestablish comm, but the team assumes a total loss of paddles to an unknown failure."

...

"Communication scrambling, perhaps?"

"Please elaborate, Mr. Eastman."

"Well, Professor, I was just thinking that perhaps once the paddles penetrated the outer sheath of the beam that the radiation emission of the beam superimposed on the communication signal would cause the signal to scramble sufficiently to lose complete comm."

"Hmmm... I'm not sure, Mr. Eastman. Recall that we sent paddles four and five to the opposite side of the beam from where the USL was, and the communication signal apparently was able to arrive unimpeded even though those signals had to go directly through the beam."

"I suspect radiation damage," Kath announced. "The paddle detected radiation, but could not identify it—similar to what happened here on Earth at Time Zero, right?"

"Could be, Miss Mirabelle. While the paddles are radiation-hardened, we are unable to test its ability to reject radiation that we have not identified."

Turning to Joram, Zimmer continued. "Mr. Anders, you've been quiet. What do you think?"

"Well, I don't know, honestly, but since we're brainstorming, I'll throw another idea out there. What about particle impact damage? I noticed that the impact density was pegged at about 68000 per second. I calculated that to be about 60 impacts per square inch per second."

"But none of the paddles ever indicated anything larger than an atom."

"You see, that's where I'm confused. How can none of this matter coalesce into larger bodies? What could possibly pulverize and energize this matter so greatly?"

"I don't know, but this is all good data, Joram," reminded Zimmer. "The media right now is having a field day over this. They're transmitting articles to their editors on the failed mission, but they are wrong. We have some very great data that has yielded some new understanding that we didn't have before. The beam is actually emitting its own light, and not reflecting sunlight as previously believed. We know that the beam physically consists of highly-quantized atomic particles. And... we still have six paddles to go."

"How is that going to help us, Professor?" Kath asked sincerely. "The first six were gobbled up by the beam. Won't the next six meet a similar fate?"

"Perhaps, but we now know how to maximize our odds for utilizing the last six better. In case we did experience radiation or particle damage, we will inject the paddles in parallel to the direction of the beam, instead of letting them approach in a perpendicular fashion."

"How will that help?" Kath inquired.

"It's like when you were a kid and stuck your hand out of the car as it was moving. When you placed it perpendicular to the flow of the air, it met great resistance, right? But when you turned your hand 90 degrees the force of the wind subsided. We're going to hope that we can avoid the 'wind' of the beam by injecting the next three paddles in a parallel fashion."

"Three paddles?" asked Joram.

"We started with twelve, and now we're down to just six. I don't want to spend them all on one remaining experiment. Instead of spreading six paddles out in 60 degree increments, we'll place three of them in 120 degree slots instead, and then if we need to we'll have a third shot at data collection with the final three paddles.

"Also, we're going to take it much slower now as we penetrate the visible extent. We were going faster than we knew we should when we hit the border at 60 kilometers per hour. So… by changing direction and slowing the speed, we'll keep our fingers crossed for some better results."

Zimmer scanned the faces of his three graduate students, probing for visual clues as to their thoughts. "Anything else you'd like to discuss before we go back to the control room, Team?"

Kath shook her head and Joram shrugged, but Reyd did have one more question to ask. "Professor, so far you've been listening to a lot of our hair-brained ideas, but you haven't shared your thoughts on this. What do you think we're dealing with?"

Zimmer gave a deep sigh and measured how he would answer the question. His answer was uninspiring. "I think we're looking at the tail of a comet."

"But the tail is potentially light years in length, and it gives off light even weeks after the comet passed by," Reyd rebutted.

"Mr. Eastman, you asked me what I thought. I gave you an answer. I honestly believe that we are looking at the tail of a comet, but an *exotic* one to be sure."

"Exotic?" asked Joram, seeking further clarification.

"If I could describe it with greater clarity, Mr. Anders, I would do so. We don't have all of the answers yet. We need the paddles to stay in the beam long enough to transmit back to us the material makeup of the beam. Then, we might be able to formulate sowme decent theories."

"Professor, do you believe the comet is responsible for the destruction on Mars?" asked Kath. "The beam occurred a few days after the damage. Did we really miss seeing it for that long?"

"It could be that the tail was there all along, but that for some reason, the matter didn't start illuminating until it reached a particular state. We know that the light is starting to fade out… it may have also faded in. I know that doesn't adequately answer your question, but again, the only word I have to describe it now is exotic. Any other questions?"

The three looked at each other and at Professor Zimmer, but they knew that for all of the questions that could be asked, the answers just weren't there yet. Well understood—and yet unspoken—was one simple fact: if paddles number seven through twelve did not perform adequately, those questions may never be answered.

As the quartet were left to their thoughts and concerns, the door to the conference room opened up. Dr. Gilroy stepped through with Stan Rodgers.

Gilroy bounded towards Zimmer with an outstretched hand. "Dr. Zimmer, it's great to see you again."

"Thank you for opening up your marvelous facility to my research team, Dr. Gilroy."

Gilroy nodded in recognition of the trio of students who stood at attention across the table. "I'm sorry that the mission didn't go better, Carlton."

"Actually, I think it went very well, Vurim."

"But you lost the paddles."

"We lost half of the paddles, and we gained a few more pieces of the puzzle, and we have confidence that we'll get even more by a better-informed application of the next paddles."

"So you have a plan of attack for continuing the mission?"

"Indeed."

"When would you like to start back up, Professor?"

"As soon as possible."

Gilroy turned to his mission specialist. "Stan, can you please round up the Flashlight team? It looks like we're back in business."

"Shall we inform the press as well, Doctor?"

Zimmer burst in. "No! I'd prefer that the press were not involved in the next phase of the mission. Besides, they got their story, and there is no need to waste their time should that story not be enhanced. If there is much to write home about after the show is over, we can hold a press conference."

Gilroy weighed this request for several moments. All eyes rested on him. "Stan, gather the team into the control room... but do not make an announcement to the press."

"Thank you, Vurim," Zimmer spoke with relieved and gracious tones.

"You realize, Carlton that this is highly unorthodox. We rely on a fairly complicated relationship with the press and their interaction in Washington."

"They'll forgive us if we have anything juicy to share with them, and if not, they won't care anyway."

Gilroy turned towards the exit as the door slowly swung shut behind Stan. "Good luck, Carlton. We really need to solve this mystery for the sake of the entire space program."

"We'll do our best, Vurim."

...

Three red dots came to rest at the end of curved lines indicating their trajectories on the map. They flanked the yellow line, indicating their position to descend into the territory from which six prior dots never emerged.

The setting felt very familiar to Joram, as he sat in the same seat of the observation room monitoring the yellow images being transmitted back from the paddles. But there were a few differences. Now there were only three images now instead of six, the observation room was vacated of the presence of the media, and several new control team members occupied seats on the control room floor—the others having been dismissed sometime before 11:50 PM, when the CalTech team reentered the control room.

In the pre-mission activity, Joram kept a close eye on Zimmer, who was wandering from station to station, communicating with the NETWORK, GUIDANCE, and FLIGHT team members. Joram also noticed the absence of the PAO, who was dismissed since the media was not invited to this second round of mission activity. The grad students all knew that this meant there would be no play-by-play commentary in the observation room. Instead, they would have to take fastidious notes on visual clues only and draw their own conclusions as to how the mission was proceeding.

"GUIDO, please continue with synchronization of acceleration at 00:15 hours local time," Professor Zimmer spoke into his headset after sitting in his chair at the FLIGHT station. A digitally projected clock in the upper left-hand corner of the mission display wall currently showed the time as 12:12 AM central time. A similar display nearby read 1 day, 14 hours, 59 minutes, and 7 seconds indicating the start of the Flashlight Mission as indicated by the separation of the Unmanned Space Lab from the rescue vehicle the day before.

GUIDO, the commonly applied name for the guidance officer responded to the command. "Roger that FLIGHT command. GUIDANCE is confirming a unified start-up pattern at 00:15 hours with paddles seven, eight, and nine ramping up to 30 km/h for 12 minutes, at which time all three units will uniformly decelerate to 18 km/h as they penetrate beam boundary. Paddles are already rotated for parallel immersion into beam in order to minimize impact of particles as previously discussed."

Satisfied with the response from GUIDANCE, Zimmer checked in on the other teams as well. "NETWORK, please commence impact and radiation detection and assessment in T minus 5 minutes,"

"Roger that, Professor!"

"Now we cross our fingers and wait," Zimmer breathed to his companion at the FLIGHT station after switching off his headset. The quiet of the room induced a tension that the graduate students were already growing accustomed to. Kath twirled her long hair. Reyd took deep breaths and tried to relax with his hands locked behind his head. Joram's hand was trembling as it waved over his note tablet.

After fifteen minutes of anticipation, the red dots were slowing down, when particle impact began. The paddles penetrated into the beam and data rushed across the monitors. Deeper into the beam they went. Zimmer heaved a sigh as the paddles were observed communicating even as they passed the point of no return for the first six paddles. Joram, Kath, and Reyd gave each other knowing glances and slight nods of the heads to indicate that Zimmer was dead-on in his suggestions to rotate the paddles away from the beam's direction of travel and to penetrate more slowly than before.

"CONTROL observing rotational acceleration in paddle number nine, currently at 0.65 degrees out of intended plane of descent. Paddles seven and eight holding at zero degrees. Attempting counter-active maneuvers to restore paddle nine to a zero degree rotation."

Zimmer responded quickly, "CONTROL, we're gonna have a very difficult time maintaining location of these paddles if we have to control them with a twenty-minute lag of communication. Please program all three paddles for coordinated automatic calibration."

After a brief pause, "Um... FLIGHT, we don't see automatic calibration as a feature on the paddles."

Zimmer flipped rapidly through a binder on his desk as he responded, "It's in the requirements document, CONTROL... section 4.23.3."

It was CONTROL's turn to flip through a binder at their station. "FLIGHT, we are cross-referencing section 4.23.3. Please confirm."

"4.23.3 confirmed."

"FLIGHT, requirement 4.23.3 was opted out of the retrofit of the paddles according to our docs."

"What?" Zimmer stood up and glared at the CONTROL station behind him. "Are you sure that 4.23.3 was not implemented?"

"Yes, sir. It says here in section 4.23.3, 'Requirement denied. Budget overrun.' Command has been sent to back-thrust on roll which is now at 0.83 degrees. CONTROL is also noticing additional yaw of the paddle in the down-stream direction of the beam. Command has been sent to correct for yaw once roll is... Um... acceleration of paddle nine down-stream is greater than anticipated... rotational acceleration increasing roll to 1.77 degrees... make that 2.16..."

Zimmer put his head in his hand as he saw the writing on the wall. At the speed of light, control signals from Houston, Texas would take ten minutes to reach the paddle. By that time, the paddle would be erratically out of control, and its yaw, roll—and perhaps pitch—would be grossly out of the reach of the CONTROL officer to correct. Paddle nine had effectively completed its service already.

"CONTROL reports a rapidly degrading roll and acceleration on the yaw... paddle nine now traveling at 85 km/h down-range... 113 km/h. FLIGHT, CONTROL requests to abort paddle nine from the flow of the beam in order to regain control. Particle impact at 27.5 degree roll is now accelerating the paddle rapidly down-range."

Zimmer spoke calmly, "How do you propose to gain control before the paddle is out of range of comm with the USL, CONTROL? You would first have to successfully control the yaw in order to point the paddle away from the beam and then accelerate away from its center."

Without responding to the original question, the voice from the other headset continued, "Down-range acceleration at... at... four... no... six..." The voice trailed off as the image and associated data for paddle nine went black.

"Did you see that red dot?" exclaimed Kath inside the observation room. "It seems like all of the paddles so far are making a rapid 90 degree turn downstream just before they disappear. What could be going on?"

Reyd was the first to offer a response. "It looks like they lost control of it and it went haywire."

"Why are they losing control to begin with? The math indicates that the particle impact is just not sufficient to knock these things off course" Kath said incredulously.

"I don't know," offered Reyd weakly, "What do you think, Joram? Joram?"

Reyd and Kath turned to notice that Joram was so absorbed in thought that he didn't even hear his name being called. Kath walked over to where he was standing against the Plexiglas wall of the observation room. Placing a hand on his shoulder, she whispered, "Joram?"

Joram turned with a confused expression on his face.

"What are you thinking about?" Kath asked now that she had his attention.

"Well, I don't know what to make of it. It took no longer than a minute for the paddle to completely disappear. It must have a very weak signal strength to lose contact with the USL that quickly. They probably need all of the power for propulsion and stabilization, huh?"

"But, did you see how the red always does a rapid 90 degree turn just before going blank?" Reyd asked.

"Yeah, I did see the red dot, but we'll have to review the data to see its actual acceleration."

All three graduate students turned back to the display. A couple of mission specialists, including Zimmer, were now standing, but a flurry of activity began when the students noticed a brief image on the paddle nine display.

"Wait!" said Reyd, maybe it still has a heartbeat after all. But, as quickly as it appeared, it disappeared.

"NETWORK?" called out Zimmer firmly.

"Yes, Professor?"

"Please get me the data which we just received from paddle nine. I want its exact location and speed. Everything, NETWORK… just get me all of the data, please."

"We'll do, FLIGHT. Give us just a couple of minutes to translate the raw data."

Zimmer realized that in the fight to regain number nine that paddles seven and eight had been mostly ignored. "CONTROL, it looks like there is movement on seven and eight. Please confirm."

"FLIGHT, we are seeing very slight down-flow acceleration, but we are noticing significant deviation in cross-sectional location."

"NETWORK, any abnormal data collection from seven and eight?"

"Plenty of minute particle impact mostly occurring on the under-side of both paddles."

Zimmer gave a brief exclamation, "CONTROL, try not to lose these… keep them under control!" Then he threw his headset to the desk and raced towards the back of the room.

Bursting into the observation room, the wide-eyed students stood riveted. "Do you see it?" Zimmer announced almost breathless. "Look at the trajectory of the remaining two dots!"

The students did indeed see 'it'.

"Why they're moving inside the beam… in a corkscrew fashion!" Kath announced.

Zimmer blurted out "That is the flow of our beam. The particles are swirling around in the beam as they travel down-stream."

"What could cause that, Professor?" asked Joram.

"I think we are indeed seeing the tail of a fast spinning comet that is spewing off some highly radioactive material. I must get back, but please continue to observe closely, and discuss among yourselves what you make of all of this. We will continue to monitor the trajectory of paddles seven and eight and collect as much impact and radiation data as possible. We're going to solve this puzzle, Team!"

In a flash, the aging—yet nimble—astronomer, raced back to his position, and placed the headset back on.

The control officer was already speaking, "should be able to control the rate of acceleration, since the direction of seven and eight is much more stable. Signal sent to counter-balance the rapidly increasing rates of cross-sectional rotation."

Zimmer shook his head as he spoke in dismay, "Are we losing these as well, CONTROL?"

"We are doing our best, Professor, but the comm signal will still require several minutes to arrive."

Zimmer leaned far back in his seat, closed his eyes, and listened as CONTROL managed to let two more paddles slip away all too quickly. He knew, however that he couldn't blame his teammates on the control floor. The lack of automatic control calibration that he placed as a requirement on the paddles was denied by some bean counter in Washington D.C., who knew everything there was to know about budgets, and absolutely nothing about what was needed to make a mission succeed. Here, millions had been spent on preparing the mission, and at least one required retrofit on the experiment paddles was expended. Zimmer was confident that with this feature, the paddles would still be collecting data and providing valuable information that would be needed to solve the mystery.

...

The clock on the small conference room wall read 01:25. The smell of steaming coffee permeated throughout as well, as all four individuals sat around a rectangular table, sipping the elixir that they needed to keep them going for the third—and final—round of the mission.

Professor Zimmer heaved a weary sigh and rubbed his blurry eyes. "Ok, so we still have three paddles, Team. As you have no doubt noticed, we have had great difficulty in controlling the first nine as they entered the beam. Because of an oversight in paddle construction, I have no hope that we will keep the final three paddles for any significant amount of time either. How do we best utilize them to understand the beam? I need every thought and idea that you can come up with to help us maximize our learning."

Reyd offered the first suggestion, "If we aren't going to have them for much time, then I suggest we ram the beam with one at full speed."

"What do you think we might learn from this, Mr. Eastman?" Zimmer inquired.

"Maybe we could drive it straight through the beam and have it emerge out the other side. I'd like to see if we can get to the center of the beam."

"Let's not forget that the beam is 12000 km wide. The paddle can obtain a safe maximum velocity of 400 km/h. It would take thirty hours to get all the way through, and we haven't had more than a few minutes with any of the paddles yet. However, I—like you—would love to pentrate as deeply as we

179

can. Perhaps we will get some imagery or sensory data telling us what is in the beam as we get closer to the center."

"Speaking of the center," Kath voiced softly yet confidently, "since we know that the beam demonstrates a very turbulent corkscrew flow, I wonder if we get to the center and all will be calm and quiet."

"Not a bad idea, Miss Mirabelle. But how to get it there? We've entered at two different speeds and angles and we can't seem to get very far into the beam. We could, perhaps, tear through as Mr. Eastman suggests, and decelerate quickly once we near the center—if we can get that far. We'll keep it in mind."

Zimmer glanced over at Joram. "Two paddles, two ideas from two team members. What do you say, Joram? If you had full control over paddle number twelve, how would you use it?"

"My idea is similar to Reyd's... drive it at full speed—"

"Boys," Kath snorted. "It's all about speed, isn't it?"

Joram feigned to ignore her as he fixed his gaze on Zimmer. "Drive it at full speed—upstream."

Zimmer gave a twitch which looked like an effort not to betray some thought which he had not shared with the team. He swallowed, cleared his throat, and proceeded in a normal tone. "Upstream, Mr. Anders? What do you mean by that?"

"I mean rather than hitting the beam at 90 degrees, I'd like to penetrate the beam at a very shallow angle with the pedal to the metal, Professor."

Looking intently at his pupil, he queried further. "Why would you want to do that? What do you intend to gain?"

"I—I don't—well, I guess I don't really know. Just a gut feeling, you can say." Anders was hiding something and even at this late hour, his transparency was readily perceived by all.

"C'mon, Joram," Kath leaned closer towards him. "Tell us what you're really thinking."

"Oh, I don't really know what we should do with the paddle. It's late, and I'm not thinking clearly," conceded Joram, attempting to deflect the scrutiny. "Professor, what do you think we should do with the paddle?"

Silence ensued for several moments. Zimmer weighed the question a little, but considered the exchange from Joram even more. Not yet ready to betray his own thoughts yet, or what he suspected to be Joram's thoughts, he wrapped up the meeting as follows.

"Three paddles… three suggestions. I actually like all of them. At this point, I'd like to start with Mr. Eastman's proposal. If we can indeed get the paddle all the way through at high speed, we might be able to make even more use of it. Depending on the outcome, we'll take Miss Mirabelle's suggestion second, and see if we might not be able to rest a paddle in the center of the beam. If we're successful, we might be able to keep the paddle there for days in order to collect images and data from the inside. Mr. Anders, your paddle will go last, since it appears to be the most reckless idea of all to go full tilt upstream, and since you have not given us a well-founded reason behind your suggestion—unless you care to do so now."

With this last phrase, Joram broke off eye contact with Zimmer and looked, instead, at the clock on the wall. He was uncomfortable with the change of expression on Zimmer's face, and hoped not to give him an opportunity to discern his thoughts. Perhaps if he avoided eye contact, Zimmer would not be able to penetrate his mind.

"All right, then," Zimmer stated as he stood from his chair, realizing that Joram Anders was not going to reveal himself. "Let's get back in there for the final push."

…

The door to the observation room closed. Reyd and Kath unleashed on Joram.

"What was that exchange back there, Joram Anders?" Kath scolded.

"Huh?"

"Don't 'huh' me. There was something fairly tense back there. You, Zimmer?"

Reyd opined on the matter. "Well, yeah. When a college professor asks you a question, it's usually a good idea to answer." The last word came out louder than even Reyd had intended.

"Look guys, it's just late… I'm tired… Besides, I don't think he really looked very reprimanding of the matter."

"Oh, come on, Joram," Kath said. "You have admired Carlton Zimmer since you were practically in diapers. You are realizing your dream of studying under him. Why would you jeopardize your standing with him with this reticence?"

Joram wanted to change the subject and defuse the tension. "Hey, I'll have you know I was out of diapers by the time I was eight."

Realizing that his attempted humor didn't exactly work as well as he would have liked, he tried a more sincere tact. "Look guys, I now know that I shouldn't have suggested going upstream, because… well, it's a stupid idea, and I'm sure I've lost better judgment this late in the evening."

"What is the idea, Joram?" Kath implored.

"No, Kath—it's—please forget it. I'll tell you someday—I promise— when we can all look back and have a good laugh about it."

Kath didn't look convinced.

"I promise," Joram stated with a tone of finality.

Realizing she wasn't going to pull it out of him, Kath honored Joram's last word on the subject. "Ok, ok… I'm sorry to be so pushy about it. Let's sit down and watch the show, shall we?"

After a brief pause, Reyd tried to loosen up a little bit. "It's too bad there aren't any couches in here to lie down on. Paddle eleven is just now being undocked. It'll be at least a half hour before the paddles are in place for deployment."

"Hey, I'll keep an eye out on the progress if you guys want to close your eyes and catch a few winks." Joram's offer was genuine and was readily accepted by Reyd, and reluctantly agreed upon by Kath. Both were grateful for the offer and quickly found a position in their seats in which they could refresh themselves for a moment.

Joram slowly paced back and forth along the front of the room, his gaze focused on the mauve carpet that was compressing under his feet. The full-length glass wall made it easy for Zimmer to occasionally peer in. It was clear that Joram was heavily burdened, and Zimmer suspected he knew the reason for his turmoil—particularly if it was due to the same concern which he himself carried with him since earlier in the evening.

The time dragged on for Joram, as he paced and weighed his concerns in his head. "What a ridiculous theory. Why did I ever suggest upstream? Will this change my relationship with Zimmer? Will he look for a replacement on his research team? I didn't mean to disrespect his authority or intelligence. What a ridiculous theory."

His mind raced. Time flew by rapidly. He heard a tap on the glass wall separating himself from the control room. Joram looked up, and saw Zimmer point to his eyes and then to his watch, as if to say, "Showtime, Mr. Anders!" Joram looked at the clock on the control room wall and then back to Zimmer with a knowing look on his face. He nodded as he wheeled around to wake Reyd and Kath. The three students resumed their vigilance on the mission as they saw a red dot indicating paddle number ten racing towards the beam. They could see the data set against the background of the yellow flickering image. 384 km/hr. The paddle was at maximum velocity, and was about to penetrate the outer extent of the beam.

The next several minutes proved tense. All remained quiet, breathless, and attentive to see how far the paddle would be able to penetrate the beam. Reyd kept glancing at his watch. So far, none of the paddles had gotten farther than approximately a few miles inside the particle-rich beam.

Exuberantly, he worked the math. "This might just work, Guys! We're looking at four miles of progress per minute. We're about ten minutes into the experiment. That's 40 miles so far."

Kath responded quietly. "Dang it! You spoke to soon, Reyd… the position is degrading." The red dot was veering downstream rapidly.

On the control room floor, sensors started failing, the image went black, the red dot demonstrated a final 90-degree curved directory, and transmission ceased completely.

Reyd stood up. "There must be some larger debris in there breaking these things up. That's just got to be the answer."

Joram rebutted. "I don't think so, Reyd. None of the sensors have detected anything larger than a small grain of sand. Wouldn't we start to see some larger objects before a large rock blasts it away? If that theory were true, you'd start to see pea-sized pebbles, then golf-ball sized rocks, and then a basketball offering that would knock it out for good. From sand to large rock without anything else in between? Maybe, but I'd think the odds are highly against it."

"So what then, Genius?" Reyd's fatigue induced a hasty and defensive posture.

Joram shook his head. "It would all make sense if the debris were larger, like Reyd proposed. I could totally see the debris start to move the paddle downstream and eventually cause it to break up. But you can't make that conclusion with the small size of the debris that is impacting these paddles. The math simply doesn't stick, no matter how fast our sand is moving through this hourglass."

Zimmer stepped into the room with a dejected look on his face. "Two paddles to go team, and it's looking like we won't penetrate this thing far enough. Kath, since Reyd's paddle could barely scrape the surface, what do you want to do with your paddle now?"

Kath looked down at the floor, and then looked up at Zimmer. "I've been thinking a little bit about Deneb, Professor."

Zimmer raised an eyebrow and wrinkled his forehead in interest. "Me too, Ms. Mirabelle. Along with any number of puzzle pieces that we haven't yet put together. What do you propose?"

"Well, I'm not sure what to propose, but we haven't yet found a vastly massive source that could cause enough gravity to distort the light in that manner. Can we do something to explore the gravity of the beam?"

"There doesn't really seem to be significant gravitational pull, Miss Mirabelle. We've navigated several of the paddles to the opposite side of the beam with respect to the USL. The guidance team tells me that there have been no abnormal course corrections due to unexpected gravitational forces."

"Then what is causing the light bending, and how can we study it?" Kath pondered.

"I'm not sure that we can even see the light bending at close range. I've been recording image data from the paddles, and the images seem to indicate no bending of light, but we'll need to run some computer simulations and rendering to compare with expected results."

After a brief pause, Kath suggested, "Professor, can we go ahead and deploy Joram's paddle next, and then confer about paddle twelve when we get there?"

"Great idea, Miss Mirabelle," Zimmer agreed. "We'll get your paddle in position next, Mr. Anders."

Joram's paddle, of course, met a similar fate. After slamming into the beam at full speed in the opposite direction of particle travel, the trajectory curved nearly 180 degrees very quickly towards the direction of the beam's flow, and the paddle spun wildly out of control before losing contact with mission control.

With one paddle to go, the team consulted sternly over the prospects of collecting any data they thought would be useful.

"I've got an idea, Professor," stated Kath as they conversed. "It seems that just before the demise of each paddle, a very rapid change of course occurs first. Maybe we're inducing too much stress on the paddles to have their position change so rapidly. As such, I propose that we revisit Joram's experiment—in reverse."

"What?" asked Reyd with a condescending tone.

"I think," started Zimmer with a glare of disdain for the tactless syllable voiced by his pupil, "that Mr. Eastman means, 'What a great idea!', but please do explain exactly what you mean, Miss Mirabelle?"

"I'm thinking that we should send the final paddle at full speed, but instead of going upstream, let's go downstream. The possibility for greater success could be anticipated simply because we'll be going in the direction of least resistance. So far, we've gone straight into the beam, and we've gone upstream. We have yet to go downstream."

Zimmer lauded this suggestion. "Absolutely brilliant! So far, the beam has rejected our efforts to penetrate its realm. Perhaps we could sneak in a paddle-sized particle that simply goes with the flow."

Looking at his watch, he concluded, "0450 hours, Team. Let's get this last paddle going. If we can inject it stably into the flow, then we'll be able to get some rest while we let the fresh morning recruits track its progress."

Least resistance appeared to be just the secret sauce that was needed for this one last paddle. Particle impact was a bit lighter than with any of the first eleven. But most importantly, as mission control nudged it farther into the beam, they saw it penetrate to depths of 50, 60, 70 miles. Particle impact was growing, but there was reserved optimism among many as this paddle had set a record among all twelve for depth of penetration. There was a growing concern, however, on the part of GUIDANCE.

"We're experiencing acceleration on the paddle, inducing a velocity greater than desired. 750 km/hr... 925 km/hr."

"GUIDO," Zimmer blurted quickly, "please put full reverse thrust possible to slow deceleration. We need to maintain constant velocity in order to maximize our depth and data collection."

"Roger that, FLIGHT, full reverse thrusters engaged, but please note that reverse thrust will only provide one tenth of the acceleration force capable with the forward direction. Acceleration continuing. 1260 km/hr. We're losing ground, FLIGHT. Please advise."

"GUIDANCE, we need to turn the paddle around, face it upstream and then apply full forward thrust to counter the force of acceleration. We need to rotate such that the plane of the paddle is parallel to the flow."

"FLIGHT, we're starting to notice a new vector of direction. It looks like the paddle is starting to take on a corkscrew trajectory. It will be difficult to coordinate a full parallel rotation."

"Negative, GUIDANCE. I also see the corkscrew rotation, but this is accompanied by a paddle roll that is coordinated with the rotation. Look. The face of the paddle is constantly facing the center. Apparently, the corkscrew is because particle impact has started to roll the paddle counter-clockwise. We absolutely must rotate now... as parallel as possible please."

"Working on it, FLIGHT. Discontinuing reverse thrust and commencing rotation."

After a grueling period of waiting and watching the trajectory continue to accelerate, the communication signal to reverse the direction of the paddle upstream was received. "1850 km/hr at commence of rotation. 35 degree rotation, 2300 km/hr. 55 degrees, 3200 km/hr. FLIGHT, without any thrust, we're accelerating more rapidly now. 4800 km/hr, 78 degrees. FLIGHT, we are corkscrewing at a rate of one spiral per 17 minutes with downrange velocity of 7500 km/hr, engaging full forward thrust. It appears as if full forward thrust is doing little to decrease the rate of acceleration. Velocity still increasing to 9800 km/hr. 11,650 km."

In nearly perfect synchrony, the voice of the GUIDANCE officer ceased with the communication of paddle twelve as the image and data on the wall monitor went perfectly black.

...

The clock in the conference room ticked loudly against the quiet and dejected mood present. The time showed that it was 0610 hours. Three heads hung low with as much disappointment as fatigue when the door opened slowly to allow the entrance of the quickly-aging Carlton Zimmer. He took a seat at the table, and his team of pale-faced research students awaited his instruction.

"In less than twelve hours, Team, we've managed to burn through twelve paddles, and are we any closer to solving this mystery than before?"

Heads shook in defeat.

"Do you mean to tell me that all three of you missed the most important discovery of the century—perhaps the millennium?" A smile grew on his face while he studied his students. Reyd leaned forward with opened mouth. Kath brushed her long hair aside and cocked her head as if to hear better. Then, the smile grew more serious, as he looked towards Joram, who blushed slightly and tried to avoid eye contact with all of his team members.

"I'm not exactly sure what's troubling you, Joram, but if it is nearly as difficult as what is troubling me about this, then I sympathize with your situation deeply."

Zimmer walked slowly to the other side of the table, hands clasped behind his back, and head lowered slightly. Pacing the length of the table two or three times, he weighed the exact words that he should use to explain his theory.

"You see—" he started slowly, still pacing, still looking down, "I'm just not sure how I'm going to be able to convince the world—" A deep, raspy sigh emerged as he stopped, leaned towards the three concerned graduate students, and placed his hands on the table.

"—that we have just discovered the tail of the first superluminal comet— the only celestial body ever observed in the history of man to travel faster than the speed of light."

Chapter

17

The prison bars echoed throughout the hall as they slammed shut behind the newest inmate at the U.S. Penitentiary in Atlanta. Paol Joonter shuddered at the noise, which resounded with finality, as if they couldn't be more sealed had they been welded in place. It was fitting for someone who truly believed that the judicial system had let him down harshly, had ruined his life. He had no reason to believe anymore that it would see justice through in the end. In the last few weeks, he had become calloused and bitter at having been thrown on death row as a first time criminal, convicted of a crime he did not commit! And what about his family? They were suffering even more than he. Their sobs for justice were callously denied by a flawed judicial system which has locked up an innocent man, and ceased investigating the real perpetrator of the crime.

Paol turned to look out of the cell. It would be his only view for most of the day. Nonetheless, he needed to see it now, as the prison guards retreated down the long corridor, leaving him alone to his new surroundings.

"Well, I say," a voice said behind him. "You 'da most odd character I ever seen in this cell, and I seen some doozies, let me tell ya'."

Paol didn't know how to respond, or who to respond to for that matter. Gazing around, he finally spotted an inmate similarly attired as himself in a very unfashionable orange and green jumpsuit sitting in a back corner of the cell with a rather large book in his lap. He was a thin black man with a very long face, and very short spiky hair. Paol would've guessed his age at around 35, but that was because he would have failed to factor in the decade of aging that occurred to his new acquaintance on "the streets."

"Fo' 'xample," the voice continued to reminisce, "there was Hans Van Kemp, the Strangla'. He never did like it when I suggested that his first name shoulda been Hands instead of Hans." He made himself laugh heartily, baring a full set of yellow teeth, which contrasted vastly against his skin. The joke was lost on Paol, who was certainly in the least humorous attitude of his life. "Then, there's Luke 'Skeleton' Stilton. Tall and skinny, but when he stared at you with those gray eyes, why you'da thought they'd start to burn a hole right through you."

"But that Rall McHerd character..." At this, Paol's cellmate shivered. "Just thinkin' of that dude is frightful. He was 6-5, weighed 350 pounds in the least. And hairy? Why he looked more gorilla than man with all that long, mangy hair runnin' down his face and body. He sent couple inmates to the hospital with who knows how many broken bones each. I's glad that it wasn't me, and that they moved him off to solitary real quick like after the second attack. They should'a done it sooner, 'xcept there was no room in the schoo'."

At the pause, Paol asked, "Schoo?"

"Schoo', or S-C-U, Special Confinement Unit," offered his chatty companion. "That's the joint where they have them padded 6- by 9-foot boxes they use to keep the really nutso jobs from hurtin' others and themselves."

With a low whisper, as if he were divulging a secret that Paol should never reveal, he leaned towards Paol and continued describing the SCU. "I hear that when ya' go to one of them boxes, ya' never come out the same. And fo' the good of society, ya' done better not be let loose ever 'gain.

"Of course, I never knew nobody to be released that ever spent any time in solitary," stated the inmate as he returned to his previous posture and demeanor.

At this point, the man placed his book on the cot he was seated next to and stood to reveal a tall and lanky frame. At six feet, three inches tall, he weighed no more that 190 pounds. It's no wonder he was afraid of McHerd. Judging by the description offered, the violent character could've snapped this jail bird in half.

As he created images of McHerd and the damage he could have done to himself, Paol inquired, "So, this McHerd character was your cellmate, and he never touched you?"

"No, sir."

"How long did you two spend together?"

"I reckoned 'bout sixteen days."

"And in those sixteen days, he thrashed two different inmates?"

"Yes, sir."

"But not you?"

"No, sir."

"Even though he had more access to you, I trust, then he did to anybody else—what being your cellmate and all?"

"Yes, sir."

"Well, then, educate me." Paol got to the point. "What do you do around here to preserve your—um—health?"

"Well, sir..." the inmate started, but was interrupted by Paol.

"By the way, the name's Paol, Paol Joonter—not sir. Judging by the way you and I are dressed, I suspect we're pretty much equal around here, so I think formal titles can be dismissed."

"Blade Slater," Blade introduced himself by extending his hand.

Paol received his hand and was surprised at the strength of the grip for such a scrawny frame. "Well, Blade, I'm glad to meet you. I think if you can avoid the McHerd treatment, you can certainly teach me a thing or two about self-preservation here."

"Well, ya' just have to find the right balance of avoidin' confrontation without demonstratin' weakness. Fo' 'xample, don't get in no ones' way, and definitely, don't get in their faces, meanin' don't yell at 'em, don't call 'em names, don't be goin' insultin' 'em or nothin'."

"But, what if somebody tries to start something with me?"

"Happens all the time, especially to new guys."

"Like me," Paol's voice quavered as he looked towards the ground.

"No!" exclaimed Blade, calling Paol back to attention with a start. "Mistake number one: weak voice. Mistake number two, lookin' down. What ya' just done, man, is exactly what ya' need to not do. Yer response should'nt'a been, 'like me.' It shoulda been 'LIKE ME!'"

Paol turned around to see if Blade was starting to draw undesired attention to the conversation with his strong voice, but since their cell was at the corner of a hallway, all he could see was the long hall leading to the exit of the ward and the bars of cells lining that hallway. This gave him comfort as he realized that he wouldn't have to confront other inmates in conversation of any form while he was in his cell.

"I follow you," nodded Paol approvingly of his new education.

With the pause, Blade accepted an opportunity to change the conversation. "By the way," Paol asked. "I trust that 'Blade' is your nickname?"

"True 'nough." Blade chuckled. "The real name's Thomas—you know, like from the Bible. Seems like nobody gets Bible names these days, but Momma liked 'em better than the names we hear now 'days."

"I don't suppose Blade has reference to the reason you're in here, does it?"

Slater chuckled heartily. "Not at all. My Momma caught me playin' with a knife when I's three years young. She says I's pretty good wieldin' the blade, and didn't even nick myself. She started callin' me Blade, and—well—it just stuck I s'ppose."

For the first time, Paul lifted the corner of his lip into a smile. There was something heart-warming and genuine about his cellmate that some of the anxiety and tension were starting the melt away.

"Whatcha in fo', Paol?" he inquired with an inspectful gaze. "Ya' don't look like ya' belong here."

Looking down again, Paol was brought back to the remembrance of his situation. Lowly and bitterly, he spat, "I was convicted of a crime I did not commit."

"No!"

Paol's head snapped, and he looked deeply into Blade's eyes to correct his mistake. "I mean," he scowled, "I was convicted of a crime I did not commit."

"That's better," Blade encouraged. "What crime d'ya not commit?"

"Murder."

Blade took a step back and furrowed his brow. "Murder? You don't look like no murderer to me."

191

Paol nodded facetiously. "Great... why weren't you on my jury?" The quip was received with more robust laughter from the veteran inmate.

With a deep voice, Blade responded half-seriously, "They don' let convicted felons serve on juries."

Paol actually weighed the irony here. Rubbing his jaw he thought out loud. "You know, they probably should. I mean, who better to spot a criminal than another criminal. If I would've had a panel of felons on my jury, I bet they get the case right!"

"I dunno, Paol... sounds like yer plan has a logical flaw."

"What do you mean?"

"Well, it's chicken-'n-eggish, ain't it? A real Catch-22. I mean, how d'ya ever convict a felon, if ya' already need twelve of 'em to judge 'em by."

Paol weighed this for a moment. In a fresher state of mind, he probably would've made quick sense of Blade's logic, but in a few seconds the proverbial light bulb came on. "Oh, right. You're talking about the very first criminal. In that case, there would be no previous criminals to create a jury out of, since this was first person accused of a crime. That's downright sensible of you, Blade... very rational.

"Well, to solve that problem, I suspect you could wait for the first thirteen accused, and then have them sit through thirteen simultaneous trials, each one serving as a defendant in their own, and then as a juror on the other twelve."

Blade frowned and shook his head. "Now what's gonna happen in that case, Paol? They'll all acquit each other, because they've all served as a team of jurors with every other accused criminal. They're all cronies together, and they'll all let each other off nice and easy. Then you're just back to where 'ya started—with no convicted felons to serve on yer jury. Don't'cha see?"

"Yeah, yeah," Paol brushed aside the criticism. "But, what if the judge mandated that at least seven of them—over half—had to be convicted?"

"In that case, I can assure you that they won't convict seven... they'll convict thirteen, sure enough."

"How can you be so sure?" Paol drilled. "That wouldn't be in their collective best interest. They would need to determine a solution that would let six of them off, while the other seven serve."

"Paol, d'ya go to college?"

"Well, yes," answered Paol, who was rather interested to see where his colleague would take him with his reasoning.

"D'ya study math?"

"Sure."

"Well, if you'd'a paid attention, ya' might'a learned 'bout game theory, boy?" Blade was starting to get rather animated, pacing up and down the cell throwing his hands in the air and shaking his head.

At this revelation, Paol was rather dumbfounded. He was actually enjoying the logical exchange with his partner, but he assumed that it was his street-smarts that gave him his ability to solve the problem. At this statement, Paol realized that his cellmate actually knew the mathematical branch of logic to which they had been addressing this hypothetical situation they had created.

"You know about game theory?"

Ignoring the question, Blade continued with his tirade. "Why in game theory, ya' see one of the prototypical case studies is the non-zero sum game called the prisoner's dilemma. In the dilemma, prisoners are given a chance to cooperate with each other, or to defect against each other. They all serve a lighter sentence if they all cooperates together, but the cooperative prisoner who is betrayed by a defectin' prisoner will receive the harshest penalty, while the back-stabber gets off free and easy."

"And if they all defect against each other?" Paol admired as he appraised the problem.

"Stiff sentences all around."

Paol weighed the outcomes out loud. "So the best solution for any prisoner is for him to defect while all others cooperate, because he'll be able to walk without any jail time, right?"

"Yes, sir."

"I think you mean, yes, Paol."

"Yes, Paol."

"So, the solution is simple! You have to join a pact with everyone to cooperate and make them understand that together, they will serve the lightest combined sentence. Then, in private, you turn against the others and defect, right?"

"No!"

"What? Did I look down again?"

"No," Blade attempted to clarify. "I didn't mean 'No, look up', I meant 'No, you're wrong.' Ya' see, every mathematician understands that the best *collective* solution is fer all to cooperate. But the best *individual* solution is to defect."

"Why?" Paol prodded.

"Because, ya' can't make a collective bargain with a bunch of prisoners and expect them to not turn and stab ya' in the back, just like you're doin' to them. There's only one state of mathematical equilibrium to the problem... everyone defects, because it's in everyone's *self-interest*."

Paol was impressed. "So, tell me. Where did you learn about game theory?"

"In that seat right over there," admitted the convict as he motioned to the seat that Paol found him sitting in when he first entered into the life of this enigmatic character.

Paol cocked his head and raised an eyebrow.

Blade understood the question.

"Have a seat, Paol." Blade motioned to another hard wooden chair, sitting by the cot on the opposite wall of the cell. He returned to his seat as well. With the pair of odd-fellows seated, Blade continued.

"I grew up right here in Atlanta, Geo'gia—on the south side, in the ghetto... or I guess I should say, the 'inner city.' Momma raised me and my two sisters and two brothers in a small one-bedroom apartment. I dunno what happened to my Pa... Ma never would tell us kids. I remember wakin' up in the middle of the night with the sounds of gunshots and sirens. It wasn't much less rough durin' the day, while we kids was outside playin' in the alleys. Ya' couldn't make it on yer own. Ya' needs support, ya' needs to rely on each other. So, by the time I was 'leven, I hooked up with a gang. I was pretty small fo' my age, so I wanted some personal protection too—had my eyes on a long blade I saw in the window of a pawn shop just down the street from where I lived. But I had no money... couldn't steal it, 'cuz it was locked up in a glass case. Thought 'bout breakin' the case with a rock or somethin', but I figured I'd never get away, and the 'ol man in the shop was a big'un who'd give me a bruisin' fo' sure.

194

"Well, I'd heard some of my type in the gang was sellin' drugs, so I figured I needed to also, so I could get me that blade. Well, it was darn easy money, so even after I bought it, I kep' sellin' the goods. Problem was, there's this other gang who thought we was workin' too close to their territory. So I had to use my blade to cut someone up."

"How old were you?" Paol asked, fascinated at the tale.

"Fi'teen… and then I's real scared when he got himself outta the hospital, but he never came after me. He had lots of problems with his Daddy beatin' him, and finally, he was just gone."

"What do you mean?"

"Disappeared. We suspected that he done run off, but nobody knows fo' sure. Anyway, there's I was in a real mess, sellin' drugs and gettin' in trouble. Ma knew what I was doin', but she never said nothin' 'cuz I gave her some of the money she needed to help with the family.

"When I turned seventeen, my main bro's on the street had this real dumb idea. They's said, 'Blade, get yo' Momma's car tomorrow fo' some real business.' I was the only one who could drive, ya' see. Well, we was drivin' along when Xavier tossed a handgun in my lap. 'Fully loaded', he said. 'Just in case.' He still never told me what was goin' down when he had me stop the car along a store front. They strolled into the store, and was gone fo' 'bout two minutes when I's heard some shots and then they come runnin' outta the store. They jumped in the car and when someone else came limpin' outta the store and started firin' at us, I took off… a little too fast."

"What happened?"

"The light at the intersection was red, but I was lookin' back in the mirror at the poor foo' who my bro's shot up. He was still firin' at us, when I heard and felt a crash. We was hit on the passenger side by another car. My buddy, X, couldn't get out, but me and Kojo, who was in the back seat, got out and ran off. Runnin' down the street we heard a voice yell, 'freeze!'". I looked and saw two plain-clothes types runnin' down the street towards us with their guns pointed at us. Without thinkin', I raised my arm and shot while runnin'. I never used a gun befo', so I was surprised when I saw one of 'ems go down. We kept runnin' but we was stupid, 'cuz we'd never get away."

"Why not?"

"Xavier was trapped at the scene, and my Momma's car would lead the cops right to her. I had no chance. My public defender tried to get me off as an accomplice to the robbery, seein' how I didn't know what X and Kojo was up to, but it was no use to try and lighten the sentence of an aggravated assault with a deadly weapon against a federal officer."

"Federal?"

"Yep, they was two feds who happened to be in the 'hood that day. What luck, huh?"

"So, here I am serving 3 years as an accomplice, and 20 for takin' down a fed… good thing I only hit him in the leg. I'd be serving 40+ if I'd'a wasted him."

"23 years, huh?", Paol shook his head sadly.

"Yep, and seven of 'ems down, but I think I'll be gettin' sprung in another five or so—fer good behavior ya' know."

"But you still haven't answered my question. How do you know so much about math?"

"Well, my Momma's brother runs a car shop, and when I was startin' to fall away, he tried to bring me back to an honest livin'. Told me how I was breakin' my Momma's heart, and if I wanted, he'd teach me to work on cars. I never took him up on it. I wanted to, but I was young and stupid and made all the wrong decisions. I had lotsa time to think 'bout everythin' when I was throwed in prison. After the first week, I thought so much 'bout how I could be helpin' my uncle at the shop, and how my Momma wouldn't have to cry every day while I'm here in jail."

"Then, I had an epiphany."

"An epiphany?"

"Yeah, ya' know a precipitous manifestation of the essence or implication of somethin'."

Surprised by this intelligent definition, Paol was knocked back in his seat. "Does this epiphany involve a vision of a dictionary?" It was an unexpected attempt at humor that even he wasn't expecting from himself, but now that he was thinking more about the poor life of this kid, and was thinking much less about his own problems, he allowed his own cares to lapse if but for a moment and returned to his previous, jovial self.

Blade slapped himself on the knee and whooped raucously at Paol's banter. "Aw, that's a good one, Paol... you're a funny man. No, it had nothin' to do with a dictionary, but if ya' ever need to borrow one, I got me one, right under here."

Blade leaned down to point under his cot, and Paol craned his neck to discover a vast collection of books, large and small, under Blade's bed.

"Have you read all of those?" Paol asked admiringly.

"Most of 'ems. Ya' see, the 'precipitous manifestion' that I had was that I could either spend a dozen or two years feelin' sorry fer myself, or I could make somethin' of the time. I mean, I'll still be young enough to do somethin' with my life when I bust outta here, ya' know? So, I decided to read and learn, and ya' know what?"

"What?"

"I really enjoy readin' and learnin' 'bout new things. It's enlightenin', invigoratin', exhilaratin', ya' know?"

"Um... hand me that dictionary, would you?" Paol smiled for the first time, and Blade responded with his most hearty round of laughter yet.

After Blade regained his breath and wiped the tears of laughter from his eyes, Paol concluded, "So, this is where you've learned about mathematics?"

"That's right," Blade said excitedly. "Ooh, hang on just a moment." He knelt down, and Paol watched him rifle through the books under his bed and mutter incoherently to himself. "Where is it now? I thoughts it was over there... Oh, that's where's I put 'All Quiet on the Western Front.'... been wantin' to read that one... some good history there, I bet, just decent... ah, here 'tis."

Blade returned to his seat with a large hard-bound text book, titled, *Applied Mathematics, Volume II.*

Flipping through the index, his fingers raced down the page, "Aha! Prisoner's dilemma," he exulted. "There ya' is, now."

Paol shook his head as he saw the page titled 'Case Study 2: Prisoner's Dilemma', and marveled at the highlighting and well-drafted handwritten notes in the margin.

"Blade, I'm absolutely flabbergasted."

"Flabbergasted!" winked Blade. "To be overcome with astonishment or stupification."

197

At this, Blade waited for Paol's snicker—his first in weeks—before returning to his whole-hearted laughter. At this point, Blade himself had an epiphany. Perhaps it was the affable, easy-going nature of his cellmate that protected him against the most hardened. How could anyone not quickly grow to love this young man? Fate had handed him a bad lot in his wrongful conviction, but at least he was placed with one of the most decent men possible in this brutal environment.

Chapter

18

The pilot leaned back in the seat of his C-320 space craft as it floated serenely through the expanses of space. The C-320 was the most recent engineering marvel at NASA. Capable of traveling at 0.6 Warp, it was the fastest space craft ever constructed. Now that it had completed a rigorous three years of testing, it was on its first mission to the outer edge of the solar system. The C-320 had the appearance of a white bullet, although on closer inspection the shape was more flattened than rounded, and had wing-like protrusions on either side. It was spray-coated with some of the highest tech material ever invented. A light-weight, elastic and resilient polymer, it protected the ship and its passengers from impacts with space objects.

Inside, the ship could be deemed cozy at best, but astronauts never seemed to use that term upon return to earth, where they almost certainly proclaim that "sardines have no idea." Even so, space explorers were clamoring for opportunities to take the new-fangled vehicle for a spin somewhere in the galaxy, simply because of the excitement of exploring the far reaches of the solar system where no man had ever traveled before.

"All systems check. Having successfully navigated through the asteroid belt and beyond the orbit of Jupiter, we've obtained cruise velocity and are on time with a rendezvous at the edge of the galaxy. The Magellan-Victoria is all systems go," the astronaut voiced into a headset and then lifted the microphone away from his mouth. "You see, Tef... everything is going normally."

"I know, Jainn, and that's what has me concerned," replied the pilot. "There's always a problem on these voyages, no matter how small or insignificant. So far, there has been nothing. It's almost too quiet, too eerie. I just want to get that anomaly out of the way, so I can relax and enjoy the trip."

Jainn shook his head. "You're too superstitious. Everything will be fine." The confident navigator reclined as far as he could in his seat and gazed out into the expanses, stars blazing in panoramic splendor from the cockpit. "Would you just look at that, Tef? What an amazing view!"

Tef reclined his seat, wanting to forget his concerns. "You're right about that, partner. I'm still surprised that we're traveling faster than any human ever has, and it feels dead still, just the hum of the ion thrust engines."

"Yeah, it definitely doesn't feel like we're moving... I mean I know that those stars are very far away but it still surprises me considering the speed we're traveling that you hardly notice us moving."

The two star-dazed astronauts enjoyed the various quality of brilliance and color that filled the black canvas behind them. Even Tef, the paranoid pilot began to relax and forget his worries.

While the astronauts were watching the spectacle overhead, they could not notice the tiny particles of ice and dust left behind from some far-flung comet, speeding by as they intersected its orbital path. However, the C-320 was very well-equipped to sense them, and alerted them to their presence with an audible alarm. Both returned their seats to a fully upright position simultaneously to assess the situation.

The pilot lowered the microphone on his headset. "Victoria reporting to mission control on a debris sensor. It appears as if we are being impacted on the right side by minute debris field at an angle of 254 degrees. We're commencing navigation first to minimize angle of impact."

Tef worked a joystick to cause a gentle and gradual roll of the craft in the direction of the stream, to allow particles to glance off the right side of the craft. Jainn monitored the sensor data of the craft and watched intently for any other alarms signaling problems while navigating out of the debris field.

Tef spoke clearly into his headset. "Mission control, we're going to pitch up at an angle of 13 degrees from the galactic plane to take ourselves away from the field. Frequency of impact detection is decreasing rapidly."

Taking a deep breath, his turned to his navigator. "Well, Jainn. Hopefully, we're out of the woods. There's that anomaly I was worried about... may it be the last."

"Yeah," said Jainn panting slightly. "I love this job, but I really hate..." He was interrupted abruptly by a jolt which rolled the craft slightly to the right. An alarm indicated some kind of breach on the wing. Jainn looked out of the right side window in order to get a visual on the incident and grew pale instantly.

"Tef, I'm seeing vapor coming off of the end of the wing!" he exclaimed. "Oh no, I'm seeing sparks... and..." His voice trailed off as he saw a white piece of debris floating in space just behind the wing. "Tef, we've sustained damage." The tip of the right wing had been sheared completely off of the craft by one of the minute particles they were attempting to avoid.

Tef continued in a business-like manner. "It looks like I'll need to continue the direction of pitch in order to pull up from the debris. We really need to distance ourselves from the portion of the vehicle that's traveling right next to us. If we veer into its trajectory, it could do more damage still."

The wing tip fell out of view as the craft continued to pitch up, but what the unsuspecting astronauts couldn't see was that the particles, although fairly sparse now, were continuing to bombard it pushing it closer and closer to the back of the craft. As it slammed into the rear, the C-320 yawed from side to side. An alarm indicated that damage had indeed been sustained in the back of the craft now and that oxygen was escaping into the vacuum of space around them. Vital cables, electronic equipment and hardware began to ooze out of the gash like blood, and each lost object was only adding to the damaged exterior as it was sucked into the volume of space.

While the astronauts struggled to regain their craft, shouting orders to each other, closing off pressurization breaches, sweating nervously, and listening to a litany of alarms, the craft began to pitch and yaw violently until the ion generators in the rear of the vehicle were severed. Tef, previously fighting the joystick, let up and leaned back in his seat

"Tef!" barked Jainn. "What are you doing?! We're spinning out of control and need to restabilize the craft!"

"We can't," proclaimed Tef calmly, while fixing his gaze somewhere out into space.

"Why not?!" shouted Jainn as he glanced all over the panel, dazed by the number of lights and alarms.

"Listen, closely. What do you hear?"

"Alarms… I hear alarms. All over the place."

"Exactly! You hear alarms. But, do you hear the engines?"

Jainn strained to listen to the remainder of his environment. He silenced all of the alarms to get a better fix on any other sounds in the cockpit. Then, he noticed the panel of flashing lights that were lost by a sea of red, yellow, and white lights pulsing from the panel. The engine failure alarms had indeed come on. Breathing heavily, he racked his brain for a solution to the problem.

"Ok," Jainn struggled to control the emotion in his voice. "Let's think this through. We need to get back there and restore power to the engines. Since the craft still has power, we haven't lost the ion generators yet."

"We've sealed off the cabin, Jainn. Nothing short of a spacewalk would get us back there, but we don't even have an airlock that we can reach. Even if we did, we have no way of stabilizing the craft."

"How bad is our destabilization situation?"

"Can't tell, the sensors have been badly damaged or lost, so I don't trust them, but if you look at how quickly the stars are spinning, my guess is that we're rolling very fast, and pitching a little too. In fact, I'm guessing we have velocity vectors in all three directions. We couldn't possibly calculate a successful jump-off from the craft."

After an uncomfortable and eerie silence, Jainn asked his pilot, "So, what do we do now, Tef? We can't simply sit here and just float off into space completely out of control! What are our possible scenarios, captain?"

"Well, in the worst case," the pilot stated in a matter-of-fact manner, "we get pulled in by some nearby object's gravitational field and we'll begin to accelerate toward it, eventually slamming into the surface and creating a deep crater."

"And the best case?" asked Jainn. "The worst doesn't sound very encouraging."

"In the best case, we become one of the universe's most bizarre objects orbiting around some planet or solar system as a frozen memorial to the mission."

Having muted all of the alarms, the astronauts sat there in complete silence and near darkness as the power being served from the damaged generators weakened. Their attention was immediately drawn to a large orange button in the middle of the panel that was sounding with a harsh, pulsating buzz accompanying it.

"Mission Abort!" read Jainn. "I don't remember seeing that button. What does it mean, Tef?"

Tef didn't get a chance to answer as a final electric pulse shot through a vein-like series of circuits throughout the surface of the aircraft. In complete simultaneity, a thousand small explosions on the surface of the craft reduced the Victoria and all of its contents to dust. For a split second, all of the oxygen remaining on board turned into a fireball of bright orange and searing blue flames, before quickly evaporating into the quiet blackness that existed before Victoria wandered into the region....

Maril Scoville sat straight up in bed. He found himself sweating profusely and breathing heavily. He clutched his chest, feeling his heart pound rapidly under his ribcage. It was as dark as the vastness of space surrounding the recently destroyed C-320 Magellan-Victoria. The harsh pulsating alarm from the C-320 cockpit panel persisted. Slowly, Maril realized that it wasn't a panel alarm at all. Instead, the noised emanated from his digital clock alarm which read 5:00 AM.

His wife rolled towards him and rubbed his back. "What's the matter, Honey?"

Composing himself with a deep breath, he whispered, "Another nightmare."

"What happened this time?"

"Tef Alline. He was... he was on a mission with the new astronaut, Jainn Tucker... and..." His voice trailed off. "And the shield failed them." He hung his head and rubbed his face with his hands.

"Oh, Honey... I'm sorry." She tried to focus her hazy thoughts to say something comforting, but was having difficulty at this time of the morning. After a few moments of silence and reduced breathing she continued, "Where are Tef and Jainn now anyway?"

"I think Jainn is on family leave with a new baby. Tef was preparing for a mission to Mars. He was going to replace the Russian astronaut on the next shift change."

Maril stood up from the bed and put on his slippers and robe.

"Will you be ok, Sweetie?"

"Yeah, you go back to sleep, Love."

5:00 AM was earlier than Maril's normal alarm. This was going to be a long day for the burgeoning rocket scientist. As a project manager over a team of 30 engineers working at the Jet Propulsion Laboratory adjacent to the CalTech campus, one of his biggest tests would occur on this day. The efforts of his team would be scoured by resident engineers and visiting authorities from Ames, Langley, and of course NASA headquarters.

Maril's project was deemed critical to the success of Star Transport. His job was to develop the Star Shield. One of the major headaches facing theorists on interstellar travel was how to protect the craft from random space debris at speeds approaching the speed of light, commonly referred to among scientists as Warp Speed. It doesn't take too much imagination to consider what could happen to a spaceship that has a head-on collision with space debris traveling at a half million miles per second. In fact, some of the mathematical modeling performed by Maril's team demonstrated that a particle of dust no bigger than one millimeter in diameter could have catastrophic effects on a space vehicle if the impact was just right—or perhaps better said, just wrong. Computer simulations demonstrated that a head-on impact on the wing of the Star Transport design would not only impale the wing, but could saw it clean off. It didn't take long for his computer models to translate into nightmares that were coming with greater frequency. In these dreams, visions of shuttle parts being ripped apart, disintegration of the entire vehicle, or sudden explosions provided more of an effect than a science fiction movie.

On the night before the design review, Maril slept tolerably well, all things considered. But on his commute down Interstate 210, Maril's thoughts were focused only on the details of the design review. Did Physon get the remainder of data from the particle tunnel? Had he remembered to ask Kelcey to print the handouts for the presentation? Did the final simulations

204

finish up overnight? His cell phone rang several times on the way into the office with all sorts of issues he'd have to solve as quickly as possible.

Problem number one occurred at 6:03. "Maril, the simulations are still a couple of hours away."

"Ok, then let's adjust the agenda accordingly."

At 6:12, the following detail was announced. "The techs are telling me we may have a problem running the demo in the wind tunnel."

"Well, those things happen. Just set up a flat panel display in the auditorium, in case we need to do a computer demo instead."

Perhaps most importantly was the call that he answered at 6:27. "Don't forget your tux at the cleaner's. The party is tomorrow night. You know I've been looking forward to this all summer."

"No problem, honey. It's just around the corner from the office, so I'll have Kelcey pick it up before her lunch break."

Finishing up another call as he entered into his office at 6:45, he thought to himself, "You know, maybe I should just get one of those ear-implants." His phone even had one of those new terabyte holographic drives where all of his favorite music and talk show broadcasts were stored.

Pocketing his cell phone, Kelcey handed him five other urgent messages that had come in that morning, briefed him on the agenda and catering for the design review, and presented him with a stack of handouts of the presentation. "I really need to give this girl a raise," Maril reminded himself for the umpteenth time as he sat down at his desk and made the final preparations for the review.

. . .

The auditorium was packed like never before. While Maril had met nearly all of the scientists present, he'd never seen so many of them at one time. He was surprised to see experts from nearly every other NASA site in the country. Johnson, Kennedy, Ames, Langley, Dryden, and Goddard were all represented. From Washington, there were policy makers and worse yet— finance committee members. He was not told that the finance committee would be represented, but he also didn't know that it was simply coincident with their visit to his father, Ballard Scoville, just the day before.

He was pleased to see that most of the 200-member team on site had come to aid or simply provide moral support to Maril's team throughout the day. Electrical, mechanical, chemical, computer and aerospace engineers were all represented in an effort to convey to the bigwigs that the project was well staffed.

At precisely 8:00 AM, while most were still enjoying the fruits, muffins, juices and coffee that was constantly replenished on the counter in the back of the auditorium, Maril began his introduction.

"Ladies and gentlemen, thank you for your attendance here today. I recognize the distance that many of you have traveled for this important review, and I am confident that you will leave here at the end of the day with all of the data that you will need to confirm that this project is making great progress and that all of your questions will be answered satisfactorily."

Maril took just a few minutes to bring his team onto the stage, introduce each member by name, and list the various credentials which they bring to the team. Pausing to allow the team to return to their seats in the front row, Maril then used his remote control to lower the lights, draw the curtains from the back of the stage, and bring the projector to life.

"As you are all aware, Star Transport is slated for an intra-stellar flight mission in the third quarter of next year. It is intended to journey towards the outer reaches of the solar system and will then race back to the center of our solar system, passing within just one tenth of an astronomical unit—or eight million miles—of the surface of the sun. The Star Shield that my team is working on will be thoroughly tested in three phases of this flight.

"The first test comprises the asteroid belt, lying between Mars and Jupiter. We know much about the asteroid belt, and the materials of which it is comprised. We believe that this will be an easy maneuver for the shield to handle, because of the low distribution of asteroids. Our computer scientists have developed a set of algorithms that can quickly process magnetic field data in order to detect the presence of an asteroid and steer clear of it. We believe that with these algorithms, Star Transport will be able to navigate through the asteroid belt at Warp 0.68. That's nearly 204 million meters per second.

"The second phase—the Kuiper Belt and Oort Cloud—proves to be much trickier. While we have discovered much recently about the Oort Cloud, we still can only theorize about its density at its outer boundary. As such, we're not convinced about the speed at which we'll be able to approach solar systems with similar clouds. However, this is typically a trivial matter, because it is commonly agreed that the amount of time traversing through such clouds is minimal compared to the time required to travel between star systems. At this point, the conjecture is that the inner portion of the cloud—believed to be denser—will only be maneuverable to Warp 0.25, whereas the outer portion of the cloud should allow the vehicle to reach speeds of Warp 0.45. Calculations show that such speeds would allow us to traverse the cloud in about two to three months. Of course, we will continue to explore these assumptions as astronomers around the world continue to map out the cloud. Obviously, we'd like to do better than to keep our fine astronauts tied up in our own solar system for so long. We'd be much happier getting them through the cloud in just a few weeks at most."

"Now, while the first two phases are involved in large body avoidance, the final test phase will prove out fine particle and heat tolerance. By traveling close to the sun, the Shield will be prone to vast quantities of high speed gases and dust emanating from the sun. It will also test its ability to withstand the higher temperatures within this region. To make the test even more problematic, Star Transport is expected to approach the sun at a speed of Warp 0.75. The speed of the craft, coupled with the speed of the solar particles will accurately simulate the effects on the Shield of particles approaching speeds that, for all intents and purposes, would be the same as traveling at the speed of light."

At this last comment, several of the visitors inched forward on their seats in suspenseful recognition of the meaning of Maril's words. If such a test could prove successful, then the more perplexing problems of Warp Speed travel would be solved. Both large object avoidance and small particle tolerance could be checked off of the list for interstellar travel. For some, the realization that such a test was literally just around the corner gave them chills.

. . .

While a litany of design reviews were held throughout the day, none were more important or more impressive than the one demonstrated in the the particle tunnel. There analysts could see the impact of small high-speed particles on the shield. Maril was on hand personally, as he felt that this was the most critical aspect of his part of the project: to make sure that the vehicle and astronauts were adequately protected from unavoidable high-speed impacts.

"Gentlemen," began Maril confidently. "I'd like to walk you down a timeline of our efforts on the Star Shield project here today. First, if I can direct your attention to the video monitors, we'll demonstrate our early materials experiments, where we studied the effects of high-particle impact on a flat, square piece of material three millimeters thick."

Maril then demonstrated a parade of materials, where he placed no fewer than twenty different three-millimeter thick sheets into the particle tunnel and revealed the effect. He showed the frustrations that were encountered when they marched through sheet after sheet that didn't make the grade. One was too susceptible to penetration. Another was simply too heavy to measure up to the vehicle specifications. Other materials were too brittle, not malleable enough, more susceptible to radiation, or had lower melting points.

"Now, if I can draw your attention one last time to the video monitors," announced Maril. Everyone turned their heads away from the speaker and back to the video display. Maril was able to convey that a particular metal hybrid composite was able to deflect all particles up to five millimeters in diameter at speeds of Warp 0.3—the maximum speed the technology allowed at the time, even though the sheet itself was only three millimeters thick.

"Gentlemen, I think the results speak for themselves. In this ultra-lightweight composite material, we have a very durable material to use as the outer skin of our Shield."

"Mr. Scoville," called out a reviewer formally, "this experiment only convinces me that we will be safe at Warp 0.3. How can we be sure that this material will work up to Warp 1.0?"

"Excellent question." Maril was prepared for this. "What you are seeing is the effect on a flat sheet, where particles are allowed to strike the surface at precisely ninety degrees. As reviewers are gathering in the wind tunnel presently, my team is demonstrating to them the novel aerodynamic shape of the shield, which will guarantee that no particle strike any part of the shield at an angle greater than sixty degrees. Our calculations prove that this would equate to a particle tunnel speed-up factor of 2.5." "But that's still not good enough, Mr. Scoville," scowled the critic. "If we only need the vehicle to travel at Warp 0.75 that would be fine. But the specification is clear. Warp 1.0"

"Yes, indeed," Maril did his best not to get irritated by the pessimism of his visitor. Besides, these were the types of questions that needed to be asked in order to find any holes in critical assumptions which could jeopardize the project or the mission. "Keep in mind that this is just the skin. We also have shield impact response sensing software that will ensure that we prevent damage to the shield or vehicle under high-impact events. For more than 99.99% of the time, the vehicle will be able to travel at Warp 1.0. However, when traveling through high-dust regions, such as the Kuiper Belt or Oort Clouds, the drive will be reduced sufficiently in these less frequent scenarios."

Maril had already put the arguments of the reviewer to rest, but added one more detail to ensure that any doubts be eliminated in full. "For those nastier space objects that are in the gray area—for example, anything that may be larger than a pea, and smaller than a beach ball—these cannot be detected with the avoidance software, these will be pulverized by the electronic disintegration mechanism layer which is placed just underneath the skin. These electronic pulses will radiate through the skin and break up these types of objects before they reach the skin. Our simulations show that at Warp 1.0, such disintegration will sufficiently break down these objects before they reach a distance of ten centimeters from the shield."

Question after question, Maril did all that he could to convince the reviewers that this most critical piece of the puzzle was ready for prime time. Now, he just needed to convince his subconscience in order to avoid all of those annoying nightmares he was having.

...

Ya Ming was a young aerospace engineer taking on her first responsibility as a team lead. Maril Scoville was impressed with the CalTech graduate turned JPL employee when he met her eight years earlier. He had been impressed enough with her work that he invited her on the Star Shield team as a team contributor. When the shield design lead left his post with NASA for a corporate engineering position, Maril felt that Ming was a perfect fit for the job. Had he seen her efforts during the wind tunnel portion of the design review, he would've been confirmed in his promotion of her.

"NASA fellows," she began, "I thank you for your presence here in the wind tunnel today. As I make my presentation to you, please feel free to interrupt to ask any questions that you may have."

Ming appeared confident enough in front of the panel of reviewers, but inside she was quite nervous about her first major design review presentation. She didn't know if she was more nervous about the presence of all of the senior visiting authorities, or whether it was the fact that the director of JPL, Dr. Rawson Cornell, was there as well. Maril thought that it would be useful for Cornell to attend, in case Ming needed any help or support during the review.

Ming continued, "Before we fire up the demonstration in the wind tunnel, I would like to begin with a brief presentation." Ming gestured to a projector screen, where her computer presentation was already queued up.

"On this first slide," she noted, "you'll see the cone-like shape of the Star Shield. We have taken measures to minimize the angle of approach of particles impinging on the shield. The design is such that 90% of particles will approach the shield at an angle less than 23.5%. Computer models show that most particles of reasonable size will glance off of the shield without harm at this sharp angle."

A hand raised among the crowd. Ming acknowledged the visiting reviewer, "Yes, Mr. Callahan. You have a question."

"While it may be good that most of the particles will deflect, it seems to me like it would only take one particle approaching at the worst case condition to impale the shield, and perhaps the vehicle," expressed Callahan.

"If you were to take cross sections of the shield," Ming answered quickly, "you will notice that the cone is perfectly circular until you get ten centimeters from the nose of the shield. At that point, the circular cross sections begin to slowly morph into octagons, which is calculated to reduce the rounding effect at the tip of the cone. Continue down and these octagons will get smaller and smaller until about three centimeters where the shape of the octagon becomes irregular. In this region, you will notice that the nose begins to point slightly downward until it comes to a point. That point actually is bent three degrees below the directional axis of the vehicle. In order to get a direct ninety degree impact of a particle on the shield, it would need to approach the vehicle at three degrees from below. While the vehicle is traveling at sufficiently high

210

speeds, it is impractical for any object to impact the shield at zero degrees. In fact, the vast majority of particles will impact at angles well below fifty-five degrees."

Satisfied with the answer, Callahan gestured to Ming to continue with her presentation.

Ming clicked on her presentation controller to advance the presentation. "On this slide, I show the layers of the shield. The skin consists of a three millimeter single-molded sheet of a highly specialized metal-matrix composite material. It is extremely light and very impervious to high-speed particle impact. It is molded into a single sheet to avoid any seams which might cause degradation in performance.

"The second layer of the shield consists of a two-dimensional array of impact sensors. The sensors relay the amount of pressure on the shield to the main guidance computer system. There are over twelve million microscopic semiconducting sensors in the array, placed in immediate proximity in order to assess not only the force of impact but also the size of the particles in question. The computer calculates the size by assessing the simultaneous force of impact on neighboring sensors. The larger the object is, the more sensors that will transmit a simultaneous reading to the computer. Size and force together are the two key components which dictate the potential damage to the shield."

Ming paused and looked around for questions, but she had apparently described the second layer sufficiently for the reviewers to comprehend the usage of the second layer.

"The third layer consists of electronic pulse generators, or EPGs which can pulverize larger particles into smaller ones just prior to impact. For the most part, the vehicle will prefer to decelerate in areas of higher density debris. However, some objects will be too large to safely deflect but too small to avoid. In these instances, the vehicle will first decelerate to an acceptable speed and will engage the EPGs. These can turn a basketball-sized particle into multiple golf-ball sized particles as soon as it approaches within twelve centimeters of the shield, even while the vehicle is traveling at Warp 0.5.

"Miss Ming," interrupted another reviewer. "How long can the vehicle sustain the amount of energy required to engage the EPGs, and how is that

211

energy restored? I trust we will not be able to place interstellar gas stations along the route, right?"

Ming chuckled respectfully and answered, "At Warp 0.5, we expect to be able to navigate through dust fields as large as 500 astronomical units. We expect these events to be rare, compared to the asteroid fields that the shield will completely avoid impacts altogether. In most galaxies, dust has coalesced to form asteroids. Only in very new galaxies, will the vehicle have to contend with large quantities of dust. The most typical use of the EPGs will be while navigating through chunks of ice scattered behind the tail of a comet. However, these will only cause the EPGs to be turned on for a very short period of time.

"I am afraid that I am not able to answer your second question, since that comes from the Star Energy team, who is handling the energy generation and consumption requirements for the vehicle. We were given a specification from the team that the EPGs must consume no more than 100 kilowatts of power in a single burst. From this, we calculated the numbers I provided before. That is, 500 astronomical units at Warp 0.5."

"If there are no further questions..." There were none. "I would now like to demonstrate the shield in the wind tunnel."

The team was able to note the deflection of wind across the shield. They paid particularly close attention to the effects of the wind at the tip as well as along the flat octagon-shaped portion of the shield. They briefly examined the effect along the curved portion as well.

One reviewer asked if an EPG demonstration could be provided, and Ming was able to oblige by leading the party into an electronics lab. She took two three-foot square metal screens and placed them upright in front of a small canon-like device. She took a couple of average looking rocks each about five inches in diameter and loaded them one at a time into the canon. The first one was fired directly into the metal screen with the EPGs disengaged. The screen was completely impaled by the rock as was evidenced by the five-inch hole in the middle of it. Ming then turned on the EPGs, which caused the shield to dance with blue glowing pulses of electricity. The second rock was fired into the new screen. The effects were vastly different. Several gasps of air and a couple of high-pitched whistles convinced Ming that her party was impressed. To finalize the effect, Ming took the screen and showed them the profile, where there were several dents in the screen, none of which were larger than about five millimeters. Then she showed them the floor below the screen where a collection of fine dust had accumulated from the disintegration of the rock.

"Miss Ming," announced a senior reviewer, "it appears to me that your team has done a magnificent job in your research and development. Congratulations on a job well done, and keep up the fine work."

Ming bowed graciously. Words nearly escaped her, until she was able to fumble out an emotional acceptance of the praise. "Thank you, Dr. Janos. I am glad to have been able to demonstrate our work here today."

...

At 8:45pm, Maril collapsed into the leather seat in his office. In the quiet of his office, the only sound he could hear was a dull ringing in his ears. After introductions, design reviews, and debriefing sessions, Maril found himself alone for the first time since walking into his office earlier that morning. Had it really been just that morning? It felt so much longer than that.

Heaving a deep breath of air and finishing off a bottle of water that sat on his desk, Maril collected his computer bag, and started to walk out of the office. He paused as he noticed a freshly pressed tuxedo bag on a hanger behind the door. He smiled and reminded himself out loud, "I really do need to give that girl a raise."

Chapter
19

"Well, what do we have here?" A prisoner sat down next to Blade Slater with a tray of food. "Looks like Doubting Thomas has himself a new friend."

Blade looked across the table at his 'new friend' with a smile. "Ever since Goat Herd here started readin' the Bible, he's been callin' me Doubtin' Thomas."

Extending a hand across the table, the newcomer introduced himself. "The name's Guntherd Schenthtzen. Some folks around here find it easier to remember my prison number, 689214—or, for the numerically challenged, Goat Herd works too."

After looking to Blade who gave an almost imperceptible nod of approval, Joonter reached out his hand to find a deceptively firm grip from the otherwise scrawny looking Guntherd. "Paol Joonter."

Not comfortable in how much he should say, Joonter decided to keep his communication with other prisoners as succinct as possible, since he still wasn't sure of the intricacies of proper communication with inmates.

"Sharp dresser," Guntherd said matter-of-factly.

Paol looked down at his prison garb and then scanned the rest of the cafeteria. With a look of confusion, he found it to be no different than any other prisoner in the commissary.

"What Goat Herd here is tryin' to say," Slater clarified for his cellmate, "is that you is pretty well groomed. Short hair. Clean shave. No tats. It gives yer wardrobe a different appearance, like it's newer than the rest of us."

Eyeing Joonter with suspicion, Schenthtzen announced, "I hear there's some fancy-pants three-piece-suit businessman due to arrive soon. That would be a real boon for those of us in a position to help him learn the ropes and keep him safe, if you know what I mean."

With a disgusted look on his face, Blade turned to face their uninvited guest, "Since when do you have any power to protect anyone 'round here? You may be able to herd some goats, but you know that wolves eat goats, dontcha?"

Guntherd pushed his tray a few inches away from him and stared down at the blank table in front of him. "Are you threatening me, Thomas?"

Turning back to cut a piece of his Salisbury steak with his spoon, Blade attempted to defuse the situation. "Be reasonable, '214. You was the one to suggest to extortin' money from my friend here."

"I ain't doing nothing different than what you're doing? You're just trying to pick his pocket by being his friend."

Could this be true? Could it be that Blade was trying to get on Paol's good side to receive favors in the form of extra money for the commissary? Or was this Guntherd character really good at manipulation. Paol wondered if he had let his guard down with his new cellmate and was too quick to abandon the rule Warron had given him to "trust no one!"

"No matter," Blade stated shrugging his shoulders. "Joonter ain't worth nothin' anyway."

"You're lying, Slater!"

"Let me rephrase my sentence," Blade responded in measured tones. "He ain't worth nothin' in here. Fo' the last three days, Paol's been followin' me 'round to learn all 'bout the prison. In three trips to the commissary, he ain't bought nothin'. So, I asked him, 'why ain't you buyin' nothin'? He says, 'I ain't got no money.' So, I asks, 'Whatcha mean? Every prisoner's got money. We all work, we all get paid—not much, but 'nough to buy stuff.' And you know what he says?" Slater turned back to Guntherd who was still looking at the table.

Blade went on after pausing long enough to know that Schenthtzen wasn't going to respond to the question. "He says, 'I arranged with the warden to send all of my money to my family.'"

"This stuffed suit's family doesn't need any money," Guntherd pointed an accusing finger at Paol. "You are full of—"

215

Slater raised his hand to cut off Schenthtzen before he could complete his sentence. "I ain't full of nothin', '214, 'cuz you won't let me eat my meat and potatoes. You see, Paol ain't sendin' money to a needy family. He's a smart man, and he learned how to survive tough competition. That business survival instinct is servin' well in prison. The reason he's sendin' his money home, is 'cuz he knew he'd be a target. If he ain't got no money, he can't become prey to nobody, includin' you, Guntherd. Sorry to disappoint, but you might wanna spread the word that Joonter ain't worth nobody's time."

As prisoner number 689214 stalked off with his tray of food untouched, Paol looked Blade in the eyes and gave a grateful nod. In the commotion of the courtyard after lunch, Paol got a chance to ask Blade about the exchange.

"But we haven't even been to the commissary once, Blade."

"I only go on Mondays, but Goat Herd don't know that, 'cuz his commissary schedule is different than ours."

"I suppose this means that I won't be able to buy anything while I'm here," Paol opined, "but that appears to be better than the ugly alternative that I just witnessed back in the cafeteria."

"I thinks you just need to wait a few weeks. Once Goat Herd's intel makes the rounds, you'll be hands off, and the dust of the newness will settle down. Then, you should have no problem buyin' anythin' you want. But, you might wanna give it to me for safe keepin' until we get back to the cell— just in case we pass one of Guntherd's goats."

...

That night, as Paol lay sleepless in his bunk, he couldn't help but think that he dodged a bullet already in his brief tenure at the penitentiary. He wondered how many more close calls he'd have with prisoners, but at least for now, he was grateful for the quick thinking of his cellmate.

How could he have such bad luck to end up in prison in the first place, and yet have such good luck to be led to the most helpful person in the entire prison? And how is it that a self-educated young man from the ghetto could be so important to the well-being of a post-graduate engineer and successful businessman? It all seemed so ironic. Perhaps it was fate. Maybe fate led Paol here to become acquainted with Blade. Perhaps Warron would soon find the evidence he needed to bring the case to justice once and for all, and when released, the roles would be turned. Whereas Blade Slater was Paol

Joonter's savior in prison, Paol would be there to protect Slater as he adapted to society in his post-prison life.

Paol gave up belief in something divine years ago. But for the first time in ages, Paol could see potential purpose—fate-guided purpose—to his ordeal. In the long dark hours of the night he wondered if there really was something called fate, and if so was it fair and balanced? Did it have the foresight to turn even the ugliest of present situations into meaningful futures? Or was fate just the godless embodiment of hope that he needed to cling to in a meaningless world?

Chapter

20

"So, you knew all along!" Kath exclaimed in disbelief, hitting Joram on the shoulder as they approached Professor Zimmer's office.

"Not all along," Joram downplayed his discovery. "In hindsight, I think Zimmer knew even before I did."

"Why do you say that?"

"Just a hunch. Do you remember the last meeting we had in the conference room at Johnson? The one where we were deciding what to do with the last three paddles?"

Kath nodded while looking intently into Joram's face as the graduate students pressed on down the long hall of the astronomy building and stopped abruptly at the professor's office door.

"I suspect that Zimmer knew what I was thinking all along, and that is why he pressed me on the matter. I saw a look of surprise when I suggested ramming the beam upstream at full speed, almost as if my thoughts betrayed me to him. At the time, I thought that if the paddles were simply disappearing, because they were being driven by the beam faster than the speed of light, then we might be able to see more of the trajectory of that paddle as it did an abrupt U-turn towards the downstream and disappeared. By seeing the negative rate of acceleration, we would be able to ballpark the speed of the particles in the beam. The bottom line is that I thought I read something in his expression that may have indicated he knew what I was thinking. I'm fairly certain that he had already guessed what the beam was doing. He just needed enough evidence to convince himself and the scientific community."

"But, how did he guess? Why would he guess something so preposterous? During thousands of years of recorded human history, nobody has ever seen anything traveling faster than the speed of light. It's so… so… unrelativistic."

"I prefer anti-relativistic," said a familiar raspy voice approaching Kath from behind.

Kath gave a start. "Oh, professor… I didn't know you were there."

"I see you two are right on time," acknowledged the astrophysicist tapping on his wrist watch as he unlocked the door to his office. Looking down the hall in both directions, he continued. "But where is…"

At that moment, Reyd appeared briskly from around the corner of the hall which Zimmer was facing.

"Ah, there is Mr. Eastman now." He opened the door and invited his research team into his office for the appointed meeting which all three students had been eagerly anticipating.

It was Joram's first time in the hallowed—almost sacred—room. It was much smaller than he would've guessed, and he couldn't help wonder how some of the brightest ideas of their day could come from such a humble office. If only he could interview the walls, painted in light beige; the desk, with its three modest stacks of papers; the laptop computer, which was turned on, but currently showed a black screen, as if to purposefully veil all of the secrets that were maintained inside.

There were shelves above every counter and desktop, housing an array of books, many authored or co-authored by Zimmer himself: "Quantum Forces of Nature", "Astronomical Phenomena: Current Research on Unsolved Issues in the Universe", "The Big Bang and Zeta Theory", "Intergalactic Space and Matter", "Advanced Particle Physics." At the end of the room was a window with blinds pulled up, revealing a portion of the rooftop of Zimmer's namesake planetarium. A hint of sunlight bathed a small corner of the office as the afternoon wore on. There was a slight hum and low tick of a wall clock above the main desk.

Zimmer invited his students to a round white oak table with four padded chairs. As they settled in, he grabbed a CalTech coffee mug filled with water, a notepad, and a pen before joining the students.

"Let me start with Miss Mirabelle's question, first."

"What question, Professor?"

"I think it was something along the lines of… 'How would he have guessed something so absurd?' Was that the question you just asked outside my office, Ms. Mirabelle?"

Kath blushed, while Joram relished this rare off-guard moment with a smile. Reyd laughed heartily at her gaffe. "Oh, Professor… I'm… I'm sorry. It was impertinent of me."

Joram's smile fell open suddenly. Was that an apology? From Kath Mirabelle? It must've been a first, he thought.

"No, no… not at all, Miss Mirabelle. In fact…" his voice trailed off with his thought. He stood up and went to his desk searching for something in one of the stacks of papers. "Ah, here it is."

He returned to the table with a crisp piece of paper recently printed out. He placed the paper in front of Kath and asked her to read the blue-highlighted portion of a news article from the U.S.A. Today website.

"In an announcement which has rattled the scientific community, world-renowned astronomer, Carlton Zimmer issued a statement from the California Institute of Technology theorizing on a discovery of 'warp'ed proportions…"

"Ah, yes… I love that statement," Zimmer interrupted. With childlike excitement, he thrust a finger at the word 'warp.' "Clever, isn't it? It's a double entendre on the word warp, meaning both faster than the speed of light, and also implying that I've just plain lost my marbles. Please do continue, Miss Mirabelle."

Stunned by his careless attitude towards the disrespect of the journalist, Kath continued slower than before. "The continually-studied yellow beam, he claims, consists of matter which is traveling faster than the speed of light—a superluminal comet. If his theory proves correct, he'll have Albert Einstein turning in his grave for defusing his heretofore unchallenged Theory of Relativity."

After a brief pause, Zimmer indicated to Kath, "If you wouldn't mind, Miss Mirabelle, please read the last paragraph as well."

"Ironically, it was this same Dr. Zimmer who—years earlier—was quoted as saying, 'it would be absurd to assume that anything could ever travel faster than the speed of light. There is a good reason why we've never observed such travel—it is because it simply cannot occur.' Now Zimmer finds himself in the awkward position of having to prove Einstein—and himself—wrong."

"You see, Miss Mirabelle," Zimmer now got to the point. "There is nothing shameful about challenging my position. In fact, they used the same word that you did, 'absurd.' The criticism is coming from everywhere. Am I truly warped? Is my position preposterous? Certainly!" Leaning over the table was an effective mechanism for gaining every bit of attention of his students. "Until I can prove otherwise." He sat back up, waiting for the questions to begin.

"Can you?" asked Reyd.

"Easily, Mr. Eastman. The data is very convincing, and once I've had a chance to convey it properly in a paper that will be published in the Journal of Astrophysics, some—but not all—of the disbelief will be assuaged."

"What do you mean by 'some', Professor?" asked Joram.

"Mr. Anders, I will be able to show evidence that the material that created that beam is traveling faster than the speed of light. But, I still won't be able to prove *how* that is happening. I do have some speculation, but scientists will continue to live in denial of the claim until they are shown how this phenomenon occurs."

"But, how did you solve that, Professor? And what evidence will you list in the paper to prove it?"

Zimmer's expression clouded over, and Kath slowly turned her head to assess what the astrophysicist was studying on the wall behind her. Finding nothing, she turned back to realize that Zimmer was caught up in a thought, or perhaps a memory, which caused him deep concern.

"A few years ago," Zimmer began with a slow hoarse whisper, still staring at the wall behind him, "I met someone who—"

All three students leaned in closer to the table when Zimmer paused mid-sentence. Returning from somewhere else, Zimmer blinked, smiled, and looked one after the other at the trio of graduate students seated before him. "I met two men who tried to convince me that Hyperwarp travel is feasible. They were very convincing. I was certain that they knew it could be done."

Reyd asked curiously. "Why haven't they published their findings, if they were so convincing?"

"Because… they were silenced."

Kath gasped as a dark expression clouded Zimmer's face.

"You mean—they were paid off?" Reyd suggested the most positive meaning for Zimmer's ambiguity after giving a concerned look in Kath's direction.

Zimmer sighed and shrugged his shoulders. "I never did get a straight answer from them as to what happened, but I have a suspicion that they will come out and share everything… it's a fascinating story."

Quickly changing the subject, Zimmer stood up, and returned to the topic of their research. "Let me come back to the subject at hand. You asked, Ms. Mirabelle, how I came to realize that we were dealing with a superluminal body. You see, shortly after paddle nine ceased communicating with the USL, there was one final heartbeat received from it. There were at least three things that didn't add up. First, the timestamp of the final blip indicated a time on the clock that was too early. Relativistic experiments show that the clock of an object approaching the speed of light will slow down. This clock had obviously slowed down significantly. Second, the modulated signal was recovered at an ultra-low frequency, indicating a huge Doppler shift. The paddle was still alive, but it was booking. Third, the positional information conveyed in that final blip indicated that the paddle had already traveled farther down the beam than it possibly could have in the allowed time. As a result, I concluded that the beam had a force that was quickly accelerating the paddles to a velocity approaching the speed of light, but in order to accelerate an object with significant mass to near the speed of light, the material in the beam must have been traveling *faster* than the speed of light itself."

After giving the students a chance to digest this epiphany, he continued. "Then there were paddles eleven and twelve. Remember how quickly paddle eleven turned downstream and spun out of control? Even Kath's paddle twelve gained acceleration way too quickly for mission control to handle it. Based on the amount of impact that was collected by the paddles' sensors, the acceleration was simply too fast. The material that was powering those paddles must have been traveling faster than the speed of light."

"But we saw the material in the beam… it was glowing yellow. How would we be able to see it if it traveled faster than the speed of light?" Kath pointed out with more curiosity than skepticism.

"Yes, you did see material in the beam, but that wasn't the stuff that was propelling the paddles. What powered the acceleration was material you could not see. The paddles were able to detect this matter, but it could not identify it."

Zimmer turned to look out the window and weighed his thoughts before turning back to the table. "I trust that all of you have studied at least basic particle physics in your undergraduate programs?"

All three heads nodded.

"Good… then you are aware that the quantum state of particles can be altered. For example, it is the weak nuclear force that causes radioactive decay, inducing some of the heavier elements to shed protons and neutrons, thus changing their atomic structure. At the sub-atomic level, fundamental particles can decay into entirely different fundamental particles. I surmise that the superluminal comet which is currently orbiting the black hole at the center of our Milky Way consists of a very large clump of quantum material. As the particles on the surface decay, they do so from a state which is able to travel faster than the speed of light to a state which is not able to travel faster than the speed of light. Once they have decayed into this state, they must decelerate quickly, shedding off energy in the form of photons which we are able to see with our very eyes."

"But what is the stuff that we can't see, and how can it break the rules of relativity to travel faster than the speed of light?" asked Joram.

"Ah that is the question, isn't it?" Zimmer pointed out. "Scientists, in general, think we know so much more about the universe than we really do. For example, for all of our observational astrophysics, we really can only see less than five percent of the universe. The remainder consists of dark matter and dark energy. Thus, for all of our knowledge about this universe, it may only apply to the five percent we can actually see. Do all of the discovered laws of physics apply to the other 95%? For example, we know that dark matter is subject to gravity. It clearly exerts gravitational forces, because that is how we detected it in the first place. Otherwise, we have no way of explaining the gravitational effects on the universe without introducing the concept of dark matter. Now, while this unseen substance is subject to gravity, it does not interact with the photon—the carrier for the electromagnetic force. If it were subject to electromagnetism, we would be able to detect its presence on the EM spectrum, but we cannot. Let me define the term 'observational physics' to therefore mean the set of universal laws which apply to everything *which can be observed*. Traditionally that which can be observed is subject to light so that we can see it. Light is nothing more than the electromagnetic force, demonstrated through its carrier, the photon. The reason that nothing observable can travel faster than the speed of light is because it is *subject to light*."

He paused again. "Let me repeat that. Nothing which we can see is able to travel faster than the speed of light because it is *subject to light*."

The proverbial light bulb came on for Joram. "Professor! I see what you're saying. Matter that can be seen—particularly baryonic matter—must travel no faster than the speed of light, because it is subject to the properties which constrain light itself. The corollary to this would be that if there is matter which is *not* subject to light—such as dark matter—then that matter may *not* be subject to the speed of light."

"Exactly!"

Joram continued his thought process. "Non-baryonic matter may indeed be traveling around faster than the speed of light."

Kath had to interrupt at this point to keep from getting lost in the conversation. "Professor, I remember the term baryon, but I forget. Is that the stuff that has the integer spin or half-integer spin?"

"You're thinking of bosons and fermions, Miss Mirabelle. So much jargon for one year of study, I know. When we talk about baryons, we are usually referring to the triple combination of up and down quarks that comprise the neutron and the proton, so really it makes up the bulk of matter that we interact with."

"That's right… sorry about that." Kath hung her head in embarrassment for having to ask the question.

"Mr. Anders, your thought was that this non-baryonic matter *may* travel faster than the speed of light, but it might be even more than that. I've been thinking a lot about this, since we left Johnson last weekend. My thought is that the real reason that this matter is not subject to electromagnetism is because it *must* be traveling faster than the speed of light. That is, once matter—non-baryonic, or otherwise—escapes the effects of electromagnetism, it is guaranteed to travel faster than the speed of light. That mystical constant, c, which we know to be equal to 299,792,458 meters per second, could be considered the escape velocity of electromagnetism. Once any matter can exceed that velocity, the electromagnetic force no longer applies. So, we cannot see dark matter, nor can we see our superluminal comet, simply because they are traveling around in the universe faster than the speed of light. Thus, they are no longer subject to the force of the photon, which we know can travel no faster than c, you see?"

Three eagerly nodding heads indicated that they did see. Heaving an exhausted sigh, Zimmer sat back in his seat now that he could tell that his researchers were beginning to comprehend these brand new ideas.

. . .

Joram Anders sat alone on a bench by a paved walkway, watching the sun dip below the top of the pine trees across the large vacant field to the West. A family of four passed through a door after their visit to the Hale Telescope, returned to their car, and drove off. While open to visitors during the day, few continued to make the long, windy drive up the mountain to enjoy the history of the aging observatory. Overshadowed by so many newer, larger and more important telescopes, most haven't even heard of the 200-inch mirror, nor realized the fact that way back in the 20th century, it was the largest telescope in the world for a while.

Distracted by a whirlwind of thoughts, it took several efforts for Kath to get his attention. "Joram. Joram!"

"Oh, Kath... sorry I didn't see you there."

"When I didn't see you in the dormitory, I assumed you must still be sleeping," she stated.

"Oh, no... I come out here every evening. I never get tired of watching the sun set from up here."

"I didn't know this was such a favorite spot of yours."

"I suppose you wouldn't... you usually sleep until well after the sun sets," Joram elbowed Kath playfully as she took a seat next to him on the bench. Eying her suspiciously, he asked, "Why are you up so early this evening?"

225

"I got a phone call with great news," she beamed. "The astronauts at Camp Mars have been recovered. They are a suffering from exhaustion, and some mild bumps and bruises, but otherwise, they're going to be just fine! The rescue vehicle just launched from Mars, and is on the way home."

Joram took in a deep breath and leaned back on the bench. "That is great news indeed! It must've been a horrifying experience for them."

"Yeah, I can't wait to hear their story," Kath stated as she turned her gaze to the West, Kath observed, "Well, I can see why you enjoy it here. Such a beautiful sunset, and so quiet." "Sunsets in Kansas could be pretty spectacular, but the horizon always left something to be desired. It was so flat. No pine trees, no mountains. Just flat, waving fields of grain."

Looking at his watch, Joram suggested that it was time for dinner. The two stood from the bench as the last strong rays of the sun penetrated the atmosphere, bathing the clouds in brilliant yellows, pinks, and oranges, contrasting them to the blue and purple of the sky.

They met Reyd for dinner in the common room of the astronomers' dormitory and the threesome engaged in pleasant small talk, but they were distracted by all that had happened in the last few weeks. The disaster on Mars, the mysterious yellow beam, the mission at Johnson Space Center, the discovery of the superluminal comet created a mental overload, and in fact, all three had been dealing with an increase in headaches, insomnia, and fatigue. Even Joram recognized in himself a diminished ambition for the work ahead of them that evening. The mental stress and exhaustion was starting to affect each researcher.

The situation was not much better for Carlton Zimmer. Being advanced in years, having been ridiculed for his near-obsessive interest in finding a parallel earth, and now enduring near rejection by the scientific community for the anti-relativistic and heretical proposal that there was an object—right in their own galaxy—which was traveling around the center of the Milky Way faster than the speed of light were each starting to add up and take their toll on the relentless astrophysicist. While he tried to put on his best face, his graduate students were not oblivious to his suffering.

"I'm worried about Zimmer," Kath said while poking at her mashed potatoes. "Have you guys noticed how tired his eyes look, and how pale his complexion is."

"Yeah," Reyd agreed. "I've been around Zimmer for three years now, and I've never seen him look so unhealthy. His whole countenance almost appears sunken, defeated."

"Which is all the more reason," Joram realized out loud, "that he needs our help in piecing all of this together. We need to convince the world that he his right!"

"But what if he's not right this time?" asked Reyd.

"You don't believe him?" Kath's jaw dropped in disappointment of her colleague.

"All I'm saying, Kath, is that there's still a lot of speculation. We can't exactly track down that comet and catch it can we?"

"Actually, we can." Joram announced flatly.

"What?" Kath and Reyd both turned their attention to him.

"I overheard Zimmer last week explain that we were going to continue to study the beam to determine its exact speed and orbital path. That's what we're going to start doing tonight. He suspects that it's traveling fast enough to orbit the galaxy once every five years."

"Five years! Absurd. I mean, if we're going to see it five years from now, why didn't we see it five years ago as well?" Reyd shook his head and wrinkled his forehead as he worked the math, mumbling numbers incoherently. "26000 light years... two-pi-r... five years..." And then announcing his results out loud. "You see, the old man may be losing it. He's not suggesting that this thing is traveling at $1.2c$, or even $3.5c$. He's talking tens of thousands of times the speed of light. I really think Zimmer may be losing it. Not that I'm criticizing—he's been through a lot recently. He might just need some time off."

"He might just need some students to roll up their sleeves and get the work done," Joram countered with a calm voice and yet a hot look in his eyes. "Let's just get in there and see what we can discover, ok?"

Too tired and drained to fight, Reyd nodded and continued nibbling on his sandwich. "Mmm... this is pretty good," he said with one cheek full of corned beef and marbled rye, a hint of brown mustard in the corner of his mouth. All three recognized it as a lame, yet genuine attempt to change the subject. Quiet settled over the table, but their thoughts were still rampant as Zimmer walked in to escort the group to the 26-inch telescope.

A glimmer of light cast the still treetops into a gray silhouette against a violet sky. Joram strained to see the yellow beam, but it had faded so much now that it was no use attempting to spot it with the naked eye anymore. No matter! He would be using Palomar-26 for the next several hours in order to continue to study the trajectory of the comet. Could it really be tens of thousands times the speed of light? Would they really get another fly-by in just five years? And if so, would they be able to take advantage of it? Even if NASA was able to inject a probe directly in its path, it would be pulverized. How could they possibly be able to study it and determine its makeup?

So many thoughts, so many questions, so many distractions. Patience is the proper prescription for just such a time. Joram had his whole life ahead of him to study these exciting and difficult challenges, and preparing himself under the tutelage of Carlton Zimmer was just the beginning of a promising lifelong adventure that hopefully could be just a small bit as fulfilling as Zimmer's had been.

...

"It might take me a while to develop that model, Professor," Reyd assessed.

"I understand. Better to get started right away then, Mr. Eastman."

"And the model may take a while to simulate. With billions of stars being flown by, it will take an inordinate number of calculations just to get hundreds or thousands of orbits, and I don't have all of the parameters yet. We still need to know the shape and duration of the orbit."

"Mr. Anders, Miss Mirabelle, and I will be working on getting you those parameters as quickly as possible. I trust that you'll be able to develop the model with placeholders in the meantime?"

"Yes, sir. But let me make sure I understand the task at hand. You want to know every star which has encountered a fly-by of about two million miles of the comet in the last 50000 years. Is that right?"

"That's correct."

"Professor, how will that help us in our study of the beam?" Kath inquired earnestly.

"Once we figure out the orbit of our comet, Miss Mirabelle, we will be able to compare it to any interactions of stars or planets with which the comet has interacted. For example, let's say that Reyd's model finds a star about

228

10000 light years away. If we can project that the comet came to within a couple of million miles of that star and any planets in its solar system, about 9,998 years ago, then we can be fairly confident that the interaction between the comet and that star's solar system will be observed by us in the next couple of years. We can keep an eye out for any and all such systems that might help us understand the makeup of the comet by determining the type of radiation that is being generated by the material that is shed by the comet as it orbits the galaxy."

"But we couldn't even detect the radiation that occurred when we were affected a couple of months ago," Kath posed curiously.

"It is true that we observed a radiation impact here on Earth as well as on the sun, and that we didn't determine what it was. However, we were blind-sided by that event. We just weren't prepared for it. Further, don't forget that NASA is bringing back samples of soil and debris from Mars with the rescue mission, and it could well be that extensive interviews with astronauts O'Ryan and Boronov might prove useful as well. Since the comet practically grazed Mars, we might get a lot of answers right there. Ideally, we'll be positioned to find a star that experienced a similar fly-by, which would interact with the star in such a manner as to generate a radiation event to be studied here on Earth in the near term. Therefore, we really need Reyd to focus on programming that model for us, so we know which of the billions of stars we'll want to focus on to study this phenomenon in the future."

"Professor," It was Joram's turn to join in on the interrogation. "If this comet has been orbiting the solar system for a long time now, why is this the first time that we've noticed the beam? You suggested that it may be orbiting every five years. Why wouldn't we have seen it five, or ten, or any number of its previous orbits."

"I think we need to figure out that there is an orbit, and what shape it entails. Remember that it was a fairly thin beam to the naked eye when it was just a million miles away. What if it were ten million or more miles away during its last fly-by. Because our solar system is orbiting the galaxy, it could well be that our orbits do not coincide very well, but have now come together close enough to observe it. Again, we won't know for sure until we get a closer look at the orbit and the speed of the comet.

"Any other questions, or shall we get to it?"

Everybody understood this invitation to be more of a command. The time for questioning an astronomer is during daylight hours. The time for action was now!

Reyd quickly assumed his position on the far side of the room, at the computer terminal where Kath once studied the meteorological effects of the wind storm on Mars. Joram and Kath sat down at the main terminal, while Zimmer assumed a position on the telescope platform in order to search for the current trajectory of the beam in its orbit. It was a tedious night of work for the team. Reyd worked as quickly as he could on programming the mathematics into the computer to simulate the comet. Joram, Kath, and the professor took measurements, calculated, took more measurements, calculated some more, and then took the same measurements and calculated all over. For Reyd's model to have the precision that it needed, they had to figure out the orbit of the comet with the utmost of quality. Otherwise, deviations in the model would contribute to gross errors in calculation as the computer calculated the projected location of the comet backwards for tens and hundreds of thousands of years.

Towards dawn, the professor handed Reyd the data to plug into the computer.

Upon reviewing and crunching some preliminary numbers, Reyd had to admit that he was wrong. "Professor, I just don't understand how this can be! Based on the absolute magnitude of the beam, and the position of is trajectory, it is in an elliptical orbit around the center of the galaxy with an orbit of 6.369 years."

"Hmmm," the professor thought out loud as he rubbed his forehead. "I was quite a bit off in my estimates. I was thinking just under 5 years. Maybe the orbit is more elliptical than I had imagined."

"No matter, Professor," said Reyd in astonishment. "This is simply massive. When and how did you know it was going so fast?"

"You all seem surprised that this thing is traveling so fast. I'm guessing that means you all missed the most important clue. Miss Mirabelle, what happens when you are standing on a sidewalk, and a large truck travels by with immense speed?"

"Well, it's normally very loud… and it generates a lot of wind."

230

"Exactly! It's very similar to our comet. When it flew by at approximately 25000c, it expelled a radiation wind that not only devastated Mars, but remember… it also took out all three satellites and the Mars Shuttle simultaneously. Remember how it was all timed in exact simultaneity with radiation detection on Earth as well as solar activity from the Sun? All at the same time?"

Here, Zimmer paused to make sure his students could see where he was going. "The truth is that those events weren't exactly synchronized, but when something is traveling at tens of thousands of times the speed of light, you don't exactly have the ability to calculate the timing of the event to as many decimal places needed. I've been thinking about the timing mystery for a long time, and the only thought I could come up with was that something was traveling a whole lot faster than it should be."

Heads nodded slowly. A knowing smile came across the face of Joram Anders as if to say, "Why didn't I think of that?"

Zimmer c, "In the meantime, we need to find as many fly-bys that we can study, so get those numbers crunching. When we return here in two weeks, we'll need to get busy studying those star systems which are closest to delivering a radiation signature from the comet in the past."

"Yes, sir," answered Reyd, spinning around in his seat to face the computer. Typing furiously and finishing with an elaborate twist of the wrist on the enter key, Reyd started executing the program on a distributed system of hundreds of supercomputers that Zimmer had at his disposal throughout a university and government intranet. For now, all that the exhausted students and their mentor could do was wait for the results.

...

For Joram, it seemed like the slowest two weeks of his life. The thrill of returning to Palomar for hands-on study of the galaxy was so much more rewarding than the textbook study of astronomy. It was like those two weeks leading up to his ninth Christmas where he had asked for that first pair of star goggles. But now, he was even more excited as the research team consulted with Zimmer over a growing list of candidate star systems for study. A few possibilities had emerged within a couple of days. With more time the list grew to dozens, and by Friday morning, just before Kath and Joram drove up to Palomar, thousands of candidates had emerged.

231

Prioritizing the list was difficult. They knew that they needed to focus on those stars whose fly-bys of the comet would be closest to reaching Earth, and yet the list of stars which could possibly be studied in the next couple of months numbered around fifty. Of those, about a half dozen appeared prominent among stars which may have had the closest fly-by. After much deliberation with his team and consideration on his own, Zimmer selected ZB-5344, a class F9 main sequence star about 27000 light years from Earth. A fly-by of the comet was calculated at just 2.3 million miles, making it a target for intense study by the team.

As the team entered the Palomar-26 observatory, Zimmer briefed his trio of research students on the agenda for the evening. "We first point our 26 to ZB-5344 in an effort to find any extrasolar planets orbiting the star. There is data in the ZB catalog suggesting the possibility of planets due to minor movements discovered in the star—wobbles that may indicate orbiting planets, especially those whose brush with the comet may have been closer than the star itself. If so, we will certainly want to study those planets for any radiation that may have ricocheted off of the planet, which might be indicative of the destructive forces of the comet on Mars. 2.3 million miles will be an interesting study, but if we can find planets which may have a closer fly-by, then those planets will be of extreme interest. Once we've detected any spectral data suggesting the location of planets, we have Kepler3 on standby for further study. I think everyone knows their duties, right?"

All three heads bobbed affirmatively.

"Are there any questions?"

After a moment of silence, Zimmer spurred the team to work. The pattern of searching for planets around the fly-by stars, relaying location information to Kepler3, and continuing throughout the star system would persist all night. They needed to work furiously to cover all six or seven stars on the short list over the weekend, because by the time the supercomputer network had an opportunity to crunch two more weeks of numbers, the short list may grow into the dozens or even hundreds of stars, all but outpacing the team's inadequate efforts to keep up with the data collection of Reyd's model.

The team communicated details noisily throughout the evening.

"Professor, the movement of ZB-5344 indicates a plane of planetary activity about 65 degrees to the plane of the galaxy."

"Kath, can you confirm that from Earth's perspective, there's a 12 degree angle, not quite edge-on, but it should narrow down the field of play."

"Based on the mass of 5344, it looks like the system should have gravitational effect on its planets to about 100 AUs. Can we calculate a field of study for the orbital area of interest, Mr. Anders?"

Effectively, in finding planets that were 27000 light years from Earth, the team was looking for a needle in a haystack. Even narrowing down the effort to just one star, the field of study was immense. The effective field of view was about 200 Astronomical Units tall by 50 wide. That represents an area which would be 10^{20} times larger than the visible area of Jupiter. So, if the team were to find a Jupiter-sized planet in such a large place, the odds of any given search yielding the location of that planet would be 1 in 10^{20}.

Of course, the team would not simply pick random points within the total possible planetary field and point the telescope there. They were able to calculate the presumed plane of the planets in orbit around ZB-5344. Projecting the orbit of the comet back in time about 27000 years, they found a point where the orbital line passed through the plane at the distance of a couple of million miles away from the star. They could then narrow down the search to an orbit around ZB-5344 which would traverse through the intersection of the plane and the orbit of the comet.

For a couple of hours, the team slowly scanned the segment of sky in question. Up. Down. Left. Right. Orbital motions around the star. The telescope worked its way around the orbit of interest. At long last, an infrared detection was discovered, indicating a pinpoint of heat in the otherwise blackness of space.

Zimmer came down from the telescope platform to inspect the data on the monitor. "Let's zoom in on that point Mr. Anders, and please sharpen the visual data, Mr. Eastman."

The students worked at the computer, each typing away at his respective keyboard.

"Miss Mirabelle, please run a full spectral analysis."

"Yes, professor."

After a few silent moments, Kath blurted, "Professor, this could be interesting. Come take a look."

Zimmer, who was standing over Joram's shoulder walked over to Kath's terminal, with Joram and Reyd following quickly behind. On Kath's screen appeared a low resolution circular shape. Towards the bottom left, the circle was filled with red, but about a quarter of the circle in the upper right was filled with a more reddish-purple color, and the upper right hand edge was nearly blue.

"Exactly right, Miss Mirabelle! 5344 sits down here," Zimmer pointed off the bottom left side of the screen. "Your temperature distribution demonstrates that the warm side of our dot faces the star, whereas the cooler side—this purplish blue color on the fringe—is away from the star. We have an uncatalogued planet, here, team. Great work—an excellent discovery."

"Actually, it was more a bit of luck than real work," Reyd pointed out. "I mean, we just happened to find a planet exactly in the orbit where we pointed the telescope. What are the odds of that?"

"In this game, odds don't matter, Mr. Eastman. It's the discovery that counts, and you can now add ZB-5344 to the list of known stars harboring the galaxy's five million known extrasolar planets. I'll contact the Kepler3 team, and they'll be able to perform a high-optics visual of the planet to see what we've got."

Zimmer dismissed the team for a break, since he knew that the moon-orbiting Kepler3 telescope would require at least an hour of calibration and location tuning before the first images of planet ZB-5344-P1 would be available for study. After the break, the team pulled chairs close to a computer monitor, and lounged around while watching a black screen with red text that spelled, "Awaiting Kepler3 Imaging." The text flashed every few seconds to garner the attention of the spectators.

"Wow… watching telescopes calibrate is like watching paint dry," Reyd broke the silence.

"Mr. Eastman, I'm surprised at you," offered the astrophysicist in mock disgust. "I personally think it's more like watching grass grow."

Exhausted and giddy, the students laughed raucously at Zimmer's humor. Another wake-up call occurred in the moments that followed, as Zimmer's cell phone chirped loudly throughout the room.

Kath jumped instinctively while Joram stood upright. In the quiet of the room, the students were able to hear the hurried voice on the other side.

"Professor Zimmer, we're shooting the first images your way right now. You've got to see this, Sir—we're still—well, we're not sure, but you'll see."

"What do you have, Mr. Jefferies? You sound like you've never seen an extrasolar planet before."

"Actually, Professor, it's quite the opposite. It's exactly like I *have* seen this planet before. Why, at a glance it looks just like—"

The cell phone went dead the moment the image came across, as Zimmer unconsciously dropped it to the floor with a reverberating thud that nobody heard.

In shock, Joram slowly stood from his seat and was the first to complete the sentence of the Kepler3 team member on the other line. The word was slow, breathy and nearly inaudible.

"—Earth!"

Chapter

21

With hands clasped behind his back, Carlton Zimmer stood erect admiring the picture on the wall in the black elliptical room. The Von Karman Bicentennial Museum at NASA's Jet Propulsion Laboratory in Pasadena was the most impressive public display ever created by NASA. The brainchild of a billionaire space explorer, the intent was to depict the purpose of continued space exploration as it relates to discoveries that help the human race understand the universe we live in. Fronting a hundred million dollars to the effort, the museum quickly became one of the most popular attractions in Southern California.

While the main room of the museum appeared to be perfectly circular, it was proportionally accurate to the elliptical orbit of the Earth. It was nearly 320 feet long by 310 feet wide. The perimeter of the room contained some digital and interactive displays containing images taken by the moon-orbiting Kepler3 telescope. Exhibits scattered around the room were situated as to replicate the locations of the orbits of Venus and Mercury, with a bright globe light suspended from the ceiling to represent the Sun. The black ceiling featured recessed projection LED lighting which gave an appearance of a night sky, accurately depicting the sky as it would appear over the JPL campus at midnight on the Summer Solstice. Light intensity varied to indicate stars with more or less apparent magnitude. Every attempt at authenticity was made, including colors of red, yellow, pink, and blue indicating differences in surface temperature and Doppler shifting.

At this moment, Zimmer was admiring the imagery of the Hourglass Nebula. Unlike most museum visitors, however, who simply admire the conical orange circles of emitting gas and the superheated blue center resembling the piercing Eye of Providence for its visual impact, Zimmer's fascination was one of nostalgia. He reminisced over the intense focus and studies that led to important discoveries about the nature of stellar winds and solar radiation which improved the safety of inner Solar System exploration.

The work on the Hourglass prevented catastrophes similar to the doomed Mercury-S55 mission, where critical navigational equipment was significantly impaired by radical deviations in solar radiation. The inability of NASA and the government to agree on the logistics, mechanics, and cost of a rescue mission to save the astronauts resulted in a black eye for NASA and a landslide loss for the President of the United States. Instead, the astronauts survived on rations for months while the spaceship trajectory was pulled into an orbit around the Sun. The orbiting tomb was a symbol of failure for nearly two decades before the orbit degraded sufficiently to eventually melt and disintegrate the vehicle entirely.

Zimmer turned away from the outer wall to look at some of the exhibits on the floor. Appropriately, on the outer-most floor display, which represented the orbit of Venus, his eye rested on a wrap-around folding panel of Earth's nearest sister planet. He remembered, as an adolescent, watching the televised broadcasts of the first Venus landing by an astronaut. Many robotic missions had already occurred on Venus, but no astronaut had ever been. Public sentiment was mixed on the excursion, considering that much had already been discovered about Venus through the robotic and satellite missions to the planet, but further, many worried about the violent heat and pressure of the Venetian atmosphere. Could the astronauts' spacesuits be designed to protect against the massive atmospheric pressure of Venus? Materials scientists were confident that the astronauts would be able to move about and be safely protected even under the extreme pressures of the dense atmosphere of Venus. Nevertheless, for many, it seemed too risky to send humans to such a hostile environment for so little benefit. But they were wrong.

An inadvertent discovery had been made by physicians who studied the astronauts upon return to the Earth. Physicals showed that heart and brain activity were healthier and stronger in each astronaut compared to their respective measured activity just prior to departure. Through subsequent study, the cause had been shown to be the air that they were breathing. Scrubbers on the Venetian surface module and the astronauts' space suits were designed to convert the carbon dioxide into oxygen, but the atmosphere of Venus also contained trace quantities of materials which did not exist in Earth's atmosphere. A particular combination of such materials was shown to produce the desired effect. A medical treatment was devised from the discovery which aided in a host of common maladies as well as severe conditions.

While Zimmer didn't have many opportunities to come down to the museum, he always made a concerted effort to visit any time he came to JPL for business. With each rejuvenating visit, he felt like a child nearly a tenth of his age as he recollected the various scenes. To him, the Von Karman museum was like a hundred million dollar scrapbook of memories that he would never have been able to afford on his own, of course.

While lost in his nostalgia, he was returned promptly to Earth by a gentle touch on his right shoulder.

"Ballard," he said. "It looks like you found me!"

"I thought I might find you here," smiled the CalTech astronomy dean knowingly. "Like me, I know that it's hard not to stop at the museum when you're in the vicinity. You remember my son?"

Zimmer's gaze was turned in the direction indicated by Dean Scoville's outstretched hand.

"Ah, yes," nodded Zimmer as he reached out and grabbed the firm hand of Maril Scoville. "How long has it been? Three? Four years?"

"Actually, Doctor Zimmer, I think it's been about six years?"

"Six? Really?" Zimmer shook his head and focused on one of the stars in the ceiling, reaching for the memories that would help him set a correct timeline. "Gosh, time does fly. How is your family—six years must put your oldest child at about twelve now?"

"Jenny is thirteen actually, and she is quite the teenager."

"Thirteen. You know, I just can't picture it... she was just a wee little thing the last time I saw her—I think that was at your father's house."

"Well, the time has certainly flown by for my wife and me as well."

"Ballard told me about your wife's award a few months ago. What an amazing honor. You must congratulate her for me."

238

"Thank you, Professor. I'll be sure to extend your greetings to her."

Ballard broke up the pleasantries. "If you two are sufficiently caught up, I think we only have about 45 minutes before the meeting. I thought it would be good, Carlton, for you to give Maril a heads up on your thoughts, so we can be better prepared for the meeting."

"Yes, and thank you, Maril, for taking some extra time out of your schedule today. We have a topic of discussion that I think you'll find rather fascinating."

"Why don't we head over to my office where we can be more comfortable? It's just in the adjacent building."

With that, the three retired from the blazing stars and nighttime setting of the museum for the more glaring light of a misty morning fog that had settled over the area. Zimmer squinted as he adjusted from the thousands of imitation stars that were suddenly replaced by a gray circle of light hovering over the haze.

. . .

"Kelcey, please hold all of my calls," Maril requested as he walked briskly by his secretary's desk.

Recognizing his urgency, Kelcey simply nodded and smiled as the group of scientists convened their closed-door session in the program manager's office.

The three visited the coat rack first where damp overcoats were hung to dry before being seated around a small conference table.

Zimmer wasted no time. "Tell me how the Star Shield project is going, Maril."

"We think it's going very well, Doctor Zimmer. We're actually fabricating a prototype of the shield right now for a test flight that should occur in August of next year. We'll put it through the wind tunnel and bombard it with all sorts of nasty space debris at high-speed, hope that it doesn't even come close to scratching the surface, and then mount it to the prototype vehicle for its flight towards the Sun."

Something in Maril's delivery betrayed him. "And, so you think it will be able to handle particle impact near to Warp speed?"

"Oh, yes, yes we do."

Realizing that any doubts or concerns were not being volunteered by the young scientist, Zimmer grew more pointed in his interrogation. "So, what is your top concern about the project?"

Not feeling a desire to be frank, Maril said unconvincingly, "Well, to be frank, I'm just not sure about the viability of the project?"

"Oh?" said Zimmer prompting for more information, while the older Scoville sat back and watched the volley of questions and answers fly back and forth over the desk.

"I don't get the impression that the Star Drive team is making good progress on their propulsion experiments. I think they've made way too many trips to the drawing board to give me any warm and fuzzies about their current status. So, what good is the effort of my team, if we don't have the rockets to propel the vehicle to high speed?"

"Well, in that case, I guess you'd be over-designed, but at least you'll know that the shield will function perfectly at speeds lower than specified."

"But, what's the point?" opened up Maril. "I mean, we put our blood, sweat, and tears into this project for years, and to what end? For a slow craft? Or worse yet… to get the plug pulled? The scenarios are bitterly frustrating."

Zimmer leaned back. "Well, I'm here to offer you an exciting possibility that would end that frustration once and for all, Mr. Scoville."

Maril sat erect in his chair with intense curiosity. "Go ahead… you've certainly got my attention with that opening."

"Well, all this time, you've been preparing to mount your shield to the front of the Star Transport vehicle, right?"

"Yes," the response from the scientist was measured. "Although, I guess it would be more correct to say that it will be *molded* to the body of the vehicle. It's pretty much like a very thick skin that we will be growing from the shell of the spacecraft."

"Well, I propose that we put it on backwards!"

…

Carlton Zimmer stood from his chair and approached the front of the room. He chose to be at the end of the table, where he could better see all of the attendees, and look each and every one in the eye. While the astrophysicist was quickly regaining status and popularity for his recent discoveries of the superluminal comet and the parallel Earth, he knew that perhaps this hour would prove whether he still had more to give to humanity—one more peak in a career of Himalayan proportions.

He paused as he calculated each participant quickly in a clockwise manner. To his left sat Vurim Gilroy, the Mars Mission manager, effectively looking for a new job, since any subsequent Martian efforts had been put on hold at NASA. Then he saw Marrak Henley, the tight-fisted director of NASA. He knew Henley would be his toughest sale, which is why he had pulled some influence and invited a pair of Southern California congressmen to the meeting, just in case Henley needed reminding who his boss was. His eyes met the friendliest bodies in the group—namely, Ballard and Maril Scoville, whose support he knew would be invaluable. This high-powered group of eight was rounded out by directory of JPL, Rawson Cornell, who sat next to Maril, irritated with the fact that he was called to this secret meeting, knowing nothing about its intent, while suspecting that his subordinate had been better briefed than himself.

"Gentlemen," began Zimmer serenely with his hands clasped in front of him. "First, let me thank each of you for your attendance here today. I am well aware that you know nothing of which I would like to address you but am grateful that you have honored me with your attendance anyway.

"It is a particular honor, considering that my views and opinions have not been held in the highest regard lately. For years, I received ridicule for chasing after a parallel Earth—the proverbial needle in the haystack. I was severely reprimanded for heretically proposing that our yellow beam was a superluminal comet. Often, my views and projects have been simply too radical to accept. I have been called by peers and press 'crazy', 'warped', 'irrelevant.'

"Fortunately, for me," Zimmer said wiping his brow in a sign of relief, "some of the criticism has been appeased. For my fortunate discoveries of late, I have been restored to some degree of respect among my colleagues, but don't expect that to stop me from doing something foolish again." A few soft chuckles were heard in response to Zimmer's colorful delivery of the word 'foolish'.

"In fact, if any of you leave here today thinking I've been restored to my senses, then you clearly must be sleeping, because what I will suggest to you today will certainly be the most radical idea that I have ever proposed. I am

241

not entirely convinced myself that it will work, but that is why I have assembled you here today, to help me assess the feasibility of such a notion or to follow up with studies of the matter in greater detail at a later date.

"Gentlemen, I propose to send astronauts to the planet designated as ZB-5344-P1…"

In disbelief, some eyes widened. Some rolled. Others widened and rolled. The first realization of Zimmer's proposal was met with a sense of absurdity.

"…Earth 2."

With the common name used, the remaining eyes narrowed skeptically.

"This is preposterous, Professor," stated Henley, who was the first to feel defensive against Zimmer for his resistance to funding the Yellow Beam mission, and then for cutting critical requirements off of Zimmer's wish list. "ZB-5344 is 26000 light years away from here. Do you intend to endow our astronauts with immortality to be able to live for the hundreds of thousands of years that will be required to travel there?"

Zimmer looked the NASA director squarely and earnestly in the eye. "Dr. Henley, it will not take that long." Then looking up at the group at large, he continued. "Remember, gentlemen, we live in a new age now. A couple of months ago, Dr. Henley's statement would have been absolutely correct. It would have impossible to travel to the ZB-5344 star system. But that was before the discovery of a superluminal object traveling around our galaxy. But now, we have no limits on the distances we can reasonably travel."

"But, Professor," rebutted Cornell. "Just because we have seen something travel faster than the speed of light, doesn't mean that we can ourselves. And it certainly doesn't mean that we will ever have the technology to do so."

"Dr. Cornell," responded Zimmer cordially. "This discovery should enlighten us to explore the possibility. The possibility for exploration becomes limitless with that discovery. We need to break through the glass ceiling that has been placed over humankind for its entire existence— superluminal travel is possible, and I suggest we get right to it."

"Professor?" called out one of the congressmen. "The funding for such research—I just don't see where we'd come up with the money needed to fund that research, especially if we really have no idea how long it will take to create propulsion faster than the speed of light."

"I agree that funding will be huge, but championing this cause will bring massive opportunity to Southern California. Besides, if I am hearing correctly from your constituents, they want to do everything in their power to find out what Earth2 has in store. Everybody is curious about whether there is life there, and whether that life is like us or—"

"—or more hostile," blurted out Gilroy. "Professor, in the few moments that I've had to consider your proposal, so many insurmountable questions come to mind. How do we get there? How can we build a machine robust enough to handle traveling that fast? Mr. Scoville, you know better than anyone the risks associated with space debris at near Warp speed! Are you willing to put the lives at astronauts at risk with debris hitting the Star Transport at rates much greater than the speed of light? How do we know that human flesh won't obliterate as it approaches Warp speed? And then, perhaps we actually get there, but then are captured and executed by a hostile species. How do you find astronauts that would be willing to do this? You realize that this won't happen in your lifetime, Professor, don't you?"

"Why not?" said Zimmer skeptically.

"Ever the optimist, you are Professor, but this time, I think you're over your head, and you won't even see it happen. I'm sorry, but this really is a waste of our time, Carlton."

"Professor," asked the other congressman with much interest. "How do you propose we go about such an effort of developing the technology to accomplish this?"

"First of all, I think you're all looking at it wrong," answered Zimmer. "What I've been considering is a much lower-tech approach then developing warp-drive capability."

With derision, Cornell fired back. "A low-tech solution to one of the most profound controversies of our day. What are you going to do? Chase the comet and hitch a ride?"

Zimmer smiled and pointed at the JPL director. "Yes! That's exactly what I suggest we do."

Frustrated at this answer, the JPL director turned his attention elsewhere. "Maril, do you have any idea where Zimmer is going with this? Does this make any sense to you?"

It was Maril Scoville's turn to stand and back up his father's associate. Zimmer deferred his position at the head of the table happily and moved back to the corner of the room to watch Maril Scoville's attempt to appease the crowd.

Addressing his boss first, he began. "Dr. Cornell, Professor Zimmer came to me just before this meeting with his suggestion, and while I agree with him that there are many questions that need to be answered, I actually like his idea quite a bit, and I think, Gentlemen that the public will be very interested in supporting all of us in our decision to move forward with the proposal. It won't cost hundreds of billions of dollars, and it might just work."

"We've been working on the Star Shield for nearly three years now—from concept to prototype. We believe that we are building something practically impervious to high-speed stellar debris."

Henley was first in probing this claim. "Mr. Scoville, as I understand it, your requirements are for avoidance of large objects and tolerance of small objects on the order of $1c$. Is that right?"

"That is correct, Dr. Henley. In open space, we are immune to space debris up to the speed of light."

Henley's voice increased in volume and speed, indicating his intolerance of this discussion. "But, we're talking about $25000c$. I don't see how you can be comfortable putting the lives of astronauts at such dire risk when you aren't building the shield to anything near to the type of condition to which you plan on subjecting it."

"Sir, with all due respect, we aren't putting anybody's life at risk yet. We are only asking for the ability to review all of the details of such a mission to determine its feasibility. Further, I expressed this same doubt to Dr. Zimmer just before this meeting, and he pointed out that we will not be traveling at $25000c$ in open space. We will do it in the confines of a comet's tail. That comet will make a way through the vacuum of space and will eject all debris that stands in its way. In that case, we need not worry about debris coming head on, but rather we must focus the study on the ability to receive bombardment from behind."

"I fail to see the difference."

"The difference is that we will accelerate gradually yet rapidly as we enter the beam, ensuring that particles propel the Star Transport to greater velocities while not impacting the shield at speeds greater than $1c$. Professor Zimmer has calculated from data retrieved during the study mission that while the center of the beam is traveling at $25000c$, there is an inversely proportional and linear relationship between the velocity of particles in the beam and its distance from the center. As long as the Star Transport penetrates the beam gradually, it will be able to accelerate under the propulsion of the matter, but it will not be subject to damage by it. It will be a perfectly controlled environment that will balance the velocity of the vehicle with its ability to penetrate the beam even farther, and thereby gain even more velocity."

"Dr. Cornell, I appeal to your judgment," wavered Henley only slightly. "Tell me that this isn't the most ludicrous proposal. Tell me that this isn't set for certain failure. Tell me that it won't be a suicide mission."

"I can't tell you any of those things, sir," Cornell said in response. "We will need to study everything in greater detail. Nobody's life is at risk if we're simply studying the possibilities."

"But we are risking our taxpaying dollars."

Zimmer stepped forward. "Dr. Henley, Dr. Cornell, and Congressmen, let me assure you that this is something that taxpayers want to see done with their money. It is rather anti-climatic to find a parallel Earth and then not be able to study it. Curiosity has got the better of your constituents, and I think your leadership in this area would only secure your job security."

Zimmer saw that the congressmen were weighing the statement and considering the fine line they were walking between pleasing constituents and funding programs with taxpaying dollars.

Henley did not look happy. "Look, gentlemen, even if we do fund this program, Congress has already allotted NASA a certain budget for this year. We will have to cancel other programs. It's not for these representatives to decide."

One congressman spoke qualified this last statement. "At least not this year, but we certainly could appeal for a larger budget for your organization starting next year, if we believe the citizens of our districts would find it valuable to do so."

With his gaze fixed on the ground in front of him, Henley paused thoughtfully for a several quiet and tense moments. Eventually, his demeanor softened. "Ok, if you think we can fund the research above our current budgetary plans, then I guess we could produce the team to do the feasibility research at least."

Zimmer smiled almost imperceptibly. The meeting had served its purpose, and he was certain that research and planning for a mission to ZB-5344 was on its way.

. . .

Before Zimmer had a chance to realize it, autumn turned into winter and winter into spring. It wasn't difficult for seasonal changes to escape the recognition of Southern Californians, since these changes only delivered slight variations in precipitation and temperature. But for Zimmer, this year was particular busy. Between his class instruction and increased research activities, Zimmer's year at CalTech flew by.

As soon as ZB-5344-P1 had been discovered, Zimmer put his Parallel Earth team to work studying the entire ZB-5344 system. Even Zimmer was stunned to find even more similarities between the Solar System and the ZB-5344 star system. Four other planets had been discovered that approximated Jupiter, Saturn, Neptune, and Venus in their appearance, size, and orbits. The only thing the team had found vastly different was the orbital plane of the ZB-5344 system. It was oriented exactly 90 degrees different to the plane of our own Solar System, leading Joram Anders to joke with the professor that Zimmer still had work to do, considering that "you didn't exactly find a *parallel* Earth yet" and that it was "too bad he hadn't been looking for an *orthogonal* Earth all of these years."

The team also spent a vast amount of time probing the P1 planet itself. Searches for signs of life—including detection of artificial light or electromagnetic radiation—proved frustrating, but Zimmer was not taken aback by this. Any studies of Earth2 dating 27000 years ago would also prove useless. Geologically speaking, 27000 years isn't much time, but if Earth2 was on the verge of civilization, then 27000 years would prove plenty of time for significant intellectual advances.

As for Joram, Kath, and Reyd, they continued studying the aftermath of the comet. They continued to scour the data from the original Yellow Beam mission and were also focusing on improved sets of data from a more controlled second mission, where the USL had been relaying data for several weeks as improved paddles were navigating the comet's tail with much greater control and were mapping out its cross-section. The only problem with the second mission is that a significant amount of time had elapsed, such that the quantity and velocity of particles remaining this far behind in the tail were now reduced significantly.

The team had ceased going to Palomar altogether these days, and were studying and measuring data in their lab on campus. They had made a couple of weekend trips to Ames Research Center in Northern California. Ames was tasked with studying the soil and debris samples returned from the rescue mission to Mars, so the team had a chance to meet scientists and engineers on the team and were able to get a first-hand glimpse of some of the artifacts and the discoveries which were being made.

Along with NASA's efforts, Zimmer and his research team were making great progress in understanding the matter left behind from the comet. Hordes of scientists around the world were jumping on the superluminal band wagon as well, which was aiding the understanding of travel greater than the speed of light, but nobody had yet stumbled onto any solid theories about the exact mechanisms required to escape the electromagnetic force, and thereby be enabled to travel faster than light. This was a complicated problem, and physicists knew that answers would take a long time to fully be understood. Some were certain that we would need one more fly-by of the comet before we could really understand superluminal travel. Outspoken opponents went so far as to be a significant hindrance in Zimmer's efforts in getting a mission off to Earth2 during the next fly-by of the comet.

Late one evening, Zimmer sat in his office reviewing media coverage of Congressional debates regarding the mission. Irritated with the press' coverage of the matter, he closed the lid on his laptop.

Shaking his head, he muttered under his breath, "Why does politics always have to get in the way of science?"

He stood up and walked over to the window of his office. He looked over the quiet campus. Sidewalks were illuminated in bright blue light, shadowed occasionally by the overhanging tree standing motionless in the still of the night. Near the circle of ground lights illuminating the planetarium bearing his name, he caught a movement out of the corner of his eye. Easily recognizable in contrast to the perfect stillness of the night, he saw the backs of a pair of students walking together along one of the walkways. Their path curved towards a building, and as the students approached, he smiled as he saw the distinct profiles of Joram and Kath. Joram held the door of the building open for Kath, who smiled and nodded as she crossed the threshold. Joram stepped in behind her and allowed the door to swing shut.

Zimmer looked at his watch. 9:43 PM. "Those two seem to always be in that lab these days, and with the evening growing late, they return for more." He would have to stop by on his way to the parking lot now—just to make sure that everything was going well with their research, and to ascertain whether they had any questions for him.

Just as he grabbed his coat off of his office chair and headed for the door, his ear implant rang softly. He wasn't used to getting any phone calls this late, but he tapped his ear to answer the call anyway.

"Carlton Zimmer speaking," he said while beginning to put his coat on in hopes of being able to dismiss the caller quickly.

"Carl," sounded an exuberant voice on the other end of the call. "How are you doing?"

"Little brother?" Zimmer was pleased to hear the pleasant voice.

"Little brother, indeed!" exclaimed Warron Zimmer. "Little enough to be in your shadow, as always… I keep hearing about you from the media these days."

Shrugging off the praise, Carlton spoke warmly, "It's been a while, Warron. I'm glad to hear from you."

"Well, I do apologize that it's so late… I've been busy reviewing a new case, and time ran away from me. I couldn't miss the opportunity to wish my big brother a happy birthday."

"Ah, yes. I should've known," Zimmer nodded and smiled while taking his coat off and reclining in his office chair with his hands clasped behind his head. "You never miss calling me on my birthday… even though I almost always find an excuse to miss yours."

"Excuse… is that what you call unraveling the mysteries of the universe these days, Bro? How is the sleuthing going anyway?"

"Well, it's been an exciting year, to be sure."

"No kidding! You found your parallel Earth, and you've discovered something moving faster than the speed of light! And now, I hear you're working with NASA on a mission to the other Earth?"

The older Zimmer sighed audibly and paused, weighing his response to this question.

Warron probed, "At least I thought I heard about a mission."

"Oh, yes… you heard," the astronomer confirmed. "It's just not going very well at the moment."

"You talking about those critics? It's nonsense. The American people are behind you on this. We all want to know about this place and you know how impatient we are when we want something. Nobody is going to stand for waiting an extra five years, when we have the time to prepare now."

"I only wish those guys were our biggest problem right now, but we have an even bigger problem at the moment—something that I did not foresee, and which may scrap the entire effort altogether."

"I'm sure it's nothing you won't be able to solve," Warron encouraged. "You've solved all sorts of tough scientific challenges in your life."

"No, this time it's out of my hands. I was in a meeting with NASA earlier this week. Turns out we can't find any astronauts who are willing to take the job. None… not one. And for this mission to succeed, we need two."

"You gotta be kidding? This must be the most exciting mission in the history of space exploration. Talk about making a name for yourself. I mean, we still read about that Ned Armstrong guy who was the first to land on the Moon. Imagine how famous the guy will be who first lands on Earth2?"

Zimmer corrected quickly, "Neil!"

"What?" asked Warron in a state of confused misunderstanding. "Can't I just sit?"

"No," Zimmer rolled his eyes. "I didn't mean for you to kneel. I was referring to Neil Armstrong, who was the first man to walk on the Moon."

In his career as well as in personal conversations, the successful defense attorney was not one to be allowed to get off onto irrelevant tangents. "Oh yeah, right... but you get the idea, Carl. The thrill of the adventure. Going somewhere nobody has ever been before. The fame. Maybe you should increase the salary?"

"It's already at twenty-five million, Warron," the professor answered flatly, and then heard a startled whisper on the other end.

"So, what's the problem, Carl? I just can't believe you're not getting any bites."

"It's actually very easy to understand. You travel through space at over 25000 times the speed of light for more than a year, hoping that the speed of light won't adversely affect you physically. Then, you stay on a foreign planet for six and a half years waiting to hitch a ride on the next lap of the comet. What if they get there and find that humans aren't exactly friendly to them? What if they land in a Jurassic era of dinosaurs excited to feed off of an exotic meal? And if you've actually managed to survive Earth2 this long, then you have to hope that NASA didn't botch one of the coordinates or round off any of their math to the wrong decimal place while trying to rendezvous with a massive object that it hurtling towards you at a pace that is faster than anything you could conceive. What if you get flung off of the comet prematurely on your return home, and you get stuck in the vastness of space with no hope of return to either Earth.

"Remember, also that all of this will take 13 years away from your personal life. That alone will take out every family man on the planet, but it is also a significant reason for rejection among bachelors as well, who view this time in their lives as significant for settling into family life or the pursuit of any other personal activity. The 23-year olds out there have a hard time coming to grasp with the fact that they'll be gone until they're 36. Would you want to give up your twenties for a likely suicide mission?

"Well, if you put it that way..." Warron's voice trailed off in a tone of defeat and discouragement—not only out of empathy for his brother, but also out of disappointment for his own curiosity. Everybody wanted to know what—or more importantly—who was on this other earth.

"Basically, we have conflicting requirements in the person that can fill the job. We need somebody who is intelligent enough to understand the science and engineering of the mission, and yet stupid enough to not figure out that we're asking 13 years of their lives for a suicide mission, or somebody who has absolutely nothing to lose."

There was a long pause in the conversation at this point. After looking at his watch, Zimmer broke the silence. "Did you fall asleep on me during that explanation, Warron? It is getting awfully late there in Atlanta."

"Um… no, actually I was just… thinking about something."

"What's that?" the elder Zimmer asked.

"Oh, sorry… it's nothing… ludicrous really… but then again…"

"Go ahead."

"It's just something you said that made me think… You said you need 'somebody who has absolutely nothing to lose', right?"

"That's right," Zimmer said with full, albeit reserved, attention.

"It's going to sound crazy, Carl, but I might be able to help you out."

Chapter

22

The two prisoners sat quietly in their cell. Paol Joonter was writing a letter in response to the one he had received from his family. Every Tuesday, Paol anticipated that weekly letter. It was his only link to the family. After reading the letter three times and memorizing every detail of the picture of his children, who appeared to be enjoying themselves at the Seattle Mariners baseball game, Paol sat down on his chair and began to write his weekly response on his clipboard.

Three feet away, he could hear the occasional deep and raspy breath of his cellmate, Blade Slater, who was enveloped in his reading "All Quiet on the Western Front." An occasional muffled vocalization was heard in response to Blade's reading, followed by the soft sound of the pages turning. Echoes of other prisoner interactions could be heard through the halls of the cell block.

Only Paol noticed any of the noises, as Blade was consumed by his book. For that reason, Paol's head was the only one to raise from his letter writing as he heard the growing thump of footsteps approaching from down the hall. A guard emerged in view and approached the cell.

"Joonter!" the guard barked into the cell needlessly, considering that the two had already made eye contact. Unlocking the cell with his laser key, the guard announced one last word "Visitor."

At this, Blade's focus returned to the present with a nearly imperceptible raise of his eyebrows. Without lifting his eyes from his book, Blade congratulated his partner for his break in the doldrums of the regular routine and bid him farewell for the moment.

Paol quietly followed the guard, remaining ten feet behind as required by security regulations. Prisoners cooed and jeered at Paol as he walked by, voicing resentment through phrases too indecent for print. Paol ignored it all, fixing his gaze to the back of the guard leading him to the visitation room, a small five-foot square box of concrete with aged fluorescent lighting. A 12-inch thick glass separated him from his lawyer, Warron Zimmer.

Paol was always encouraged by these visits, since he remained hopeful that Zimmer would bring some significant news in his parole process, but generally, all updates were less than encouraging. The process was moving forward, at a typical judicial pace, but Zimmer was still seeking a significant piece of the puzzle that would help accelerate the process. After months in prison, Paol was growing frustrated and hopeless.

After briefing his client on the current status, Paol could tell that there was no reason to get his hopes up during this visit either. After a typical exchange where Warron gave Paol details, and Paol gave Warron his appreciation, Paol felt something a little different in the countenance of his lawyer during a pause in the conversation.

"Paol," began Zimmer, not knowing exactly how to begin.

"I don't think I've ever told you that my brother is Carlton Zimmer, the astrophysicist."

"No, I don't remember ever hearing that. I read in the news that he has been involved in some pretty amazing discoveries this year."

"He is working presently on a mission to Earth2."

"Yeah that sounds quite wild."

"Actually, everything is proceeding quite nicely, as far as the mission is concerned, but there is one snag that is jeopardizing his efforts of ever getting to explore this new Earth."

"What's that?"

"Nobody seems willing to accept the mission."

"I thought NASA was stacked with astronauts and candidates ambitious to become astronauts."

"Well, I think the Mars scare has been effective at keeping astronauts on pins and needles, and frankly, every astronaut—as I understand it from my brother—feels that the mission is simply suicidal. They see too many unknowns that could easily go wrong, and the commitment is large. It will be

13 years before the astronauts return. So there they are. NASA needs a pair of astronauts for the most exciting mission in the history of our planet, and they can't even find one."

Paol gave a low whistle. "I guess I hadn't been following closely enough to realize the specifics. That is a long time."

Sitting forward in his seat, Warron spoke intently. "I'd like to make a suggestion, Paol."

Paol's face contorted, not knowing where this was going. He indicated to his lawyer to proceed with the suggestion.

"NASA is very eager to find individuals to fulfill this mission. The United States—heck, the world—is very eager. I could get you out of here, Paol, if you would accept to do this."

Paol blinked rapidly and cocked his head to the left. Measuring his response, he continued, "I'm not sure if I understand what you're saying."

"I'm saying that I think it would be in your best interest to trade in your orange jumpsuit for a blue spacesuit, Paol. Serve your country on this mission, and when you return, I can practically promise that you'd be pardoned by the president. Besides, by the time you return, I'm almost certain to have cracked this case open."

"Warron," Joonter spoke with complete surprise. "You just told me that the mission is suicidal. If I wait here, I might be able to see my family again someday."

"No," Zimmer shook his head. "I didn't say it was suicidal… it's the press and the astronauts who say it is suicidal. My brother thinks there is actually a good chance for success."

"So, I put my life in the hands of one person, who is certainly biased towards making this attempt."

"Paol, I would trust my brother with my life. I have talked to him at length about this, and I believe him—the mission can succeed."

"Why should I believe him?"

"That's what everyone said when he was looking for his parallel Earth. It's what they said when he first discovered an object faster than the speed of light. Nobody believed him—but they were forced to in the end. Look, I'm not going to pressure you into this, but I think it would be an incredible opportunity to do something with your time instead of sitting in this cell. I

254

might get you back to your family within the next couple of years instead of taking 13, but that all depends on if I can find the smoking gun that lands the right person in your place."

Warron Zimmer stopped there, as he realized that Paol was enveloped in a flurry of thought. Weighing the options, his mind raced. He envisioned the scenarios—perhaps he would spend many long years in a prison cell, or maybe he would be returned to his family sooner than expected, or maybe he should invest the 13-year side trip to regain his life on his own terms, once and for all.

"I'll do it."

Zimmer was dumbstruck. "Don't you want time to think about it?"

"Warron, I didn't get to where I am—" he stopped to look around. "—Or I should say, where I was—without waiting long enough for someone else to take the opportunities away from me. In business, I always acted fast, trusted my instincts, and more often than not, they served me well. My heart tells me that the world needs to know about this other place, so why should I sit here doing nothing, when I have the opportunity to do something more—much more."

"But there are no guarantees. You may not come back."

"Are you changing your mind on this, Warron? I thought you trusted your brother with your life. Besides you didn't ask me just for kicks. You thought that it might just make sense."

Warron smiled.

"So, I'll do it, but under one condition."

The smile was erased. "What condition?"

"I get to bring my cellmate with me."

"What?" Warron asked in amazement. "You want to bring a hardened criminal in a maximum security prison on the most dangerous undertaking of your life?"

"Well, you just asked one person in that category to do this? Why do you think there are no others in here that could do the job? He is one of the most gifted people I've met—a real self-taught genius who has read up on every subject imaginable in the seven years he's been here. Besides his intuition and quick thinking has preserved his *and* my health in this hell hole. And he has something in common with your brother. "

255

"What's that?" Warron asked excitedly.

"*I* would trust him with *my* life."

…

Blade Slater could detect an expression of bewilderment on the face of his fellow inmate when he returned. Barely looking up from his book, he inquired, "Good news, I hope."

"Well, I'll let you be the judge of that."

In curiosity, Blade closed his book, set it on his cot, took in a deep breath and gave his cellmate his full attention. "Well, go on, then."

"You remember that planet that was discovered several months ago?"

"Yes, I do."

"Turns out my lawyer is the brother of the astronomer who discovered it. NASA is working on a mission to fly there, but they are having a hard time rounding up astronauts."

"And how 'xactly do they plan on flyin' to a distant planet. Why… that'd take fo'ever to get there!"

"They're going to hitch a ride on the comet that was discovered in conjunction with Earth2."

Blade looked skeptical but waved on his partner.

"Well, they can't find astronauts to do the job."

"Mmm…" came the confused grunt of Blade. He was trying to figure out where this was all going.

"My lawyer suggested that I should take up NASA, and that way whether he is able to clear my name or not, by the time I return, I'd get a nice presidential pardon, admiration of the whole world, and an entry in history books fer ages to come."

"How long's the mission?" Slater inquired.

"Well, there would be training for about five years."

"That's some time!" Paol's cellmate interrupted

"And then it would take a year to get to the planet, six and a half years there, and another five years to get back home."

Blade easily and quickly worked the numbers in his head. "Why that's twen'y years from now. No wonder they can't staff that job. Such a foo'hearty thing to even think 'bout it. And I s'pose ya' done told him you'd think 'bout it." Blade shook his head and managed a hearty laugh.

256

"Not exactly—I told him I'd bring you with me."

Blade's laugh and smile vanished as quickly as the understanding registered. Growing disinterested in the conversation, he picked up a book, and said, "What was ya' thinkin'? I ain't doin' somethin' so foolish as that!"

Paol pulled his chair around in front of Blade's and sat down to face him. "Look, Blade—this is an opportunity to do something no other man has done before. And you'll get out of here as well."

"Now, why would I wanna go off fo' twen'y years, when I'll be sprung from here in abouts five? It's darn foolish, Paol."

"So tell me, what do you think is going to happen when you do leave anyway?"

"Well, I'll make me a respectable citizen. You know that!"

"How?"

"Get me a job... have a family hopefully."

"Blade, you have no education, and you're a convicted felon. Who will hire you?"

"I'm educated—You know that."

"I do—but they don't. There's no formal education to back you up." Paol's tone grew more serious, more important. "Look, Blade, think about what you'll do for mankind—for the knowledge of science. Think of how much you'll learn becoming an astronaut. That's something you won't learn by reading all of the books in the Library of Congress."

"Paol, listen to ya'self. You got a family. Ya' just can't go off and leave 'em fo' twen'y years."

"I could rot in here until I die, Blade. My family will be proud of my contribution. What do you plan on contributing before life is over, Blade?"

"Oh, I wanna contribute too, you know that. But, I think I can contribute in plenty of other ways to please my neighbors and my God."

"God!" Paol snickered in derision. "I know you've been studying those world religion books, but look around you, Blade! There can't be a God."

"I think you're wrong. There's a God."

"Why would a *just* God throw me in here, then?"

"I 'spect it's fo' the same reason he gives all of us trials in this life of ours. Was it *just* of God to put me into a family in the ghetto, whereas some kids is put in the 'burbs? What's important is not that we have adversity but how we deal with it. We can choose to get *better* or we can choose to grow *bitter*."

"So you think everything happens for a reason, huh? Everything is just as God would have it?"

"No, I don't!" answered Blade in a deep voice. "Ever'thin' is not as God'd have it. God'd not have us abusin' little children. He'd not have us murderin', stealin', liein'."

"Then why does he allow it to happen?" Paol asked incredulously.

Blade gave a deep breath, and reached under his pillow for the only book that he didn't keep under his bed, but instead on top of it. It had a worn black cover, and thin, embossed sheets, which crinkled as he opened it to the place he desired. Reading from the page, he spoke in a confident tone:

See, I have set before thee this day life and good, and death and evil;

In that I command thee this day to love the Lord thy God, to walk in his ways, and to keep his commandments and his statutes and his judgments that thou mayest live and multiply: and the Lord thy God shall bless thee in the land whither thou goest to possess it.

But if thine heart turn away, so that thou wilt not hear, but shalt be drawn away, and worship other gods, and serve them;

I denounce unto you this day that ye shall surely perish, and that ye shall not prolong your days upon the land.

"It seems, Paol, God wants us to choose fer ourselves. It's a test, Paol—to see who is worthy to live in His presence. He'ss given us commandments, and we just needs to choose. Look, I don't know all the answers. That's why I still read. But, what propels us as a race to survive, to thrive, to go fo'ward, if there's no purpose to life? And how could there be purpose in *life* if there's no purpose in *death*. Without somethin' more, why do we do so much? As a race, we've had plenty a' challenges—plenty a' opportunities to just lay down and give it up. But we've never done that. Why not? I think it's because there's somethin' inside us—a God-made spirit—that drives us."

Paol thought for a moment, desiring to steer the conversation back on track. "If there is such a grand purpose, Blade, then think of what this mission could add to our knowledge of that purpose? Will we find another God-fearing people on Earth2? Will we understand better this universe really is made by intelligent design?"

Blade's head stared at the concrete floor, his body expressionless.

"Blade, you told me that you wanted to make up for past mistakes—that you wanted to be a productive citizen of your country and community. What better opportunity than this mission? Think of how proud you'll make your mother and your uncle!"

Invoking thoughts of his family, Blade replied with a choke in his voice, "If this could erase even a little bit a' the hurt I gave 'em, then it'll be worth it. But, if I dies, then it would only make the hurt worse."

"I'm not so sure," Paol rebutted. "They would think of you as a hero. Even that legacy will erase the pain."

Blade stood from his chair and slowly walked to the bars which held him back from the things he was eager to start doing in life. Paol remained seated, but his gaze was fixed on his cellmate with great interest. After staring off into the distance for a couple of minutes, he turned to face Paol. His look was stern, the eyes intent. Realizing he had no response to Paol's last argument, he had to respond, "I'll do it."

Chapter

23

"Bottoms up, Gentlemen."

Paol Joonter drained his pint-sized bottle of clear blue liquid immediately, but Blade Slater hesitated slightly. Glancing over at Paol, Blade gained the confidence to follow his lead. As soon as the pair had completed the instruction, two prison security guards pulled out their wand-like laser keys and the sound of metal against concrete ensued as each pair of hand and ankle cuffs dropped from each prisoner—a sign of quasi-freedom that the two prisoners would now enjoy.

"As a reminder to both of you," began the prison warden, "the contents of the fluid will remain attached to the blood stream for nearly three weeks. Therefore, every two weeks, a member of my staff will remotely monitor your consumption of the beverage by video feed. You will continue to be monitored by a central team of minimum security guards from Knoxville, Tennessee. You may not leave the borders of the continental U.S. and any attempt to get within 50 miles of a border must be preapproved and done under accompaniment of a federal officer or guard. For you, Mr. Joonter that means you must be very careful on home leave. Your home in Washington State is only 90 miles from the border. I wouldn't wander to far north if I were you."

"Understood," Paol acknowledged the order.

"Mr. Edwards," said the warden as he turned his attention to a young man standing to the right of the prisoners. "I release these prisoners to the custody of NASA."

Edwards thanked the warden and escorted the pair to a van, waiting to drive them to the airport. As the pair left the prison building dressed in brand new street clothes, Slater paused on the front steps in a dreamlike state of wonder at his release.

"What's the deal with the blue water, Paol?" Slater asked as they walked a few feet behind Edwards. He continued to gaze around at the outside of the prison and took in views which were new. He had not seen anything but the same concrete walls, whether inside the prison cell, or outside in the prison court. Trees, flowers, grass, cars and pedestrians passing by… it all seemed so new.

"It's a little concoction that was invented several years ago. It's called a minimum security beverage, or MSB."

"But what's it fo'?

"It's a cocktail of chemicals—all FDA approved, I assure you—which will track any individual in the USA."

"The devil, ya' say."

"No, really. It works like this. Each prisoner has a specific ratio of two different chemicals. The combination of these chemicals will prevent the passage of a high-frequency signal. Around the US, there are transmitters which send a constantly-emitting variable-frequency signal. That signal disperses until it reaches your body. The chemicals in the blood stream will reflect the exact frequency which is tuned to your chemical composition. It then bounces back to the receiver, and based on the location of detection and the time of flight, your exact location is calculated and mapped in Knoxville. So, it's like a tracking device which you can't get rid of no matter how hard you try."

"And it stays inside the body fo' three weeks?"

"At least."

"And there's them transceivers placed all over the US?"

"You got it."

"And they can cover the whole country?"

"Except for the non-continental states."

After a pause of reflections with some low, quiet grunts, Slater spoke up. "What if I get me a transfusion?"

Paol appreciated how quickly this thought came to him. "Who's going to do that?"

"Maybe I got me a friend or uncle who's a doctor."

"Well, what would happen is that you would fade on the map, go blank, raise an alarm, and have local law enforcement at the doctor's office within minutes. Your friend would either have to turn you in or spend time in jail himself for aiding and abetting a criminal."

"Ok, but what if I decide to hop on an airplane and fly outta the country?"

"You have to register all air travel. If you're on a flight that you haven't registered for, your speed will become an alarm, the flight will be tracked by radar, and the plane will be diverted to land in the States by federal law enforcement jets. The bottom line is that there have been thousands of petty criminals tracked this way. Instead of being stuck inside of jails for months or years, they are able to continue a semblance of a normal life. They can work, be with their families, and as long as they keep themselves clean, they can serve their sentence.

"It was actually invented to track cattle on open ranges. Ranchers would get an alarm if the herd wandered towards the edge of the network and be able to track and intercept cattle more quickly. Politicians dealing with prison over-crowding realized that it could be used to track criminals more cheaply, without the expense of putting them in prisons."

"But, what if the criminal goes back to his old behavior?" Blade asked.

"Well, because they are very trackable, it's nearly impossible to get away with subsequent crimes, because they can be tracked back to the scene of the crime, and then they are taken back to jail. Some opponents claim that it actually hurts crime, because people know that if they have a free pass on small crimes, then they are more encouraged, because they know that even if they're caught, they can be back in society after a conviction. There really isn't a whole lot of data to back up the claim, though."

"Right over here, Gentlemen," Edwards interrupted the conversation as they arrived at the vehicle. Edwards took the driver's seat, while Paol and Blade went to either side of the back.

Before climbing in, Paol looked over the top of the car at Blade as he opened his door. "I know what you're thinking, and I know you won't do it."

"Do what?" Slater asked raising an eyebrow curiously.

"I know you're not planning on escaping, Blade." He said with a wry smile.

"Oh, really… and why not?"

"Frankly, you know that the mission would abort, and I'd be sent back to prison. You wouldn't be able to live with the guilt. You should know that many have tried to escape, but none have ever succeeded. Besides, I know that you are a changed man. You want to give back to society and repent for past doings. You wouldn't be able to do that as a man in hiding and on the run from the law."

As the car engine started, Blade shot back, "I wasn't thinkin' 'bout doin' it myself. I'm worried 'bout you doin' it to me." He smiled and ducked into the back seat, leaving Paol standing with a mock expression of disdain at the offense pronounced by his good friend.

"So, Mr. Edwards, you work fo' NASA, then?" Blade asked the driver as the car pulled onto the street.

"Yes," Edwards replied, looking up into the rear view mirror. "By the way, call me Physon."

"So, whatcha do fo' NASA, Mr. Ed—I mean Physon?" Blade pressed the conversation out of excitement for his newfound freedom.

"I am an engineer working on your mission. I'll be providing some of your training and instruction regarding the details of the mission."

"Tell us all 'bout the mission."

"Well, frankly, we don't know all of the details just yet, but when we get to Houston, you'll be fully briefed on everything we know to date. There are a couple of years ahead of us to get all of the details ironed out. However, the gist of it is this. You get in a spaceship, you travel to ZB-5344-P1, study its geography and any inhabitants that you discover there, and return home to tell us all about it."

"So this ZB… P1… is the official name of the planet?" Paol interjected his question into the conversation, growing curious about what lay ahead of him.

"Yes. Earth2 is its common name among those of us here on Earth1, but it is the first planet to be discovered around the star entered as ZB-5344 in the most comprehensive Milky Way star database. Thus the official designation is ZB-5344-P1."

"Hey, Physon—I got a question," Blade asked playfully. "How do we know that it's Earth2? Maybe we're Earth2, and it's Earth1?" A roar of laughter came from the back seat. Paol shook his head at his partner's easy joviality.

As Physon looked again into the rear view mirror, Paol felt obliged to explain. "You'll get used to it. He's fond of laughing at his own jokes. It kind of grows on you, and can be contagious sometimes. Even if it isn't the best joke in the world, I've come to appreciate how his laughter made prison life a lot less gloomy."

Physon nodded and replied, "Well, Blade, we know that we're Earth1, because we are light years ahead of Earth2—literally."

"Whatcha mean?" Blade asked inquisitively.

"Well, everything we observe here on Earth1 regarding Earth2 happened 27000 years ago, so that just goes to prove that it is 27000 years behind us in history."

Blade's distorted face proved that he was weighing this comment. Maybe he wasn't as smart as he thought he was, considering that this remark from a trained engineer seemed so ludicrous that it must instead have been absolutely brilliant. Maybe Blade was over his head, but he felt to rebut the comment anyway. "But that's just because it takes light 27000 years to reach—" Blade stopped abruptly as Physon started to snicker.

In between hearty fits of laughter, Blade managed to admit, "Ah, ya' got me, Mr. Physon—ya' got me there."

Paol nodded slowly. "I told you so, Physon—the silly joking can be contagious when you're around this man."

. . .

Paol and Blade sat alone at an oblong table in a small conference room. Blinds were open to reveal a large workspace, with occasional passersby, each engaged in their workday tasks. Each of the recently released prisoners had a notepad and pen in front of them emblazoned with the NASA logo, as well as a beverage which Physon had retrieved for them after they entered the room.

As he sipped his coffee, Paol closed his eyes. "Ah, so much better than the stuff back at the pen."

Blade appeared indignant. "Really? I've been cheated then," he said as he sipped on his can of coca-cola. "Mine tastes just the same." He could barely finish the comment before smiling and adding a spurt of choked laughter.

Conversation was suppressed, as each man was consumed in his own flurry of thoughts due to the abrupt change of events in their lives. It would certainly take some time to adjust now that they were no longer confined to their small prison cell. With the muffled sound of an occasional conversation taking place on the other side of the window, and the ticking of an old analog clock—a tremendously contrasting relic in this center of futuristic facility— the door to the conference room swung open and a pair of individuals entered the room.

Physon Edwards introduced Paol and Blade to Vurim Gilroy as the program manager for the Earth2 mission. Vurim took each hand and shook it warmly and vigorously. "I'm thrilled to meet both of you. On behalf of NASA, the United States of America, and indeed for every citizen of the world, thank you for accepting such an exciting mission of discovery."

Gilroy invited his new acquaintances to take a seat, as he and Physon took seats directly opposite of them. Physon opened a notebook on the table, while his boss laid down a thin manila folder on the table and folded his hands on top of it.

"Gentlemen," he began after taking a drink from his bottle of water. "We have a little over five years to prepare you for this mission. Let me explain first what the mission consists of, and then I'll tell you how we plan to get you ready for the task.

"A spacecraft, called Star Transport, is currently under development at the Jet Propulsion Laboratory in Pasadena, California. This craft is a horizontal take-off and landing vehicle, designed to require as little facility as possible for launching and landing the spacecraft. It requires no launch pads or lengthy runways. It has a self-contained, highly-efficient, low-weight, and low-volume fuel reservoir for anti-matter nuclear propulsion. Only due to recent advances with sub-atomic replication were we able to generate the type of propellant needed for such an engine. As such, there are no external rocket boosters required as is the case with more conventional rocket designs. This is imperative as it allows for planet-hopping without requiring booster equipment on each planet. Its five-engine design is capable of speeds at 0.1 Warp currently."

Paol, feeling overwhelmed from this rapid-fire briefing glanced over to Blade, who was copiously scribbling details down on his notepad. He looked as if everything was making sense, and Paol figured that it probably was. Here, the engineer was having a harder time keeping up with spaceship construction than was the unschooled convict.

"The spacecraft is—um—cozy. There are just two main compartments; namely, the cockpit, and the SAR chamber. All flight activities naturally take place in the cockpit, with the pilot seated on the left and the navigator on the right. Behind the cockpit is the main hatch for entry and exit of the vehicle. The SAR chamber is required for regeneration of all fuel, water, and nutrition. Waste is recycled in order to increase the range of the spacecraft, but even so, the engines are not 100% efficient—they do lose some heat and exhaust that cannot be reclaimed by the SAR. The vehicle requires refueling where raw materials can be obtained to reproduce the necessary fuel.

"Because of the immense speeds that the craft will obtain, the entire skin of the craft will be coated with a shield that will prevent a breach, by avoiding or pulverizing any objects which gets hurled at the vehicle. At the same time, this shield will allow the tail of the comet to propel the vehicle at speeds of 27 KiloWarp—that's around eight billion meters per second. In other words, fast—so fast that nobody can comprehend what it means to travel at these speeds."

Gilroy paused after this description of the Star Transport allowing for questions to be asked. Blade spoke up immediately.

"How do we knows what health effects there is with humans travelin' at these speeds? I mean... won't we get torn to shreds up there?"

"Actually, no... we don't believe that you'll be harmed in any way. Physicists are rapidly converging on a set of mathematical models which are very encouraging. They suggest that traveling faster than the speed of light merely requires the escape of the electromagnetic force. It turns out that the mechanics of escaping EM isn't at all destructive to the atoms which comprise any physical body."

266

"But we won't be subject to electromagnetism?" Blade's question was animated.

Edwards looked intently at Gilroy who was weighing the answer. "That's right."

"Absurd!" responded Blade in agitation. "Without the EM force, we'd be nothin'. All the molecules that make me who I am are kept together because of EM. Without it, the finger attached to my hand will float off into space. The hand attached to my wrist? Same thin'. Wrist? Arm? Shoulder? Like I said, we'd be shred to pieces without electromagnetism. It's—it's—it's responsible fo' darn near everythin' we 'xperience in life."

"Well, this led physicists to some concern, but as Dr. Zimmer reiterated, there must have been an answer to that question, otherwise there would be nothing keeping the comet together once it had obtained warp speed. It turns out that recent mathematical models indicate that once matter obtains warp speed, it enters a state of suspension. All atoms effectively remain frozen in place. While it is true that there is no electromagnetic force to keep atoms together, there are very small sub-atomic particles which act as a glue to keep everything intact."

"But without electromagnetism, how we s'pposed to see or hear anythin'? Light and sound travel in EM waves, y'know."

Dr. Gilroy leaned closely over the table. "Blade, have you ever heard of cryogenics?"

Blade instantly realized where this was going. "You mean yer gonna freeze us? I thought the technology was still unproven and dangerous. If traveling the speed of light don' kill us, then freezin' us certainly will."

"No, no..." Gilroy asserted. "We won't be freezing you at all, but we believe that warp speed yields effectively the same result. You will be suspended in time. It's like being frozen without having to lower the core temperature of your body. In fact, even the 98.6 degree body temperature that you will have at that velocity will remain suspended until you slow down below the speed of light. It's really like stopping time. And why shouldn't it be? Einstein gives us the relationship of time and speed. The faster you go, the slower time goes. Once you hit the speed of light, time stops. And now we know the reason why... because the EM force fades to zero. The strength of electromagnetism yields to weaker quantum forces that simply preserve the state of the body traveling faster than the speed of light in freeze-frame as it were."

Blade's mind kept whirring with excitement over these newfound theories. "Ok, so then if we have this comet that's goin' faster than the speed of light, and it's frozen, why is there a tail? Shouldn't it simply stay frozen? If the freeze theory is right, then tell me how's it sheddin' matter."

Gilroy sat back in his chair with a smile. "You really think through everything, don't you, Blade? Let me answer your question with a question. What do you think happens when an object traveling faster than the speed of light strikes another object which is not?"

Blade thought for a moment, but Gilroy didn't give him enough time to think through his answer. "The tail of the comet is due to material stripping away from the comet because of particle impacts. As it hits matter in front of it, tiny atomic-level explosions result that cause the matter to unfreeze and drop back to sub-warp speed."

Blade was not appeased. "When we're ridin' in the tail of the comet, won't we be bumpin' into other matter? Won't our spaceship tear apart?"

"No, because it only happens when you hit matter which is subluminal. By the time the Star Transport obtains warp speed, you'll be comfortably in the middle of the tail with nothing but particles that are traveling faster than the speed of light. You will gradually accelerate towards this point and then gradually decelerate away from this point, all under computer control. Effectively, you'll be riding behind the comet, which will block everything... kind of like a windshield keeps the bugs from hitting your face as you drive on the freeway."

"But won' the computer be frozen too? I mean, once we's travelin' faster than the speed of light, there'll be no control of the system." Blade volleyed back across the table.

At this Gilroy leaned back, and cocked his head while wearing a playful smiled. "Ah, did I forget to mention the time bombs?"

Blade's eyes grew into large circles, while Paol quickly whipped his head forward as if to hear better.

"In the last several months, we've come to understand that superluminal matter is not subject to the speed of light. The other forces, however, remain in tact. In our case, in order to start moving the ship back out of the tail,

268

we'll use the weak nuclear force to our advantage. By calculating the half-life of a heavy metal, we can combine the exact ratio of masses between a certain gas and the decayed material. At a point where we desire, the decayed matter will be of sufficient mass to cause an explosive reaction with the gas. The explosion will be used to propel the vehicle back out of the comet's tail. Once the ship has hit the outer reaches of the tail, where matter is traveling at sub-warp speeds, it will act as a breaking system that will slowly decelerate the vehicle. Once the Star Transport is traveling less than the speed of light, the computer will be able to take over and make course corrections based on its position. Of course, since the computer is coming out of a deep sleep, it really won't know initially where it is at. It will use image sensors to scan the sky around it in order to calculate its exact location and then put the spaceship back on track with its rendezvous with Earth2."

After a pause, all that Blade could muster were the words, "Time bomb."

"Oh, don't worry about that Blade. The explosion will be very small, not enough to damage the ship, of course. It's no more harmful than the explosion of fiery gasoline that occurs in your car's engine."

Paol was dumbstruck by all of these concepts. "Sounds a whole lot like sci-fi to me," he said in deep, serious tones. He wasn't appeased by Gilroy's response.

"It is—at least for the next couple of years. As we refine all of these mechanisms and concepts, we'll need to do extensive testing to see if we can pull it all together. We remain optimistic that we'll be able to pull it off."

Questions flooded the minds of both Blade and Paol, and as quickly as they could come, Gilroy did his best to either answer them or defer them to their normal course of training. In due time all questions would be answered. He did proceed to tell them of the mission in its basic form. Hitch a ride on a comet tail, orbit the Milky Way, visit another Earth, study it for a few years, and return with oodles of data.

Blade asked one final question at the end of the two-hour overview briefing session. "Dr. Gilroy?"

"Yes, Blade."

"Why'd we get tapped fo' this job? Ya' gotta have hundreds of astronauts more capable of this job. We don't know nothin' 'bout bein' astronauts. It don't make sense."

Gilroy sighed. "I think you know the answer to that question, Blade. Our astronauts think it's too much of a commitment at best, and suicidal at worst."

Paol interjected. "So, give it to us straight, Doctor. I'm guessing you're a man with a conscience. Tell us—if you wish to continue to sleep at night— what are the odds of the mission?"

"Well... that's impossible to say, Gentlemen."

"Humor us, then," Paol goaded. "Tell us what you *think* the odds of success are. It sounds like there is just so much that could go wrong, don't you agree?"

"There certainly is, but we have five years to get everything as perfect as possible. After we're done, and Star Transport takes off from Edwards Air Force Base, all we can do is put it in the hands of God."

Gilroy gave no indication that he was going to answer the question. Paol gave every indication that he wasn't satisfied with this approach, but for the time being, he deferred questioning to allow the briefing to continue.

"Let's turn to logistics," Gilroy said after an insufficiently basic briefing of the mission. There simply wasn't enough time to answer every question and placate every fear just yet.

"Typically, an astronaut candidate comes to us with a set of skills that is mandatory for mission training. Neither of you have any of that, so the first step will be to make potential astronauts out of you. A physical, intellectual, and training regimen will be required to make sure the basic sciences and physical conditioning result. Further, you will both need to be trained as jet pilots and will need to log hundreds of hours of flight time in order to get you comfortable with the concepts of flying. Only then will real mission training begin.

"Your schedule will be as follows. You will wake up at 5:30 AM every weekday morning. Personal trainers will meet you in the gym on Mondays and Thursdays at 5:45 AM. You will be at the gym until 7:00 AM. You will have one half hour of personal preparation before reporting to the astronaut candidate cafeteria for breakfast. At 8:15, you'll be in class, learning aeronautics. At 11:00, you'll turn to the simulator to get cockpit training on the XJ-20 fighter jet. Lunch is at noon, and then at 1:00, you'll return to the classroom for instruction on mathematics and physical sciences. Teachers will finish with you at 4:00, where you will then have an hour and a half to yourself for any personal business you'd like to attend to—email, laundry, etc. Dinner from 5:30 to 6:30, and then on to the library for personal study after that. You'll need to be back in your living quarters by 9:30. Lights should be out no later than 10:30.

"Of course, this is just for the next several weeks. We'll be mixing it up with field trips to Edwards air force base for in-flight training, you'll be tutored on psychology, philosophy, and other social studies in order to know how to relate to any sentient beings that you discover on the planet. Eventually, there will be a host of other astronaut training—spacewalking, scuba diving for weightless conditioning and functioning, wilderness survival training, medical training, emergency procedural training, atmospheric pressure conditioning, mechanical and electrical engineering, earth sciences, orbital mechanics, earth and space navigation—let's just say, you'll know everything that you could possibly need to know by the time you launch several years from now. This is a crash course which will be about as mentally difficult as a PhD program and as physically grueling as boot camp.

"So, gentlemen! Good luck, and enjoy the adventure."

After a deep breath and pause, Gilroy stood up. "Mr. Edwards will give you the tour of the facilities from here and answer any logistical questions that you have."

He paused as he walked through the doorway. With his hand on the lever of the door, he turned back and said, "One in three."

"Come again?" asked Paol.

"Let's just say that if you were going to play Russian roulette, you'd load four bullets into the revolver—not just one. Those are your odds, Gentlemen, but this is strictly my opinion, and it is utterly off the record." Gilroy took a deep breath. "It was a fair question, Mr. Joonter, and it deserved an answer. But, I trust you to not repeat it—to anyone." His intent gaze passed from Joonter to Slater to Edwards. No words were exchanged, but everyone understood each other clearly. Gilroy's words were not to be repeated or the entire mission would certainly be jeopardized.

Observing the look of terror in the eyes of Joonter and Slater, he attempted to comfort the pair. "If it's any consolation, I feel confident that those odds will improve by launch time."

It was very little consolation.

...

The next morning, the alarm clocks went off at 5:30, just as Gilroy had promised. Blade rubbed his blurry eyes and let open a wide-mouth yawn as he turned off the alarm and rolled away from it, falling back to sleep. He was quickly wakened up by a loud rap on his room door. He sat up, and looked at the clock. 5:32 AM.

"Who's there?" called out Blade with an annoyed voice.

A cheerful voice pierced the door. "It's Paol. Time to wake up."

"Oh, man... what on Earth?" Blade mumbled as he shuffled his feet across the cool floor, rambling incoherent phrases with an occasionally articulate word, like "ridiculous," "tired," "unbelievable." Wearing nothing but briefs, he cracked opened the door and protected his eyes from the blinding light in the hallway outside. "Whatcha want, man?"

"Blade, get dressed. We're due at the gym in 10 minutes."

"It's too early fo' this!"

"You heard Gilroy. 5:30 AM!"

Blade closed the door, and Paol listened through to hear his partner cursing lowly as he shuffled around the room getting ready for their first day of training. Abruptly, the door opened, and Paol, leaning against it, almost fell into the room. Blade looked disheveled, but he was at least attired in a sweat suit that was given to him for his workout sessions.

At the gym, the trainers got acquainted quickly with the physical capabilities of each man. Paol was noted for having more endurance than his counterpart, but Blade had spent some time at the gym at prison, developing upper body strength. Both had their work cut out for them, and their trainers spent the session showing them the various cardio, flexibility, and weight-training exercises that they would need to do. Both were expected to return to the gym each evening after dinner.

"But we'll be swamped hittin' the books," Blade objected.

"The books will be meaningless if we can't get physically prepared for this mission!"

Blade nodded and accepted the order without further criticism.

Throughout the day, the recently released criminals were introduced to teachers and flight trainers as well. Large quantities of downloads to their iText Readers indicated the vast reading and memorization assignments that were given to both. Cockpit acronyms, pre-flight checklists, safety guidelines and more were given to them on just the first day in the simulator room.

Upon leaving the simulator building, the pair squinted in the bright sunlight and found their way to the cafeteria, with the help of some other NASA employees who happened by when they realized that they were hopelessly lost on the sprawling Johnson Space Center campus. Paol opted for the chicken Caesar salad with breadsticks, while Blade chose a bowl of Italian minestrone and a club sandwich.

"How we gonna learn all this stuff 'bout the airplane?" Blade asked after blowing on the soup in his spoon to cool it off. "We got tons to start memorizin' tonight, and we ain't even been to the classroom yet!"

"Well, we begin by beginning now," Paol said reaching in his shirt pocket for his iText Reader. Turning on the blue-white display he asked, "What does HMDS stand for?"

"Uh… Head-mounted display system," said Blade and then slurped down his soup with an approving nod of his head. "Mmm... good stuff."

"Close," encouraged Paol. "It's Helmet-mounted though."

"Well, the helmet mounts on the head, don't it?"

"Yes, but it's the display that we're talking about, and it mounts on the helmet."

"Ok, wise guy," said Blade, pulling out his reader to continue the duel. "HOC!"

"Hands… off Control. Right?"

"Yeah, I started ya' off light, so fer extra credit, can ya' name the two types of HOC?"

"Easy," Paol said with a snicker indicating that his companion was taking it way too easy on him. "There's gloved control, where the position and motions of the hands are calculated through glove-mounted motion control sensors. And there's optical-sensing control, where image sensors continually scan the cockpit for visual detection of location and motion."

"Ok, since ya' seem to have soaked up everythin', what's the pros and cons of the two systems."

"The gloved system can utilize finer motion controls. For example, to indicate a right roll maneuver to the aircraft, the right index finger makes one clockwise rotation. For a left roll, the right index finger makes a counter-clockwise rotation. You can use the same finger for both motions. However, with optical-sensing control, there is a chance that the optics will not be able to discern the direction of the roll, so the right index finger is used for right motion and the left index finger has to be used for a roll to the left."

"Nice job, Paol. Now, can ya' tell me what the right middle finger is used fo'?"

Paol hesitated and strained to remember. "Yeah, I remember talking about this one—give me a moment." Rubbing his forehead and straining to remember, there was just so much that brain could absorb from the first day of instruction in the simulator room, and the teachers really did fire-hose them. Thinking out loud, he continued. "I'm sure they talked about the middle finger gesture. I just—just don't remember." He looked up at Blade for an answer. "You stumped me, Blade. What is the middle finger used for again?"

Smiling in triumph for finally stumping his fellow astronaut, Blade stated matter-of-factly that "of course, when pointed up, the middle finger gesture is used to indicate someone's vehement displeasure with another individual to whom the back of one's hand is extended."

Paol chose the worst of all times to put a large bite of salad in his mouth, as he laughed involuntarily at the joke that was played on him, and the salad found its way back onto the plate. After wiping his mouth with his napkin, he turned towards Blade, doubled over in laughter. "If I were a less civil man, I would try the gesture on you to make sure I got it right."

"Hoo boy that was a good one," Blade said as he struggled to regain his breath. "But, all kiddin' aside, I think it should be used as a legitimate signal."

"Yeah? And why is that?" Paol said trying once again to consume his chicken salad.

"Just think 'bout it, Paol. If I'm caught in the crossfire, and my plane gets riddled with bullets, I'm gonna be in such a state of panic that I ain't gonna remember no hand signals—except one. When I realize that I'm so totally screwed, I'll extend both middle fingers to indicate my vehement displeasure with the bastard that gunned me down, and it will save my life, as I hear the pleasant cockpit voice say, 'Thank you fo' choosin' to fly the XJ-20.

Fo' yer safety and protection, the vehicle will now eject yer seat into the atmosphere.'"

Curiously, Paol poked at the display of his reader while Blade finished the joke. His smile was quickly replaced with an open-gaped mouth. "Unbelievable!"

"What?" said Blade as he tried to peer in at Paol's LCD display.

"I just searched the XJ-20 manual for 'middle finger' and it came up with this: 'Extend both middle fingers towards the top of the vehicle in order to open the canopy and complete seat-ejection sequencing.' Looks like you're not the first to think of that clever little usage of the ubiquitous hand signal."

Blade continued to chuckle while concluding the conversation with a final thought. "Great minds thinks alike!"

"Ok," Paol said steering the pair back on track. "We need to finish this lunch, and get back to business. What does MPS stand for?"

"Main power system," Blade fired back quickly. "When comin' up from a cold start, the first step is to switch on the MPS."

"And then what?" Paol drilled.

"Uh.... Put the ignition in standby... er... idle the throttle, and the OBC, or on-board computer, takes over fo' the rest of ignition sequencing."

"You are a quick study, Blade Slater," Paol approved with a bow of the head. "I'm glad to have you as my partner on this adventure."

Humbly, Blade deferred the recognition. "Ah, we got a long way to go, my friend. I suspect that we'll be needin' each other lots to get through this effort."

Noticing that time was limited, they finished their lunch quickly and quietly, each consumed in his own thoughts.

During the afternoon, classroom instructors were impressed that both students were farther ahead of schedule than expected. Expectations were high for Paol, but nobody could've imagined that a high-school dropout and drug-dealing convict would already have a strong grasp of trigonometry and calculus. His math instructor attempted to stump him with question after question on differential equations, analytical geometry, infinite series, trigonometric equivalences. Blade was able to work through nearly everything, balking only occasionally for a quick prompt from the teacher. Paol was much more rusty, having been farther removed from some of the

275

more abstract concepts. Blade seemed naturally geared towards the subject, however.

Paol was quicker than his younger cohort in a chemistry overview, but both performed admirably in both static and dynamic physics. Blade, however, was much softer in the computer sciences. He had studied these topics, but had little opportunity for hands-on study or experimentation during his prison years. Paol understood this field through many years of experience.

As the pair left the classroom at 4:15, they conversed lightly but felt the weight of the mission that lay ahead.

"Boy, this reminds me of my college days," Paol reminisced.

"It's a darn shame I didn't apply myself and go on to college. Learnin' is so exhilaratin'. If I only knew then…"

"But here's your second chance," affirmed Paol with a smile and slap on the back.

"This time'll be different, fo' sure. This time, I'll take the bull by the balls."

Paol gave a start at the imagery invoked by this adage. "I don't think you want to do that, Buddy."

"Why not?"

"I think you want to take the bull by the horns."

"Nah… from what I hear, everybody takes the bull by the horns… I'm takin' it one step farther." Blade laughed jovially and enjoyed his newly coined saying. Paol appreciated his partner's optimism.

"Anyway," Paol redirected the conversation. "Looks like we survived the first day, Blade 'ol buddy."

"Not yet, we ain't."

"Why not?"

"Tons of books to hit tonight, and Kai ordered me back to the gym too."

Shaking his head in understanding, Paol replied, "I'm starting to wonder whether we're more likely to die during the mission or before the mission."

…

The embrace was powerful and emotional. Tears fell freely on each shoulder and even the three bystanders were moved to emotion. Closest to Paol Joonter and his wife were their two teenage sons, ages 12 and 16. Paol

276

looked at them through blurry eyes, trying to imagine what they would make of their lives while he was gone. By the time he returned from his mission, they would be in their 30s.

Blade Slater stood farther off, in the corner of the room. His lips were tightly pursed, and his eyes glistened with tears, which had not yet rolled down his cheeks. His emotion was one of joy seeing his dear friend reunited with his family after the long months apart. But it was also filled with the emptiness of not having a family to call his own. While his mother visited him a few times shortly after he had been sentenced to the U.S. Penitentiary in Atlanta, her visits became farther apart, until finally he lost all contact with her. His uncle visited a couple of times as well, but they weren't encouraging to Blade. Instead, they were just reminders of how he had failed and missed the opportunity that his uncle had offered him. How could he have been so stupid? His thoughts were broken as he heard his name.

"Blade!" It was Paol. "I'd like you to meet my family." With his arm wrapped tightly around his wife's waist, he introduced Blade to each of family member, and Blade graciously received his sons with a warm hand shake, but his wife refused Blade's hands, preferring instead to throw her arms around him and kiss him on the cheek.

"Thank you, Blade," said Joyera with red and swollen eyes. "I was made aware from my husband's letters that when I couldn't be there for him—you always were. It meant so much to me that Paol had been placed in the great company of a decent and good man."

There was no sound of sobs from Blade, but the tears which had previously been contained now flowed freely down his face. "I'm so glad to meet you all. Paol's told me all 'bout each of ya'."

After brief cordialities and deepened introductions, Blade excused himself. He was glad to meet Paol's family, but he also knew that Paol needed time alone with them.

"I'll just head be headin' back, then," Blade stated awkwardly. "You all have so much to catch up on."

"Are you sure you won't at least come have dinner with us?" Joyera asked imploringly. Blade felt like family to her, through the descriptive closeness to which she had grown by reading each of her husband's letters from prison.

"Ah, no, Ma'am. Thank ya' kindly, but Kai—that's my personal trainer—has given me strict instructions to be in the gym every evenin'."

"Well, Blade, it is a pleasure to meet you. We'll be seeing you soon."

Paol waved his family ahead of him, and as they left the visitor's lounge at Johnson, he confronted his friend. "You gonna be ok, Blade?"

"Just fine," Blade assured him. "So much to study anyways. And I got some sleep to catch up on this weekend too."

"Ok, buddy," Paol was still hesitant to leave Blade, but he knew he had to spend as much as time as possible catching up with his family. "I'll see you Sunday evening. You have my cell phone if you need anything in the meantime."

Blade nodded and waved Paol on with the back of his hand imploring him to catch up with his family in the parking lot. As he walked back to his room, an odd feeling came over him—a feeling like maybe he did have a family after all. At least there was a group of people who he felt had his best interest and concern at heart, and that was enough for Blade. His pace to his dorm room quickened, and his resolve to succeed on the mission was strengthened.

After dinner, Paol and Joyera left the boys in the hotel room watching a movie, while they drove to a nearby park, and enjoyed a fresh summer evening listening to the ducks splashing in the center pond which reflected the antique gaslights of the park. While spending a significant amount of time simply holding each other and considering the misfortunes that came into their lives over the last year, they also discussed matters of vast importance to the family.

"Joy, Dear," Paol whispered after kissing his wife on the cheek. "Do you think I made the right decision? I agreed to the opportunity without consulting you, simply because I knew that I would have plenty of time to change my mind before heading out into space."

"I think you said it exactly, right, Love." Joyera spoke in a soft yet reassuring voice. "There are still six years that you will at least be away from prison. In the meantime, we will be able to see each other on the weekends."

"But you and the boys won't be able to come every weekend to visit, you know."

Joyera sat up on the park bench and looked intently at her husband. "The boys and I have discussed this, and we agree that we need to move to Houston to be closer to you."

While Paol had wondered about this option himself, he didn't think it was a realistic scenario. "But Dear, we have such solid roots in Seattle. And the boys will leave all of their friends and activities behind."

"There will be friends and activities here, too. We just realize that there won't be a father—and husband—in Seattle. The boys will each be out on their own by the time the mission is underway, and then I would be left alone in Seattle."

"But your family—"

"You are my family." She reached up and grabbed Paol's head in her hands to make sure that he looked into her eyes. She was always a determined woman, and Paol could tell that her resolve in this matter was stronger than ever.

"Besides, Warron will clear your name within the next six years, and then you will be a free man."

"And if he doesn't?" Paol spoke antagonistically.

"Then all the more reason to move here, so we can at least have the next six years with you. And all the better for you, because that would be six less years in prison. The way I see it, the worst case scenario is that you remain here in your astronaut training program for the next several years. The best case is that at some point your name is cleared, and then if we choose to, we can return to Seattle. Either way, you made the right decision in getting out of that prison, Paol."

Paol stood up and took a few steps towards the pond with his back to his wife. After some thought, he turned back to his wife. "Honey, I have to decide now whether I am committed to this or not. It is all or nothing."

She shook her head. "I... I don't understand. You wouldn't go through with the mission, would you? I mean... you're just waiting out your freedom here instead of in prison."

"If Warron does clear my name, I still have to go through with the mission. I can't just leave Blade to go back into the pen. I can't abandon him."

279

In disbelief, Joyera took a moment to process this unthinkable piece of data and responded, "So, you would choose him over me? I don't understand, Paol."

"Joy, he has become like a brother to me. He saved me from hell in that prison. His attitude, humor, and intellect insulated me from pure torment. I to think of what it would have been like had I been cellmates with the 'Strangler' or with Rall McHerd—a violent man I had only heard about, but nevertheless suffered through a number of nightmares because of."

With a snort of disdain, Joyera now stood on her feet and turned her back on her husband. As she felt his hands on her shoulders, her closed eyes released a tear down her cheek. "Joyera, you know I love you. Please don't be mad with me. Try to put yourself in my shoes. If Warron is able to obtain my freedom, I have to make a choice between returning by your side as we both want to, but I would have to do so at the cost of my integrity to Blade. I would have to send him back to prison. It is not an easy decision, but I think you can respect the fact that there is a good man—a decent friend—a brother—who I cannot stab in the back. I can't use him as a stepping stone to escape prison on parole and then ask him to go back there once I am freed."

"But, they'll find somebody else to work with Blade."

"No, Darling. They are extremely desperate for astronauts. You have to know how desperate they are by digging up a pair of maximum security criminals to do the job. They are really rolling the dice on us. If I am freed, and I quit the mission, the entire effort is in jeopardy. Blade will return to prison, millions of taxpaying dollars will have been squandered, and the hopes and dreams of the world will come to naught."

She now turned to face him. "Oh, so that's what this is about? Becoming a hero to the world? Gaining immortality in the history books? Paol, you probably won't even return—everybody is saying that this mission is suicidal."

"No, no. Honey," Paol sighed as he saw the discussion heading in the wrong direction entirely. "First, you're allowing the media to convince you of that. They want the public to think it is suicidal, because it creates drama and excitement, and that's what the media needs to sell their lousy services. Further—I don't care about being a hero. I just want to sleep at night

280

knowing I did the right thing, and sending Blade Slater back to prison would be crushing to me—if not to him. If you tell me that you would rather me go back and wait for Warron to find the smoking gun in prison, then I need to do it now, before this goes too far."

Tears flowed more freely now from Joyera's eyes. "Paol, what do you want me to say? If I say yes to the mission, I'll lose you for twelve years at least and maybe forever if anything goes wrong in the vast distances of travel that you'll be assuming."

"If you say no, then you may only be able to enjoy seeing me through a thick glass window for the rest of our lives."

"At least I'll have hope of seeing you freed."

"Will you? Do you think you'll still have hope in ten or fifteen years from now? The trail to any evidence will have cooled too much to ever hope for. But I do see one thing—"

"What's that?" She looked into his eyes that were now moistened with emotion.

"This isn't an easy decision for either of us. Should I go back to prison and hope that something will happen soon? Or should I go on with the mission, and not know for another 20 years whether we will be able to enjoy together what remains of our lives."

Joyera began laughing nervously. "Do you know what is wrong with us women?"

Paol's mind worked this question at a million miles a minute. This was certainly a loaded question, but then again when would he have the opportunity to have a woman ask him that question ever again. But maybe he was being tricked into something. In the end, he opted for the only safe answer that he could give.

"I didn't know there was anything wrong with women."

With genuine laughter, she bowed her head. "Nice try—do you really expect me to buy that? Anyway, since you are unwilling to give an answer, I will. Women fantasize too much about their happily-ever-after. All along, I had convinced myself that we would move to Houston, wait a few more months, have your name cleared permanently, move back to Seattle, and live out our perfect little lives happily ever after. And then when those unrealistic expectations are not met, our worlds are shattered beyond repair.

"But I have to accept that there may be a different happily-ever-after for us, which is that we move to Houston, enjoy our weekends together thoroughly for the next six years, and become famously admired for giving up our father and husband to the heroic service of his country and world. I guess, sometimes in life, there are things larger than ourselves—larger than life itself. I mean, what does our existence on this planet mean unless we are engaged in bettering the world for generations to come? Your efforts in learning about Earth2 will be indispensable in gaining the knowledge we crave and need to understand our universe better, and to progress—not as just a self-centered all-important view of the universe that revolves around us, but rather a universal community of beings who share the universe with brothers and sisters that today we can only imagine are out there."

"We don't know that we'll meet anybody on Earth2, you know."

"You will, Paol—you will."

"How can you be so sure?"

"We women may be optimistic to a fault, but our intuition can't be refuted. I've always felt that there is something out there bigger than just ourselves. Can we really be so egotistical to think that we evolved as the only intelligent beings in the universe? In the vastness of the galaxies, what makes our little solar system so much more important than the trillions of other stars out there? Or—on the other hand, if we really are created by an all-powerful God, can we really think that he created trillions of stars just to populate one little planet with sentient beings? Why would he waste his time creating all of the other stars, planets and galaxies when one little star called the Sun would do?

"No, Paol—there are others out there, and I should be less selfish to keep you to myself when you have the opportunity to discover them for us. You should go on this mission—but I want you to do everything in your power to make it succeed. You are a great man, Paol Joonter—too great for your efforts to fail and be in vain."

Words escaped him, not that they would have helped anyway, as he was too emotional at this point to be able to speak. Instead, he chose to hold his wife close to him. As he felt her head on his chest, he also noticed his heartbeat, and in that heartbeat, he felt something different—something that he had never quite felt before. He realized that his wife was right—that his life was somehow meant for something greater and that the inhabitants of Earth1 needed to learn about Earth2. He was the man chosen—either by God or by fate—to discover for his own race something of vast importance, something so vast that it might even be paramount to the future of Earth1.

Chapter

24

It took months for Paol and Blade to feel comfortable with their new routine. Going from the prison to astronaut training was like night and day. They found themselves exhausted before breakfast due to the torturous workout of their personal trainers, but that was just the beginning, of course. Flight simulation required intense focus and reflexes, while the barrage of coursework took every last bit of energy.

Naturally, they looked forward to the weekends, where they could catch up on rest, and more casually work through their physical routines and their memorization and study. But the weekends just never seemed long enough. Muscles were sore when the alarm went off on Monday morning. Eyes were bloodshot from reading their iTexts and flash cards. Headaches seemed as if they were simply trying to stretch their brains faster than they could absorb it all. As a result, they were thrilled to hear of their first flight field trip. Their flight instructors would be escorting them to Nevada, where a range of in-flight tests would take place. They would eventually need to log hundreds of hours of flight experience before they could even be considered as astronaut candidates. The week-long trip was intended to give them the first couple of dozen hours under their belt.

At an abandoned Air Force base in central Nevada, the two students felt like visitors to a military ghost town. The teachers, however, were familiar with the location and knew that it had the best conditions for flying. The weather was typically sunny and strong winds didn't normally occur, but if they did, they typically occurred around sunset, when the instructors wanted new pupils out of the air anyway, since the longer shadows could deceive pilots flying at near-mach speeds.

Physon waited for Blade with the flight instructors on the tarmac during a particularly dry, hot day. His olive green flight suit simply did not breath well, and he sweltered inside as evidenced by the sweat beading up on his forehead just under the raised visor. As Blade came rushing out of the barracks making the final adjustments on his flight suit, Physon rolled his eyes.

"Sorry there, Gents," Blade said gasping for breath. "These duds is harder to adjust than I thought they'd be." Blade grabbed at his crotch. "And awful uncomf'able too."

Blade's flight instructor couldn't resist the opportunity to mess with his pupil. "You think these are bad. Just wait to see how bad you chafe after spending a few years in that spacesuit."

Blade's eyes grew as big a golf balls, while Paol smiled widely at the gesture, and queried Blade's instructor, "So, Arjen. I don't remember seeing the hand gesture for grabbing yourself. Should we have practiced that in the simulator so we know how to adjust for it out here?"

Playing along, Arjen responded, "There was never an intended gesture, but the computer misinterpreted it occasionally as a dive maneuver, so we had to reprogram the dive signal to prevent it from happening again after the last accident."

"Accident?" Blade leaned closer, his face glistening with sweat, mostly from the heat, but partly because of the anxiety of his first solo flight.

"Yeah, we couldn't figure it out for the longest, but after collecting enough data from the black boxes, we finally pieced together what was going wrong. Why, even Metch here had a nearly fatal moment while adjusting himself."

Arjen gestured to Paol's flight instructor, who shrugged his shoulder and tipped his head in affirmation. "It can happen to the best of us."

"That does it!" Blade spat. "Take me back to prison. This ain't gonna work out!"

"Now, Blade," said Arjen. "I'm just kidding about the accident."

"I know that," said Blade. "That's not why I'm callin' it quits. This monkey suit is so hot and uncomf'able that I'd rather crash and burn than to stay inside it fo' 'nother minute."

"Let's get you up in the plane, Blade. It'll be better when you get out of this heat." Arjen's former playful voice was transformed into a tone of serious business.

The XJ-20 experts walked their students through vehicle and suit inspections, instructed the new pilots to climb into their cockpits, drop their visors, and buckle themselves in to the seat. The pair of instructors then returned to an air conditioned building and put on communication headsets as each sat at an override control terminal which the instructor could use to gain control of the aircraft should either student make a mistake in flight.

Paol and Blade turned on his headset and waited for instructions, as they sat side-by-side on the tarmac. They made eye contact with each other along the way, when Paol gave a thumbs-up to his colleague across the way. Blade nodded his head slightly and bared his white teeth through a forced smile. He was extremely nervous about his first flight, but he was comforted in knowing that he'd be up in the air with his good friend. He took a deep breath realizing that that there was a safety net sitting at a control panel on the ground below.

"XJ-1, do you copy?" came the voice over the communication channel.

"Roger, Ground 1," replied Paol.

Another voice repeated the question. "XJ-2, do you copy?"

"Yes, sir!" Blade attempted to exude confidence in his response, but his voice crackled dryly.

"XJ-1, initiate startup sequencing."

Paol engaged his HOC, turned on the main power supply, and waved his hands in the proper gesture to engage ignition. He heard a soft rapid clicking noise and a high-pitch whistle that grew higher until it was out of audio range. The jets kicked in, and Paol confirmed that all systems checked.

Similar displays indicated successful startup in the control room as well.

"XJ-1, please confirm startup."

"Startup successful, Ground 1."

"XJ-2, initiate startup sequencing."

"Roger, Ground 2." This time Blade's voice was all business. While his hands trembled slightly, he was focused and ready to fly. "Startup successful, Ground 2."

"XJ-1, you will take-off on runway 3. Please proceed to runway."

"I'm on my way, Ground 1."

"XJ-2, please proceed to runway 1."

"Roger, Ground 2."

The planes proceeded in parallel away from the buildings and as the pair started for their respective runways, the pilots gave each other some final encouragement.

"Good luck, XJ-2," Paol spoke.

"See ya' back on the ground soon, XJ-1."

After taxiing to the end of their respective runways, the new pilots waiting for their next instruction. Paol glanced down the long runway, distorted by the heat waves rising from the black asphalt. Blade looked to the stillness of the blue sky and then glanced to his right and strained to see his companion across the way. The distance was too great to see more than a dark silhouette in the cockpit of the adjacent airplane.

"XJ-1, XJ-2. You are both cleared for takeoff. Proceed when ready."

Paol and Blade responded affirmatively. Paol engaged the throttle first, and Blade followed soon behind. Superheated gas emerged from the engines of the airplanes as the flight instructors watched the planes amble down their respective runways while glancing back at the cockpit video on their control terminals to make sure that the advance of each pilot was successful for takeoff.

Paol's visor display indicated full speed, and with his left hand he slightly curled his fingers skyward. A smooth motion ensued as the aircraft nudged its way off the ground and into the air. Within moments, Blade's aircraft roared off the runway and into the sky as well. The flight instructors could hear the roar of the engines for a couple of minutes. Within ten minutes, the binoculars of the instructors became useless. They switched off their headsets and conversed.

"Not bad for a first takeoff, huh?"

"Yeah. I saw a little veering down the runway from Blade, but he was pretty steady in the air."

"I always remember my first time when I see these newbies lifting off. It was so much easier than I feared."

"Yeah, I expect these guys to be pretty excited when they get back. After getting the first flight under the belt, you can't help wanting to get back up there. It's just plain addicting."

Once in the air, Blade and Paol separated themselves as instructed gaining sufficient altitude to do some free maneuvers. This helped them gain a feeling for the real aircraft instead of the simulator back in Houston. While Blade continued heading north, Paol veered off to the east.

Blade watched the four blue flames of Paol's jet engines propel him away. "XJ-1, this is XJ-2. Where ya' takin' that bird of yers?" he inquired.

"I think I'll head over to the Great Salt Lake. It should be interesting to see the salt flats from high in the sky."

"Uh… is it ok to fly there?" The tone of Blade's voice made the statement sound half like a question, and half like a reprimand.

"We can fly anywhere we want, XJ-2… as long as we have enough gas to return home."

"Ground 2, is this true? Are we allowed to fly anywheres? There ain't no restricted air space fer us?"

"Affirmative, XJ-2. Your display will warn you if you are converging on any other aircraft in the vicinity, in which case you will be able to take evasive maneuvers quickly enough."

"I'm just surprised that astronaut candidates are allowed to fly with no restrictions."

"XJ-2. You are not quite at astronaut candidate status yet, but your status as preparation for the Earth2 mission gives you permission to do just about anything you want."

A smile came on Blade's face as he let his left arm extend outward to indicate a hard left bank. Arjen sat forward in his seat perplexed by the sudden hard change in course, while Paol's instructor, noticing the movement glanced away from his cockpit display with concern.

"What's wrong, Arjen?"

His concern was answered with a raised hand gesture from Blade's flight instructor. "XJ-2, you are engaged in a vastly sudden change in course heading. Is everything ok?"

"Never better, Ground 2."

Growing more direct, Arjen probed. "Where are you heading, XJ-2?"

"Well, I always wanted to see Vegas. I'm headin' to Las Vegas, Ground 2."

Arjen sat back in a seat shaking his head and smiling at Blade's playful exuberance. "That's a negative, XJ-2. There is heavy air congestion in Southern Nevada—not recommended for a first flight."

"Ground 2. D'ya not just say I could goes anywhere I want?"

Arjen's smile evaporated while Metch started snickering at his partner's sudden dismay.

"That is true, XJ-2. But I don't recommend going there on a first flight. There will be plenty of time to do a fly-by of the Strip."

"So why's it ok fo' Paol to head to Salt Lake City—that airport's much busier than Vegas, ain't it? Nah—I'm headin' to Vegas, Arjen. See ya' in a couple of hours."

"XJ-2," said Metch now, trying to compose himself. "This is Ground 1."

"Go 'head, Ground 1."

"Put twenty on the roulette wheel for me, would you?"

Blade and Metch enjoyed a hearty laugh, while Arjen still disapproved of Blade's joy ride.

"Paol, can you talk some sense into your partner?" Arjen asked sincerely.

"Hey, Blade," called Paol.

"Yeah."

"I think Arjen is right. Why don't you choose a different location? Maybe you could spot a movie star in Hollywood."

Arjen's eyes grew wide at the thought. "NO... no... Las Vegas is just fine, XJ-2."

Laughter filled three of the headsets simultaneously. Ground 2 had become the butt of the joke, but it was all in good humor, and spirits continued to fly high as the two aircraft vectored off in opposite directions— Paol flying northeast to the Bonneville Salt Flats, and Blade venturing southwest towards Las Vegas.

"Just remember," added Arjen. "You have to stay within 100 miles of the border, or else you'll get tagged by law enforcement. My orders are clear—I will override if you get too close."

"Roger that, Ground 2!" The response from Blade was filled with excitement as he peered towards the south keeping an eye out for Las Vegas.

The next five minutes passed in relative silence. Blade and Paol continued to acquaint themselves with some of the responses to various hand gestures, but there were no significant stunts performed. Arjen and Metch continued to monitor the progress of their pupils, but all was calm, until a voice rang out over the headset.

"Ground 1, why am I seeing—"

Metch leaned forward in his chair and breathed an expletive.

"What happened?" As soon as he asked, he realized that the answer was an obvious one. The cockpit display for Paol's XJ aircraft went immediately dark.

"XJ-1, do you copy? This is Ground 1. I've lost your display. Please respond."

The silence grew more disturbing with each passing moment.

"XJ-1, do you copy?"

"XJ-2, this is Ground 1. Do you copy?"

"Yes, I do, Ground 1."

"Can you identify XJ-1's location?"

"Negative, Ground 1. XJ-1 is not on my radar."

"XJ-2, can you proceed to a heading of 175 degrees?" The request was moot, as Blade had already performed a hard bank. With his display focused on the last known location of Paol's jet, Blade abandoned his trip to Las Vegas, and began pursuing after Paol. After pulling out of the bank, Blade gave the signal for rapid acceleration. His body was pegged to the seat as the fire of the engines thrust the aircraft forward with violent force.

"Not so fast, please, XJ-2," implored Arjen. "There is no reason to jeopardize your own safety over what is probably just a communication glitch."

There was no response from Blade, as he continued to accelerate.

"Blade, I can take over control of your aircraft. Please throttle back on acceleration. I doubt there's anything to worry about."

"What if there is?"

"Then there's nothing you'll be able to do about it anyway. You can't exactly pull up beside Paol and offer him a ride, you know?"

Blade's acceleration continued.

"Blade, listen to reason, please."

290

Just as Arjen was about to take over the controls, he noticed that Blade's acceleration was dropping. His speed leveled out.

"This ok, Ground 2?" Blade asked simply, yet dejectedly.

"Just fine, Blade. I understand that you are worried. At your current speed, you should at least be at his last known position in about five minutes. Keep an eye out in case he has turned his aircraft back towards the base, ok?"

"Roger." Blade's responses were automatic, as he focused all of his efforts on the manual pilot of his aircraft. His eyes strained to look for Paol in the distance, but for several minutes, he saw nothing but the horizon defined by the indigo sky above and the auburn terrain below.

Eventually, a wispy gray line was discerned in the cloudless sky.

"Ground 2, I think I might be seein' his trail."

"Keep us posted, XJ-2."

Within a couple of minutes, Blade was able to see a wavy gray cloud of smoke already starting to dissipate in the breeze.

Following the line to its end, Blade roared into his headset. "He's down. XJ-1's down."

"XJ-2, can you give us coordinates. We'll contact emergency personnel and local rescue operations as quickly as possible."

Blade peered down at the mountainous terrain where smoke continued to obscure the crash site. An occasional flame pierced the gray and black cloud of smoke, while his attention was captured by an occasional glint of sunlight reflecting off of metal pieces scattered on the ground.

Breathing heavily, Blade's voice cracked into his headset, "Ground control, I've locked on the coordinates of the crash site. Latitude 40.584, Longitude -115.407." It's 'bout 500 feet below a steep mountain ridge."

Metch was already on the phone with the Air Force, who promised to contact local emergency support and dispatch a helicopter from Hill Air Force Base in Ogden, Utah.

Arjen continued to communicate with Blade, as Metch relayed developing information.

"Blade, based on your description of the crash site and the plume of smoke leading up to it, I have every reason to believe that Paol would've had enough time to eject safely. He must've had at least three to four minutes from first incident to impact. Can you cruise above Paol's last known altitude and hunt for a parachute?"

"Roger, Ground 2. I will continue to circle the area until I spot him or run outta fuel."

Blade circled to his left, then to his right, he criss-crossed large sections of the mountain range and the foothills below, all while maintaining rapt vigilance on the terrain below him. His eyes focused intently on the surroundings, looking for any sign of Paol's parachute, or any sign of human activity at all for that matter. This was a very remote section of the mountain range, and while he could see a few roads penetrating the range from the west, they all ended well before the crash site, where the terrain was steep and rocky with dense thickets of evergreen barring the way to the cirque where Paol's plane continued to smolder.

Occasionally, Blade would mutter under his breath so that he couldn't be heard over the headset. "C'mon, Paol... where ya' at? Why can't I spot no parachutes. It's been a half hour already. He should'a sent up a flare by now fo' cryin' out loud."

As Blade continued scouring the landscape for his colleague, he discovered something about himself that surprised him. Not since the botched robbery attempt back home had he been under such stress and concern. During those youthful years, where each mistake compounded the effects of the previous, he had plenty of time to replay the scenario over and over in his concrete cell. He realized that panic was his worst enemy in that scenario, and it cost him dearly.

But now that was all different. Why was he able to maintain focus and composure? As the minutes passed, he found that he felt the stress of the scenario, but none of the panic or fear. He realized both mentally and emotionally that panic would not serve him here that there was nothing he could do to change the past. He realized that Paol was beyond his help, except that he could continue to search and relay his position to rescue teams had he parachuted safely before the plane slammed into the side of the mountain. As he glanced towards the western horizon and watched the Sun lowering in the sky, he realized that time was running out on finding his partner before the day was over, and yet he knew that it would serve no purpose to worry over the circumstances. He simply needed to utilize every last bit of time available to him searching instead of panicking.

"XJ-2, this is Ground 2, do you copy?" It had been the first time in nearly an hour that Blade had been distracted by his flight instructor.

"Yeah, I'm still here, Arjen."

"XJ-2, you are running low on fuel. Please return to base."

Blade's response surprised himself again. "Ground 2. It looks like I can lower my altitude gradually to 18000 feet and buy myself another fifteen minutes of search time safely, as long as my descent back to the base is also sufficiently gradual." Blade was surprised simply because he expected to have been agitated by the order to return to base and shout a stream of expletives for being asked to leave his companion helpless. His calm, calculated response was as surprising to himself as it was to Arjen.

The response from ground control was not immediate. Blade figured that Arjen and Metch were consulting, but that did not bother him. He welcomed the pause for every precious second of searching.

After a minute, Arjen's voice crackled over the headset again. "Blade, we can give you ten minutes, and then I will have to take over control to bring you home safely."

"No need, Ground 2." What more could he do? It would do no good to waste his time arguing only to have Arjen take over the controls of his airplane anyway. He repeated: "No need... I accept the ten..."

His voice trailed off as his eyes grew wide with shock. At first, he couldn't believe his eyes. Blinking a few times, he tried to refocus his eyes to the north, where he saw a pillar of yellow-gray smoke rise in the sky at a curved angle. A flare! Could it be Paol? No, it was too far to the north! Surely, he would not have floated that far away from the trajectory of the aircraft. Either way, he had to hope beyond hope, and he banked his XJ-20 to the north to investigate the source.

"XJ-2, I didn't copy on that last response," A hint of concern was apparent in Arjen's voice.

"Sorry, Ground 2. I'm headin' north to investigate a flare."

"Did you say flare, XJ-2?"

"Yes, sir! A flare!"

293

Blade dipped to an altitude of 12000 feet, about 3000 feet above ground level. He was determined to get one good look at the source of that flare. He wanted to make sure that it was Paol and not some distressed outdoorsman.

As he spotted the blue-white parachute draped on the branches of a towering cottonwood tree, his relief was immediate. Heaving a deep sign, Blade smiled fully as recognition dawned on him. Flying directly over the site of the parachute, he could just make out a human shape in the olive green suite about fifty feet away from where the tangled parachute perched.

"Ground 2, I have a positive ID on Joonter. Please point rescue crews to a visible parachute near latitude 40.672, longitude -115.380 fo' recovery."

"Will do, XJ-2. Please return to base."

"Yes, sir," affirmed a jubilant voice from the cockpit of the surviving XJ-20 aircraft. In one last burst, Blade banked hard into a corkscrew pattern and slammed his thrusters after coming out of the maneuver. It was his way of telling Paol both visually and audibly that help was on the way.

...

The embrace was joyous and painful—joyous for Blade, but painful for Paol. After hearing a low grunt, Blade released his grasp on his companion.

"What's wrong?" Blade asked.

"Bruised ribs." Paol wheezed and coughed softly, so as to not aggravate the condition.

"So sorry, Paol... I'd no idea."

Paol returned to his hospital bed and sat down softly. He lifted his legs onto the bed and reclined back. The head was tilted up so that he could relax while talking to Blade. Blade grabbed a seat and pulled it close to the bed.

"How hurt are ya', Paol?"

"Not bad, really—just a couple of bruised ribs when I slammed into the tree, and a twisted ankle from the fall to the ground after cutting myself out of the tangled parachute."

"You hit the tree that hard? From what I recall, there wasn't many trees in that landscape. D'ya mean to say ya' couldn't'a landed on the ground?"

Blade shrugged his shoulders in embarrassment. "The wind was really sweeping me along, and I just couldn't seem to get down before those trees flew up at me. So I hit the tree, crashing through the branches and took a six-inch thick branch right in my side."

Blade winced to acknowledge the pain. "That must'a been awful."

"That wasn't even the worst part. So there I am dangling about 30 feet off the ground in a spaghetti of ropes and canvas."

Blade's eyes grew wide at the thought of Paol's predicament. "How'd ya' get outta there?"

"Well, I just dangled there for a few minutes in order to collect my thoughts and my breath. The adrenaline of ejecting and parachuting took its toll on any intelligent thought process. As my heart settled down, I knew that my best option was to release my chute straps and work my way down the tree. So I worked my way out of most of the harness and swung myself up to the branch that I had hit. It was strong enough to support my weight, so I worked the remainder of the harness off, but only then did I realize that my waist and legs were hopelessly tangled in cords. I reached the chute's survival pack, and unzipped the main compartment. I grabbed the knife and cut myself loose. Then I cut the pack away from its cords and threw it and the knife to the ground.

"I will say that it took some thought to work myself off of that branch, but one by one, I lowered myself to other branches until I ran out of room and had to eventually drop the last fifteen feet to the ground. I grabbed everything else up and ventured away from the clump of trees in order to launch the flare out to the west, hoping somebody in the valley below the mountains would catch a glimpse. I heard your plane off in the distance, so I figured it was somebody looking for me too."

Paol stopped to take a couple of shallow breaths. He would've preferred to breathe deeply, except for the jolts of pain that shot through his side and back.

Blade took advantage of the break and asked, "How'd ya' end up so far away? I was lookin' fer ya', but I never thought to go that many miles away until I spotted the flare."

"The seat ejects with more velocity than I expected it to. I know it has to clear the craft, but because I was already tilted at an angle, it shot me to the north like a cannonball. From there, the wind continued to push me farther away."

Blade couldn't imagine what horror this all must've been to Paol. He shook his head and gathered himself for the next question. "So what happened up there, Paol? What went wrong with the plane?"

"I'm not really sure. I got a warning alarm on engine two, and when I looked back, I could see thick, black smoke coming from under the wing. I couldn't see where it started. But the plane started to veer to the left. I tried to correct it, and it almost seemed to work, but then I heard and felt a large jolt, and the plane continued rolling to the left again. The nose also started to pitch downward. I'm ashamed to admit that I started to panic, after I heard no response from Ground Control. I couldn't figure out why Metch didn't talk to me, or take over controls directly."

"He couldn't, Blade. He lost comm with you. He said it was total blackness."

"Well, there I was all alone, and panic was setting in. I couldn't remember emergency procedures, was straining to recall hand gestures of any sort, so I was completely at the plane's mercy. The plane had probably rolled about 40 degrees to the left or so, when a memory came racing back to me— a memory that saved me, but it didn't come from flight instruction. It came from lunch. Lunch saved my life."

"Lunch?" Blade snorted. "How on earth did lunch save yer life?"

Paol showed Blade his middle fingers with a smile.

An expression of recognition appeared on Blade's face. "You mean..."

"Yep, the middle fingers."

...

Blade returned to Johnson while Paol spent two more days at Hill Air Force Base, recovering from his injuries. Both were given the time as leave from all training in order to recuperate. During that time, Blade spent many hours in his room, reviewing the accident. Nightmares consisted of vivid descriptions of the crash scene, and a couple of times, he saw in his dream Paol's lifeless body lying next to the smoldering debris.

"I can't do this..." he would say to himself. "How can we possibly reach Earth2, when we couldn't make it across Nevada... This really is suicide... All of the astronauts were right... This is just nuts."

Through his discouragement, he had decided that he couldn't go on. Gilroy gave the pair an extra week to recover. Paol did his best to get Blade

296

to talk, to work through the issues, but Blade grew more inward emotionally. Paol tried everything, and with one last idea, he made an inquiry to Gilroy.

"There is one person who might be able to talk some sense into him," Paol shared with the program director.

Gilroy listened intently.

"He speaks highly of his uncle—he was Blade's only role model when growing up… the one person he looks up to even today, and regrets not listening to when he had the chance."

"Where can I find him?"

"I don't know. Blade lost contact with his uncle many years ago, but I know his name and where he was last known to live."

"We'll find him," Gilroy promised. "We've spent too much money on this project, and we can't let it fail now."

…

Blade received a knock on his door, but didn't answer. Paol opened the door slightly, and called in to the darkened room to his partner, who acknowledged him with a grunt.

"Blade, I have somebody here who would like to see you."

Another grunt—this one his last, as the door opened, and he instantly recognized the figure standing there. Quickly, he rose from his seat. "Is it—is it you?"

"Thomas."

Tears formed in Blade's eyes and began to roll down his cheeks. Choking back sobs, he fell into his uncles arms as the two enjoyed a long-missed embrace.

As Blade released his grasp, he spoke with a crackle. "Uncle Jes, how'd ya' come to see me here."

Looking at Paol, Blade's uncle replied. "Let's just say that you have a good friend that wanted to reunite a long-lost relationship."

Blade looked curiously at Paol. "Why—how'd ya' ever find him—I tried to mail him that letter after we come here, but it wasn't delivered."

"Well, Blade," answered Paol. "The federal government seems to do a good job at finding people who need to be found."

Blade nodded, understanding that Paol had pulled some strings, and wondered how many federal organizations needed to be employed in the search.

"I'm going to let you two catch up," Paol said, excusing himself from the room. Blade just stared at his uncle with great excitement, as he heard Paol's footsteps down the hall.

"Where's my manners? Do come in," Blade said. "It's not exactly the biggest place fo' entertainin'."

Jes nodded approvingly. "Actually, it looks like you're moving up in the world." A knowing smile was offered, and a hearty laugh ensued as Blade quickly understood the reference to his prison cell.

After exchanging some pleasant memories, Jes brought Blade up-to-speed on his life. After losing his job, he moved to a small town south of Atlanta, claiming that he always wanted to get out of the big city. He got a job as a mechanic and has enjoyed the small-town lifestyle ever since.

"As for you," Jes changed the subject. "Not much catching up needed. I know everything about you, Blade. The media's published just about everything except your auto-biography."

Blade chuckled softly. "Well, that'd be tough, Uncle, seein' how *I* have to write my auto-biography."

"That's the point—if they could figure out a way to do so, I reckon they'd do it too." Jes flashed a wide smile of pride at his nephew.

"Blade—" The tone was clear. Blade knew what his uncle was going to say. It was the whole reason for his being here. "I understand you're thinking about giving up this opportunity."

"I can't do it, Uncle—it's just suicide."

"Really? It doesn't look like you're dead yet to me. In fact, it looks like you're doing quite well. This environment suits you well. You look better than ever, Blade."

"When I saw my good friend's plane on the ground engulfed in flames—well, I guess I'm 'fraid, Uncle."

"Afraid of dying?"

"Maybe I'm 'fraid of dyin', maybe I'm 'fraid of failin'… and Paol's got a family and all—if he don't make it back safely—"

"Well, then. Why don't you just make sure he makes it back safely? You've already done that once by helping rescue him after the crash."

"I can't make a promise that I can't guarantee. The odds are stacked against us, and there's too many things outta my control. Millions of things could go wrong, Jes."

"But it only takes one thing to go right, Blade—the one thing you said 'yes' to. The mission just might succeed. Have you considered that?"

"Oh, I dream it up occasionally, but it don't seem as real as the nightmares of how it might just as easily end."

Jes heaved a burdened sigh. "Your momma is so proud of you, Blade."

Blade sat upright at the reference to his mother.

"She talks of you all the time—how she knew you had greatness in you from when you was born. You know, Blade, the only reason she stopped seeing you was because she couldn't bear to see you locked up like that."

"I know that," Blade whispered.

"And she was real worried, Blade—real worried—that her tears only made it worse on you."

"They did."

"I hope you never for one day thought that she didn't love you after those visits stopped."

"No, sir. I always knew. She never told me nohow, but I always knew."

Jes looked deeply into his nephews eyes, as he saw him gaze off into the distance. Tears began to flow again. "I'll do it."

Jes leaned forward in his chair. "Do what, Blade?"

"I'll go on with the mission. I won't break her heart again, Uncle—I won't do it anymo'."

Chapter

25

Six years had passed since Joram Anders, Kather Mirabelle, and Reyd Eastman began their graduate studies at CalTech. Since then, all three of them had received their doctorate degrees in astronomy and had filled post-doctoral positions as researchers with Carlton Zimmer. During those years, they had helped discover a superluminal comet as well as the first extrasolar planet with specifications nearly identical to that of Earth. While each had opportunities to work for different research institutions, all had decided to stay on for the time being with Zimmer, mainly because they were interested in continuing the study of the superluminal comet and had a host of experiments lined up to gain a greater understanding of its origins, construction, and operation.

At the moment, however, they had set their work aside to be a part of the event that their research had made possible. They were filled with nostalgia as they began to realize that their years of research were about to be put to practice. Reverently, each took positions in the back row of the room. Even though they were the most responsible for the discoveries, they were too absorbed to notice the irony of being placed in the position of least prominence among the crowd. 0020`Ahead of them, several rows of padded folding chairs held occupants of diverse backgrounds. Some were huddled in pleasant conversation, while others waited intently for the table ahead of them to fill. The vacant table was covered with a black velvet cloth and skirt. Four black chairs sat empty behind the table, while four microphones and two tumblers of ice water had been prepared for the panel that was to assemble presently. Name placards located on the front of the table indicated the two scientists and two astronauts who would shortly be attending the press conference.

Behind the table, a wall-sized banner provided a photographic backdrop. It depicted the deep blackness of space, its depth implicated by the thousands of stars of varying brightness and color. A thin yellow beam cut through the mural at a gradual curve, while a smooth silvery-black spaceship with three blue-white rocket engines thrust the vehicle towards a rendezvous with the beam. In the middle of the mural, the artist had placed a depiction of Earth in a three-quarter illumination. A spotlight recessed in the center of the ceiling acted as the imaginary sun shining down on the blue planet with its swirling white clouds. At the end of the yellow ray, was an identically apportioned planet almost too small to make out. Written in brilliant gold letters above were the words:

Earth2 Mission – ST3
Joonter / Slater

The researchers studied the banner, admiring the artist's efforts in capturing the essence and emotion of the mission. Just as Kath's eyes began to moisten with emotion, she noticed a few heads turn towards the door at the front of the room. She elbowed her colleagues on either side of her, in order to focus their attention on the spot that everyone else was now monitoring. Through the door, Dr. Gilroy led the procession to the table. Paol Joonter and Blade Slater followed, with Carlton Zimmer in close pursuit. The crowd now stood and in unison respectfully began to applaud this historic group of individuals.

All four men had become household names in the United States and throughout most of the world for the roles they assumed in the Earth2 mission now in its sixth year of its preparation and twelfth digit of its funding. The media portrayed these individuals as both champions of space exploration and consumers of $267 billion in wasteful spending for which nobody would reap the benefit for at least a dozen years, even if the low-percentage mission actually succeeded.

Only after the men took their seats at the table, did the applause taper off. Throats cleared, and the shuffling noise of chairs on the tile floor indicated the adjustments being made to settle comfortably into the press conference. Gilroy spoke first and addressed the audience with prepared remarks, which he read from a yellow manila folder that he opened flat onto the table.

"Ladies and gentlemen of the press, esteemed colleagues of NASA, and dear dignitaries, we thank you for your presence here today, and trust that you are as excited as we are to enter the second phase of the Earth2 mission. These two unlikely and yet extraordinary astronauts—" Gilroy paused while gesturing to his left where Paol and Blade sat donning their teal spacesuits. "These two astronauts have been examples of inspiration to all of us. Even in the most desperate and unfortunate of circumstances, their stories have given us hope to overcome our difficulties, to correct our own courses with courage and determination. In the last five and a half years, these two fine gentlemen have become some of the highest caliber astronauts that I've ever had the privilege of knowing. Perhaps it is the nature and complexity of their mission, but I can say without any reservation that they have done everything humanly possible in preparing themselves to face any obstacle they should encounter on this mission. Tomorrow, we will bid farewell to these men, as we send them on a journey of more than 150,000 light years. We commend them to the far reaches of our galaxy as ambassadors of Earth1 to the inhabitants of Earth2. Never in the history of scientific study does one mission have the promise of so much learning. We are eager to take our learning of this universe in which we live to new heights previously unanticipated."

Addressing the astronauts directly, Gilroy concluded, "Mr. Joonter, Mr. Slater, may God speed you on this journey to bridge the inhabitants of the Milky Way."

Paol and Blade bowed graciously to their program manager and to the audience as an even more generous ovation ensued.

Through the din, Kath turned to Joram. "Look... I have goosebumps."

Joram nodded understandingly. "I know. It's overwhelming to be a part of this. We all feel it, Kath." Through the years, Joram had to proverbially pinch himself for the role he was taking in the scientific community. Under the tutelage of Professor Carlton Zimmer, some of the most exciting and unprecedented research of the century was taking place. And he—a humble

302

farm-boy from Kansas with a passion for star-gazing—was a part of that effort.

Joram leaned forward and looked over at Reyd as Kath's eyes followed. Without words, he concurred knowingly through a wink and a single nod of his head. The experience was clearly surreal for each.

"Now," continued Gilroy, "we will be pleased to hear a few remarks from our esteemed astronauts, and then we will open up the session for questions and answers. Mr. Joonter, you have our attention."

"Dr. Gilroy, thank you. Thank you for your leadership of this mission, your encouragement through the difficulties, and your meticulous oversight of so many details along the way. Your example and efforts over the last few years have given me great confidence that everyone involved has made every effort to provide the mission with the highest opportunity for success."

Turning to face the audience, Paol continued. "Ladies and gentlemen of the press, I thank you for your attendance here today. Because of your efforts in following this mission from its most unlikely beginnings until this very moment, you have made the world aware of the exciting future facing Earth, our galaxy, and indeed the universe. While I know there have been skeptics, I do not scoff. There certainly were many occasions when I found myself in their camp."

A few chuckles filled the room, mainly because of the way in which Joonter rolled his eyes, conveying the overwhelming nature of the preparation which he and his companion endured.

"Your reporting of this mission, both encouraging and critical has helped fuel a healthy and needed debate over the necessity of this effort. I applaud each of you in raising awareness of the issues, the difficulties, the risks, and the benefits that such a mission could entail. Tomorrow, we turn the page in the history books to a new chapter. Many of you will be in the envious position to write this chapter, and I can assure you that my companion and I will do our part to give you the best possible material. Thank you."

The audience applauded vigorously as Paol expressed his gratitude with a slight bow of his head, and a tip of the baseball cap, emblazoned with the ST3 mission logo.

Once the applause died down, Dr. Gilroy spoke clearly and proudly into his microphone. "Ladies and gentlemen, please give your attention to Mr. Slater for a few comments now."

Blade had been scanning the crowd the entire time, and had mapped out those who were friendly to the mission and had easily honed in on those who were clearly antagonistic. He was encouraged that the overwhelming majority of journalists were proponents of the mission, and this gave him the ability to speak comfortably.

With deep, yet hushed tones he began, "Ladies and Gentlemen, this is a most humblin' experience. Many years ago, I made a mistake—a most terr'ble mistake. I thought I'd pay fo' that mistake the rest of my life. As I sat in a cold concrete cell, while many my age was makin' somethin' of their lives in school and college, I suspected that my life was over befo' it'd begun. But somehow, fate plucked me outta that cell, and put me here. It is a position I do not deserve—a position I did not earn—a position fo' which there's many more who'd qualify better. I ain't the most eloquent, and I ain't the most learned, but seein' where my life was and where it is today, I am the most fo' knowin' that where there's breath, there's life. And where there's life, there's hope. And that's what I bring to the mission. In a world where doubt and despair are more common than hope, I intend to use the latter in this mission. I'll work with my colleague and dear friend, Paol Joonter, every day we're together fo' the next twelve years with hope. I'll fight to make this mission a success, and bring back hope to all the world. When we come back to ya' a dozen years from now, my hope is that the word 'impossible' will be replaced with 'hope', 'cuz if two average guys can safely travel so far at speeds which should tear us to microscopic pieces, then I think Mr. Joonter and I certainly have a case to make fo' hope!"

With this last word, Blade realized that his voice elevated gradually throughout his speech. What began as a soft tone, ended in a piercing trump. The contrast and intensity of the ensuing moment of silence was broken by a controlled whisper: "Thank you."

The audience leaped to their feet and applauded vehemently. Each felt the emotion and determination in Blade's delivery. While the applause continued, videographers raced to upload their recordings over wireless links to a mass of vans, buses, and trailers outside. In a flash, Blade's speech was delivered around the world, interrupting television programming everywhere. His speech, while delivered in simplicity, would become instantly famous, and media, would latch onto the word 'hope' as an endearing connection to Blade Slater, and the ST3 mission.

Once order was restored to the room, Gilroy laid ground rules for the question and answer session. Each individual was entitled to ask one question of any of the four panelists when he gave them the floor to do so. With hands aloft, Gilroy selected a front-row participant to begin the questioning.

"Mr. Slater, thank you for reminding us of hope. Can you tell us of a time when you needed to reach deep to find hope while preparing for this mission?"

"One time? Why I could tell ya' of a hundred fo' sure." Blade stated sincerely while shaking his head. His voice softened as he continued. "But, I can tell ya' of one time where I had to reach very deep. Paol and I—we had to do some wilderness survival trainin' in some very rugged areas. The worst, fo' me, had to be the time we were told to jump out of a plane in the Arctic Circle. It was a long cold drop to the ground. As the ground rushed up at us, I have to say that I's too 'fraid to enjoy the view, but when we landed, my breath was taken away. We was in this small valley, with mountains towerin' 'bove us on either side. A lake at the end of the valley met a glacier comin' down the chute 'tween two mountain peaks. As we walked to the edge of the shore of the lake, there's icebergs so big I had to look up to see the top of 'em. I never saw anythin' so amazin' and beautiful, and was taken back such that I didn't even remember that it was darn cold and I was put into the middle of the wilderness to survive on my own.

"Well, Paol pulled me back to reality, and we used our global positionin' devices to locate where we were and where we needed to go. As we studied the terrain, we saw that we had a fifty-mile journey to get to our destination— the Anaktuvuk Pass. There's an airport there where our support team would be waitin' fer us to take us home. We located a valley pass connectin' the lake with the Anaktuvuk valley, where the outlet of the lake cut through. It was at the end of Spring, so the river was pretty swollen, and there's all sorts of ice blocks floatin' down the river, but we needed to make good time, so we pulled out our sponge kayaks—little things in the pack, but when ya' put 'em in the river, I's surprised at how big they swell up, and make a perfect floatin' craft.

"At first, it was a nice float, but then the river picked up as we went through a narrow steep part of the valley. Over a small rapid, I didn't even see that large chunk of ice churnin' at the bottom of a small drop. When I hit it, I flipped over into the river, and slammed my shoulder 'gainst the ice. Pain shot through my arm, and at first, I tried to swim to the shore with my good arm, but I knew that the current was too strong. I had to use the other arm. Reachin' overhead, I could feel my whole arm convulse in pain, but with big strokes, I's able to power myself over to the shore with as few strokes as possible.

"I fell down onto the shore exhausted and hurtin', but worse, I started realizin' that I was freezin'. Within moments, Paol brought his kayak to shore, and was by my side, warmin' me up with a fire and a wrap. As dusk was settin' on, we had no choice but to camp right there that night. I slept on my other side, to make sure I didn't put any pressure on my shoulder. In the mornin', I was still in pain, but was glad to discover that it was just a nasty bruise. We were just six miles into our journey, and I was devastated when Paol mentioned that we'd lost my kayak—it floated downstream, and our only hope was that we'd find it just a little way down.

"Mile after mile we walked that day. We never did find the kayak. In the afternoon, the valley started to open up, and I heard a splash just behind us. Spinnin' 'round, I saw this monster of a grizzly bear, splashin' across the river 'bout 30 yards behind us. I suspected that he was comin' to get his dinner. When he dragged himself on shore, he shook his fur of the icy water, stood on his hind legs and stared at us intently. He stepped slowly towards us, and I was just standin' there frozen. I mean—where's I goin with a ragin' river to one side of me and a sheer cliff on the other. Good thing my partner had the sense of mind to climb onto a ledge nearby, wave his arms frantically, and make some noise. I thought it would just agitate him, and at first, he looked to charge, but then he got a sniff of us, turned and bolted.

"I thought I'd never be so scared again, but then two days later, as the canyon started widenin' into a marshy plain, I saw somethin' outta the corner of my eye across the river. I looked across to see a gray wolf scramblin' down a mountain. At first, I wasn't sure if he'd seen us, but then he bolted towards the river, and stood erect on the bank, just starin' at us, and bearin' his yellow-white teeth at us. We continued to walk, as if to pay him no attention, and he simply followed along the bank, keepin' an eye fixed on us. I could also see some frothy drool in the corner of his mouth, and I couldn't help but wonder if he was plottin' to get at us fo' some meat to chew on. My heart raced, and my stomach was all in knots fo' nearly an hour, as he continued to follow on the other side.

"At one point, Paol here stopped and turned to me. He pointed out that the river was widenin', and we knew that it also meant it was gettin' shallower too. We worried that the current would be easy to traverse fo' the wolf if we went much further. In fact, we could see 'bout three miles downstream, where the canyon opened up to the Anaktuvuk valley that the river was splittin' up into a delta. Had we continued on, the wolf woulda had no problem gettin' to us had he wanted us bad 'nough. So we waited there to see what the wolf'd do, and he waited to see what we's gonna do. There we was at a tense impasse, and we could do nothin' but wait until the sun set. We don't know when the wolf left, as we could see an occasional reflection of light off of his eyeballs, even after it was pretty dark. But I do remember sleepin' next to nothin' that night, worried 'bout where that wolf was. Maybe he was gonna work his way downstream, cross over and then come up to greet us. Then, very early in the mornin', we heard the most eerie and hauntin' group of howlin' in the distance. By our recknoin' the pack was high up on the mountain across the other side of the river, but my skin crawled with each new chorus of howls that echoed across the canyon walls fo' the rest of the night.

"At the first sign of light, we peered across the river. There was nothin' there. As the light grew brighter, we grew more confident that the wolf had gone on—moved up hill with the rest of his pack, we s'pposed. We packed up as quick as we could and made fer it downstream, where we hoped to reach the Anaktuvuk valley befo' that wolf came back.

"'Round noon, we had left the mouth of the canyon and entered into the vast expanse of the Anaktuvuk. We saw loads of caribou that day, and we worried 'bout whether they'd cause us any trouble. While they knew we were there with 'em, they kept their distance, and in some cases, bolted away from us when they thought they's gettin' too close. Miles passed, and we didn't feel like we was makin' good progress, 'cuz the valley's so long. We'd hoped to come 'cross the Anaktuvuk village, but we saw no signs of it that day. When we set up camp that night, however, we could see in the distance—only 'bout ten miles away the dim electric lights of the tiny Anaktuvuk village. It was such a welcome sight as I never thought I'd feel. It wasn't much of civilization to be sure, but it was more than we'd hoped fer in four days of adventure.

"While we sat there enjoyin' the shimmerin' lights, we were treated to a light show of even more impressive caliber. The Aurora Borealis—wow! I was awe struck at the curtains of yellow, green and electric blue that waved 'cross the sky. It was mesmerizin', and at some point durin' the light show, I drifted off to sleep, and I done slept better that night than any while I was in the Arctic, I'll tell ya' that much.

"Well, to make a short story long," Blade chuckled to himself for his inversion of the common cliché, "The next day, we marched on and arrived at the pass late in the afternoon, where the Nunamiut eskimoes was waitin' fer us and took us in—quite hospitable they was... Well that was it—the most frightenin' adventure of my trainin'. It took a whole heap of faith and hope to get through that."

The room stood still, riveted by Blade's dramatic story-telling. All felt as if they had experienced some of it for themselves, and so they remained rooted in their seats. After a brief moment, a tentative hand raised into the air. And then another, until most were clamoring to ask the next question. With a point of his finger, Dr. Gilroy yielded to another for the next question.

"Mr. Joonter," beamed an eager journalist with large spectacles in the front row, "Since your colleague has shared his most concerning experience with us, how about you? Can we hear about your biggest trial?"

"I suspect that most would assume this to be the plane crash in Nevada, and I will attest that it was my most frightening moment to that point in my mission, but there were worse. The Alaska experience that Blade shared with you was truly bothersome, but remember that we had to endure many different wilderness survival training adventures over the last few years. One very big concern with our mission is the unknown elements of Earth2, and while the highest powered telescopes have been focusing their attention on that planet for the last several years, there is still very little that we really have

308

come to understand about the geography and climate of that planet. Besides, since we are 27000 light years away from there, the data we do have is from the very, very distant past. While scientists believe that we will be subject to very similar conditions that we have here, we don't know if we'll be subject to generally warmer or cooler climates, and whether we will have to face more extreme biomes than here on Earth1.

"Because of this, we received wilderness training on the most extreme of all environments our planet has to provide us. Blade has given you one example of this by recalling the Anaktuvuk as his most harrowing adventure. I will share the Anavilhanas for mine."

Paol looked at his companion with a smile, and noticed the very expressive Slater grow wide-eyed at the mere mention of this word. He exhaled strongly through pursed lips while nodding in agreement with Joonter.

"Once we had completed our tundra adventure, mission trainers sent us to the Amazon for our rain forest adventure. Leading up to the experience, we spent months studying up on the resources and dangers of that area. Our task was to parachute into a very remote area a couple of miles away from the Black River, navigate through the dense forest maze of archipelagos called the Anavilhanas with our sponge kayaks (and by densely, I'm talking as much about insects as I am about trees or the islands along the river!) and find our way down to the Amazon and on towards Manaus, nearly 50 miles away.

"As we broke through the canopy on our way to the ground, we remained for a few minutes in the underbrush taking in the scene. Never had we anticipated such a diverse environment. Dark even at midday, we could not look up through the trees to see any portion of the sky, and while at first, we could see no life, we knew the forest was rich with hiding birds, insects, and other animals. The incessant cooing, whooping, chirping and burping made us reel, as we looked without success for the source of this orchestra of sounds.

"Leaving our parachutes, we ventured towards the west, where we had seen the river on our way down. What at first was a minor annoyance quickly became an unbearable bane—insects! All shapes, sizes, colors. Some airborne, some under our feet, some dropped from tree branches. At one point, I quipped to Blade that there must be a million insects out here, to which he knowingly replied, 'thirty million, Paol.' He pointed out that it was a fact that he had discovered during his study of the region. At first, I laughed, assuming he was simply trying to lighten the situation with his trademarked humor, but once we returned home, he proved it too me in the book he had read. To this day, however, I still wonder how on earth there are so many insects in that jungle, considering the number of birds there as well. I would think that the thousands of birds we heard on our trip would've had to make a dent in the insect population.

"At any rate, we did receive some respite from the insects, and I'd like to say that it was welcomed, but it was not. During several occasions, our focus on insects was diverted to predators. Shortly after reaching the Black River, we launched our kayaks along the river, and were engulfed in a maze of long thin islands that run with the current of the river. Some of these islands were just several feet wide, but miles long. Navigating through them was a chore. At first, we assumed that as long as we caught a downstream current, we would be safe, but on a couple of occasions, the channel between two islands became too narrow to navigate, and we were forced to walk our kayaks across the island to another channel on the other side.

"Anyway, as tense and stressful as it was to walk along that river in Alaska with a wolf on the other side, this river didn't exactly protect us from predators. Our first predator experience was preceded by a high-pitch screeching that raised the hair on the back of my neck. Looking over at the bank, I saw leaning on a branch of a tree in the river, a jaguar eying us with clearly malicious intent. I was relieved to be on the river instead of on the bank, and I thought that we were surely safe from the big cat, but much to my horror, the animal lurched and then dove headlong into the river. Seeing the thing swimming straight towards us, I nearly panicked. We couldn't out-paddle him, for he was paddling with much more ability than we could.

"Not knowing what to do, we had hoped that the beast couldn't take on our kayaks, but we continued to look behind us with the cat in pursuit. Blade was just ahead of me and to the right, and I saw him look often over his left shoulder. Eventually, the thing gained on me and clawed at my kayak. I swatted at it with my paddle, but I didn't have a good swing since the thing was directly behind me, and I dared not try to stand or pivot my body for fear of capsizing in the river, where the jaguar would certainly have the advantage over me.

"I was so focused on the cat that I hadn't noticed that Blade had slowed and pulled behind my foe. Likewise, the cat was so focused on me that he hadn't noticed Blade either. Then I noticed Blade lift his paddle high over his head and bring it down on top of the jaguars head with crushing force. The cat howled in pain and instantly relinquished its grip on my kayak, sinking into the water.

"Blade quickly pulled beside me, and the river seemed deathly quiet while we looked all around for evidence of the cat's location. Would he spring up from the river and fly at us for our attack? After about a minute, I noticed an object slowly emerge to the surface about fifteen feet behind us. The cat glared at us, opened its mouth to reveal sharp fangs and bellowed in a manner that seemed to rattle the entire jungle. Worried that he would recover and make a fresh attack, we prepared ourselves with handguns. We weren't eager to unload ammunition so quickly, because we still had at least three days ahead of us, but we certainly didn't want to deal with this cat any longer. Fortunately for everyone involved, the jaguar thought better of its plan, slipped back to the shore, and disappeared into the dense vegetation.

"As dusk settled over the river, we found a beach on one of the Anavilhanas islands and set up camp there. With all of the scares in the jungle, we did two things to survive each night. First, we lit and kept a fire burning, in the hope that nocturnal predators stayed away from light, perhaps out of fear of human populations. Second, we took turns sleeping, or at least that was the theory. I found it very difficult to sleep at all. With the calls of nocturnal animals, and the sound of rustling brush on one side of our camp or the splashing river on the other, my attention was constantly focused on trying to gaze into the darkness to assess the source of each new sound or movement.

"One night, while Blade was sleeping, I saw an anaconda try to sneak into camp. While throwing a rock into the sand on one side of it, I diverted its attention while rushing to the other side with my switchblade. I stabbed down with the blade clenched tightly in my fist, thrusting the blade clear through the snake about a foot below its head. I rushed away as the thing started writhing all over the place with my knife staking it to the ground. It wasn't until the morning when I went back to reclaim my knife, and I had noticed the snake, and my knife missing. After a search of the surrounding area, we found the dead snake draped over the branch of a tree with my blade still lodged tightly in its neck. It took some exertion to reclaim my weapon, but I was not about to leave it behind. I figured I might need it again, and again before this was all over.

"As we were preparing to launch our kayaks for what should have been our final morning, a black caiman shot out of the water from underneath my kayak. This thing was frightening beyond all belief. With the body of an anaconda and the head of an alligator, I was completely unprepared for this attack. Quickly, the thing latched onto my arm with powerful jaws and sharp teeth. I dropped to my knees in pain. My arm burned as teeth bore down to bone. Thanks to Blade's quick acting, I was spared from certain amputation, as he got behind the monster and stabbed him with his switchblade. Turning to deal with this new threat, it dropped to the ground and slithered aggressively towards Blade. With one shot of his gun, Blade ended the threat as quickly as it began with an efficient shot between the eyes. The last thing I remembered was looking up to see Blade's horror-filled expression, a bloodied blade in one hand, and a smoking handgun in the other.

"Blade quickly dressed my wound, wrapping a towel tightly around my arm to stop the bleeding, but the damage was significant, and I figured I would not be able to use it to continue paddling down the river. With some thick vines and other materials that we had available in our packs, Blade fastened a makeshift tow-line between the kayaks, and tugged me down the river slowly. That day, we didn't make it to our destination as we had expected, so we camped one more night. I was finally able to get some sleep, but was awakened by a call and nudge from Blade. Gaining my senses, I noticed that Blade had just whacked my good arm with a long stick he had in his hand. And then I saw him thrashing at the ground with the same stick. I looked down at the ground and noticed that with each jab at the earth, Blade's stick was driving a bright blue frog back into the jungle. Here while we had dealt with predators of such a large scale, we were completely unprepared to deal with such a little menace as was the poison dart frog that Blade had discovered climbing up my arm.

312

"The next morning, Blade knew he had to get me to Manaus for medical attention. If the damage done by the caiman wouldn't start a threatening infection in my right arm, the growing deep purple spot on my left arm left from the toxic secretions of the frog would do me in.

"So, while I was completely helpless, here was my partner, paddling with all of his strength to get us downstream as quickly as possible with my dead weight dragging behind. Well, fortunately for me, as you know today, my partner did deliver me to Manaus quickly, where I was attended to, and then rushed by air back to the States for continued attention and recovery on not one, but two badly damaged arms."

"So, clearly, I have to say that if we do land in some harsh environment on Earth2, I'll take Alaska over the Amazon any day."

The astronauts continued to be probed on their training experiences for about thirty minutes. Questioning varied widely from light-hearted to optimistic, to skeptical, and occasionally downright angry. The nation, and indeed much of the world had formed vastly polarized opinions of the mission, and that became all too apparent, when the professor of astronomy was drilled by an antagonist reporter.

"Professor Zimmer," called out one reporter, as a corner of Zimmer's mouth turned downward almost imperceptibly in recognition of the tone with which his name was called.

Zimmer's eyes quickly located the reporter, standing tall over the seated crowd. His forehead was wrinkled as his brow reached for a receding hairline. Salt and pepper hair coupled with thick inquisitive glasses indicated that this was a seasoned veteran, and Zimmer thought he recognized the individual from one of his many press conferences over the years.

The reporter introduced himself as "Cartier Landry, of the NPC."

Zimmer managed a cordial smile, as he thought to himself, "Ah, yes... how could I forget Mr. Landry of the National Press Corps. Wasn't it just two, maybe three years ago, when we butted heads over the parallel Earth. What was the word? Preposterous? Ridiculous? I would've thought that I'd convincingly won that battle now that Earth2 has been discovered. And yet here he is."

"Yes, Mr. Landry. Go ahead," Zimmer was pleasant in outward appearance, but was preparing for verbal fisticuffs inside.

"Pundits, statisticians, and actuaries all over the world have placed their odds on this mission, and yet NASA has not come out with any official statement against these individuals. Nor has NASA released any mission prognosis themselves." Landry paused, to shoot a brief glance over to Dr. Gilroy turning his eyes only, not wanting to waste precious energy on moving neck or body muscles to physically turn towards the mission manager. "I understand that NASA will maintain a veil of secrecy over what is really being said about the prospects of this mission, but you," his eyes now shifted back to Zimmer, as a condescending smile formed on his face in at attempt to goad the astrophysicist into saying something newsworthy. "You, professor, are not accountable to that organization. Are you willing once and for all to state your gut feel as to the success of this mission? What odds would you ascribe in light of what the world is saying."

"Mr. Landry, it would be rash and imprudent of me to give you a number that would indicate my personal belief on the prospects of the mission.

"Assume with me that I give you a number, any number. If I give you a number that is less than 50%, and the mission fails, then it looks like I called it. If I give you a number greater than 50% and the mission succeeds, likewise, I must've known what I was talking about. If I give you exactly 50%, you will complain that I'm not courageous enough to take a stand on the matter. Let's say, I believe the mission will succeed. Why would I give you any number other than 51%? If I say 80% or 90%, don't I get just as much credit for calling it right as I do for saying 51%? Further, 51% is a safer number if the mission should fail, because then my reputation has some leeway for having some doubt in its success. So, I am unwilling to give you a number.

"To be honest with you, however, this is a mission without precedent. We have never attempted anything like this in the history of man. We have invited experts from professional astronomical and cosmological organizations the world around to brainstorm, troubleshoot, and review critical mission data. We have given this mission every level of success, but there is no empirical data from which any statistician could reasonable ascribe odds to its success. They can make guesses about how reliable specific mission components may be, but these are just that—guesses. And when you add guesses to guesses, you get nothing but numbers from this community of experts between 0% and 100% which are just that—guesses.

"Now, I know that this answer isn't going to satisfy you or your readers, so let me tell you a little about what I believe to be true. I believe that this mission can succeed. If it does succeed, we will have gained priceless scientific, cultural, and sociological knowledge. We will learn more about the universe that we live in certainly more than any other mission in our history. And isn't that something we can all agree on? Don't we all desire to better understand this universe in which we live. I truly believe that we do, and that I have attempted to dedicate my life's work to this cause."

After Landry studied a set of facts on the clipboard he was holding, he continued. "Professor, my data indicates that this mission will have spent at least $230 billion conservatively. Can you say that the gain will compensate the discretionary loss of so much money?"

"First, Mr. Landry, I wouldn't use the word loss, but rather investment. Second, I think I already answered that question with the word 'priceless'. You really can't put a price tag on learning, since knowledge isn't purchased or sold—it is earned. That said, we have invested billions, and if the mission fails, then if nothing else, we will learn from those losses, and then take another stab at it. I will agree with you, Mr. Landry that money can be used to purchase goods and services that we need as individuals, but does money really mean anything in the grand purpose of the universe? I am no philosopher, but my guess is that we will not take any of our money with us when we depart this life. I do, however, strongly believe that as we depart, any intelligence that we have obtained and shared will be left to the inheritance of our children. They will benefit much more from our knowledge than they will our money."

Landry refused to back down, and grew impatient with Zimmer. "Yes or no, Professor. Do you believe that this mission can fail?"

"Absolutely, there is chance for failure, but as I've stated, I believe there is a chance for success. What we gain from the success is priceless—I repeat—priceless. What we lose is money. But let's not forget that with every failed mission in life, comes learning in and of itself. And that learning can be applied to increase the odds of success the next time around."

"Professor!" barked the irascible reporter. "We would lose more than money. We lose two exceptional men. Does their lives not count for anything to you?"

Zimmer stood and rebuked Landry with calm yet vehement tones. "Mr. Landry, you have falsely accused me of negligence of human life. The entire team have spoken directly to both Mr. Joonter and Mr. Slater, and the risks—which they have assumed of their own volition—have been accepted by both individuals."

Zimmer looked at both astronauts, and each nodded affirmatively.

Backing down from that angle, Landry asked "You mentioned that there would be a next time. When you say that, I trust you are referring to the next time we throw hundreds of billions at ST4, right?"

"Throw, Mr. Landry? Is that a synonym for the word lose that you used earlier? I think I was clear that this is an investment of money, not a waste of it."

Raising his voice in agitation, Landry began to border on dramatic. "Investment?! Why not invest it in food for the hungry, shelter for the homeless? Instead, you have chosen to 'invest' the money in the execution of a pair of lowly criminals!"

"Mr. Landry!" It was Gilroy's voice which objected. He launched himself out of his chair, and buried his fists on the table as he leaned over to peer hotly as the insolent behavior of the journalist. "That is enough. You have gone beyond objective reporting in favor of setting personal agenda, and even beyond that you have now slandered these two astronauts. Your questioning is complete."

The word 'complete' was offered with irrefutable finality. Landry glared back at his opponent, but eventually slinked into his seat, as the nearby security detail took a couple of steps out of the darkened corner of the room, prepared to pounce on anyone to whom Gilroy gave the order. Gilroy sat down slowly, but refused to take his eyes off of Landry, until the latter broke off the staring contest with an awkward attempt to scribble notes on his clipboard.

Utter silence was broken by a deep parched voice at the front of the room. "Dr. Gilroy, may I say somethin' to answer the question?" All eyes turned to Blade, whose face was expressionless. Gilroy, not sure of whether

316

Slater would help the cause of the press conference or not, hesitantly yielded to the request.

"Mr. Landry, I don't think ya' meant those words, and I suspect ya' might regret havin' said 'em later. Fo' yer benefit, I'll just say that I assume these was spoken in the heat of the moment. I do see where you're goin' with the concerns over the financin' of the mission, but let me allay any and all concerns as to the motivation of my companion and me in acceptin' this mission. Neither of us was forced to do this, and there was no premeditated decision by the government to seek a couple of felons as lab rats in some super-warp experiment. Paol made his decision in the presence of his lawyer, and I made my decision in the presence of Paol. No government agent spoke to us 'bout this opportunity until after the decision had already been made.

"What's more, if you're worried 'bout me takin' this course of action just so I could break outta the pen', then let me just remind ya' that I would be free of my obligation to society in just under a year right now. Why would anybody choose to go on a 12-year mission away from his home planet when he's just a year away from purchasin' his freedom. It makes no sense. So, let me say now, on the eve of my departure from Earth1, I am not doin' this fo' any selfish purpose. I'm doin' this fo' the good of mankind.

"Let me say somethin' 'bout my companion here too. While I have got to know Paol Joonter in the last few years, I can tell you that this is a man who was convicted of a crime he did not commit. He was setup, plain and simple. I've talked to him in confidence, and I can assure you that his sacrifice is great. What's more is the sacrifice of his family. They was not too terrible interested in the idea at first, and I mean, who would be? They won't see their husband and father fo' twelve years! But in time, I saw 'em change their attitude. They went from consternation to utter pride. When they look at Paol, they see a hero who is makin' a tremendous sacrifice fer his country and fo' scientific discovery and progress—and he's doin' it at great risk, as you point out, sir.

"So, Mr. Landry, believe whatcha will 'bout this mission, and 'bout the pair of us who's goin' out there tomorrow. Paol and I know in our hearts the reasons fer us doin' this thing, and that's enough fer us."

After this speech, the atmosphere was tense and electric, and all were glued to their seats, except for one person, who stood slowly in the back and

317

began to slowly applaud this astronaut for his stirring words. Kather Mirabelle was quickly joined by Joram, who propelled himself out of his seat and began applauding even more loudly. Within moments, all were on their feet, applauding with excited anticipation for the mission. Landry alone remained seated, with a glare that bored down on Blade. How dare this crude, uneducated man best him in his attempts to spread his doctrine and gain more disciples to his ridiculous cause?

...

The press conference had been a success, even beyond Gilroy's wishes. All of the major television stations were broadcasting video clips, quotes, and commentaries on the event, while Americans remained glued to their television sets. Talk was animated and cheerful around the water cooler at work, over the fence with neighbors, in shopping malls with complete strangers.

"Where did you get that 'Paol and Blade' T-shirt?"

"I grabbed one of the last ST3 bumper stickers on the store shelf just yesterday."

"OFFICE MEMO: Don't stay home to watch the launch! We'll broadcast it live in our large conference room."

"I heard the President is going to meet with the astronauts in the morning to wish them well."

All were cheering for Paol and Blade. There was so much support that the skeptics were compelled to hold their peace until after the excitement wore off. They figured that they'd get their chance after the spaceship disappeared into the yellow beam. After a few weeks, life would be back to normal, and they could again begin to sow their seeds of discontent.

Carlton Zimmer's research trio thoroughly enjoyed being at the press conference. Excitement and energy proliferated the room, but they were even more excited for their next opportunity.

"Blade, Paol, I'd like you to meet some friends of mine." Carlton Zimmer was beaming to make the introductions, and had looked forward to doing so for years. "This is Kather Mirabelle, Joram Anders, and Reyd Eastman—my post-doc research students, who helped to discover the superluminal comet, shortly after the Camp Mars incident."

318

Hands were extended warmly between the astronauts and students. Blade was the first to speak after greetings had been fully exchanged. "I'm so pleased to meet all of ya'. Thanks fo' yer hard work in discoverin' Earth2 and makin' this opportunity possible."

"You're thanking us?" Kath queried in stunned appreciation. "You two are making the hero's journey along with a tremendous sacrifice that few could ever step up to."

Paol stepped forward and put a hand on Blade's shoulder. "You know, Kath, I find that some of the most important heroes in life are those unsung heroes who never make the headlines. It is a shame that my partner and I garner all of the attention from the media, when it is all because of your efforts that we are even in this privileged position to begin with."

"Excuse me, Mr. Joonter," Reyd interrupted softly.

"Oh, you can call me Paol."

"Paol, then—there's something I've been curious about."

"Go on," Paol smiled.

"I'm a bit perplexed about your attitude—actually both of your attitudes. Tomorrow, the two of you leave on an extremely dangerous journey, ranging through expanses of the galaxy that just a few years ago, nobody thought ever to be possible. At best, you won't see your family for a dozen years, and at worst, you'll suffer a horrendous death in the expanses between stars, or maybe you actually reach Earth2, find it to be hostile, and suffer death there, or the Star Transport fails in one of a million ways leaving you to float endlessly through space, or—"

Kath stabbed Reyd in the ribs with her elbow. "Would you get on with the question? What are you trying to do anyway—convince them to back down now just 24 hours before launch?"

Reyd blushed. "Sorry, I didn't mean—"

Blade laughed heartily at the exchange between Kath and Reyd, while Paol simply gestured for Reyd to proceed with the question.

"Well, you say this is a 'privileged position'. How have you formed such an attitude?"

Paol tried to ease Reyd's embarrassment. "Thanks for asking, Reyd. It's always good for me to remind myself of my personal reason. Let me assure you that I've thought through every horrible scenario that you have, and many more than those. Further, let me state that the decision isn't as easy as I might let on with my language. Leaving my family behind like this is a very, very difficult thing to do. But, I take comfort in believing honestly that there is more purpose in a life given in service to others. Sure, I could wait for my acquittal in prison, and then return to the business sector and continue to build products and earn profits, but how does that help my fellow man? This is a fulfilling opportunity that I trust will give more to the world than I otherwise could contribute. In short, this is what will make my life meaningful.

"That said, it is easy to think that I am just doing this to save my own skin—meaning, I have been convicted of a murder I did not commit, and this buys me time for my name to be cleared. However, it is harder to make a case for my friend here. When the opportunity was presented to him, he scoffed at it—didn't even give it a thought before saying it was crazy. He did the numbers, he knew that he would probably be out of prison before the spaceship even left the ground. He might have his freedom today on parole. But, in the end, he could sense what a big opportunity this was for this country, indeed this world."

"Off the record," Joram spoke up for the first time during the interchange. "The media is frenzied about the odds of this. You can't turn around without seeing some update on the odds in Vegas. Does it bother you guys that most think this won't succeed?"

Blade let out a groan.

"Every time I hear the naysayers, I remind myself of Christopher Columbus. Most people laughed him to scorn, and fo' six persistent years, he tried hard to convince people that you could sail a ship towards the west to get someplace that's in the east. Ludicrous, ain't it? It's no wonder nobody believed him. Finally Spain took a risk on him and provided him with the support he needed. It was awful brave of him to do it, but I remember readin' a quote from Columbus that showed me why he had faith that his mission would succeed. He said:

"With a hand that could be felt, the Lord opened my mind to the fact that it would be possible to sail and he opened my will to desire to accomplish the project. This was the fire that burned within me, the fire of the Holy Spirit urging me to press forward."

320

"Now, I'm not much of a religious man, and I certainly ain't felt no Spirit urging me towards Earth2, but I believe that this mission—this exploration—can succeed. First, Columbus—as an insider—believed in himself and his mission. He knew things that the critics didn't ever know. I can tell ya' that with what I've seen in the last few years, what the critics don't understand, is that every possible brainstormed problem, issue, and hurdle have been addressed. The odds fo' success are certainly maximized. Second, there's no question that we have the technology to succeed. Columbus was able to succeed with far less. Further, Columbus set sail into uncharted waters—there was no evidence that this new path would get him anywhere, let alone to the discovery of a new world. On the other hand, we actually did discover our new world befo' we're settin' sail. We also know the exact path to take to get there, and the computer's all programmed and ready to go. And that's that, friends. There's no use in thinkin' it can't be done, because it can."

"Thank you, Blade, for the Columbus analogy," Joram congratulated, shaking his head at his own lack of faith. "For the first time, you've given me hope that our work of discovery won't be in vain, because until you return with all of your stories, data, and materials, I've often felt that this discovery is really meaningless."

"Well, Joram, you just keep discoverin' those amazin' things out there, and when we return, you'll have to catch us up on all that we missed out on, ok?"

"Deal!" Joram nodded and smiled enthusiastically.

The door opened to the room where the group was convened, and all attention was diverted to a rather anxious looking mission commander.

"I know that this has been a rather brief meeting," Vurim Gilroy directed his comments to Carlton Zimmer and his students, "but there is a busy preparation schedule ahead for these two, and they are going to need their rest for the big day tomorrow."

Zimmer reached out his hand to the astronauts. "Gentlemen, thank you for the interview. This has been a most pleasant exchange. Godspeed on your journey tomorrow. We look forward to seeing you about twelve years from now."

321

Chapter

26

The sky to the east turned to a milky blue, forecasting another arrival of the Sun. Despite a few wispy clouds that began to glow on the horizon, the Florida morning was crystal clear, and dead still. The weather was fitting to the mood of those who awoke early to witness history. As the wind held its breath, so did the thousands of spectators gathered at various locations around Kennedy Air Force Base. In the center of this group of people, several strong search lights flashed up from the launch pad onto the star of the show.

The Star Transport interstellar vehicle stood erect on the launch pad high above the ground. It was supported by three large fuel-bearing silo rockets. Each white silo was attached to the spacecraft with large bands, one under each wing, and another under the body. While Star Transport would not have the luxury of being launched into space in this manner from Earth2, the Star Energy team took advantage of this launch to minimize the consumption of the fuel that would be required for the trip home.

The Star Transport, at the center of everyone's attention, had been considered by many an uninspiring work. As black as the depth of space it would traverse, it was designed to absorb every scrap of energy as it hurled through the darkest reaches of the cosmos. Its propulsion system was a combination of nuclear and exotic fuels, but all other electronics—including lights, computerized equipment, navigation panels, and communications devices were powered purely on electromagnetic collection panels that made up the entire body of the craft. The collectors were designed to suck in all of the solar and cosmic energy in the vicinity of the craft, much like a vacuum cleaner. For this reason, the body had no shine or luster. In fact, it largely resembled a lump of coal, and wouldn't have been mistaken for the star of the show, had it not been for the staring crowds and the flood of blue lights, mixed with the white flashes of camera equipment.

The body was entirely seamless, except for a nearly invisible door in the back of the craft. There were no stark edges or lines to be seen anywhere. The final design of the Star Shield was a thin, transparent, but practically impenetrable compound which was sprayed onto the craft with precision jet spray robots. Once cured under extremely high temperatures, it was as smooth as glass, and harder than anything known to man. Also lacking were windows of any kind. The two-man crew would instead rely on a series of image sensors surrounding the aircraft to provide visual details of their environment.

The fuselage had the appearance of a shark, consisting of concentric ellipses that grew towards the center of the body and tapered off slightly at the back. The nose was tilted downward very slightly into a curved point designed to deflect debris away from the vehicle. Direct impacts with the nose were calculated to be about five particles per billion. In preparation for even this most unlikely scenario, the shield was sprayed on to a greater thickness of five inches at the nose, whereas the rest of the body was given two to three inches of protective coating. This black resembled that of a clown's nose on the front of the vehicle.

Working back from the flight deck, the wings gradually tapered off of the fuselage. It was clear that the entire body was molded as one piece. No bolts or rivets anywhere. Gradual curves leaving the elliptical sides of the fuselage formed thinly flattened airfoils to create the wings. In the back, the tail stabilizer curved away from the fuselage gradually. This was the image for thousands of onlookers and millions stationed at television monitors around the world as the sun broke the horizon far across the Atlantic Ocean. Broadcasters added to the drama with lavish countdown ceremonies, colorful commentaries and exclusive pre-taped interviews with the astronauts and engineers behind the ST3 mission. Having tested the Star Transport during a couple of rigorous test flights—first around the moon, and then the sun— this was the third such launch in the history of the spacecraft. But, of course, this was the mission for which NASA was grooming the Star Transport all along. And while the ST1 and ST2 missions certainly drew the attention of many, this is the one that had the world enraptured. This is the one where suddenly-famous astronauts Paol Joonter and Blade Slater would say farewell to loved ones and the inhabitants of Earth1 for more than a decade.

The family of Joonter, as well as Slater's uncle and mother sat front and center in the VIP stands just above the astronaut preparation facility. Wide-eyed spectators waited anxiously for the emergence of their beloved astronauts. Joram, Kath, and Reyd joined Professor Zimmer on the left-hand side of the stand, and watched as the scene unfolded down below.

Launch specialists zoomed about every direction whether in car or on foot. Some hurried about, while others barely moved. Security forces held back crowds, which were cordoned off from access to the tarmac, and all were clamoring for a view of the scene.

At long last, two large doors to the building slid open, as a procession of specialists filed out double-file. Camera flashes further lightened the dawn as Joonter and Slater quickly came to view, attired in deep blue spacesuits and beaming smiles. Each looked up to the VIP room, waved, winked, and blew kisses to their loved ones. Spontaneous applause erupted, and even the driest of eyes were threatened with emotion. Shouts of "I love you", "Good luck", and "Godspeed" could barely be heard through the din.

After a brief pause, the procession continued towards the launch pad, where an elevator whisked the two heroes along with a pair of attendants towards a platform just below the rear of the Star Transport. As the bay door opened, the attendants unrolled a ladder from a spool on the platform up into the bay of the spaceship. Within a minute the ladder stopped, and the attendants returned to the side of the astronauts. Joonter turned to look over the platform, gave a brisk wave with his right hand, and blew one last kiss with his left. In an instant, he climbed out of sight, into the belly of the vehicle.

An attendant scaled the ladder behind him. Because the Star Transport was placed upright, getting strapped into the cockpit seats was nearly impossible without assistance. The attendant harnessed Paol into his seat while the astronaut held on to a bar on either side of the seat to keep from sliding out. The attendant again emerged on the platform, but quickly disappeared inside the craft again with Paol's blue space helmet in hand.

Once Paol's assistant emerged from Star Transport a second time, this same sequence continued for Blade, but not before he could give his final farewell to the crowds with a full-tooth smile and two thumbs up. Cameras zoomed tightly into his radiant face, giving field correspondents plenty of material to work with, touting the efforts of the heroes during training, invoking the encouraging example of Slater's life in overcoming challenges, and praising NASA for their visionary efforts.

Once both astronauts were secured, the attendants left the platform, and gave a signal towards the mission control tower. They quickly rolled the ladder back onto its spool and confirmed the complete sealing of the door.

Blade's head turned slowly to his comrade. Noticing the movement out of the corner of his eye, Paol turned to see a very anxious and wide-eyed expression on Blade's face.

"What's the matter, Blade?"

"I's just wonderin' what we got ourselves into here, Partna'. Why this is some fool dumb thing we're doin', ain't it?"

"Now, Blade—" said Paol softly. "You aren't getting cold feet now are you?"

"No, they've been cold 'bout five years now. I'm just now recognizin' it."

"Blade, what better thing could you be doing with your life right now?"

"Anythin' better than committin' suicide quickly comes to mind."

Paol grew agitated and surprised by this comment, and scolded his fellow astronaut. "Blade! You were the one who convinced me that this mission has a perfectly fine chance of succeeding. Why are you second guessing that now?"

"C'mon, buddy," said Blade. "Ya' can't nohow tell me that ya' don't often think 'bout the fact that we know so little 'bout what we're gettin' into. I mean, nobody—nobody!—really knows anythin' 'bout this ride we're gonna hitchhike on. Look, we have no clue 'bout the real effects super-warp travel is gonna do on a livin' bein'. And, we don't know nothin' 'bout Earth2 that ain't more than twenty-seven thousand years old. Fo' all we know, evolution has advanced to the point that we're gonna have to run from dinosaurs or cannibals fo' five years, waitin' fer our bus to return."

"Dinosaurs and cannibals?" Blade asked curiously. "Is that the worst you can think of? Why I'm far more concerned about lawyers and politicians."

"Say wha—" Blade looked at Paol's half-hidden smile and realized a bit later than he should have that he was being joked with. Blade responded with grateful laughter that helped to strengthen his resolve.

Just then, a voice from mission control was heard coming from no particular location in the cockpit. In fact, it sounded as if the noise was formed inside the ear. "Star Transport Pilot, all systems are a go for take-off in T minus 2 minutes."

"Copy that, Ground Control," replied Paol.

The voice continued, "Please provide cross-check of onboard systems, ST3."

Paol quickly worked through a checklist of systems.

"Avionics: check."

"Communication: check."

"Computation: check…"

When Paol had completed his checklist, Blade raced through a list he had also been working on.

"Propulsion: check."

"Navigation check."

"A/V check…"

"Mission ST3, it appears that all systems are check, and launch will commence in T minus seventy seconds." Then in a less robotic manner, the voice asked. "Star Transport, is there anything you'd like to tell the inhabitants of Earth1?"

Paol took a quick breath and replied, "To the citizens of the world, we thank you for the opportunity, and can't wait to return with the knowledge you wish to gain from this expedition. To our families, we love you and hope the years will pass as quickly for you as the distance will for us."

And then, a final word from Mission Control before the final countdown. "Godspeed, ST3."

Anticipation grew with each second that passed. "T minus fifteen, fourteen… T minus ten, nine, eight, seven, six, five, four, three…"

In a sudden blast, rockets roared to life and exploded into a fireball that lit up the Florida morning even more effectively than the low-lying Sun.

Spectators struggled to determine whether they should shield their eyes or cover their ears. The vehicle lifted gently off the ground, cleared the launch pad, and then quickly shot the Star Transport into the atmosphere. The roaring of the rockets gradually subsided giving way to the cheers of the crowd. All were applauding, yelling, and whistling enthusiastically as their beloved astronauts approached the upper reaches of the atmosphere.

Paol and Blade sat silent in the darkness of the cockpit, enveloped in the discomfort of rapid acceleration and intense vibration. They had experienced this multiple times in the simulator, but this time it was real, and that knowledge multiplied the difficulty of the situation, not to mention the churning of their stomachs.

Medical personnel watched abnormal vital signs in both astronauts with guarded concern. While nothing they saw was unexpected, they also knew that the elevated heart-rate, body temperature, and rapid breathing were not desired.

A sudden jolt shook both astronauts in a tense, yet anticipated moment. Through the darkness of the flight deck, the astronauts knew that this was the moment of separation. The two wing-mounted silo rocket boosters separated from the Star Transport, and the high-tension straps whipped rapidly away from the body. The astronauts braced for one final jolt, when the third silo was to be released. In an instant, the vehicle lunged upwards, while nauseated stomachs lurched in the opposite direction. Blade closed his eyes while Paol inhaled deeply.

At long last, the astronauts exited the atmosphere and the ride became more smooth and comfortable. Slowly, as the astronauts realized that the worst was behind them, vital signs began to stabilize—for both the astronauts, and mission control personnel.

"Piece of cake, huh partner?" Paol reached over and slapped his navigator in the arm.

"Yeah, I can't wait to see what super-warp's gonna feel like." Blade shook his head slowly.

A voice from the planet they just departed sounded in the cockpit. "Star Transport Pilot, please provide physical check."

Paol replied "Pilot reports no major physical problems—a slight nausea. That's all. Over."

"Star Transport Navigator?"

"Is my head s'pposed to feel this way? Sheesh!"

After a brief pause, a voice continued, "Navigator, medical staff reports some head stress reported in your vitals, but nothing out of the ordinary… so, yeah… it should feel that way for a while. Guys, I regret that we don't have any beverage service on this flight, but we do have some in-flight entertainment."

With that, the light began to grow throughout the cockpit. The flight deck transformed into a virtual planetarium. The dome shaped roof shone with stars, and the bright curved outline of the blue and white Earth dominated the left side of the display. Drawn to the light, both astronauts turned their heads to the left and gawked at the display.

"Wow," was the response from a wide-eyed Slater, whose word was more breathed than it was audible.

Paol turned his head back to the right to see his navigator's face full of stunned expression. "Pretty amazing, isn't it, buddy?"

"Ground control, thank ya' fo' the show," Blade expressed, as he looked back to his left. "These views are simply amazin'… it's just like lookin' out a real window."

When systems engineers considered the body of Star Transport, they knew that the astronauts would need an unprecedented view of their surroundings for proper flight and navigation, but they also wanted every square inch for the collector panels to ensure a sufficient supply of energy for the entire trip. The solution was to place miniature high-resolution cameras around the fuselage to provide a full panoramic three-dimensional image.

This seemed like a great idea, except that early demonstrations proved that the quality of the video wasn't realistic enough. Psychologists noted that simulated scenarios with video-game quality proved that participants would be emboldened to take unnecessary risks. With improved video quality, responses were more scenario-appropriate. As a result, engineers pushed themselves in the design of the video until they obtained near perfection in image quality. In an experiment, less than one out of a thousand could discern the difference between a real image seen through the window and a projected digital scene through the high-quality display.

Time stood still as the astronauts enjoyed the quiet and stillness of space as Earth floated quietly below them. The tranquility of the view was in stark contrast to the turbulence of life down below: people scurrying in all different directions, horns blaring in morning rush hour traffic, sirens attending to emergencies of all kinds, gunfire in war-ravaged countries. It didn't seem possible that the still blue of the ocean, the silky white of the clouds, the extensive sands of the deserts, nor the deep green of the forests could ever have induced such chaos.

Within minutes the Earth faded behind them, in spite of their necks craning to catch as much of the show as possible. Eventually, the duo had to concede that their home was gone—for more than twelve years. While hearts hung heavy, they knew that the best thing they could do was to just look forward—and that's exactly what they did, for their first task lay exactly straight ahead of them in full view.

...

"It's so big," Paol gasped.

"Sure is, Buddy," the navigator agreed with a huge grin.

"It's just that—you know—you see this thing in the sky night after night, and you just don't realize how big it is. It's—well—I can't even comprehend its size. Just look at that crater there, for example. How big do you think that thing is? I'm guessing I could get lost in that thing."

"You mean that one there with all them rays comin' out of it?" Blade indicated with his finger straight out from his arm and one eye shut to focus in on the object in question.

"Yeah."

"Why that there is the Copernicus Crater. A couple of those early Apollo missions landed jus' south of there. That's one nasty impact there, to be sure."

"Why do you say that?" Paol looked over at his navigator

"Well that hole's 'bout 50 miles wide, and—" Blade paused for effect, sensing the eager stare of his partner. "—and over two miles deep! Good luck climbin' outta that hole, if ya' ever fall in."

Blade turned and looked at Paol. "See those white rays comin' outta the crater? They're 'bout five hundred miles in every direction. How hard must two things hit each other to send dirt and rocks flyin' that far?"

Paol pursed his lips and let out a low whistle. "I'm trying to imagine the view from the rim of a crater that is two miles deep."

"Well, don't try," Blade shrugged. "There's nothin' like it on Earth. Even if you're standin' atop Everest, the base of the mountain is only 'bout two miles below. Even then, ya' wouldn't get an idea 'bout what a two-mile deep hole looks like 'gainst the flat land you're standin' on."

Silence ensued in the cockpit as Star Transport raced towards the moon, on an apparent crash course. Eventually, the vehicle steered away to make its way around to the other side, where the astronauts would rendezvous with one final fuel stop. A moon orbiter with a trio of astronauts awaited the arrival of Joonter and Slater to top them off and give them that extra burst to speed them on their way towards Jupiter, which was projected as the closest spot to catch the super-luminal comet as it passed through the solar system again.

"Moon Orbiter, this is ST3," announced Paol. "Do you copy?"

"Loud and clear, ST3. What is your ETA?"

"We are currently at an orbital distance of 175 miles, and are anticipating arrival to your orbit in about 27 minutes."

"We look forward to seeing you, ST3. Over."

Blade scrutinized the navigational display for any deviance in calculated trajectories, or orbital velocities for either the Star Transport or the Moon Orbiter, but this was a mere formality, as the computers controlled everything exactly according to plan.

While Blade monitored the computer displays, Paol maintained a constant vigil on their surroundings to make sure that nothing orbiting the moon might cross their path. Ever since NASA constructed the first astronaut base on the moon, the amount of space debris jettisoned by spacecraft, satellites, and rocket ships had increased greatly, and there were a couple of different orbits which posed greater hazards. Having past uneventfully through both, Paol turned his attention to picking up a visual on the moon orbiter. He strained to see, but with the sea of bright stars, it was difficult to catch a glimpse of the fuel orbiter, and the angle of light from the sun did not help his cause.

"Blade!" Paol announced abruptly. "There she is. At two o-clock with an angle of declination about five percent."

"How'd ya' spot her? Against the backdrop of the moon, she's so small."

"I finally spotted movement with respect to the stars just above the horizon of the moon. Anyway, I think we're in perfect position, aren't we?"

"Yes, sir… I'll radio ahead." Blade switched on his radio. "Moon Orbiter, this is Star Transport Navigator. We have a positive visual ID, and are closin' in."

"ST3, we see you as well, and are ready for rendezvous."

The vehicles closed in slowly. Paol took over manual control, in order to ease the Star Transport just over the top of the orbiter, passing within just a few feet of each other. As the orbiter passed below, and out of sight, his heart started racing. To know that he was so dangerously close to another spaceship, and that both were racing at tens of thousands of miles per hour. The smallest mistake could mean disaster.

"ST3, we see you overhead, and are taking over the negotiation."

"Roger, Orbiter." Paol breathed a deep sigh of relief to know that the pilot below him was now in control of nudging the two vehicles together.

Silence ensued for a couple of minutes before a sound of a thump caused Paol and Blade to lurch forward. Wide-eyed, the two looked behind them and saw a round portal open on the rear bay door. The round face of an astronaut, with a large tuft of blonde hair floating above his head emerged in the hole with a beaming smile.

"Star Transport. Permission to board your vessel?"

"O'Ryan!" exclaimed Blade with a mile-wide smile. He would've bounded towards the visitor to greet him warmly, but he was still becoming accustomed to weightlessness, in spite of all the zero-G training on Earth. Further, Star Transport was very short from floor to ceiling, so the astronauts had to move around a very confined space. Garrison O'Ryan, on the other hand, floated swiftly and effortlessly through the cabin to greet the ST3 companions.

"Why—the last time we met, I thought you's all against gettin' back up in space," Blade stated as he took a firm grasp of the visitor's hand.

"Me too, Blade—me too. I fully expected never to come back up here after the incident on Camp Mars. I still shiver to recall the destruction and the weeks of waiting and wondering."

"What made you get back in the saddle, Garrison?" Paol now joined in the exchange.

With pride, O'Ryan answered, "You two!"

Paol and Blade looked at each other, confused by this answer.

"Like the rest of the world, I've been watching this whole mission unfold. I've read the interviews in the magazine, listened to the press conference updates, and I realized that if you guys could have the courage to travel tens of thousands of light years, the least I could do would be to travel the a few light seconds to help top off your fuel tank before making the long voyage."

"Well, we appreciate ya' makin' the trip just fer us, Garrison," said Blade gratefully.

Paol continued to catch up with their astronaut friend, "How's the family, Garrison."

"Great, thanks—everyone is just great. Had you heard about the baby?"

"Yes, we did—we also heard that Timmer wasn't exactly thrilled."

"Funny—when he first found out that he was going to have a little sister, he was quite agitated. 'Send her back!' he demanded. But now, he seems to enjoy playing the role of big brother. He loves helping her with her bottle, but he still thinks diapers are icky".

"Well, they is icky," Blade agreed with a comical shudder and contorted face, to which the group laughed readily.

"So how are you guys feeling anyway?" Garrison asked with genuine interest in his pair of comrades with whom he had spent more than a few hours in training.

"We're doing well," Paol spoke for both. "Leaving Earth was a bit of a trying experience. But the headaches are gone, and the stomachs as good as ever—except for the want of something a little more solid in them. As we adjust to weightlessness, NASA is keeping our diets fairly soft."

O'Ryan shook his head, and asked again. "No, I mean how are you *feeling?*" He hung on the last word for a moment to help clarify its meaning.

"Ah—you mean emotionally," Paol looked at Blade and a brief silence ensued.

After a deep sigh, Blade commenced. "We ain't gonna kid you, Garrison—it ain't easy comin' to realize you're leavin' everythin' behind fo' more and a dozen years—" He swallowed hard. "—Or worse." His voice trailed off.

Paol stepped up to complete his partner's train of thoughts. "We really have no clue if we'll make it back, right? You go through every imaginable horrible scenario. I didn't see Camp Mars first hand, but I saw plenty of pictures. The thing that annihilated your home up there—well, that's the thing we're hitching a ride on, right? You can't find a wind tunnel in the Solar System that can shake this tin can up enough to know that it will hold up in the barrage of particles traveling at twenty five thousand times the speed of light. Then, how many hostile settings can you think of for this planet that we haven't the foggiest notion about. But you know what's worse than thinking about all of that, Garrison?"

Garrison shook his head silently.

"What's worse is thinking about it over and over for the next twenty-seven thousand light years of travel."

"But it's supposed to go in a blink of an eye," said Garrison in amazement. "As far as I understand what the physicists are saying, you guys are going to sleep through most of it."

"Really, Garrison?" Paol's eyes narrowed as he probed the astronaut's expression for any clues to help him discern his thoughts. "Why, then, did every astronaut—including yourself—refuse the opportunity to come on this mission?"

O'Ryan was not prepared for this loaded question. He stammered through some unconvincing vocalized pauses, and weakly mumbled words like "family", and "Mars." After collecting himself, he admitted. "Guys, I know—this isn't anywhere close to a slam dunk, and I thought through many of the same issues, but even if I did want to go, I was still traumatized from the Mars incident. Besides, I couldn't leave my young family. My son would grow up without his father—he would be 19 years old when I returned. My baby would be a teenager before she even had a chance to meet her father. You wouldn't go either if you were in my shoes."

"Nope. I wouldn't." A blank look of bitterness swept over Joonter's face, and in a blink, every moment since his arrest flashed through his mind in an instant—the unjust verdict, the ridiculous sentence, the red-eyed and tear-stained face of his wife, the plane crash in Nevada, his injuries in Brazil, and now this—a mission touted as a certain suicide by many rational individuals.

A voice over the communication system interrupted his thoughts. "ST3, this is Moon Orbiter do you copy?"

Paol turned his head towards the cockpit, but in his mental state, he found himself rooted to the spot. Blade grabbed hold of the side of the vessel, and spun himself around awkwardly. Making his way towards his seat, he sat down and placed a headset over his right ear.

"This is ST3. We copy ya'."

"Fueling is complete, and we are ready to untether, but I think you have one of our crew on board."

"Yes we do," Blade said. "He says it's more cozy here, and he's thinkin' 'bout takin' a spin with us."

"That's a negative ST3," the voice replied with a chuckle. "Tell Mr. O'Ryan that he missed his opportunity, and will have to wait for the ST4 mission now. Over."

"Copy that, Moon Orbiter. We'll have yer boy back with ya' in a short moment. Over." Blade slowly pulled the headset off and placed it in its compartment next to his seat. He allowed the weightlessness to distance himself from his seat, and turned around to the other two astronauts.

"Well, Garrison. You go have a safe ride back home. We'll have a lot of catchin' up to do in, say, twelve years or so." Blade offered a firm handshake.

"Godspeed, gentlemen. I do wish you all the best."

"Thanks, Garrison," said Paol with a tight-lipped smile. "Don't worry about us. We're going to do everything imaginable to make this mission a success."

O'Ryan nodded and winked at Joonter, as he backed out of the spacecraft.

"Hey, Garrison?" Paol called out as he began to shut the portal through which he had entered.

"Yeah, Paol."

"I'd appreciate it if this exchange remains off the record. I don't want Joyera any more worried than she needs to be while I'm gone."

"Absolutely, Paol. Everything we talked about stays right here until you guys open this hatch up at Kennedy." And with a quick wave of the wrist that hatch sealed shut again, with a sound that reverberated like the bars of the cell at the penitentiary.

Paol and Blade strained to hear the detachment and departure of the Moon Orbiter, and when they were absolutely certain that there was no audible sign of their fuel tanker, they slowly returned to their seats and watched the diminishing figure of the orbiter in the video monitor on the domed ceiling. Craning their necks backwards in their reclined seats until the dot of the spaceship was no longer visible, they realized that they had seen the last thing from their home planet for more about a dozen long years ahead of them.

In an instinctive impulse to latch on to anything that would continue to connect them to their home planet, their heads turned to the left where the miniscule blue and white Earth sat a little less than half illuminated from the Sun. Diminished by the immense horizon of the moon below them, it was hard to fathom how they used to live there along with nearly ten billion other inhabitants. How utterly small and insignificant it seemed in the vast panorama of stars that filled their little planetarium. Speechless, they paid their final homage to this place they used to call home and then mechanically set a course in the opposite direction for a destination that was indiscernible among all the thousands of stars in their view.

...

"Looks like we're half way there, Buddy," Blade announced.

"Is that so?" Paol replied lifting his eyes from the monitor where he was reading the navigational display. The data demonstrated that Star Transport was now "204,975,___" miles from Earth and "204,974,___" miles from Jupiter. The reason that the least significant digits were blank was simply because they were hurtling towards Jupiter at several hundred miles every second. At these rates, the odometer changes so quickly that there is no way to perceive anything in the lower digits.

"You know," began Paol. "Time seems to be going by faster than I thought it would. I thought that sitting in the same seat hour upon hour would get tedious."

"I thinks it helps that NASA gives us a good schedule to follow," surmised Blade. "The daily activities seems broken up pretty well."

"Good point! There really is nothing on the schedule so lengthy as to make the time go slow. Between meals, exercise, scientific experiments, journals and logs, reading, and communications, the day does go by quite naturally."

"I understand now why they told us how important it is to stick to the schedule. Our bodies are used to the night fo' sleepin', and the daylight fo' bein' awake. But up here, all 24 hours are exactly the same. The body needs the schedule to keep from gettin' into some whacky state. I was thinkin' when I woke up this mornin' that the body would be used to, say, a 27 hour schedule if that's how fast Earth rotated. I wonders what kind of schedule the body would naturally fit into if there was no night or day. I could see things gettin' totally random, and that would be unhealthy, since there'd be no regular pattern of sleep."

This became food for thought, and both astronauts were silent in their musings on this matter, as they stared—literally—off into space. Jupiter was a focal point of much staring to be sure. First, it was their next destination, and further, it was directly in front of them, but even more than that, it was quickly becoming the most recognizable object in the sky. Occasionally, they would force their planetarium to turn to a different location, and most often they would choose to turn 180 degrees around, to watch the sun growing more dim and cold. It was shrinking and they knew that in the coming days, Jupiter would begin to appear larger than the Sun.

A series of three soft chimes directed the astronauts' attention back to the control panel in front of them. In large letters, the display splashed the text, "Communication from: Joyera Joonter." It had been eight days since their departure from the Moon, and Star Transport was now far enough away from Earth that communications between the vehicle and its home base now required well over a quarter of an hour before arriving at its destination. As a result, there were no conversations per se, just messages sent back and forth at regular intervals of the day. Immediate family had a phone number they could call to leave a recorded message. Mission control specialists would then package and send these conversations up at regular intervals up to a few times each day. While Blade's uncle or mother had stopped calling when they were unable to speak to Blade in real time, Joyera continued to call her husband once or twice every day.

Paol eagerly grabbed a headset, and placed it on his head to receive the message from his wife. "Paol, my love, as I continue to monitor your spaceship on the computer, you are getting so far from Earth that it is really starting to set in now that we will be apart for a long time. But, the days still go by quickly. The media still call for interviews and updates. I can't go out in public without being thronged by people with encouraging remarks and compliments. You are a real hero, and I'm so proud. Oh... the boys... I almost forgot. They received an invitation to the White House by the President's son. They say they're 'wildly ultra-dimensional'—kids and their slang these days. I still haven't decided if I'm going to Paris, but NASA's public relations office is putting on quite a bit of pressure. They fear that if I refuse the offer from President Chartier, she may take offense. The problem is that I know it will remind me of our tenth anniversary in Europe. It's going to feel empty there without you, Dear.

"Regarding your last message, I'm about half way through Seddy's book. I agree with you that his theories on extra-terrestrial intelligence evolution are quite interesting, but I have to point out they are just that—theories. We still haven't discovered a single intelligent communication coming from anywhere in the Milky Way. I know, I know... distance between stars, dark energy interference, yada yada. I do have to reiterate, Paol... please be careful on Earth2, and don't take anything for granted. Even if you find intelligent beings, don't take anything at face value. Unless the same human seed was used to fill inhabitable planets, we can't assume anything that anybody says or does. Just... just be careful, Love!

"Well... gotta run now. I'll look forward to hearing your voice when I return home this evening. Have a great day, and tell Blade I said hello... poor fellow. It must be hard not having any family to talk with, especially at this time of such change. I'm sure he could use some encouraging words. I love you, my hero!"

Paol slowly removed the headset and mechanically returned it to its holster beside his seat. He looked over to notice his companion lying back with his eyes closed and a peaceful smile on his face. He reached out with his right hand to get his partner's attention, and then drew it back, thinking it was better not to disturb him in such contemplative peace and relaxation. Instead, he slipped the headset back on and listened to Joyera's message a couple more times. Hearing her voice helped him feel that she wasn't so far away, even though he knew that hundreds of millions of miles were beyond his comprehension.

After perhaps a half dozen times through the message, he again removed the headset and after looking down while replacing it in its compartment, he was startled by an apparent flash on the video display. Slightly worried, his eyes shot all about the domed display, looking up, to the left, right, behind, and straight ahead. Nothing appeared out of the ordinary, but had there not been a flash of light out of the corner of his eyes?

"What's up, Partna'?" Blade asked curiously, having sensed the sudden movements of Paol. Noticing Paol's wide eyes glancing about in different directions, he restored his seat to its full upright position, and was restored from his meditative state to full attention.

"Nothing—I—think" was Joonter's reply.

Blade's stare was persistent. "I'm thinkin' that was a bit less than convincin' there, Paol. What happened?"

"No, I—I just was putting up the headset and I thought I saw—"

Paol's sentence was cut off abruptly at the second flash, which equally caught both of the astronauts by surprise. Neither directly saw the brief flare that flashed directly in front of the Star Transport, but there was no denying a brief and sudden explosion of white light directly in front of them.

Blade forced a smile onto his face. "No, wait! Ya' know how much I love guessin' games. You thought ya' saw a flash of brilliant white light out in the front of the ship, didn't you?"

Since both were now staring at the video display with both eyes fully open, Paol couldn't see the expression on his companion's face, but having familiarized himself with Blade's playful inflections, Paol responded, "Why, how on Earth2 did you know that, Blade?"

"Lucky guess, Partna'… lucky guess."

Complete silence in the cockpit added to the tension, when all of a sudden.

"Whoa!"

"What the—?"

A third, nearly blinding flash occurred.

338

"Blade, can you see?" Paol questioned, while shielding his eyes. "I was practically looking at that thing straight on."

"I know what ya' mean." Blade's eyes were closed, but he was feeling around the control panel when he saw a fourth and fifth flash through his eyelids. Locating a compartment underneath the panel, he pulled out a pair of dark glasses and put them on. Shielding the top of his eyes with his left hand, he squinted through his glasses, while searching the darkened control panel for the right button, as a few more flashes occurred with increasing frequency.

"Ah, there ya' are," Blade addressed the button of interest. In a moment, the flashing ceased, as the planetarium quickly transitioned from video display to cockpit lighting. Both astronauts were left squinting and blinking rapidly, as the lights came on.

"Thanks, Buddy," Paol said. "Good thinking, on shutting off the display."

"Sure thing, Cap'n, but what the heck is goin' on out there."

"That's a good question." Paol was reeling from the excitement, but quickly regained his focus, and went to work. "Can you start a communication to Ground Control? Send them a video feed starting at time 14 hundred 12 hours. Give them a full 360 video. I know we only saw flashes directly in front, but let's not rule out any pertinent data. Let them know that I'll provide them with full diagnostic reports in ten minutes. I'm going to head to the back of the ship first, to make sure mechanical and life support systems aren't impacted by the event. I'll be back in 2 minutes."

With that, Paol quickly flipped himself out of his seat and drifted towards the back of the vehicle, and the cockpit was a blur of activity. Paol opened and closed panels, took note of monitor and gauge levels, while Blade threw on his headset and spoke out his message while fervently working with the buttons and touch screens on the control panel.

While floating horizontally and holding on to a handrail with his left hand, Paol worked through the panels and meters with his right hand, when he started to feel a tug on his left arm. Star Transport was beginning to slowly lurch. He fixed his gaze towards the front of the ship in order to assess the change in direction of the vehicle.

"Blade! Why are we drifting downward?" Paol shouted to gain the attention of his companion in the middle of his message to NASA.

"—at least eight or ten flashes in increasin' frequen—hold on—we're moving. Yes, Paol. You're right we are pitchin' fo'ward gradually. Um—debris detection, Paol... debris... the nav-comp says we're goin' through a debris field. You might want—you should come buckle up buddy, I don't know what kind of course correction this system's gonna do to us. Uh. Mission Control, please corroborate event. Do the flashes correspond to debris detection event? Over."

Blade flipped off the recording and pushed the transmit button. "Gimme yer hand, Paol," Blade partially fastened his seat harness with his right hand while looking back and extending as far as he could with his left hand.

Paol grabbed his partner by the hand and around the wrist, as the latter gradually pulled him back into the cockpit. He clumsily tossed himself into his seat, and both engaged full seat harnesses.

"Ok, Cap'n... d'ya ever remember hearin' the Star Shield team mention flashes? Could this thing be zappin' debris? Would that cause the light?"

"Makes sense, Pal. All of the flashes were almost directly ahead of us, which is where the impact of debris should be occurring, but you're right. I don't remember being prepped for the extreme light show. By the way, what is our heading now, Blade?"

"Looks like we're 'bout 0.8 degrees below ecliptic and 2.3 degrees to the left side."

"Aha! Here we go." Paol exclaimed while working one of the monitors. Pointing to the screen, he presented his findings. "Right there. An asteroid about 50K miles down range. The computer estimates it at about five hundred meters wide! That's definitely an object worth steering around."

"Ya' think the flashes was debris from the asteroid, then?"

"I think we can figure out if it was." Pointing to a monitor, Paol described his assessment. "You see, the first flash occurred right here around 14 hundred 15 hours. We should pass the orbit of the asteroid at about 14 hundred 28 hours. That means the debris on the other side should cease around 14 hundred 45, say 50 at the most. We'll try to fade up the video display around 14 hundred 40 hours to see. In the meantime, we'll want to capture the entire video, and Star Shield sensor data and wrap it up for NASA."

"I don't gets it, Paol. They tolds us that the trip through the belt would be easy."

"They said that it was a very, very low probability that we would experience any debris. They based their calculations on their map of the asteroid belt and our timeframe through here, but it is purely statistical. Even NASA doesn't know all of the tiniest asteroids that orbit up here. The space is too big to categorize all of the smallest rocks. Either we just got really lucky—"

"Uh—dontcha mean unlucky, Joonter!" Blade corrected.

Paol smiled appreciatively. "Either we got really unlucky, or perhaps this indicates a much more dense field in the asteroid belt than was previously estimated. I mean NASA has sent hundreds, if not thousands of probes up here, you'd think that would be sufficient to get a decent idea of density. But then again—" Paol trailed off as he noticed another slight course correction. The ship had leveled off below the asteroid and was traveling parallel to the ecliptic plane of the solar system. Likely, this meant that they had cleared the bottom of the asteroid already.

"Then again," persued Blade. "The asteroid belt is 'bout 2 billion miles in circumference. Even if two thousand probes have come out this way, that's still one fer every million miles of circumference. That's hardly sufficient to know what's really out here."

"Aha!" Paol interjected triumphantly. "Look at monitor five. The computer is beginning to collate data sets from the Star Shield."

Paol swiped his finger across the top of the monitor, where a blue 3D line drawing in the shape of the Star Transport demonstrated itself on the monitor. After pressing the playback indicator, the video showed an accelerated time lapse of collisions with the Star Shield indicated by red flashing dots on various parts of the front of the spaceship. An impact counter went from a start of zero to nearly three thousand.

"I'm so glad you turned off that video display. Could you imagine how bright it is out there right now with a peak of several impacts every second?"

"Well, at least we know that the shield is workin'."

"Indeed." Paol nodded and sighed, in realization that the pair had successfully come through the first of what could be many challenges and risks in the years to come.

...

The ST3 mission control room was a much larger and more active facility than the room in which Professor Zimmer and his research contingency used for studying the yellow beam just over six years ago. Rather than just two rows of flat work stations, there were sixteen independent stations scattered throughout the large floor, with each station serving two mission specialists. The stations had sizeable work surfaces with eighteen inch walls at the back of the station where mounted stacked glass monitor panels filled the back wall. Each station and wall jutted out at a 30 degree angle on either side, providing a second set of wall-mounted panels, giving each specialist a wrap-around work space. The angle allowed for efficient usage of both monitors, as specialists could quickly see data from both screens equally well.

The stacked glass panels were a relatively new and costly technology. When turned off, the monitors appeared as little more than a stack of four panes of glass, each just three millimeters thick. Each panel is separated by a vacuum space of five millimeters, and together, the panels were all encased in a single, light-weight housing. When turned on, each panel was independently controlled by any computer capable of multiple parallel image generation. The computer manages pixel transparency independently, such that any portion of the screen can be fully transparent, fully opaque, or any degree of transparency in between. In this way, a portion of the screen can be opaque, while others can be partially transparent to allow seamless overlapping of multiple images. This can be useful when engineers wish to see a model of Star Transport on the back screen with overlays of surface temperature on another, an astronaut position on a third screen, and air quality on a fourth. Each pixel projection is controlled by a system of lasers mounted in the bottom of the display on the edge of the glass, and each pixel is projected onto a curved bubble inside of the glass pane in order to provide image shifting for parallax control. For a single engineer looking straight on to the display, parallax is not an issue, but the concept of parallax adjustment on curved pixilation is necessary to allow multiple viewers to see the same stacked images without image shifting. If one viewer is sitting to the right of the screen, then his angle of view would otherwise cause images to appear shifted, thus distorting the stacking of images. The computer takes this problem into account by shifting the image for each panel onto different pixels for viewers of different angles.

The front wall of the room contained a main mission control monitor 20 feet tall and 40 feet wide. It was flanked on either side by two smaller monitors, each of which was only 10-15 feet in diameter. On the center of the main control, a computerized image depicted the planet Jupiter. A thin red circle tightly hugging the planet showed the orbit of the Star Transport, with a small dot indicating the current location of the ship. On the opposite side of the planet, at the right edge of the screen a curving yellow line emerged and disappeared on the display, indicating the predicted course of the superluminal comet, and its flyby of the largest planet in the Solar System. Star Transport was clearly using the planet as a shield from the intense radiation field anticipated from the comet in a high-tech game of hide and seek.

From a curved theater-like balcony, which is used as an observation deck, a large gathering of media, NASA officials, and politicians were gathered. Seated on the front row on the right side of the balcony, Professor Zimmer sat with his three post-doc astronomers, Joram Anders, Kath Mirabelle, and Reyd Eastman. There was an obvious tension throughout the room, with all eyes glued to the central display.

"Professor," Joram whispered as he leaned over in his seat towards his white-haired mentor. "What are your thoughts on the matter? Our calculations indicated an arrival of the comet nearly a half hour ago."

"No need for worry yet, Mr. Anders," Zimmer consoled his colleague. "A thirty minute discrepancy on an orbit of nearly six and a half years is not outside of normal statistical deviation."

Joram nodded, but his pursed lips and narrowed eyes indicated that he was clearly not placated. Two minutes later, he inquired, "We've only seen one orbit of this thing, Professor. What if it doesn't return?"

"And why would it not return, Mr. Anders?" Zimmer responded into Joram's ear to avoid disrupting the focused silence of mission control personnel. "A collision is outside of the likelihood of possibility. As you know, this thing orbits in the sparseness of the Milky Way periphery where a collision with a large enough deterrent for such a speedy object is extremely unlikely."

"Do you think, then that we simply didn't account for everything in our calculation, Professor?"

"Undoubtedly!"

"We have studied the equations for years. What variable could we have overlooked."

"It's not what we overlooked, Mr. Anders, but rather what we couldn't calculate."

Joram tilted his head and looked Zimmer squarely in the face.

"While I feel confident that no major collisions have occurred, I wouldn't be surprised at all if the comet hasn't had some resistance to its orbit from space dust, rocks or other small sized asteroids from nearby star systems."

"Of course!" Anders stated loud enough to obtain the attention of several field correspondents seated around the group. It was so obvious that he wondered why he hadn't thought about it himself. His face flushed as Kath scowled at him for his irreverence. Leaning closer to the professor, he regained himself. "But, Professor, if these minor collisions could slow down the comet and cause a delay, couldn't they also impact its course?"

"Certainly, but I don't believe that it will be significant. Work the numbers, if it will satisfy you. A thirty minute delay is only 5 ten millionths of the entire orbit. Even if we wait several hours, the change is miniscule. I suspect the same will be true of the orbit."

After a moment of silence, Anders continued. "Professor, I've been concerned about—"

Joram was interrupted by a raised hand of Professor Zimmer, who leaned forward in his seat as if to obtain a better view of the Mission Control floor below. A certain level of bustling ensued with some shifting in seats, and a couple of engineers stood and rushed about to various workstations.

Several more engineers stood as the main video display began processing the clear path of the superluminal comet, significantly closer to Jupiter than previously anticipated.

Several chattering voices were heard, but above the din, a voice of the mission control commander came from the back of the control room floor. "Trajectory team, please adjust calculations of comet's orbit and upload immediately to ST3. Comm, please notify ST3 that we have received confirmation of the comet and that once the onboard computer has adjusted its trajectory assignment, they are to proceed immediately to rendezvous. Congratulations, Team! ST3 hyper-warp phase begins now."

Kath enthusiastically embraced Joram and went to plant a kiss on his cheek, when she noticed his ashen complexion. "Joram?" she asked wrinkling her forehead in confusion.

Joram responded by shaking his head in confusion with a shrug of the shoulders. He turned to Zimmer to notice a similarly fallen countenance. "Professor, I'm worried about—"

Zimmer shot a knowing wide-eyed glance at Anders along with a rapid, yet subtle shake of the head. "Not here, Joram."

Kath squeezed Joram's hand for his attention. He turned and leaned towards her ear. "I hope I'm wrong, Kath. We'll need to do some thorough reviews and crunch some big numbers, but there may be a chance that—"

"Mr. Anders! Not—here!" Zimmer's voice was soft enough to not be heard above the chatter of the room, but was as stern as Joram had ever remembered. He stopped short, and began to comprehend that his mentor was absolutely right. Being overheard in this group of individuals could prove detrimental.

Chapter
27

"There she is again," exclaimed Blade, "just comin' over the horizon."

"Yeah, I see her," Paol's jaw dropped. "What a show!"

Paol Joonter and Blade Slater had already spent several days hugging the surface of Jupiter while waiting out for their ride to Earth2, and yet they certainly had not tired from the celestial show they were enjoying. They found Jupiter to be simply mind-boggling as they closed in on it. The radiant colors, and turbulent cloud patterns provided an eerie, almost frightening backdrop, as if the planet was trying to swallow the tiny Star Transport into its violent atmosphere. They had also been able to see all four of the Galilean moons, each so vastly different in appearance. Now, while they hovered above the wavy equatorial clouds of Jupiter, they could see two of Jupiter's moons simultaneously.

They had already been enjoying the view of Callisto directly overhead. When he first saw the moon up close as the vehicle approached Jupiter, Paol was stunned to find that it looked like an inhabited planet due to the appearance of city lights scattered all over the otherwise dark and ruddy surface of the satellite. Even after Blade had explained to him that the bright white spots on Callisto were nothing more than fields of ice at relatively higher elevations, he still found it eerie to look upon and imagine civilization on such a small, remote, and frozen moon.

With Callisto perched high above the domed ceiling of Star Transport, Europa now began its rise above the Jovian horizon. In stark contrast to the dark regions of Callisto, Europa is covered by a light, deep permafrost. With the appearance of dirty snow the surface is mingled with a dusty brown crust

346

and watery ice. What really distinguishes Europa, however, is the deep brown lines scattering along the face of the planet in all different directions, as if the surface had been clawed by a very large cat. Neither Paol nor Blade could conceive of the violent geologic forces at work to cause this vast scarring all over the face of the moon.

"You know, Blade," said Paol in awestruck wonder, "We've seen four pretty amazing and starkly different moons here around Jupiter. After we travel the circumference of the Milky Way on this mission, I can't help but think that it would be a walk in the park to come explore the moons of Jupiter after we get back home."

"Ah that would be somethin', Paol. I don't know if they'd let us have a go at it though. They've been talkin' up the Magellan mission fo' years, where they send off astronauts to explore and map the Solar System. It always comes back to a price tag that Washington won't pay fo'."

"It seems likely," Paol mused, "that if this mission succeeds, it will open up a whole world of possibilities. It would prove that if interstellar travel is possible, then intrastellar exploration would certainly be a safe proposition, and would look like pocket change compared to the costs of this mission."

"Well," Blade snorted. "I thinks we first need to cross this bridge befo' we can comes to the next one."

"Agreed. I guess I'll just sit back and enjoy the show." Paol reclined his seat and clasped his hands behind his head, enjoying the view of Callisto overhead with Europa straight ahead and the dominating surface of Jupiter to the left.

A series of chimes pulled the astronauts back to the mission at hand.

"Message from: Mission Control," Blade read the display. "Let's haves a looksy shall we, Partna'?"

Paol remained in his position of repose. "What's it say, Blade?"

Blade read the display. "It says, 'Show time, boys! The superluminal comet passed by at oh-eight hundred six hours. While its approach was later and nearer to Jupiter than anticipated, we have ascertained that the mission is a 'Go' for hyper-warp phase. Please ensure that data set 13009 is uploaded, configured, and operational before proceeding to rendezvous with the yellow beam. This is the final communication from Mission Control until you emerge from superluminal speed on your return to Earth1. Please confirm message and proceed with mission. Godspeed, gentlemen!'"

Paol quickly pulled out of his dreamy enjoyment of the celestial view around him, and became austere and business-like. "Navigator, please respond affirmatively to the message from Mission Control. I will work on installing the 13009 patch to the computer for correct navigation to the comet tail."

Paol worked the control panel in front of him furiously and efficiently as Blade typed and sent his response to Earth1. As Blade sat back in his seat, Paol also paused briefly and turned to his partner.

"This is the moment we've been waiting for, Blade. Are you ready for this?"

"There's no backin' out now, Cap'n."

The two reached out and clasped each other by the right hand in a tight grip. With intensity, they stared deeply into each other's faces, both attempting to assess the readiness of the other. Without further need for words, the moment sealed their intent to do everything possible to proceed with the mission and succeed. They could read the expression on each other's face and realized that they could strictly rely on the loyalty of the other from this precise moment in time to the day they step back onto Earth1, over twelve years in the future.

Turning back to the display, Paol and Blade silently read, "13009: Installed & Functional!"

"Full speed ahead, Cap'n," Blade confirmed. "Full speed ahead."

In an instant, the Star Transport accelerated through its final orbit of Jupiter. The computer had assumed full navigational control via the 13009 data set, and as a result, Paol and Blade only needed to sit back and enjoy the ride.

After about a half hour of travel, Star Transport had locked its course directly for the path of the superluminal comet. Paol squinted at the video display for signs of anything out of the ordinary.

"Ain't gonna work, ya' know," Blade guessed Paol's thoughts.

"What's that?" Paol inquired.

"You tryin' to stare down the path of the comet. You know that thing has left the solar system already."

"Yes."

"And ya' also know that our ride is currently travelin' faster than the speed of light, right?"

"Yes."

"Well, there ain't no use tryin' to see it. It's out there alright, but we ain't gonna be seein' it. It's gonna be a few Earth1 days befo' any of the dust from that thing slows down enough to be seen."

"I know, I know," Paol sighed. "It's just that it's hard to have confidence in something you can't see."

Blade attempted to convince his counter-part, "But Earth-based astronomy could sees the comet path through non-visual radiation, right? We don't have to see it with our own two eyes if somethin' else detected it with certainty."

"But what if the calculation of the path was wrong? I mean, space is so vast out here that we're trying to find a very thin line of the comet's path. If the calculations are off at all, we won't be able to intersect such a thin object. It would be like finding a needle in a haystack."

Paol stared blankly at his companion.

"At night."

Still no response.

"Blindfolded."

"So," Blade replied, "You're sayin' ya' don't believe NASA? They's confident that they caught the path, and they's given us data set 13009 to make sure that we intersect it."

"I understand that *they* are confident," Paol responded. "All I'm saying is that if I could see the darned object, I'd be able to know for myself."

Blade sighed and spoke softly, "*Therefore we are always confident, for we walk by faith, not by sight.*"

"What?" Paol asked looking directly over at his navigator, to see a contemplative look on his face.

Blade turned to gain eye contact with Paol. "It's from the apostle Paul. The very same who said '*Faith is the substance of things hoped for, the evidence of things not seen.*' Ya' see, Paol, what the apostle understood is that you can actually believe in things without seein' 'em. There's been billions who believed that God was their Creator, and they ain't seen Him either."

349

"You see, I just don't understand that… why do they believe something they can't see?"

"Didn't I just answer that question?" Blade responded waving his hands in great animation. "It's faith, man… faith."

Paol was clearly unimpressed.

"Look, Paol, faith's really the drivin' motivation fer everythin' in life. When the Sun sets in the evenin', you don't worry 'bout it gettin' dark fo'ever. Ya' have faith the Sun will rise in the mornin'. When you see that Sun, ya' get outta bed, and go into the office, 'cuz ya' have faith that you'll close that big business deal that will provide fo' yer family."

"But, that's different, Blade. I have faith in those things, because I know they will work. They worked in the past, they can work again in the future. Religious faith is so much different."

"Is it, now?" Blade raised his eyebrows as he stared piercingly at his companion. "The faith you talk 'bout is based on evidence of yer experiences in life. Religious faith ain't so different. In fact, Paul used the word evidence—evidence that there's a supreme Creator who guides and directs yer life—evidence that miracles happen even today. We may not read 'bout lepers gettin' healed, or people walkin' on water, or water turnin' to wine, but in the day to day life of millions who's developed faith, they'll tell ya' that they've seen miracles in their lives."

"Have you, Blade?" Paol inquired softly. "Have you seen miracles in your life?"

"Why—of all the people to ask the question, I'd expect you to be the last, Paol. You know more 'bout my life than any other person on Earth1, but let's review anyway. A black boy's born in an inner city ghetto, gets no decent education, has little support of family, and little future to speak of. He robs a bank, shoots an officer, and finds himself servin' hard time, all befo' becomin' an adult. Where's that black boy today? He's a world famous astronaut with a well-rounded, self-taught education on the most historic and audacious space mission ever attempted. Some may look on that as a coincidence, but as fo' that black boy himself, he sees it as a true miracle, Paol—a true miracle."

Paol sat for a moment in silence, contemplating these last words, but persisted in his skepticism. "What about my life, Blade? What miracles have there been in my life? I was wrongly accused of a crime I did not commit, separated from my family, sentenced to life in prison, and as a result my life was ruined due to a legal technicality."

Blade turned his head away from Paol and stared out at the vast collection of stars. Paol could see focused concentration on his face during the intent silence. At last, he spoke softly, yet confidently. "Purpose—," he hung on the word to make sure Paol would understand, "isn't always seen through the *windshield*, but often through the *rear view* mirror."

Paol squinted and drew his lips into a tight line. He laid his head on the back of his seat and closed his eyes. He wasn't sure what to think. Could there be a purpose in all of this? Purpose to the injustices he and his family had suffered? The only purpose he could see in being separated from his family and risking his life was to appease the curiosity of his fellow man, who had been seeking extra-terrestrial intelligence for many generations. It all seemed so unnecessary.

...

"Cap'n, we've reached maximum velocity." Small beads of sweat betrayed Blade's anxiety. Wide eyes formed large white circles, as Blade focused on the navigational display ahead of him.

"Well, Blade, here we go, then," Paol stated with a deep breath. "Proceed to ease us into the path of the comet."

The Star Transport was traveling at maximum velocity in the direction of the comet's path exactly parallel to its orbit. Astronauts Joonter and Slater had officially begun the 'suicide' part of their mission. All knew that the most dangerous aspect of the mission was to insert themselves into the path of the comet, where debris shed from the superluminal rock was traveling at tens of thousands of times faster than the speed of light. Although microscopic is size, these tiny particles would soon slam into the back of the Star Transport and propel the vehicle on its course towards Earth2—if all went well. If it didn't go so well, these tiny particles would penetrate the Star Shield, the Star Transport, and the pair of defenseless astronauts.

Their hearts were racing in quiet apprehension as the displays ahead of them showed a model of Star Transport easing closer to a yellow line, representing the path of travel of the comet. In due course, they received their first impact sensor detection.

"Right topside wing impact," Blade indicated. "Zero point six seven five warp. Sensor function normal. No aberrations in systems."

"Looks like your faith in NASA's faith was well-founded after all, Mr. Slater. We are certainly in the neighborhood of our ride."

Whether Blade actually heard this or not, Paol could not know. Certainly, Blade didn't acknowledge the statement, either because of his intense focus, or because he simply had nothing to say in response to being right on his belief that data set 13009 would provide the correct coordinates for their rendezvous.

"Another right topside wing. Zero point six seven five warp."

"Where are we to the galactic plane, Blade?"

"Pretty much dead center."

"Hmmm... let's stay the course. We've received two topside impacts. Makes me suspect that the comet tail may be slightly above the galactic plane, but we need more details to extrapolate correctly."

"How 'bout this one: right topside... uh... make that two right wing topsides. Zero point six seven six warp."

"Ease us up out of the galactic plane, Blade. We need the particles to hit us straight on, or we may get pushed right out of the path. Let's correct the heading for direct parallel travel as well. I want to get enough of these rare impact events to help us stabilize a more parallel entry to the beam."

"Yes, sir... I'm correctin' the headin' by plus zero zero three five. I also have two more topside wing impacts, and one topside fuselage. All sensors and systems still functional."

Blade and Paol worked on course correction for an hour—longer than they had hoped to, but they eventually found the orbital plane of the comet to be slightly elevated above the plane of the Milky Way, by about fourteen thousand miles. While NASA was able to detect the radiation impact of the comet's fly-by, all they could use to calculate the trajectory was the single event as registered around the world's ground-spaced telescopes as well as the instruments orbiting the Earth, Moon and Mars. They quickly calculated an estimated trajectory, which proved accurate enough to ballpark, but not precise enough to give an exact orbit. Rough calculations of the comet's orbit were calculated at four thousand miles above the galactic plane, plus or minus twenty thousand miles. The calculation proved to be about ten thousand miles off, but was close enough to give Star Transport enough high-speed particle impact data to allow it to correct its course.

Once they had received a direct particle impact rate of 98%, they began to steer the ship once again towards the center of the beam, where the extremely high-speed particles would propel them towards their destination. Soon, the spaceship was being peppered by particles of comet powder at the rate of several hundred per minute. They watched the data eagerly: rate of impact, average direction of impact, maximum speed of impact, sensor health. No detail was missed by the pair, as they began to immerse themselves into the comet's path. Their minds raced, and both thought frequently about the last time NASA attempted to inject man-made objects into the yellow beam several years ago. At the end of the experiment, the comet tail managed to pulverize all twelve paddles that were injected into the stream. Now, these two clung to the hope that NASA got it right in creating an experiment which would not prove to be the thirteenth fatal failure against the violent nature of the comet. Paol and Blade had to admit that so far, everything was going according to plan. The Star Transport had made its way deeper into the beam than before, although the tension was only growing greater as they watched the speed of impact grow.

Blade broke a rather tense moment of silence, pointing to the display. "Looks like the maximum impact speed is nearin' the speed of light, Paol."

Paol swallowed hard. "Zero point nine two warp."

The astronauts stared at the display watching this rate increase slowly and steadily: 0.93... 0.94... 0.95.

"How you feeling, Buddy?" Paol looked over at his companion, who was looking a bit pale.

"So far, so good, Partna', but we've got a long way to go to reach our ultimate velocity, and this tin can is shakin' more than I'd like it to. If it continues to rattle like this, I don't think the thing's gonna stay together at twenty-seven thousand times the speed of light."

"You know—", Paol began.

When Blade discerned that Paol would not finish the sentence, he quipped, "Nope... can't say I do know... especially since I don't know what you're thinkin' I know."

Paol gave a slight smile of appreciation for Blade's attempted wisecrack in this most tense of situations.

"I was just thinking out loud—it's nothing really."

"Now, go on… tell me whatcha thinkin' 'bout."

"I was just wondering if we should turn this ship around. I really agree with you—this thing can't take the beating it's going to receive, can it?"

"Paol!" Blade exclaimed in disappointment. "Don't even tell me you're serious 'bout that. Why, just exactly whatcha think NASA is goin' to say when we tell them that we've done chickened out on their multi-billion dollar mission. D'ya think the President'll pardon us still? Besides… how would ya' be able to live with ya'self, knowin' that ya' backed out."

"I'd *live* with myself better if I were *alive*, Blade."

"You really believe that? C'mon, Paol. You know we gotta do this. We can't back out fo' no reason. We accepted it. We trained fer it. We live by it… and maybe—but hopefully not—we die by it."

Paol grew agitated. "You fool!" He shouted. "You'd rather kill yourself over a principle than accept defeat?"

"Defeat! Who says we've been defeated? Nothin' but yer cowardice, Joonter. Fo' someone who knows so much 'bout science and business, please tell me how you missed so much 'bout principles and life. This thing, Paol—it's bigger than you or me. We were born, and someday we'll die. After you're long gone, who's gonna care 'bout yer pittance of a life and the successful business ya' built up. Earth1 will keep on spinnin', people will keep on livin', and you'll just be six feet under the ground. What purpose will yer life have if ya' selfishly live it fo' yerself. You have the opportunity to do somethin' great—somethin' very, very few people get the chance to do. Whether ya' live to return to Earth1 or not, yer legacy will be better served by yer tryin' this mission instead of slinkin' back home to some prison cell, while ya' hope that yer lawyer comes up with some way of gettin' ya' back to yer no-purpose existence of closin' business deals and inventin' stuff that nobody really needs in the first place. Big deal. Others would do it if you's never born anyway. This here—this is what I call livin'. And if I die doin' it? So be it. At least people will remember Blade Slater as the first person to attempt warp-speed travel. Others will be inspired, follow perhaps in my footsteps, until they succeed at it. Now that is livin' to me."

354

Paol grew sullen, but undeterred. He spoke quietly, but firmly. "Blade, listen to reason. The Star Transport is getting a very violent treatment. You can feel the pounding we are getting." Paol pointed to the sensor impact display. "Zero point nine eight warp. We're only facing the beginning of the storm with particles hitting us at zero point nine eight warp. The vehicle will not be able to hold together when we get bombarded with particles traveling five orders of magnitude greater. Don't you think we can provide more data to NASA if we return the ship in one piece? The engineers will be able to analyze the data and beef up the ship for a more successful run at it."

Blade bowed his head and closed his eyes. Remaining in this position, he finally answered his partner. "I'm hearin' ya' loud and clear, Paol. And, what I'm hearin' and realizin' is that yer heart's just not in this thing." He looked up into Paol's face. "I do think the mission is a failure, but mainly because the mission can't affo'd doubt—it can't affo'd self-absorbed fear. If this was goin' to work, it was gonna do it by an unflinchin' resolve on both our parts. Do I feel the ship heavin'? Do I feel it shakin'? Yeah, I do. But, I also look at the data in front of me, and I see that we ain't lost a single system yet. Not a single sensor failed. I think we don't know exactly what this ship is capable of. We're almost in the portion of the tail that is strictly goin' faster than the speed of light. I say if we really want NASA to have the data it will need to make the next mission a success, then we need to wait until the max—no—until the average impact is one point zero zero warp. At that point we'll—"

Blade stopped dead in his tracks. He lifted his head up, whirled it around to the right, to the left. His eyes widened. He glanced back over at Paol, and saw Paol clutching his seat with a dead-ahead stare that sent chills down his spine.

"Paol, d'ya see it too?!"

"Red... everything... is red."

"Yeah, I know, but why?" Blade blinked rapidly. Red still. He squinted. Red. He rubbed his eyes briskly with the palms of his hands. Red. Everything was still visible, but it was all cast in a deep red. The video displays, the cockpit lights, his pilot. Everything was red.

Finally, a bright red flash took both astronauts by surprise, forcing their eyes shut. Both men held their hands tightly over their eyes. Blade laid his head back against his seat, while Paol had leaned forward with his elbows on his knees and hands still covering his eyes.

They remained in this position, not daring to peek, not daring to move. The violent heaving of the Star Transport and the bright red glare left them helpless. They were now at the mercy of the debris that was propelling them forward. For a couple of minutes, both astronauts had resigned themselves to certain calamity, when suddenly, the violent shaking ceased, and a quiet calm overcame the cockpit.

Paol was the first to move a muscle. Lifting his head slowly, he removed his right hand from his face and opened his eyelid to just a thin slit. He saw no red and risked opening his eye all the way. Everything looked normal. He opened both eyes and looked all around him. He saw Blade with his head back and his eyes covered.

"Uh, Blade... I think it's safe to open your eyes again."

Blade slowly pulled his hands away from his eyes but left them against his temple to form a small tunnel through which he could look while keeping his eyes shielded.

"Well that was strange," he admitted while folding his hands in his lap. His head still lay back against the seat, as he dared not move, fearing that it would disrupt the delicate equilibrium between normality and redness. While sitting in this repose for quite some time, he heard a gasp from Paol.

"I don't believe it!" Paol exclaimed.

"What is it, Cap'n," Blade looked over.

"If the data is to be believed, we are being impacted by particles traveling twelve hundred times the speed of light. And Star Transport herself is now traveling at zero point nine seven warp."

"Look here, Paol. Take a look at this chart. It shows our velocity relative to our time. Right here—about one minute ago, ya' see our acceleration had been pretty linear, but then ya' see this sharp turn, and our speed increased severely in just a few seconds. I'm guessin' this was around the time everythin' went red. After the sharp rise, there's another significant bend in the curve right here, where the acceleration settled back down. It looks like the ship wanted to be launched into superluminal velocity, but hit the ceilin' just below the speed of light."

"Can you overlay that with the particle impact speed?"

356

Both astronauts gasped when they recognized the correlation. The moment where the acceleration curve turned sharply upward was the precise moment the impact sensors measured their first 1.0 warp particle impact.

"Whatcha make of it, Paol?" Blade inquired.

"I don't know, but it looks like even the tiniest of warp-speed particles packs a real big punch, don't you think? For us to be vaulted from just over zero point five warp to zero point nine seven warp in a heartbeat indicates that the power of the warp speed particles is something far greater than we can imagine."

"If that's so," thought Blade, "then why'd the propulsion seem to end at zero point nine seven."

Paol's voice grew more excited as he brainstormed through ideas about what they were experiencing. "It actually looks like it stopped around zero point nine six. We're still accelerating, just more slowly. I'm thinking that we've hit some physical barrier that is making it difficult on the particles to push us past the speed of light, even with all of their might."

Blade's hands typed quickly on a pair of touch screen panels. Another graph emerged. "And how d'ya account fo' this?"

Paol frowned and wrinkled up his forehead. "This graph is curious. If I'm reading this correctly, then right up to the point where we had our first warp-speed impact, we were slowly going deeper into the tail of the comet. As we did so, the particle speed increased pretty linearly. But right when we reach the warp speed boundary, the particle impact speed quickly jumped from one point zero zero to 1203 warp almost instantaneously. Where are all of the particles in between?"

"Could there be some dead zone where particles can't travel? Perhaps once ya' hit the speed of light, there's a quantum step up to twelve hundred?"

"I don't know, Blade. I just don't know."

"Well, this superluminal physics is all new science, Paol. The next generation of scientists are gonna eat up this data. Shall we head back and give it to them? What are yer orders, Cap'n?" Blade stared eagerly into Paol's face.

Paol's fear was replaced with renewed enthusiasm at these fascinating discoveries. "What are you talking about, Slater! Go back? Now? And miss out on all of the scientific discoveries we're about to become famous for?

357

Besides, can't you feel our ride? It's never been smoother. I don't have a clue as to why we aren't being ripped apart by the violence of the particles, but I'm not one to be ungrateful for not being pulverized. Hold the course steady, Navigator. This mission is just getting started."

Blade's heart leapt and a broad smile grew on his face, as he leaned back and watched the Star Transport on its path towards Earth2.

. . .

"Zero point nine nine, Cap'n," was the report from the navigator.

"It looks like we're going to get there after all, Blade. I just zoomed in on the vehicle velocity chart, and it's definitely not asymptotic to warp speed. The projections indicate that we'll reach the speed of light in about two minutes."

"Paol?"

"Yes, Blade."

"D'ya think we'll be makin' that leap from 1.00 warp to twelve hundred warp?"

"I don't know… it's as possible as anything, I suppose."

"D'ya think the Star Transport will be able to handle that sort of velocity transfo'mation? I mean a particle of dust is already… well… a particle of dust. What if warp speed only pertains to the realm of atomics? Couldn't we also be transfo'med into independent dust molecules when we make the leap?"

"Maybe so, but if I know you, you won't be content not knowing, right?" Paol had a twinkle in his eye as he smiled at Blade.

"Oh, the lost sleep!" Blade blurted playfully. "I thinks we've just gotta forge ahead, come what may, or I'll never rest again wonderin' what could'a happened."

"That's what I thought," Paol nodded. "Zero point nine nine five. We're only traveling about one thousand miles per second, or about three and a half million miles per hour less than the speed of light now."

"When ya' say it that way, it doesn't exactly seem imminent, does it?" Blade shook his head.

"And yet the computer calculates that we're less than a minute away now."

Both astronauts held their breath, as hearts pounded relentlessly, knees bounced nervously, and remaining bits of finger nail chattered noisily through teeth. Their eyes barely blinked as they focused on the display: 0.995… 0.996… 0.997. Mercilessly, it seemed that the anxiety would never end, as the display hung onto 0.999, until long after the anticipated event should've happened.

"Ya' thinkin' what I'm thinkin', Partna'?" Blade spoke softly.

"Now, let's be patient, Blade. I know we had expected to be at one point zero zero warp by now, but maybe it'll just take a little longer."

"I don't think there's gonna be a one point zero zero, Paol. I thinks we've reached our physical maximum."

Paol slammed his right fist into his left palm. "No! I don't accept it. Just a little longer, Blade. It would be too anti-climactic to not hit warp speed. Besides, if the comet tail particles can do it, then there's no reason why Star Transport can't."

"I don't know, Paol… maybe it's entirely different material all together. Anti-matter? Dark energy? Who knows? Maybe the subatomic makeup of that stuff out there's ever so different than the raw material found on Earth, from which you and I and this ship's made up of."

Paol's fist pounded on the display in fury. "No, No, NO!"

Zero point nine nine eight.

"Blade, steer us farther into the beam, will you? We need to get to the deepest part, where the fastest material will certainly push us over the threshold. We're only getting pushed at 10K warp. We know that the fastest stuff will be going nearly 30K, so I think we just need to push deeper in."

Blade feverishly worked the navigational controls for a couple of minutes, and eventually confessed. "Can't do it, Cap'n."

"What?! Why not?"

"All nav systems are on automatic control, and I can't get it into manual?"

"Why not? Is the manual control system damaged?"

"Dontcha remember, Paol? Once we start comin' outta the beam, the computer takes over. It's a failsafe mechanism that NASA employed, in case the effects of superluminal travel incapacitated us to the degree of not bein' able to fly the ship properly."

"Ugh! Stupid engineers! Did they not think that perhaps we would be lucid enough to need to fly the blasted ship on our own? What idiots! We've got to override the system somehow, Blade. When we come out of the beam, we're going to be nowhere near Earth2 for the computer to recognize the celestial signature. What will the computer do to try to get us to Earth2?"

"I think the abort sequence'll kick in. The computer will not recognize the star signature fer Earth2, so it will look fo' the signature fer Earth1, at which point it will calculate our trajectory back home."

Paol's face grew red with anger. "We were this close, Blade!"

"Yes, but there's no shame in goin' home now, Paol. The ship aborted the sequence, not us. And we will have lots of data to provide. I'm guessin' if it's at all possible, another mission will launch durin' the next pass of the comet."

"Geez... that's another six years to wait, Blade."

"A small moment in time, compared to the history of man."

After a brief pause, Blade saw Paol's face grow even more red.

"Blade! Close your eyes."

Instantly, Blade realized that everything was growing red as before. Both astronauts tightly closed their eyes and covered their hands over them to avoid another red flash.

"Paol... d'ya think we're makin' the leap to warp after all?"

"Alas, no... I think we're coming back out of the quiet zone of the comet tail. As soon as we feel the choppiness return, I think it will be safe to open our eyes, at which point we'll see the current impact speed will be something less than one point zero warp."

Shortly, both astronauts felt a sharp jolt and a return to the violent shaking of the vehicle that had been a concern before. Slowly, they both opened their eyes, and saw the current average impact speed at 0.99 warp. As expected, they were leaving the path of the beam, and would shortly be on their way back to Earth1.

"Well, buddy, looks like a fairly anti-climactic mission, huh?" Paol reached over and placed his right hand on Blade's left arm.

"Yeah. There goes any hope of this story bein' written down fo' the ages."

"I don't know," Paol said wryly. "Authors can find ways to write about anything. I suppose there'll be somebody out there desperate enough for a gig to write our tale."

Blade chuckled. "I feel fo' the poor sap who gives up his day job to write 'bout us."

The pair laughed nervously about their situation, but deep down, the disappointment could not be assuaged.

. . .

Paol and Blade sat sullen and reflective. Since Star Transport's computerized navigation system had full control of the vehicle, there wasn't much else either could do, except wait out the ride. Their thoughts went a million miles a minute, as they reflected back on the many experiences they shared together: the prison cell, the astronaut training, the sublime views of Earth and Jupiter along with their moons as well as the stars and asteroids.

Neither could help feeling the depressive anti-climax of the situation, but they also felt the privilege of the opportunity, and yet both felt guilt and shame for secretly contemplating their future. How would they be integrated back into Earth life, and what directions would their lives lead there? Wouldn't this provide them the easiest way out of the difficult situation? Of course, Blade's prison sentence had long since past, but would Paol still be pardoned, or would he return to penitentiary? Would they be anticipated with the same heroic fanfare with which they left Earth just a few weeks earlier, or would they be ostracized and seen as the symbols of failure for a mission that cost too much and never should have been attempted? Would they continue to pursue their new careers as astronauts, and perhaps even attempt another ST mission to explore and map the solar system, or perhaps to even make another go at Earth2 six years from now?

Paol tried to distract himself by studying the stars overhead. He had become so used to the sky above him when they journeyed from the Moon to Jupiter, but everything looked so differently now that they were heading in the opposite direction. Frankly, he didn't know exactly how far away they were now either, considering that they had been propelled quite a way down the beam before they were ejected from the stream of particles.

Through this train of thought, his stomach dropped. How far had they come indeed? How long would it take them to return to Earth? For some time, they had been traveling nearly the speed of light, and this was taking them very quickly away from their home. Certainly, they must first send a communication to Earth. Once they received a response, they would be able to time their distance to the Earth by the round trip time of the communication. That way, they could calculate whether they would have enough fuel to race straight to Earth at full speed, or whether an emergency mission would need to be launched to reclaim the Star Transport in a reasonable timeframe.

As he began to turn to Blade to ask him to relay a message to Earth, he was interrupted by the voice of his companion.

"Cap'n," started Blade softly. "I'm not sure I understand what I'm seein' here."

Paol looked down at the display to which Blade was pointing. It read: "Celestial reading locked, trajectory to Earth2 calculated."

"Blade, when did you first see this?" Paol asked in dismay. "Something must be wrong."

"Just now, Paol. Why I's just starin' off into space, and I saw this display flashin'. When I touched it to acknowledge the message, well... this is what it said. Whatcha make of it, Partna'?"

"Somehow, this hunk of junk thinks it has found a pattern in the stars that matches the Earth2 region of the Milky Way. But, it should've found Earth1 instead."

Paol started typing on one of the displays. Instantly, it provided a map of the galaxy. It pinpointed Earth1 and Earth2 on far extremes of the display. The Star Transport was represented by a green dot extremely close to Earth2!

"Oh, my... oh, my!" Blade exclaimed nervously. "Why didn't I thinks of this befo'? Stupid, stupid!"

Joonter looked over to see his navigator taking his seat harness off and leaning towards the edge of his seat. His hands trembled violently as they fumbled on the touchscreen panel ahead of him.

"What is it, Blade?" Paol spoke quietly, almost daring not to ask for fear of the answer.

Paol stared intently at his companion as he threw himself back in his seat and started laughing uncontrollably.

"What are you laughing at?!" Paol exclaimed. "Star Transport is thoroughly confused about our location, and you're laughing? I'm not sure you understand the gravity of our situation, Blade. Unless this thing can be convinced of its error, we might just float in space forever!"

"Doncha see?" Blade looked at his partner incredulously. "Wasn't we supposed to fall asleep when we hit warp speed?"

"Yes, but we didn't." Paol answered simply. "Instead, we fell out of the beam at zero point nine—" He stopped short. "Wait... are you thinking what I think you're thinking?"

"How would ya' know if ya' fall asleep if you're asleep the whole time?"

"Blade, don't be so ridiculous. When I wake up in the morning, I know that I fell asleep the night before." Paol's voice hinted of agitation.

"Sure enough. But that's *sleep* sleep. This wasn't exactly the same. Instead of sleeping, we were in some sort of suspended animation. Dontcha remember? They told us that everythin' was supposed to just stop?"

Paol grew wide-eyed. "Blade! If that's so, then the only way we came out of the beam, was when the nuclear expulsion device propelled us away from the beam. What's the status of the nuclear systems?"

Blade turned his head towards Paol with a jubilant look on his face. Pointing to the screen ahead of him, he said, "Looks fo' ya'self, Partna'."

Joonter read the display. "Nuclear Expulsion System #1: Detonated. Nuclear Expulsion System #2: Pending. This means the system to get us to Earth2 *has* gone off, and the system to get us back to Earth1 is still waiting for our return trip!"

"So we really have been out of it for a year now?" Paul asked.

Denial turned to disbelief and disbelief to doubt. As the situation slowly dawned on the two space travelers, they began to realize that they had just come through the beam, twenty-seven thousand light years away from Earth1 after all, and never even realized it until now. They had slept through the whole thing, and not a thing had gone wrong with the mission as they had supposed.

"Can you look at the rest of the list for any system abnormalities, Blade? How's the general health of the ship after coming through the heart of the beam?"

"It looks like we got three impact sensor failures: two on the right wing and one on the tail stabilizers. All other systems are reportin' normal status."

"Not bad," Paol smiled. "This thing really held up better than anybody could've hoped for. We will need to inspect those three failures and any other body damage in general. We may need to patch some holes in the Star Shield before heading back to Earth1, but with just three failures out of thousands of sensors, I'm feeling pretty good about our trip home."

"What's our ETA to Earth2, Cap'n." Blade asked.

Paol looked at a display to his left and reported his findings. "About 137 hours. We'll be there in less than 6 days, since the beam gave us such a nice boost. We're still traveling at warp zero point eight three."

Blade leaned forward and stared into the video display looking for any indication of a blue-green planet in the distance. He saw two red circles flash on the display.

"Is that what you were looking for?" Paol asked. "There's Earth2, although we only see a sliver of light, since we're largely on its dark side, but over here is Sun2, already the brightest object in the sky."

"We're really doin' this, ain't we Paol? We're really on our way now."

They continued the journey with full smiles, giddy laughter, and more than a few tears of relief. Having survived the jump to hyper-warp speed and seeing their main target now almost plainly in sight, their confidence in the mission grew by leaps and bounds.

...

Six days later, as measured by their forced sleep cycles, they neared the planet and descended into orbit. Their eyes hurt as they strained to see details on Earth2. They wanted to pick up any clues as to the nature of this new planet. While it certainly looked exactly like the planet they had left so far away, their apprehensions grew as they wondered whether they would be entering a friendly or a hostile environment. Thoughts wandered through their minds. Would there be dinosaurs? Cavemen? Or was an advanced civilization ready to meet them? From this altitude, they could discern no signs of civilization, but this did not concern them, because they knew they were still too far away to recognize much of anything man made. The fact that they only had occasional glimpses through cloud layers complicated their observations.

364

They orbited several times as they tried to piece together the topography of the planet. Star Transport was continuously taking photos and mapping unclouded images to a map display on the main console of the cockpit. As shapes began to form, the astronauts were stunned at what they appeared to be discovering. Shapes that looked remarkably like the Horn of Africa, the Aleutian Islands, and the archipelago of Japan formed on the screen.

"I can't believe it!" Paol responded increasing vehemence as the map grew to be more and more convincing of an exact copy of Earth.

"It doesn't make no sense," agreed Blade. "I mean with plate tectonics and all, whose gonna think that this planet would be in the same geographic phase as Earth? All the continents could be in totally different positions."

"Well," replied the captain shaking his head in disbelief, "the researchers did tell us that all indications was that Earth2 was as identical as possible to Earth1 in every way: distance from Sun, axial tilt, time of revolution and rotation, mass, temperature and composition. I still would not have imagined the same exact geographic makeup."

"Looks like Florida just came into view," Slater pointed to the map as both astronauts looked at the real-time imagery and noticed that the iconic North American feature was clearly outlined below them.

It took quite some time for the astronauts to adjust to the shocking reality that in almost every way, the geography of Earth2 was identical to Earth1. Eventually, it occurred to them that their mission was not to orbit for the next six years.

"So, where do you think we should land?" asked Paol. "Mission control gave us guidelines to land in a temperate zone, but even they did not know the continents would line up like this."

Blade stroked his chin. He pondered the question seriously, knowing that in all likelihood, the decision would change the entire course of the mission. Thinking out loud, he said, "We don't 'xactly know how advanced this planet is. Could be, we're just showin' up at the dawn of civilization."

"Um… I don't think so, Partner," Johannsen's voice cracked with anticipation. "Just look for yourself."

Slater focused his attention to the direction of Paol's finger, and what he saw caused his eyes to grow wide with concern. "That looks a whole lot like farmin' goin' on down there."

As Star Transport flew past the Mississippi River delta and up into the Midwest, they could see tiny squares with different shades of greens and browns.

"Well, that just solves it for us," Blade announced firmly.

"What do you mean?"

"We should land in Kansas," Blade pursed his lips and nodded fervently. "We're gonna be lookin' for hospitable. The Midwest is the place fo' sure."

"Ok, then," Paol agreed with the assessment. "Let's get this thing down to Kansas then. "Can you load the coordinates for us, Blade?"

"Yes, sir!" Blade zoomed in on the North America region of the map that was still being constructed by the computer, and registered a location in the Midwest that he believed would be close to the Heartland of Kansas.

It took several orbits of slow and turbulent descent before the Star Transport dipped below the highest cloud layers. On their final approach to North America, it felt like the Atlantic Ocean would go on forever. A stillness settled over the cabin, as both astronauts held their breath in anticipation.

"Down there!" Blade exclaimed in excitement as a line of tiny islands running from North to South indicated that they had reached the edge of the Caribbean Sea. At the speed they were traveling, Star Transport quickly passed by Puerto Rico, Hispaniola, and Cuba before the familiar Florida coastline came into view once again. This time, they were low enough to spot something that convinced them of a modern society.

"Buildings," Paol whistled lowly. "Looks like a pretty advanced civilization down there."

Passing over the Gulf of Mexico and into the Southern States, they continued to see widespread evidence of a large population. As coastal communities gave way to small towns and farming communities, they began to realize with some trepidation that they would have to engage with a society of beings and stay as safe as possible for the next six years.

"I s'ppose this really is a parallel Earth," Blade stated hesitantly.

Joonter hadn't even heard his companion's reply. As his eyes grew wide in recognition, he scanned the terrain below rapidly, almost frantically.

"Whatcha see, Paol?" Slater stared at his companion with deep interest.

366

"It's not what I see, Blade! It's what I don't see. Take a look, that should be Atlanta right there."

As they passed by the city, Slater looked for anything out of the ordinary, without success. Eventually, Joonter pointed out what Blade was missing.

"No roads!"

Blade Slater was aghast. "You're right! How could there be cities with no roads connectin' them?"

Paol Joonter breathed heavily and responded in between gasps. "I don't know, Blade. I do not know. Maybe these are ancient civilizations that have no living intelligent life in them, and the roads have simply returned to their natural state."

"Wouldn't we still see some asphalt or some indication of roads? Indentions in the terrain? Somethin'?" inquired Slater doubtfully.

"I don't know, Blade," replied Paol, "but I suspect we're about to find out."

"D'ya wanna land down there, Cap'n, and have a look at Atlanta... –ish?"

"No," answered the pilot simply. "Let's go land in Kansas just like you suggested. I think you're right that if there's a civilization down there, our best bet for safety is in the Midwest."

After plugging in the coordinates as best as Slater could estimate on the map, the Star Transport computer system calculated their trajectory to a landing site that was an as flat and indiscernible as any. It could be Kansas, Oklahoma, or Nebraska as far as either of them could tell. But it should be close enough for a hopefully successful start to their mission.

As the vehicle began a sharp descent towards a patchwork of farmland, they could tell that there was a thriving and active farming community. Their hearts leapt into their throats as they felt both intense excitement and a healthy anxiety for what they would discover. Regardless of the fact that missing roads were a red flag as to the condition of the civilization they were about to encounter, it was undeniable as they descended that these crops were being tended to. They were extremely well cultivated, and not the product of years of neglect, let alone the decades or centuries that would be required to erase roads from the ruins of cities.

Now more than ever, Paol and Blade worried whether these people would be friendly towards them or whether they would be advanced enough to understand war, greed, and distrust.

After a long quiet period of contemplation, they felt the reverse thrusters kick in, and the vehicle decelerated until it touched down with a vertical landing in the middle of a large field of dry wheat. The descent was so rapid that they could barely focus on their visual surroundings. Sentient beings were certainly engaged in farming, yet the complete lack of roads indicated a completely missing infrastructure and certain isolation between the farmers and the city dwellers of Earth2. At long last, Star Transport touched down softly, and everything came to a standstill, as the engines shut down quickly.

In the still quiet of the cockpit, labored breathing accompanied the astronauts as they looked straight into a field of wheat as tall as the Star Transport. The wheat swayed in a gentle breeze.

Neither astronaut was lost by the fact that they would eventually need to leave the vehicle and explore their surroundings, yet they felt glued to their seats with fear and anxiety.

Eventually, the tension was broken by Slater. "Oh, no!"

"What's wrong, Blade?" Johannsen leaned towards his navigator with great concern.

Slapping his forehead, Blade replied, "I forgot to get a change of address form from the post office."

The raucous laughter from Blade and a feigned sneer of disgust from his pilot bounced around the cockpit, while immediately outside of the Star Transport, a quieter atmosphere persisted. Birds chirped in the strong sunlight, while the sound of wheat swaying in the gentle breeze suggested that the astronauts had touched down on a peaceful planet vastly resembling their own home world. As the superluminal comet raced away from them on its six-year orbit of the galaxy, they were optimistic that this would be a hospitable place to live as they waited for their ride back home.

18254291R00210

Made in the USA
San Bernardino, CA
06 January 2015